P9-CLH-231

Reign the Earth

ALSO BY A. C. GAUGHEN

Scarlet

Lady Thief

Lion Heart

Reign the Earth

the elementae

A. C. GAUGHEN

BLOOMSBURY
NEW YORK LONDON OXFORD NEW DELHI SYDNEY

First published in the United States of America in January 2018
by Bloomsbury Children's Books
www.bloomsbury.com

Library of Congress Cataloging-in-Publication Data
Names: Gaughen, A. C., author.
Title: Reign the earth / by A. C. Gaughen.
Description: New York : Bloomsbury, 2018.
Summary: Having sacrificed her freedom to establish peace with a neighboring kingdom, Shalia discovers that she has the power to control earth the day she marries Calix, whose only motivation is to eliminate the Elementae.
Identifiers: LCCN 2017024397 (print) • LCCN 2017038892 (e-book)
ISBN 978-1-68119-111-9 (hardcover) • ISBN 978-1-68119-112-6 (e-book)
Subjects: | CYAC: Fantasy. | Four elements (Philosophy)—Fiction. | Ability—Fiction.
Classification: LCC PZ7.G23176 Rei 2018 (print) | LCC PZ7.G23176 (e-book) |
DDC [Fic]—dc23
LC record available at https://lccn.loc.gov/2017024397

ISBN 978-1-68119 936-8 (Aus)

Book design by Kimi Weart
Typeset by Westchester Publishing Services
Printed and bound in the U.S.A. by Berryville Graphics Inc., Berryville, Virginia
2 4 6 8 10 9 7 5 3 1

For my brother Michael,

Who was born with a heart too big for his body. You may have technically evened out, but your eternally ginormous heart is my favorite thing about you. I love you, one quarter mile at a time.

Jitra
Desert
Land Bridge
TRIFECTATE
Trizala
Nomikos
Tri City
Kyrikatos
Summer Palace
Liatos
Communes
Mercia
Sayma
Urre
Zilarra
Kobrea
The Wyverns

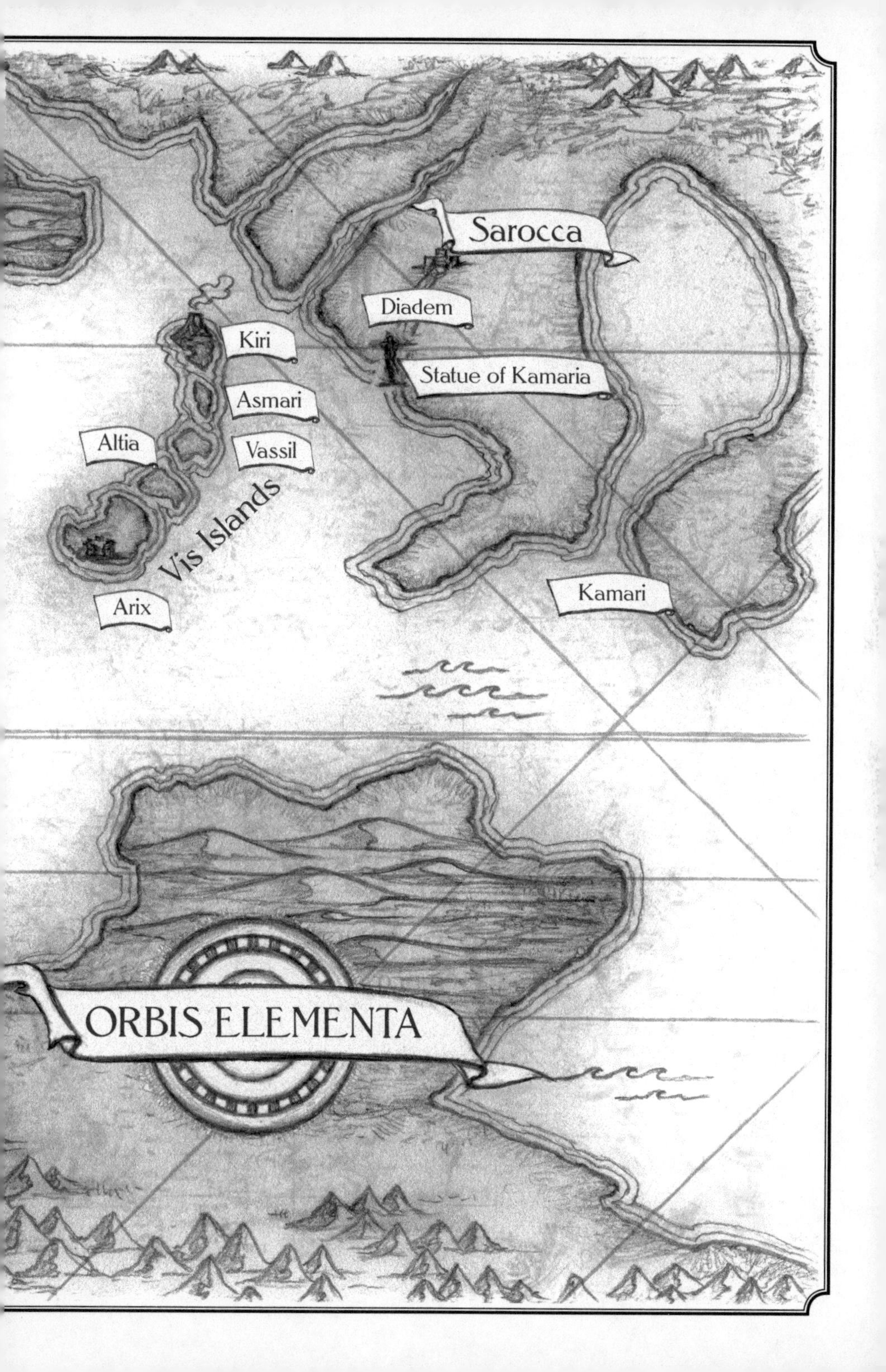
Sarocca
Diadem
Kiri
Statue of Kamaria
Asmari
Altia
Vassil
Vis Islands
Arix
Kamari
ORBIS ELEMENTA

Reign the Earth

Poison

There was a scorpion in my tent.

I stared at him. The moon was bright, but only a little of its light filtered in. The scorpion walked carefully over the sand, his tail raised but not ready to strike. He moved slowly toward where I was meant to be asleep on my bedroll.

With a deep breath, I held up my hand. "By the power of the desert, I command you to stop," I said.

In return, he curled his tail up, his body tilting down so the tail could flick out with poisonous aim.

I laughed, leaning forward and scooping him up. He stayed tense and primed for a long moment, but scorpions and dragons had nothing to fear from each other, and he remembered that after a while, crawling tentatively on my skin. I moved to support him so he wouldn't fall.

"Come to wish me good luck?" I asked him, stroking the stiff shell of his body. With a deep sigh, I confessed, "I think I need it." His tail flattened further, but flipped up again when I stopped.

When the tent flap moved to the side and a shaft of moonlight pierced my tent, I gasped, sitting up and sheltering him in my hands.

"Good," Kata said. "You're awake." Then she saw what was in my hands and jerked away. "There are less lethal ways out of a marriage, Shalia."

Laughing, I let the scorpion go and lifted the back of the tent so he could scuttle away. I jumped out of bed as she came in. She lowered her hood at the same time that the tent flap closed, and it seemed like the pale silver of her hair sucked up all the luminescence of the moon.

"Kata!" I cried, throwing my arms around her. "You came!"

Her arms tightened around me, and the unsteady rock of our hug knocked us over. We fell onto the sand giggling, nose-to-nose. Like it used to be. "Of course I did. I came as soon as I heard. I'm sorry it took me so long."

I smiled at her. "You're here now. And we have so much to talk about."

Her answering smile was watery as she looked at me. "You're getting married," she said, her voice softer. "How do you feel?"

"Short," was the first answer that came to mind, and her nose wrinkled. I wasn't short, and I knew she was about to point that out to me, but I sighed. "I think queens are supposed to be taller."

Our noses touched. "I've seen him," she told me. "He's not much taller than you, if at all."

A breath filled my lungs, full of questions, full of *what does he look like what does he stand for why does he want me what do you know*, but it didn't matter. In just a few hours I would be his bride, and I would find out soon enough the answers to all those questions.

But tomorrow I wouldn't have Kata. "Are we doing it?" I asked her.

She grinned. "Tonight? You're supposed to be up before the dawn."

"We both know I'm not sleeping much tonight. Besides, it's bad luck to break with tradition."

In answer, she tugged my hands, pulling us both up from the sand. We stuck our heads out, looking around for my brothers or uncles or anyone else who would stop us. "Is Rian with you?" I whispered to her.

"Yes," she whispered back, tugging me forward.

With no one in sight, we ran out of the tent, hand in hand, feet sliding in the sand. The sky was clear, the moon bright enough to guide us, but so much colder than her brother, the sun. We ran faster as the sand became more compact. Our clan was camped right outside the city, ready for the morning, when I would greet the sun, my husband, and a whole new life all in one day.

Coming upon Jitra was as strange and magical as every time before. Rolling dunes disappeared, leaving a blankness on the horizon, and the shifting sands slid away as solid earth appeared beneath. A hard shelf of rock then parted to reveal a narrow cleft, wide enough for a single person, the mouth of a staircase leading down through the cliff into the city.

Jitra was a city cut into the rock. Long ago a powerful river had eroded a sloping path that was as wide across as ten men. From there, the desert clans had carved into the walls, forming massive dwellings, shaded and cool, eternal and unyielding. The river still ran in a narrow vein cutting through the mountain rock until it cascaded off a cliff at the end of the city, giving my nomadic people their one fixed source of water.

It was a holy place.

Kata always had a hard time finding it. She wasn't a clanswoman, a fact I tended to forget until times like this, when she couldn't find her way to this sacred city. Her fingers, pale and strange on my dark skin, clutched mine tighter as I led her to the break in the earth, and we plunged into darkness as we descended the steep, narrow stone stairs into the city.

We slowed at the bottom of the staircase. I could hear city guards somewhere ahead and tugged her to the side. Another path burrowed deeper into the mountain rather than out into the city, and I led the way, sure of my steps as I would always be in Jitra.

Another staircase, older, less even, twisted around the rock and deep into the ground. Along that staircase, the air changed from the hot dryness of the desert to a damp that clung to the walls and our fingers.

It was there that Kata became more confident in her steps, keeping pace with me, able to tell where she was going instead of being dragged. After a few more wild steps and a laugh that echoed, the passageway opened into a huge cavern, and the massive underground lake that was the hidden treasure of the mountains.

The moment I saw it, I halted, and Kata slammed into my back. I barely noticed her as I looked around us.

Hundreds of thousands of tiny droplets of water hung suspended in the air around us. The fine scatter of mist caught the glimmer of a far-off shaft of moonlight at the surface and refracted it, sharing it among the tiny beads of water until the whole cavern looked like it had swallowed all the stars of the night sky.

I laughed, delighted, and Kata moved forward, letting the drops break over her like tiny kisses. I touched them with my fingertips, watching the little bubbles break into smaller and smaller pieces, still suspended, still standing at attention for Kata.

The cave knew her. In this place of water, her power was strong, beautiful, *magical.* As I gazed over such wonder, I felt spirits pressing close around me, protecting me, filling me with faith. Tomorrow would be perfect, and this marriage that would take me away from my family would be the beginning of a long and eternal peace.

My sacrifice would protect my people.

Kata turned in a slow circle, a happy smile on her face, and the water coated her skin. In the desert she was always dry, her pale skin cracked and sore, aching for the water, but here she was whole. Here she was everything she was born to be.

Her power, and the way the world responded to it, was the most stunning thing I'd ever seen.

And then, at some unseen command from her, the water droplets fell, those around me slipping over my skin like a tiny burst of rain.

The light dimmed without them, and I went for the torch on the wall, scraping my hand as I grabbed it. I struck the flint. When it flared to life, I saw Kata skimming out of her desert clothes, tossing them to the side as she dove into the water.

I put the torch back in its holder and followed her, jumping into the water with a massive splash, the sound mixing with our laughter and skittering around the whole cavern.

"Oh," I said, standing in the shallow water as I saw red blooming in the water.

"What did you do?" Kata said, looking at the blood coming from a short gash on my hand.

"I thought I just scratched myself," I told her.

"Here," she said, but before the word was even out, her hand touched my hand, and I watched the small wound close up and fade, the scar turning pink to white in the space of a breath.

"How do you do that?" I whispered.

"It's the water," she told me. "I can feel the water in your skin, in your blood. I can make it answer my command."

I had known Kata so very long, and yet I understood so little about her abilities still. "Thank you," I said as her hand fell away.

She waved at me. "I love this place," Kata said, shifting to float on her back. I kicked my way over to her, floating on my back beside her, looking up at the long mineral spines that hung above us like wet, shining teeth.

"I know you do," I told her. "Now tell me about your trip. Did you find the earth temple?"

"It's called an Aede," she said. "And yes."

I looked at her, my heart suddenly aching. "So they're all open now, and you can rest." I looked away. "But I won't be here anymore."

"Rest." She stared at the ceiling. "All the powers have come back to the world, yes. But I can't rest, Shalia. Can't you tell? There's nothing different? Nothing happened to you when I opened the earth element?"

I put my legs down so I could look over at her. "Not this again."

She did the same. "You have the potential for an elemental power. I know that you do. And nothing changed when I opened the other elements, so it *has* to be earth."

"Just because I think of you as my sister doesn't mean we actually are."

She drew a breath like my mother did when we were being difficult. "Shalia, it's not about families. Maybe it was, years ago, but when my people were murdered, the elements—they found places of extreme power and hid. Until I let the elements out again, no one could use them."

"I know all this," I told her. "I know that's why you left, to go find these temples and crack the elements open like an egg. But it doesn't mean I'm an islander."

"No," she said hotly. "It means *everything* changed when my people died. It means that anyone can have these powers now. I have no control over who receives them. They're everywhere in the world, not just in the islands. And I can feel it in you, as certain as whether or not you're breathing, that you have a power. The elements have been awakened. This was the last Aede, so you should be able to use your power by now." She frowned, looking into the water. "If I did it right. No. I'm sure I did it right."

When she first told me I had the potential for an elemental power, I had been thrilled. She could control water, and over time she had even developed the ability to heal things. I was in awe of her, and it would have been so exciting to share that with her.

But I couldn't, not ever. I'd accepted that—probably around the time she kept leaving me, kept choosing these temples over our friendship. "I don't have a power," I said again. "And it doesn't even matter."

"It does," she told me. "Now more than ever. Your future husband has declared the Elementae to be traitors, and their powers illegal. More than that, he's persecuted them."

"All the better that I don't have it, then," I told her. "Can't you just stop? Can't we just swim and enjoy being home?"

Kata looked so hurt that I immediately regretted my words.

"I'm sorry," I said immediately. I shook my head, scattering droplets in the water. "I knew this wouldn't be easy for you."

"Easy?" she said softly. "Aside from the fact that his father murdered my people and he doesn't seem to have very different beliefs, I might not ever see you again."

"No," I said solemnly. "Don't say that. We'll see each other again."

"I've been helping Rian," she admitted softly. "With the Resistance. Do you know about your brother's cause?"

"Only what I can manage to overhear from Father yelling. But I do know that whatever Rian is doing in the Trifectate, the king thinks this marriage will stop Rian from doing violence to him and the king will stop doing violence to the desert people."

"By putting you between them," she said. "Don't you see that?"

"Yes," I told her. "Of course I do. But better between them than standing to the side as they burn another one of my brothers in the sand. Because next time it could be Rian or Kairos in Torrin's place." She looked at me like I was foolish and young, and I huffed out a sigh that rippled the water. "Kata, I would have been married soon anyway. I could have married some d'Skorpios boy, or I could marry this king. I could protect my family for once. I could have my marriage mean something."

"You're just as fierce as your brothers," she told me. "I'm not faulting you for that. I just don't think you know how dangerous this will be."

"Peace is always dangerous," I said.

"Maybe," she said. "But have you even wondered why he wants a desert bride? He was supposed to marry a rich princess across the sea. Why is it more essential to form peace with the desert than with them?"

My mouth drew tight, and I returned to floating on my back.

"Shalia," Kata said suspiciously. "You know something."

"You won't like it," I said.

"*Shalia*," she insisted.

"I think he's looking for this," I told her. "The lake."

I couldn't hear her moving in the water anymore. "What makes you think that?"

"As part of the marriage agreement, they're sending some men to pore over Jitra and the mountains," I said. "They said they believe the desert is sheltering Trifectate dissenters and want to search it, but I think they're looking for something else. And this is the only thing I can imagine they're looking for."

"You can't let them do that," she said, gripping my arm.

I raised my head. "Don't worry," I insisted. "No clansman would ever willingly let this place be discovered. The only things that could threaten us are lack of water and the spirits turning on us," I said. "They'll hide this reserve as best they can. Even you can't find your way down here, and the water pulls you." I looked at her. "If something happened to the lake—would that hurt your power?"

"No," she said, shaking her hair. "This water is pure and powerful, but the Water Aede is in the islands."

"Good," I said.

"If I had told you it would take my power away, would that change anything?" she asked. "What can I do to make you refuse this marriage?"

I gave her an angry look, but I wasn't sure what to say. I couldn't stand the idea of her being hurt, but what could I really do to stop this from happening?

"I believe this marriage is a dangerous mistake," Kata said. "And worse, it will cut you off from those who could give you aid. It gives him everything and leaves you powerless."

"No," I said. "It will make me queen, and it will keep my family safe. And it costs us nothing."

"Our friendship is not nothing."

I met her eyes for a long moment. "Which is why no one can take it away from us. No matter where we are."

She nodded, still unsure, and I moved closer, drifting by her side, hoping I would always have her by mine.

Welcome to Jitra

We left the water, and Kata used her magic to pull the moisture out of our hair and clothes, a glittering mist that lifted off me and swirled back into the lake.

We snuck out of the city and back to the sleeping camp, smothering our giggles as we rushed to our beds in separate tents. I pretended to be asleep when the women came to wake me up and start preparations for my marriage.

They rinsed my feet, my hands, my neck, rubbing oil and ilayi blossoms into my skin until the tent smelled like crisp fruit and sunlight, even in the darkness. One cousin insisted I should open my robe a little, to show the valley between my breasts, but my mother clucked her away.

"A wedding is not about lust," my mother said, smoothing my robes into place. "It is about trust and partnership. Alliance. Faith and faithfulness."

"It's a *little* about lust," my cousin Cora muttered. Mother gave her a warning look and went to fetch more flowers.

I grabbed Cora's hands as soon as Mother turned away. Cora was married, and more than that, she lived in Jitra and knew more ways of the world. "What if he doesn't want me?" I whispered to her. "What if he *doesn't* lust for me?"

She laughed, and she held my palms open and stroked her fingers over them. "You?" she said. "You are the most lovely clanswoman alive. Why do you think he chose you?"

Because of Rian. Because of Father.

"Everyone speaks of your beauty. The wild desert rose," she told me. She laughed and lowered her voice. "And often they say very foul things about what they would like to do to a beauty like you. So trust me, you incite lust."

My cheeks flamed. "Oh."

"Oh, indeed," she told me, and kissed my hands. "Make him happy, little flower, but take a little happiness for yourself as well."

"Happiness?" said another cousin. "You'll be a queen. You'll have jewels and gold—you'll live in the City of Three and everyone will love you! How could you not be happy?"

I tried to smile, but another cousin grabbed my hands. "And the clothes!" she said. "They're scandalous, but you'll look so beautiful people will riot in the streets."

"And no one ever goes hungry there," said another girl.

My mother came back in, and her quick eyes brushed over my cousins. "Cora," she said. "Take the others and go fetch some food. It won't do to have Shalia faint right off the ledge, will it?"

"No, aunt," Cora said, bending her head to her. "We'll be right back."

The girls tittered and laughed as they filed out of the room, beaming back at me.

My mother drew a breath and came forward to me, taking my hands. "You're shaking," she said, meeting my eyes.

"I'm nervous," I whispered.

She smiled, smoothing my hair back. "You haven't been yet. You seemed so calm when we first spoke about your marriage."

I nodded. "I know."

"What are you afraid of, my little flower?"

I looked down at the ground.

"Tell me, Shalia," she said, pulling me down onto a bench.

"It just seemed so simple before—I would marry someone anyway; why shouldn't it be this foreign king? Especially if it stops our people from being murdered."

My mother's hands tightened on me, and I cursed my words. I had lost a brother when Torrin died, but she had lost a son.

"I don't want to leave everyone," I admitted in a hushed voice. "I don't want to leave you." My hands gripped hers painfully tight. "I feel like such a coward," I told her.

She wrapped her arms around me, my cowardice hidden in my mother's arms. "I know what we've asked you to do, my love. You are giving up your family and the desert, but you're making a brave choice for us. You are doing what your brothers, with all their swords and valor, can never accomplish—you are bringing us peace, and life, and safety."

I held her tight, not wanting to tell her that I would give it all up if it meant I could stay a child one day longer. If it meant Kata and I could swim on in the lake forever, and I would always be surrounded by my clan.

"I don't know how to be a queen," I protested.

She petted my hair. "Don't be silly, my love. You know exactly how to be queen."

I shook my head.

"Just look to us, Shalia. This new country, they will be your family now. You will teach them as you've taught Catryn and Gavan. You will support them as you do Aiden and Cael. Sometimes, you must even chide them as you do Kairos." She sighed with a smile. "And hopefully they'll listen to you, unlike him. You are your father's daughter, my love, and you can't help but lead."

I sniffed, pulling back to look at her. "I'd rather be like you," I told her softly. "You would never hesitate to do something that would save the clan, no matter the cost to you."

Her mouth trembled a little, and she gave a soft laugh. "I hesitate all the time, my love. You will stumble, just as I have. But you will persevere. You are a daughter of the desert and your feet—and heart—will never fail you."

She took me into her arms again until my tears were finished.

My cheeks were barely dry before my father came into the room. He kissed my mother gently and came to me, taking my hands.

For the first time in my life, I didn't want to meet his eyes, scared he would see my indecision, my confusion, my fear.

"You look beautiful, daughter," he said to me. "I never thought I would see the day when you became a wife. How can you have seventeen years already?"

I sniffed, and my father tugged my chin up so he could see my eyes, desperately holding back tears. His face changed, filling with worry that looked strange on his warrior's impassive scowl.

"You're frightened?" he asked.

Taking a deep breath, I nodded slowly.

He tucked me against him. “You don’t have to marry. You can stay with me all your days,” he told me, soft into my ear. “I won’t mind.”

A little laugh jumped out of me at the idea, so close to my own thoughts a moment ago. But I thought of my mother’s words, my brothers’ lives, my clan’s safety, and resolve twisted around my spine, making me strong. “No. I want to marry him.”

He pulled back a little. “You’re certain, my girl?”

My skin glowed, the brown shining until it looked like dark gold. My breath shook as I smoothed down the light blue robes, running shaking fingers over embroidered threads of every color for luck, for wealth, for love, for babies. Everything was in place—everything was just as I had imagined it—but I felt like the shed skin of a snake, still holding shape but hollow inside.

And yet, I could give no other answer. I nodded.

He touched my chin to urge me to stand straighter, and I did. His hands rested on my shoulders as he looked me over. Father’s eyes came back to my face, and his lips curled into a small smile as he gave me a single, solemn nod.

Mother placed a gauzy cloth in my father’s hands. He bowed over the gift, and she bowed back to him, then came forward and kissed him as he stood straight.

He smiled at her, and I wondered if my husband would look at me like that. If he could ever love me without knowing me first, choosing me and not my father’s position, my brother’s head, my people’s pride.

My father held back the tent flap, and my mother nudged me forward. Outside my tent, the whole clan was assembled, waiting for me.

I shut my eyes for a moment before I greeted them. I could do this. This was for them. This was for my people, my family, my clan.

And that would give me strength.

The sun hadn't risen yet, but it was close, the sky flush with wanting for the light. Caught in the half world between night and day, my family came forward to bless me. The women murmured behind us, speaking words to the Great Skies, calling down blessings to me as the men of the clan filed in behind the women.

The women parted, and my breath caught. In the light of day, Rian's dark skin was paler than I'd ever seen it from the years of living outside the desert's unrelenting sun, and his hair was cut in a strange, short style.

My oldest brother gave me a lopsided grin. "Kata ruined my surprise, didn't she?" Rian said, coming to wrap his arms around me.

I pressed my head into his shoulder, hugging him tight. "I knew, but that didn't ruin it," I told him. "I'm so happy to see you."

He pulled back. "I wouldn't miss this day, Shy."

"Even if I'm marrying *him*?" I lifted my eyes to his.

The grin fell a little, and he kissed my temple. "You don't have to do this," he told me softly.

I met his eyes and squared my shoulders. "I'm sorry. I know it's not what you want," I told him. "But I want to do this."

He sighed, hugging me again. "Don't be sorry," he said. "Be happy."

I sniffed, letting go of him. He kissed my cheek once more and stepped back.

Rian held up a red thread knotted with gold coins. It was heavy as he placed it around my neck, and I looked at the coins, staring at the foreign seal printed on the face. They were Trifectate coins, and tomorrow, when I left the desert to go live in my husband's country, they would be my currency. My brother's strange and hidden life in another country would now be my future.

He kissed my cheek. "For wealth, little sister. That you never want for anything."

"Will you stand with me?" I asked.

"I don't think that will endear you to your husband, Shy. As little as I like giving up my right as the eldest, I think my presence would only remind him of the Resistance, not peace."

"At least you're here," I murmured, squeezing him.

Cael gave a solemn look to Rian as he stepped up to me. "Even though Rian can't be there, you won't stand alone," he told me. He showed me a white-and-black thread woven together. "You are desert born, and you will never be alone."

Aiden was next, giving me a blue thread knotted around a mountain cat tooth. "For ferocity," he said, pinching my nose. "Show them what the heart of the desert truly is."

Kairos took my hand. Osmost, his hawk that was always on his shoulder, sprang up at this, shrieking into the sky. Kairos held my hand and tied the light blue thread around my wrist. "Keep your secrets," he said with a flash of his bright smile. "A woman needs secrets."

My two little siblings were next, Catryn and Gavan standing together. They presented one thread, tied around a small purse. "I made the thread, and he made the purse," Cat explained. She put it around my neck.

"It's full of seeds," Gavan said. "In case they don't feed you."

"So you never go hungry," Catryn corrected.

Gavan shrugged. "Same thing."

They stepped aside, and the rest of the clan came forward, stringing threads over my neck. The women began to sing, a low keening cry.

As each thread was placed over my neck, I was struck by the weight of the threads that weren't there. The cousins who had died fighting back the Trifectate. The women and children who had starved when we couldn't find food without our best hunters. Our numbers had dwindled, and yet the spirits of those we'd lost pressed close upon me, clinging to my skin like the smell of burning bodies on the sand.

I carried death into my marriage.

Kata was last, never part of the clan, but she came to me and squeezed my hands and kissed both of my cheeks. "I have to stay hidden," she reminded me. "But my heart is with you."

I nodded and hugged her tight. She let me go and gave me one last, sad look before going to stand by Rian.

By the time the clan was done, it was nearly time. My neck was heavy, and everyone stepped back from me.

The sun was coming up over the dune, and I faced the entrance to the city as it did. Standing before my clan, I was the first thing the light touched, and as it hit my face, the singing rose. The sunlight and the sound filled up the hollow space inside me, and I shut my eyes, trying to trap it there, trying to hold the power and peace of the desert within me always.

My father came forward with the cloth, laying it on my shoulders and wrapping it lightly around my head. "The next man who sees your face will be yours forever," he told me.

And then we began to walk. The women behind me broke down the tents and packed them in our quick, efficient way, but from then on, I was not allowed to look back. I was not allowed to stop.

Instead I moved forward, feeling the sand filter through my sandals, rushing over my feet, urging me onward.

Peace wasn't a thing that came swift and easy. Peace took courage and faith, and I had those. I would make my family proud, and through my wedding I would protect them for once. For always.

Charlatan

When we came to the break, my father went first, leading us into the city as Osmost took to the air. The long staircase was dark after the unending, unshadowed light in the desert, and it took a disorienting moment to adjust.

In the darkness, I thought of the night before, sneaking down to the lake that called to Kata.

I wondered if I would miss the sand as she did the water.

The sunlight broke on us at the end of the stairs, and we walked out into the wide avenue of Jitra's stone-carved dwellings.

"Dragon!"

I turned to see my uncle embrace my father, then turn to my mother and haul her off the ground. She was small, like my sister, Catryn, and I wondered how it would be to feel so delicate within a family. To be a woman who bore eight children, a woman of iron and bone, and still look fragile.

"D'Falcos clan welcomes you to Jitra," my uncle said.

"D'Dragyn clan is most welcomed," my father said, bowing to him at such formality.

"And our little bride!" my uncle cried, turning to me. He was not like my father. He was tall—most desert men were—but he was soft where my father was battle scars and rock.

And it was silly to call me little. I was only half a hand shorter than he was.

"Uncle," I said, sweeping my wedding robes back and giving him a bow before he laughed and hugged me.

"It is a miracle," he said. "The Trifectate and the clans in one city without any of it on fire."

My heart went tight and my mouth ran dry.

"Saying things may wish them so," my mother said, patting her brother on the arm. "Don't."

He huffed out in protest, but she silenced him. "Is the procession ready?" she asked.

He smiled at her and nodded.

As we moved through Jitra, everyone came out of their houses, offering threads and blessings to me, and then followed us. It was a long labor, and Jitra sloped down sharply, so much that I felt like my body tilted back as we walked down, my feet moving forward but my head leaning away, torn between my future and past.

My clan was around me in a cloud, but they all suddenly stopped and whispered and giggled. They parted enough to let me see why.

There was a man there, standing across the river. He stood beside a girl, younger than I was. They both had pale skin and dark, shining hair. She wore some kind of fashion that was like a robe but bound tight to her body with ribbons, but he was magnificent. I knew it was the traditional garb of the foreign men, but his clothes were cut so close to his body they seemed indecent, and hidden behind my covering, I let my eyes wander. He had powerful legs and a narrow waist, shoulders that seemed wider than my hands outstretched. The kind of shoulders that could surround a girl and make a fortress with their strength.

And eyes. Such eyes. They were green, bright as fire, lashed thick in black and so powerful their heat leaped across the distance.

He was looking at me.

He nodded, slow and respectful. Though he couldn't see my eyes, I swore his met mine.

My cousins and family closed around me then, pushing me along. *Please*, I prayed to the Skies, *let that be my husband.*

We kept walking, and I caught glimpses of the foreign man as he processed down as well, meeting with others dressed in similar uniforms.

Maybe it wasn't my husband. Perhaps that woman was his wife, and I still had yet to know my fate.

We reached the edge of the city, and the clan stopped. Cael came forward, leading me to the very edge of the cliff. Beside us, the river that was the life-giving vein running down the center of Jitra came to an end, dropping over the cliff and pooling thirty feet below.

As I held my breath, Cael helped me down the old, slick ladder of rock to stand on the ledge beside the pool. I looked up, and my family was only shadows against the bright glare of light.

Cael touched my arm. I let out a breath and allowed him to lead me forward to the Teorainn, the small bridge of rock that the river had cut under. I could feel the thunder of the water and the falls vibrating beneath my feet.

The Teorainn was only feet wide and not much longer across, the very limit of Jitra and my world, and at the sight of it, my heart pounded.

Keeping my eyes away from the thousand-foot drop on the other side of the bridge, I looked over, and my heart matched the thunder of the falls.

As if I had wished him into being, the handsome man I had seen earlier was standing there, his hands behind his back, looking regal and stately. *It must be him. It must be my husband.*

I looked at him, in his perfect grandeur, as if expecting some signal. But he couldn't see me looking through the cloth, I remembered. I knew he had a younger brother—this must be the man beside him, slightly taller and more severe, his nose twisted, his face hard and brutal like it was carved from the rock around us.

Of course, I couldn't be certain. One of them was my husband and one of them was his witness, and I suspected I wouldn't know for sure until my husband was the one to remove the veil.

Cael stood behind me on the small landing and nudged me toward the Teorainn. I could see the pool to my left and the infinite, terrible drop on the right.

A gust of wind pushed me a little, and I sucked in a breath, trying to plant my feet.

It was unnatural, a desert girl so high above the earth. I was a dragon, a scorpion, not a bird.

I stepped forward and froze. I was shaking so hard I didn't trust myself to take another step. My whole body was trembling, and I couldn't look up, staring at my feet and the rushing water beneath the bridge so long the rest of me felt off-balance too.

I am going to fall.

Uselessly, wildly, I put my arms out, trying to balance, and it didn't help. My heart was pounding in my throat, and I couldn't even cry out or look for my brother. I was *alone*, and I was going to die.

Arms caught me, but it wasn't Cael—my savior was in front of me, and my hands landed on stiff black cloth. I looked up to see the broken nose of the second Trifectate man on the bridge.

My heart sank as I realized my girlish hopes of the handsome man becoming my husband were wrong. Certainly it didn't matter—despite his nose, he wasn't ugly, by any means. Besides, I wasn't marrying him for his face—and he had just saved me from falling a thousand feet, after all.

He took my shaking hands, his skin warm and rough against mine, and the shaking calmed. "Come," he said, loosing one of my hands. I drew a deep breath, and my heart beat heavy and hard as he took the end of the cloth and unwound it from my face.

Our eyes met in truth for the first time. I drew a slow breath in, and something within me shifted, moved, sliding around my chest and pulling tight, shivering down my spine.

But then it was like the shiver was contagious, and the earth jolted, shaking and moving, threatening to throw us off the Teorainn as I gasped, clinging to the black cloth on my husband's arms.

It wasn't my imagination either; someone shouted, and my husband caught me, holding my arm and waist, so close to holding me tight in his arms that I couldn't breathe.

A moment later the world seemed to calm, and the guests all looked at one another, murmuring about what had caused the tremor. My husband took my hand again.

"What was that?" he asked.

I shook my head, mute. I had no idea.

He looked past me to Cael. "Is the bridge still stable?" he asked, shouting over the water's roar.

"Mountains break and move," Cael said. "Jitra is eternal."

My husband's eyebrows lifted, looking at me. I opened my mouth to start speaking the words, but he spoke before I did.

"Come," he repeated. "Meet your husband."

He pulled me along the bridge as my heart stopped. *Meet him? Hadn't I just . . .*

But no. It couldn't be.

The one with the broken nose brought me to the apex of the Teorainn and easily stepped around his brother. Behind him, as Cael did for me. His brother's witness, and not my husband.

I couldn't help but shake. They had done it all wrong—it was my husband who was supposed to remove the covering, who was supposed to have that magic moment of unveiling. No one else. Not a brother. Not a *charlatan*!

How could he have not known this error? My mother had schooled me for *weeks* on every moment of what would happen at this ceremony—had no one told the same things to him?

My true husband really was the handsome one I had first seen, first wished for, his green eyes bright and captivating, staring at me like he was waiting for something.

He squeezed my hand, and I realized I was supposed to speak. "We've come to the ends of the earth so that we may journey back together," I said, so soft it was little more than a whisper. "Here I leave the maiden, the daughter, the child. Here I become a wife, one part with my husband."

I saw his lips move, saying a version of the same, but I couldn't hear him over the river water and the violent rush of blood in my ears. *Wrong. It was all wrong.*

I turned to Cael, and he handed me the bunch of flowers in his hand. I tore off the heads, filling my hands with multilayered blooms, and turned back to my husband. *Husband.*

My husband held out his hand, and I put some of the blooms into it. He looked at me, and we spoke the final words together, words my cousins made me practice late into the night until I knew them by heart.

"Today we release our former selves like flowers unto the wind. Today we become one."

I opened my hand and he did the same, letting the flower petals drop a little before they caught the wind and swirled up, a few coming back toward us and the rest flying out into the air.

Then his hands were on my waist and he pulled me closer. I turned back to him and sucked in a gasp. He paused for a moment, and his warm breath ran over my lips before he pressed forward, kissing me. His lips were dry, and I stood still, wondering if I was meant to do something else. He let me go all at once, and despite Cael's words earlier, I did feel alone.

No one in my family told the Tri King that his brother had made a grave blunder, but it was all I could think of. We were taken to the great hall of Jitra, and the raucous celebration that usually followed a wedding was delayed as my father and husband sat at a long table, and the families were introduced. My father shook hands with my husband's brother, and he bowed his head respectfully, saying his name—"Galen." Galen straightened and swept his arm behind his sister, saying her name—"Danae." They stood stiffly as all my siblings save Rian were introduced to them, and my husband watched, his chin raised, staring at them coolly.

Then the families parted like water, the desert to one side, the Trifectate to the other.

"My siblings and I are the Three-Faced God incarnate, the Holy Rulers of the Bone Lands and the vastness of the Trifectate, and we have taken your daughter as one of our own," my husband said. He looked at me, standing with my siblings behind the table, and his eyes held mine for a moment in a way that made me smile and stand straighter. I had done it—I had said the words, and this was my reward. Peace. "And I will care for her as family should. And in so doing, I pledge to lay down my arms and leave the desert unmolested."

"We promise to do the same," my father said. "We will keep our borders and leave the Bone Lands free from any retaliation from our people, and we will welcome the Bone Lands into the desert. We will be at peace."

"Peace," my husband echoed, and he raised his cup to me as documents were brought forth. They drank from a shared cup and signed the papers, and then my husband quit the table, coming to me. Great feast tables were brought out, the remnants of the treaty signing removed, and music played. His hands slipped over my waist and everything else was forgotten, my heart stuttering with nerves. "Come with me?" he asked.

I smiled brightly at him and nodded.

The sky was dark and had taken all the heat of the day with it, and as soon as we stepped outside, I shivered.

"You're cold," he realized. "Take my jacket." He started unbuttoning what I'd thought was a shirt. It never occurred to me in all the time I'd seen Trifectate men that they might have *more* clothes under the black. He put it around my shoulders, and it was warm from his body.

"You must have been so warm today," I said, pulling it around me.

He shrugged. "I'm certainly not used to desert heat." He tugged the jacket straighter on me, then let his hands settle on my waist. It was the closest I'd ever been to a boy not my brother. I knew I was staring at him. He was . . . beautiful. He had a wide jaw, a sharp, short nose, and black hair that fell rakishly over his forehead.

His handsome face *almost* made up for his brother removing the veil. Almost.

I reached up and smoothed his hair back, and he smiled. His thumbs stroked my waist, but it felt oddly ticklish.

"Are you pleased by this match?" he asked. "By our marriage?"

"Of course," I said quickly.

"Are you pleased by me?"

I met his eyes. They were direct, forceful, like staring into the sun. "I think so," I said.

He nodded. "Your happiness is important to me."

"It is?"

His hand touched my cheek, stroking it gently and nudging my chin down. His thumb touched my lower lip, and then his mouth followed it. I waited, patiently, to feel the things my cousins spoke of—heat, and electricity such as a summer storm had never seen.

But they never came.

But they would. He was handsome, and we were married now—it was simply a matter of getting used to each other.

He pulled back. "I am yours," he said. "Entirely."

I smiled at him because I knew this was supposed to please me, but I wasn't even sure what that meant. I was devoted and committed to this marriage, and him, and the cause they both represented, but was that the same thing as being *his*? I didn't know.

"Do you know what's strange?" he asked, touching my cheek again. "I don't even know your name."

"Shalia," I said, stunned. He had never asked? Never once, in all of this?

But then, I hadn't asked for his name either. This marriage had never been about us.

"And I'm Calix," he told me. He smiled. "I'm sorry to have kissed you without knowing your name, Shalia."

It sounded . . . silly. This whole thing was silly. I smiled at him, putting my hand on his chest carefully, wondering what it would take to lay claim to the heart beneath my palm. "The past doesn't matter," I assured him. "Our future together does."

He nodded, kissing me again, and I pressed my mouth against his, wondering if I was supposed to push harder to feel something. Or maybe this was just what kissing felt like, and my cousins simply exaggerated?

He broke off, smiling. "We will have a grand future together, wife."

"Come!" Kairos said, striding to me with a wild grin on his face, his shoulder missing a hawk. "Shy, bring your husband for a dance!" he ordered. "And, Your Highness, please convince your sister to dance with me!"

I looked around him to see Danae slipping away into the crowd.

"Calix?" I asked hesitantly.

"I'd be honored," he said, smiling.

I drew him into the crowd of dancers, and I let go of his hand to hold up fistfuls of my robes. The dances of my people were fast, complex, and intoxicating, stomping and jumping, twisting to brush against the person you were dancing with. We barely entered the crowd when I was overcome with cousins and brothers and even my sweet little Catryn, swinging me around and laughing, pulling me away from my husband.

I saw a flash of silver-blond hair, and I turned away from Aiden, finding it again and going toward it. Kata's hood had only fallen for a moment, but I saw her face in the crowd and pushed my way toward her.

By the time I got to where I'd seen her, she was gone. I looked through the crush of people, but I couldn't see her.

My husband came to my side, catching my arm. "Who was that?" he asked.

"Who?" I asked.

He squeezed my arm. "I saw someone. A girl who looked like an islander. You were walking toward her."

I pulled my arm away from him. "There *are* no islanders," I said sharply. Too sharply, perhaps, but his father had eradicated Kata's people.

His eyes cut to mine. He drew a deep breath, and the edge in his eyes faded. "Forgive me," he said. "It must have been the light. Would you care for a drink?"

I tried to force myself to smile, but it felt like a flicker of fire over my face, barely there and gone again. "Yes. Come; we'll drink together."

He nodded.

When I took him to the tables of wine, I saw his brother at the tables ahead of us. Smiling, I opened my mouth to call to him, but his eyes flicked over both of us with quick efficiency, and he turned away.

"So this isn't made from grapes?" my husband asked.

Shaking my head to try to forget his brother's slight, I told him about the ilayi wine and cactus wine from the desert plants and offered him a glass of each to drink. Rather than sip as I expected, he upended each, much to the encouragement of the other men drinking.

I smiled and laughed, and he put the cup down, smiling back. "Your people are easy to impress," he said to me, looking at the other men raising their glasses to him.

That stung a little, but I ignored it—surely he meant it as a compliment, and even if he didn't, all the resentment between the Trifectate and the desert would not be erased in a single night. "They are far more impressed by dancing," I told him, offering him my hand in invitation.

He hesitated and opened his mouth, but my family interceded, Catryn tugging me into the fray as my brothers pulled Calix, showing him how to dance. I even saw my cousins trying to force Calix's stone-faced brother onto the floor, and the rock floor rumbled as we pounded it with our feet. I watched my father and mother dancing close in each other's arms, and my heart swelled with joy—my husband and I were married, my people were safe, and it wouldn't be long before my husband looked at me in the way my father had always looked at my mother. We would be safe, and I would be loved.

Heavens and Stars

I danced until I couldn't breathe, and my whole body was hot and damp with sweat. I saw my sister sitting on a bench to the side of the hall, and I went to her with a laugh, sitting down beside her. "My feet are going to fall off," I told her.

She kicked her own feet up. "Liar. Our feet will never fail us."

"Maybe they will after a wedding. Are you having fun?"

She gave me a bright smile. "I like the dancing."

I grinned back. "I like it too." It struck me suddenly that tomorrow I would leave her, and I wouldn't see her for a long time. Tugging her closer to me, I pressed kisses into her hair.

She tried to twist away. "Shy!" she whined. "What are you *doing*!"

"Kissing you," I told her. "I'm going to miss you."

This stilled her. "You're really going away tomorrow?"

I nodded.

"But you'll be back, won't you? As soon as you have babies, they'll need to be blessed here."

Babies. Stupid, foolish idiot that I was—I'd forgotten about the night, where he would put his hands on me in a way no one ever had. In a way no one else ever would. I'd been so nervous about everything else I'd forgotten to be nervous about *that.*

Suddenly I felt like I couldn't breathe. "Yes," I said softly. "They'll need to be blessed here."

"Then you'll be back soon. And you won't treat me like a baby when you return," she told me, wriggling away and pecking my cheek before she ran off to join the dancers.

My head spun, and I stood, going outside the hall.

The desert night was brutally cold, but it was the only thing that kept me from heaving. My blood seemed to pound so heavily behind my eyes that it hurt.

I gasped for breath, drinking in the cold, trying to soothe some part of myself.

"Rough night?" Kairos drawled, appearing from the darkness like a wraith. My brother had that strange way, always sliding about the world like he knew of secret passageways the rest of us couldn't see.

I jumped, but he grinned at me and tucked my hair behind my ear. "What are you doing out here?" I asked.

He shrugged. "Didn't feel much like dancing."

"Even with that pretty Tri Princess?" I asked.

He gave a wry laugh that I didn't quite understand. "She's not for me, Shy."

I sighed. "You're so picky. You can have your choice of women; you always could."

His shoulders lifted. "There are many people who you'll care about in your life, little sister. But there will only be one who moves the heavens and stars for you. And that's what I'm looking for. What we *all* deserve. And I haven't found that yet. But I'll know it when I do."

I tipped my head back to take in the stars, thinking of all our ancestors who lived up there. "What we all deserve—except me, you mean."

I looked to him and his eyes met mine, but he didn't move. Thinking. Trying to double back on his words. "You could love him. You only just met him."

"How long do you think it takes?" I asked. "Until you know you're in love?"

He laughed. "I'm not sure there's a standard measure."

Could I ever love my husband so much? Did I even know how?

He sighed again, putting his arm around my shoulders and squeezing. He kissed my temple and whispered, "None of us knows what fate has in store, little sister. There's love for you yet."

I leaned against him, nodding.

"Besides," he told me, "I'm going to find a way to come with you."

My heart leaped, but the thrill faded fast. "You can't," I said. "You're needed here."

"No, I'm not. I'm not the strongest brother, or the oldest, and I have no desire to marry anytime soon."

"Father will want you for his Shadow," I said.

Kairos lifted a shoulder. "If Father wants me as his clever little spy, I won't say no. But even if that's my destiny, I will learn a great deal more in the arms of the Trifectate than in the desert."

A shadow swooped by us, and I heard Osmost call out a warning scream.

Kairos grinned wolfishly. "And Osmost thinks the Tri City has rats for him to hunt."

I shook my head. "Father asked if he could send attendants with me. The king said no."

He waved this away. "You'll see," Kairos said. "I'll figure out a way to be there. To protect you."

My mouth opened, with the same protest I'd had for years with five older brothers—*I don't need to be protected.* But despite my brave words, tomorrow was full of everything unknown and all I wanted was to feel a tiny bit as safe as I had my entire life.

"I hope so," I told him with a sigh. "I should find my husband."

He nodded to me, and I went inside.

Calix met my eyes across the hall, but he didn't have a chance to come to me. My family swarmed around me, all the women fluttering cloths of light blue, hiding me from the men. They huddled me out of the hall like a secret and took me to the rooms we had been given.

They started to take my threads off my neck, then open my robes, and I pulled away. "Stop, stop, please," I begged, and Cora caught my hands.

She met my eyes. "Women have much to fear in a world like ours, cousin. But the bedroom is yours to rule."

She pulled at my robes then, and tears gathered in my eyes as they took my clothes, pushing me into the prepared bed with soft blankets and many pillows. They lit wax candles all around the chamber as I clung to the bedding, trying not to cry.

My mother touched my hand, and I jumped. She smiled gently. "I know it's frightening," she told me. "But soon it will be wondrous, the most loving, intimate act two people can share with each other."

I nodded at her, but at that moment, I didn't believe her. Cora and a few of my other cousins kissed my face and my hands, and then they were gone.

The room was warm with so much fire, but I was shivering. It wasn't long until I heard the noise of men climbing the stairs.

I watched in terror as the door swung open and my husband was pushed inside before the door shut sharply.

He looked at me for many moments. "You're making the sheets tremble," he said.

I clutched them harder.

He came closer to me. The men had pulled at his clothing so it was askew, but still on his body. He sat on the bed, and I refused to let myself move away from him.

He drew a slow breath and didn't touch me. "You're nervous," he said softly.

I wanted to tell him that "nervous" utterly failed to describe the feelings inside me, but words didn't come out of my mouth.

His eyes rose and looked at me, and I blinked, staring back. "You're young by any measure, and close to ten years younger than me. Tonight will be painful. I wish that weren't so, but it is."

I hugged my knees, willing myself not to cry.

"Do you know why I wanted this marriage?" he asked.

I looked at him, shaking my head a tiny bit.

"My people need peace," he said softly. "And hope. And I think that settling things with the desert will help, but having a queen, having children—it will show my people that we are not meant for war now. We are for family and peace."

His eyes watched me, and I thought I needed to respond somehow, but I didn't know what to say.

"You—watching you today, dancing with your family, you can become those things to me, Shalia. A king . . . a king has little place in his life for emotion, for weakness. But I believe that you will make me stronger. I believe that you will save my people."

So many thoughts stuttered and stopped, tripping over one another in my mind. I wanted to save my people too. I wanted family and peace. But how could we have family without emotion? Was emotion the same as weakness? I had never known it as such.

Before I could say anything, he caught a bit of my hair and tugged me gently forward. He pressed his mouth to mine, slowly, and petted my hair. He opened his mouth, and I mimicked him.

I didn't feel love, or lust, or heat. I felt frightened and far too aware of where my hands were and how to move my head.

He stopped kissing me as he took off his clothes. "It will only hurt once," he said. "And then we will have a family together. And our peoples will have peace."

I wanted all those things. Family, children, and peace. I nodded, trying to want this. To want him.

When he got into the bed with me, to my utter shame, I cried. His hands touched my arms, and a sudden, desperate instinct to flee rose up in me and I tried to push him off.

"Stop," he said, holding me fast, his hands gripping my arms. I froze, feeling tears slide out the side of my eyes. He sighed, and his hands gentled and rubbed the skin on my arms until I could take a breath. "Stop," he said again, even though I was already still, panicked beneath him. He swallowed, his throat bobbing and moving, and he sat up, backing away from me. He turned from me and sat on the edge of the bed, rubbing his face.

"I'm sorry," I whispered, the first words I'd spoken since he'd come into the room.

He didn't look at me. "Maybe this was a mistake."

Even as a tiny flutter of hope lifted my heart that perhaps I wouldn't have to do this, my stomach felt like lead. "If we don't consummate the marriage, it will be invalid."

He turned and looked at me with an edge of suspicion. "Is that what you want?"

Silently, I shook my head. No. I had come this far, and I couldn't fail now. *It will be wondrous*, my mother had said. *The most loving, intimate act two people can share with each other.* I clung to her words.

"Tell me about your home," he said, and I drew in a breath, confused.

"My home?" I repeated.

He gave a ragged sigh. "Yes," he said. "Or ask me a question. Talk to me of anything until this doesn't seem quite so frightening for you."

I both appreciated his kindness and also felt a sting in his words that made me feel like I was failing in my duty, but I drew my knees up, hugging them. "Was that the only reason you wanted to marry me?" I asked softly. "For peace?"

He looked at me, his eyes sharp and assessing. "I want to embrace the desert with friendship instead of arms," he said, but the answer still felt coy to me. "Why do you ask?"

"You want to send your men to the desert," I reminded him.

He nodded, leaning back on the bed. "Yes, my quaesitori gather knowledge and intelligence. We know so little of the desert. And of course, it's rumored that your brother is gathering Trifectate dissenters to the desert."

"What is it you wish to know of desert ways?" I asked, ignoring the part about Rian. He would never endanger us by bringing his rebellion here—Father, if nothing else, would never allow it.

He drew a slow breath, and the suspicious edge was back in his eyes. "Can I trust you, wife?"

"Of course," I told him, frowning.

"I'm searching for something. Something infinitely precious to me."

The lake. "What is it?" I asked, my heart beating faster.

"What do you know about sorcery?" he asked me.

"Do you mean the Vis peoples, the islanders?" I asked, averting my eyes from his. "I know they're gone."

"They are no longer one and the same," he told me. "The Vis may have disappeared, but their foul magic has spread—we have seen it even in the Trifectate."

I looked at him, unsure how to respond, unwilling to betray how much I knew about such magic. "Foul?" I asked.

"Oh yes," he said, shaking his head. "Their power deceives and destroys. It can burn a house to ash and take the air from your lungs. It is truly the darkest threat of all. Because of that, I'm searching for an elixir that renders their powers useless," he said. "It is the only way to ensure peace and safety for my kingdom, my family." He looked at me a moment. "Our family."

"But couldn't the powers also be used for good?" I asked. I had never known Kata's power to hurt us—in fact, her ability to find water in the desert often meant the difference between life and death.

He didn't look at me, and he was still a long time. "There's a prophecy," he said quietly, "that an Elementa will be the one to kill me. My father thought he prevented that prophecy from coming true, but now . . ." He stopped, then sighed and shook his head. "That power has taken everything from me. Everything I ever cared about. It is the single most vicious, dangerous thing in this world. And if I don't get that elixir, it will take my life."

Heat flushed my cheeks at the finality of his words. "And you believe this elixir is in the desert?" I asked. "Very little can survive in the desert."

"I've been assured that it is," he said. "Given to your people to protect."

"I have never heard of such a thing," I told him honestly. "Perhaps my father would know."

"You cannot tell him," Calix said, turning his face to glare at me, hard and serious. "If you do, I will know there can be no faith between us as husband and wife."

"But why?" I asked. "He may know the answer."

"We may have peace, but your father still knows me as his enemy," he told me. "It has to be done carefully, and my hope is to find it without him ever knowing."

Anger rose in my chest, tight and hot. "You mean because you believe he might not let you have it if you find it."

"I do not want to be set up to oppose your father," he said, touching my hand. "For both our sakes."

Better between them than standing to the side as they burn another one of my brothers in the sand. I remembered my bold words to Kata the night before; I had never thought that they would come to bear quite so rapidly. "Why did you tell me?" I asked softly.

"Because you are not my enemy," he said, tugging my hand to his mouth so he could kiss it. "You are my wife. And keeping this secret will prove that I can trust you as I so desire."

He continued to apply gentle pressure to my hand, making me come toward him in the middle of the bed, and he stopped when I was right in front of him. I licked my lips, still frightened, but it wasn't as paralyzing as before. "Can I trust you?" I asked, but I knew the answer before he said it. I could never tell him about Kata, or about the lake, or everything I knew about the elemental powers.

He nodded, his face grave. "Always," he told me, coming closer and kissing me again. My heart thudded against my chest, but I swallowed down the fear that rose up with it. I could take a little pain—I was a queen now. I could do this.

Everything felt strange—his mouth against mine was slick and intimate, and I couldn't stop from jumping every time he touched my skin. As the barriers between our skin disappeared, I felt vulnerable and exposed, my muscles tense and unsure.

When the worst of the pain struck, I cried out, and he told me it would be better after that. I bit my lip and tried not to let him see me cry, but I couldn't help but feel tricked by my mother's words and my husband's promise—instead of some wondrous act, it felt like he had betrayed whatever delicate trust he had just spoken of. Instead of two people made whole, I felt like I had fractured.

The Dragon on the Wall

The next morning I woke with the sun, and my husband was asleep in the bed beside me. I stared at him for barely a moment, and I inched my way to the bottom of the bed, trying to get out without waking him.

The sheet pulled away from me, and I cringed at the rush of cold air. I wanted something to cover myself with, and more than that, something to curl into and never emerge from, something to help me forget the night before. Shame, I realized. I felt ashamed, and it was a foreign feeling in my breast.

I stood from the bed, shivering. My wedding robes were folded neatly in the corner, and I picked them up. It seemed strange to wear these clothes twice, but I had to leave and I didn't care what I wore to do it.

My sandals were beneath the robes, and I left them there. I needed the sand and the stone beneath my feet to remind me that there was something unchanging left in the world.

Jitra was more quiet and still than I had ever seen it. The celebrations would have gone on late into the night, and now it left the walkways empty for me. Ducking between two rock-hewn homes, I found the narrow entrance in the rock that led below the city to the place I was looking for. I moved easily along the steep staircase despite the lack of light. Desert people could hear the whispers from the earth, and I had long since learned the language Jitra spoke.

The staircase ended, and it opened into a room. I lit the torch there, careful to replace the flint. It crackled to life and filled the cool room with sudden heat, revealing the secret of the chamber.

There were names carved into the wall, hundreds of names in small, cramped writing. I moved down along the walls, dragging my fingers over the names like I could call out to my kinsmen.

"Oh."

I gasped at the voice behind me, dropping the torch and spinning to face my husband's brother, then jumping away when I felt the heat of the fire on my legs.

"Easy," Galen said, rushing forward. He caught up the torch and placed it safely in a cradle on the wall, immediately close to me.

I stepped backward.

"I didn't mean to scare you," he said. He shook his head, turning back. "Good day."

Maybe it was the spirits of my family that made me bold, or maybe it was just that I wasn't used to being poorly thought of, but as his foot touched the stair, I called, "I would like to know why you don't like me very much."

He stopped, his hands on the wall, making his shoulders hunch up. "What makes you think that, Shalia?"

His use of my name seemed harsh, but I remembered him looking at Calix and me and then walking away the night before.

"You didn't speak to me last night. You don't wish to speak with me now." I smiled a little. "I don't think I've seen you smile yet."

"I'm not much for words," he said.

Was that all it was?

He pushed off the stairs and turned, his back against the wall, watching me. "Why would it matter, if I like you or not?"

I was about to be alone for the first time in my life, in his country, where I knew nothing and no one, but I couldn't think of a way to answer that didn't make me sound like a scared little girl. "You're my husband's brother," I told him.

His eyes narrowed on me. "Family is more important to the desert clans than it is to the Trifectate."

I wasn't even sure what he meant by that, but it felt like a rebuke. Nodding to him in what I hoped was a dismissive gesture, I turned into the darker part of the cave, going to the person I was really saying good-bye to down here. I traced his name on the wall.

"This place—it was made by Elementae?" he asked.

I shook my head. "I don't think so. Jitra has been here since the beginning of time."

Galen looked above him, suspicious, as if the walls could attack. "In the Trifectate, it's treason to use such power now. Punishable by death." He sighed, looking over the wall with my family's names. "A great many beautiful places the Elementae built have been demolished to serve the pleasure of the Three-Faced God."

"It is treasonous to remember their gifts?" I asked.

He looked at me, his eyes guarded. "Yes."

"Why?" I asked.

His eyes moved to the stairs and back to me, and I felt a shiver of warning run down my spine. "You cannot question the will of the Three-Faced God."

My chin rose, and I felt the familiar defiance of being a little sister to so many brothers rise up in me. "But I will be queen."

"Especially when you're queen," he said.

Our eyes met in the flickering light of the cave, and I wondered if he knew how he looked—severe and looming, his shape made larger by the shadows cast off from the flames, his eyes staring into mine and turning black against the brightness of the fire.

"What are these markings?" he asked, touching the stone next to us.

My mouth was dry for a moment. "This is where we keep our dead," I told him, looking back to the wall and the person I hadn't said good-bye to yet.

He looked at the ground.

I watched him, amused. "They aren't in the earth," I said. "They're on the walls."

He looked at the walls, aghast, and I smiled.

"You fear death," I said.

"Sometimes," he said. He looked at me, his powerful stare hitting me. "You don't?"

I went to the wall, tracing my fingers over the names. "For myself, I suppose. I don't want to die. But I'm not afraid of death, or of the dead. When we carve their names here, they stay with us. They live in the earth beside us. And eventually, their names wear away and they pass on, with all their family around them."

He came beside me, touching the wall. "These are names?"

I nodded.

"They look like little pictures."

"Everyone has a symbol. For you, and then for your family."

He ran his fingers over a line. "Some are much longer than others," he noticed.

I traced one with a sigh. "Long means you're further away from the head of the clan. You need more explanation."

"Who's that?" he asked, looking at my fingers. It was two symbols, a rabbit and a dragon.

"My brother Torrin," I told him, pulling away from the wall.

"How did he die?" he asked.

I closed my eyes and pressed my forehead against the rock, cold where I remembered the unrelenting heat of my brother's body being burned in the sand, returning his life to the Great Skies. "You killed him," I whispered. "His death was the reason my father finally agreed to talk peace terms with your country."

"*I* didn't kill him," he said sharply.

"You are a part of the Trifectate. Your brother says you and your siblings are the Three-Faced God incarnate—whether you held the sword or not, you were part of it." I felt his eyes on me, silent for a long time, and wondered whether it was wise to speak to him that way. I took my fingers from the wall and pressed a kiss to them, then brushed them back over my brother's name.

I turned to face Galen. His eyes glittered in the torchlight and it was hypnotic, engrossing. "This border has been disputed for five years. The desert people have aggressed just as much as the Trifectate. It's not as if I decided to attack your people on my own, on a whim."

"But you started it. Five years ago, you came to the desert with death." My cheeks felt hot, but despite knowing that criticizing his warfare would not endear me to him, I didn't check my words.

"I did not. That wasn't my decision."

"You are what you represent," I argued. "You know just what I mean. The Trifectate started this."

"Only after the desert stood with the islands in the war," he said, crossing his arms.

"But you *crushed* the islands," I insisted. "There was no reason to come for the desert."

"Ask my brother," he said. "He's the one who issued the order. I was not commander then."

"And so you take no responsibility for it?" I asked. "You are commander now. You have been for a long time."

"Would that make it easier?" he asked, and his voice was low, and harsh, and totally arresting. "You lost a brother. Your family sacrificed you in a marriage to buy peace. Would it make it easier to blame me and not my brother?"

My breath stopped in my chest. The light flickered over us, making our shadows move even though we were still. "I chose this marriage," I told him. "I know why I did—and that has everything to do with the number of names on this wall," I said sharply. "I didn't come down here for company—or an argument. I wanted to say good-bye to my brother."

The flame crackled on the wall as we looked at each other for a long moment. "Of course," he said finally. "My queen. Forgive me if I spoke out of turn."

I raised my chin and made for the stairs, hoping he wouldn't follow me. I took a last look at the names on the wall and prayed that my sacrifice would leave blank spaces there where my kinsmen would live instead of die.

When I looked back, Galen's head was still bent, and I liked the idea that a queen had replaced the pitiful girl from the night before whose courage had failed her when it came time to finish what she'd started.

Blessed Vessels

I returned to my rooms to find a storm of people there, women packing and men moving things, desert people and Tri guards alike. My husband should have been swarmed by people, given gifts and blessings by my clan, but he stood alone, his hands folded neatly behind his back.

"Where were you?" he asked as I drew close, kissing my cheek sweetly.

"Walking," I said. "Saying good-bye."

He nodded once. "In the future, I would prefer not to wake up alone."

I looked at him, trying to determine if this was a command or an intimacy, something he was sharing with me. "Of course," I said. "Have the clansmen already gone?" I asked.

He thought, and then nodded. "Oh, you mean the ones bearing gifts? I had my servants take them. Your family has not arrived yet."

Embarrassment flushed over my face. Those gifts were meant to be a clan's blessing on the newly married couple—he had turned them away, and I wasn't sure if I should tell him so. "Are the horses ready?"

"The carriage is."

"A carriage? Through the pass?" I asked.

He looked at me. "Yes. You, Danae, and I will ride in the carriage. Galen will defend us from horseback."

"*Defend* us?" I asked.

"Your Highness, Shalia," Kairos greeted us as he walked in with Mother and Father, bowing to the king. And me, I suppose. He straightened without being bidden and kissed my cheek, and Osmost swooped in to sit on his shoulder.

"She is your Highness now too," Calix said stiffly.

Kairos's hand stilled on my arm, but he gave my husband a bright, teasing grin. "Little sisters can never be high to big brothers," he told him. "Besides, I'm still a son of the desert, and she is queen of the Bone Lands now. But more importantly, it's going to rain," he said, a sly smile on his face.

I caught my breath.

Calix scowled. "Why does it matter if it's going to rain?" he asked.

My father heard this and came closer to us, his giant scimitar on his hip. "It's going to rain, Kairos?" he asked.

Kairos nodded.

"You'll have to go with them," my father said. "Lead them through the pass."

"This is not necessary," Calix said, glaring at Kairos, who was trying to restrain his smile and utterly failing. "And we don't have room in the carriage."

"I have my own horse," Kairos said.

"The pass gets very dangerous in the rain," I told Calix gently. "And I haven't traveled it enough to help the way Kai could."

"Yes," Kairos said cheerfully. "And to repay me for my gallant service, I happily accept an invitation to your castle to stay with my sister," he added, looking at my husband.

Color rose in Calix's cheeks, and his mouth drew tight. "A guide would be most welcome. But unfortunately we will have to leave you at the end of the pass; it won't be necessary to join us for the whole journey."

Kairos's smile grew tighter. "I'm sure it would be a comfort to my sister. Clans are very close; it would be difficult for her without any family around."

"She's my queen," Calix said. "I will be her comfort."

"Kairos attending Shalia is an excellent idea," my father said with a single, authoritative nod.

"Please," I said. "I'd like him to come with us."

My husband's face froze for a moment, and then he smiled at me. "Of course, wife." He pulled me close, kissing me.

Father made some sort of growling noise at a man kissing his daughter in front of him, and by the time Calix released me, Kairos and my father had turned to gather Kairos's things. I tried to pull away, but Calix gripped my hip. "Change into fresh clothes," he said, looking at my robes from the day before. "And don't contradict me."

The first part of our carriage ride was over wide and easy terrain along the mountain ridge. Rising with the land, I could see the desert to the left, burning gold until the sight shimmered and blurred on the horizon, and the craggy, impassable mountains on the right.

We were headed for the tunnel pass, a narrow road into the mountain that led to a wide, old land bridge thousands of feet above the river. I had never traveled far enough to know if this river came from the ocean to the west or perhaps from the same river that fed Jitra, but it rushed its way out to the eastern sea. The land bridge was the sole connection between the desert and the Bone Lands to the south. It was in the pass, somewhere in the darkness, that Torrin had died, fighting against Calix's men.

The carriage tilted downhill, and I caught my breath as we pitched.

"You're unused to carriages?" Danae asked. She sat across from me and my husband, her careful eyes regarding me.

I nodded. My stomach felt tight and stormy, and every bump and tilt reminded me of the pain from the night before. "We walk most places. We ride horses around the edge of the desert, where the sand is packed firm and their hooves can manage it. We are never so . . . enclosed."

"Miserable but safer," Calix said. "No random arrows flying at your head."

I turned to look at my husband. "Does that happen often?"

Calix's shoulder lifted and he reached for my hand, swiping his thumb over my knuckles. "People try. People fail. We will keep you safe, my love."

I held his hand in both of mine, surprised by the endearment. Did he love me? Was I meant to love him already?

"Calix is being dramatic," Danae said, looking to her brother. "The Three-Faced God will never let you be hurt, Shalia." I looked at her and she looked away again.

"Will you tell me of your God?" I asked Danae. "I don't know much of your religion."

Danae's smile was gentle. "What do you know?"

"That you three are the God incarnate, yes?"

She nodded, looking out the window again. "Yes. When I was born, the third child, my parents rejoiced," she said, and her smile grew a little tighter. "My father said the Three-Faced God had told him that his three children were the God Made Human. That we would be the most powerful rulers the Bone Lands had ever seen." She held out her hands in a triangle, pointing one of the ends at me. "With three faces, you can only ever see two, at the very most," she told me. "The third will always be hidden. Calix, he is the face of truth and justice. Galen is the face of honor and strength. And I am the hidden face, the piece that separates honor and truth, and also binds them together always."

Her fingers broke apart, the triangle gone, and she sat back.

"Is there such an incarnation in every generation?" I asked.

"No," Calix said. "The Three-Faced God has ruled for many years, and we are his first blessed vessels."

The carriage rolled into the pass at that moment, plunging us into darkness, and as I bumped and shifted against my husband, I wondered what kind of power it took to declare yourself a god.

Just after we cleared the pass, a heavy rainfall started, and out the carriage window, Kairos looked immensely pleased with himself. The army made camp in a field while we continued on to a keep that sat arched over the mountain road, ready to guard against an insurrection from the north. Desert men, I realized. This castle would defend the Bone Lands from clansmen.

We entered a courtyard to the left of the road, and there a full household of people stood to greet us. The head man rushed forward, eager to show his obeisance, but my husband stepped from the carriage, putting his hand inside for me to grasp. "All we require is a place to sleep tonight, Vestai Atalo. Certainly no such displays are necessary." He paused a moment. "And we will collect your taxes before we leave in the morning. You have accrued a hefty sum, have you not?"

The man blanched a little. "Of course. But, Your Highness, the new queen—"

Calix beamed at this, sweeping aside to reveal me as I stepped out of the carriage. "Yes, Vestai, you are the first to lay your eyes on her beauty."

The man bowed, touching his forehead once, twice, three times. "Your Highness," he said to me.

I looked at Calix, unsure of how they acknowledged such supplication. He wasn't looking at me, though; he was watching the man bow.

"Thank you," I ventured.

He scuffled back and rose up, looking at me fully for the first time, his eyes running every which way over me like I was some immensely foreign thing.

Wanting to shrink from his study of me, I turned to my husband. He took my hand, leading me inside. "Send food to our chambers, Vestai," Calix ordered. "And to the others, if they wish it, of course."

The man was striding to keep ahead of my husband and lead him to our rooms. "Of course, Your Highness."

The man opened a door for us, and Calix strode into the massive chamber without hesitation. My eyes were drawn helplessly upward to the ceiling, where tiny glass pieces had been affixed like stars. "Oh," I gasped, turning to take it all in.

"One of the many wonders of this castle, Your Highness," Vestai Atalo said. "It is said to grant blessings on those who sleep beneath these stars. A fitting chamber for a newly married couple."

"Thank you, Vestai," Calix said. He gestured toward the door, no longer bothering to acknowledge his host.

"Thank you—Vestai?" I asked, smiling at him.

He nodded. "My title, my queen. I am Atalo."

"You are no longer required, Vestai," Calix said. He was looking at him now, glaring, displeased.

The man dropped his gaze and left the room without a word.

"You can wash up in there," Calix told me, waving a hand. "Quickly. The food will arrive soon."

Confused, I wandered in the direction he had indicated. There was a smaller room, and it seemed to have a stream running through it, welling in a small basin. There was also a huge basin that I could have lain in, and it had curled horns of metal pointed into it with handles.

I tried one, and water spat out, splashing my dress. I yelped with glee and let it fill, getting enough water to wash my feet, hands, and face.

"You're happy," Calix said.

I turned to see him in the doorway. "Do all Trifectate castles have this?" I asked, stepping out of the basin and braiding my hair back. "Water, all the time?" He looked at me, his eyes skimming over me.

Then he moved forward. "This is the only one with an open stream of water. It was built by a heathen who worshiped water.

Now that the desert peace is secured, this castle will be tumbled and a new one—a Trifectate castle—raised in its place," he said, sitting on the bench and tugging his boots off.

A heathen who worshiped water—an Elementa, I realized. *Kata's people.*

He stood, going to the basin that was still full of water. He sat at the edge, dipping his feet in.

"Here," I said, reaching for a cloth. "Let me."

He looked suspicious. "You wish to wash my feet."

My cheeks burned. Was that a bad thing? "It's . . . for my people, it's a sign of care. Of respect. We don't often have water, so washing is a thing of honor."

His stern face didn't ease, but he reached out and touched my cheek. He nodded once, clearing his throat. "Very well. Thank you."

I bent over the edge of the basin, rolling up the legs of his clothing, and I ran the cloth gently over him, cleaning off the dust from the road.

"My mother did this for me," he said, his voice quiet.

"Of course she did," I said, smiling softly at him. "She wanted to care for you."

He stopped me. "You care for me."

My mouth felt dry. "I . . . I believe I will, when we know each other better."

His gaze was careful, but amusement tugged at the corner of his mouth. "Have you ever been in love before, Shalia?" he asked.

I drew a breath in and shook my head. "No," I said. "I've never even met many men outside my family."

His fingers touched my cheek gently, thinking. “It’s a frightening thing, to care for someone like that.”

“You’ve been in love?” I asked.

He nodded, his hand falling from my cheek. “Or at least I thought I was. I was young. She died,” he said. “A long time ago.”

My heart ached for him. “I’m sorry,” I offered. “In the desert, we believe a person’s spirit is indestructible. It means the people you lose are always with you.”

He wasn’t looking at me now. “It’s strange that you would say that. I thought I saw her,” he said. “Last night. Like she was giving me to you.” He shifted. “But we do not have the same beliefs,” he told me.

I didn’t know what to say to that, so I kept washing, staying silent for several minutes.

“Enough,” he said.

I stopped, straightening up. He stepped out of the tub and pressed a kiss to my temple, and led me out into the main chamber and our bed. Our food arrived, and I ate a little of a roasted game bird, enjoying the hot meal after so much traveling.

But then our dinner was done, and my husband pulled me close to him on the bed. It seemed like our conversation was a crumb, a tiny piece of sustenance that I could slowly gather to make into a real connection between my husband and me, but it didn’t make our night together more comfortable, or enjoyable, or any of the things my mother talked about. I wondered how long it would take, how many crumbs of conversation and care I would have to hoard to feel those intimate feelings.

When my husband finished and held me close to him, I thought perhaps it was the same as being tall, or short—maybe my mother and cousins just enjoyed this more, and I would enjoy it less, and it wasn't something that could develop or change—it was just a fact of my body.

I closed my eyes, trying to be satisfied with that idea, but I couldn't help feeling disappointed.

Secrets Like Armor

The next morning, I found my desert robes gone and something else in their place, a thing like Danae wore. It was just a single, wide, very long piece of red cloth and a length of silky ribbon.

Frozen in bed, I stared at it as my husband dressed. "Calix," I asked. "What do I do with this?"

He looked at it. "Put it on."

"Will you ask Danae to help me?"

He leaned against the wall, crossing his arms as he looked at me, his mouth curling into a smile. "No need. I suppose I've taken enough of these off to figure it out."

Aiden had bragged about a girl he'd been with once. My mother caught wind of it, and he ended up carrying the girl's heavy pack for a month. I desperately wished Mother were here to make my husband reconsider bragging to me.

He came to me, pulling the red cloth from the bed. He held it up, a flimsy curtain between us. "Come," he said. Despite the cloth, he still watched me as I stood from the bed, and he looped the cloth around my neck when I was before him.

He evened out the sides of it, letting his fingers graze my skin, and I wanted to pull away.

He spread out the pieces of the cloth so that they covered my breasts, and the long, wide ends overlapped and formed a skirt low on my back, leaving much of my skin bare. It hadn't looked strange on Danae, but I hated the way it felt. Exposed. Displayed. Unprotected.

"You are stunning," he said, running his hands along my sides, pulling me closer to him.

I didn't feel stunning, and I clutched my arms. "I'm cold," I told him with a shiver.

He stared at my body for a while longer, and then his finger touched my chin, drawing it up higher. "Then I will get something from Atalo to cover you with," he told me, moving away.

He left me, demanding a coat from the vestai as I stayed within the chamber. He brought it to me, a thin silk garment that skimmed my arms and went the length of the dress to the floor. There was no way to close it, and it hung open over the foreign clothing.

We left with as little ceremony as we'd come the night before. As we walked out to meet Danae and Galen, the wind kicked up and caught my dress, ruffling the light fabric, but it felt so cold on my skin I stopped and sucked in a breath, rubbing my arms.

Galen was staring at me, his hard eyes fixed and shocked like I had stepped out naked from the castle. I *felt* naked. I couldn't move forward.

"What in the Skies is that?" Kairos asked, appearing behind me.

I looked around. "The clothing?" I asked.

"Clothing?" he repeated, laughing. "You look like a bobcat in butterfly wings. Like a—"

My mind filled in any of the awful words I had been thinking.

He sighed, drawing his wide desert scarf off his neck and pulling it around my shoulders. "Like you're frozen," he said softer, rubbing my arms.

I held the scarf tight around me, nodding. He kept one arm on me as he walked me to the carriage, his watchful eyes considering Calix, Danae, and Galen all in turn. Kairos was about to help me into the carriage when he murmured, "They will never take the desert from you, Shalia. Don't fear."

I nodded, clutching his hand, more grateful for having him with me than I knew how to say.

We stopped again that night, shackled by the slow progress of the army. By the third day, I didn't even want to open my eyes and look out on this new kingdom. I wanted to go home. I wanted to be warm again, feel the heat on my skin and the bright, sustaining love of family wrapped around my heart.

And yet, when we readied the carriage that morning, Danae stretched and said to me, "We need fresh air. Will you join me in a ride, my queen?"

Osmost swooped, catching something up in his jaws, and Kairos smiled. "Osmost thinks it's an excellent idea."

The wind blew across my face, fresh and cold, and I nodded, wrapping Kairos's scarf more tightly around me. "That would be a welcome change, I think."

Kairos helped me onto my horse before mounting his own, and Calix scowled and got into the carriage alone. I saw Galen ordering his soldiers about, and Danae led me into the column. At the shout of a man on horseback carrying a flag, the army lurched forward with loud, coordinated stomps.

It wasn't long before there was a clearing in the trees, and I saw a green valley below us.

"We're in Nomikos, the northernmost part of the Bone Lands," Danae told me. "Just for a little while longer." She held out three fingers on one hand, raising up the knuckles like the legs of a spider. "People call the Trifectate the Bone Lands because it looks like three fingers—three great mountain ridges running into the sea." She tapped her fingers one by one. "Nomikos, Kyrikatos, Liatos." She wiggled the tip of her middle finger. "And the City of Three is here, in Kyrikatos. We'll make Kyrikatos by the end of the day, and hopefully the City of Three in another day."

"The Bone Lands are vast," I murmured, looking out into the green. "Is that forest?"

She shook her head. "No, those are mostly farmlands. There were forests around here, but they've been culled and are starting to regrow. The shipbuilders in Liatos get their trees from the mountain regions now."

"My father always said you had strong farms. You feed your people well."

She smiled. "Yes. One of Calix's first acts as king was to improve our farmlands. His quaesitori found that the land can be fortified so that it won't grow fallow as often, and it's worked very well."

I frowned. "What's a quaesitori?" Weren't they the men who Calix wished to send into the desert?

"They are men of knowledge," she said. "They study the ways of the world. Calix has been very enamored of their art ever since we were young."

Kairos drew his horse up beside mine. "I can't quite imagine him as a child," Kairos said. "Your mother must have had her hands full."

"I suppose so. It was only my father who would ever chastise him, even before my mother died."

I looked at Danae. Her posture was straighter now, and she looked only ahead. I couldn't imagine losing my mother so young—or ever. Even being away from her for a few days felt like someone was pulling my insides out.

Her shoulders lifted. "But no one could ever really discipline Calix anyway. From a very young age, he wasn't just a prince, he was a god. It changes things." Her shoulders dropped back down. "And then he became a king, and his will became his undeniable asset. It might have been the only thing protecting me and my brother when foreign kings and even our own vestai would have taken the crown away. And our lives, I'm sure."

"Was his early reign so difficult?" I asked her, quieting my voice.

She nodded. "It has taken a long time to achieve peace. For all of us." She laughed, a sharp, short sound. "But yes, being the younger sibling of a god is complicated."

"But you and your brother are also gods, aren't you?" I asked.

She looked at me. "Yes. But the faces of the God are never entirely equal." She shook her head.

"Don't bore her, Danae," Galen said, riding up the column to Danae's side.

"I'm not bored," I assured him. "You were raised very differently from us, it seems."

Galen's jaw worked, but Kairos chuckled. "Yes, well, having older brothers upon older cousins upon uncles means someone is generally willing to thump some discipline into you." Kai laughed. "Though it's the girls who are the worst. All that pinching."

"You must be an accomplished fighter," Galen said to Kairos. "You should teach me how to wield those scimitars."

Kairos shrugged and held out his arm, and Osmost swooped, making Galen jump. Osmost grabbed Kai's covered wrist, then hopped to his shoulder, opening his mouth and giving Kairos an affectionate *kik-kik-kik* noise that almost sounded like he was laughing. "Me? I'm not much of a fighter," Kairos said, his smile turning sly. "When you have four older brothers who could pound you into the ground, you learn different skills." Kairos held out his hand with a thick leather glove to guard against the bird's claws, and Osmost jumped to it, letting Kairos bring him in close to pet his feathers as Osmost glared at Galen. "But a scimitar is just a big sword, really. Watch out for the pointy parts."

I expected Galen to be insulted, but instead his eyes narrowed at Kairos, and I wondered if he understood the truth—with four older brothers who could pound *anyone* into the ground, Kairos was by far the most dangerous.

Osmost's head cocked, and Kairos winced as his claws dug in. Osmost leaped into flight, winging fast and high, and Kairos reined in his horse. "Stop," he said sharply, looking around. "Shalia, go there," he said, pointing to a break in the rocky wall on one side of the road.

"What is it?" I asked.

"The hawk's letting me know there's danger," he told me.

"What kind?" Galen asked.

"He's a *hawk*," Kairos snapped. "He's not specific."

"Go with your sister," Galen ordered. I still hadn't moved, and I looked to Kairos, who didn't come closer. "I'm not leaving her alone by the side of the road."

Kairos nodded at this, wheeling his horse over to me. No sooner did he turn than a cry rose up, and men started flooding out of the trees around the road. My horse reared, but I held on, locating a break in the rocks and urging him toward it as Kairos followed close behind, shouting at me.

I practically leaped off the horse to get lower and deeper into the small space, and Kairos moved in front of me, his gleaming scimitar drawn as another row of guards closed off the break in the rock.

Beyond the guards, men were rushing at each other, but they all seemed to look the same, their uniforms indistinguishable to my eyes. I didn't know how the soldiers could tell good from bad.

And then a man came perilously close to the line of guards, and I saw a green dragon stitched onto his coat.

And the dragon looked frighteningly like the symbol for my family.

Then I saw only red as a knife slashed across his throat and blood poured out. He fell, and Danae stood behind him with a knife in her hand.

She met my eyes for a moment, and I saw no fear there, no hesitation.

"Shalia, back!" Kairos yelled, and I saw the guards fighting, someone breaking through and raising his sword to my brother.

Kairos was a force to be reckoned with when he had a blade in his hands, but it didn't calm the fear rising in my chest. The dust from the road rose with the fervor of so many moving bodies, and it was hard to tell who was coming for whom.

The man Kairos was fighting fell, but two more sprang on him. In wartime, desert men carried two scimitars—and knew what to do with them—but Kairos was only wearing one today.

They set upon him viciously, and his sword flashed as he fought them both off.

Then a third appeared, brandishing a knife and heading for my brother.

"Kai!" I screamed, launching forward, everything else vanishing in my need to protect him.

Kairos turned as the man made his move, and one of the others raised his sword.

A cracking sound boomed above me, and I looked away from Kairos to see where it came from. Then the mountain moved, blocking out the light as a boulder sheared off the rock overhead and came crashing down.

Kairos dropped his scimitar and dove for me, hitting my body and dragging me down as the rock crashed, too large to get into our small corner. Everything shuddered, and more rocks swept down over us as the boulder slammed into the road, stilling before it rolled and fell off the other side.

The sounds of the fighting were loud, but no one was near us now. Dust rose thick around us, and I couldn't breathe, coughing against Kairos as he kept me down and away, and it felt like he was sheltering my thundering heart as much as my body.

A dense curtain of dust hid us away from the fighting. The men who had been attacking him were broken on the ground, their bodies still and red.

Almost like the rock knew what I wanted.

I sucked in a breath, and it was thick with dust. I coughed it out as my heart pounded and I fought to get in any clean air, my chest tight with panic.

My hands were tingling, and it was more than the rush of fear—I had felt this before. On the bridge, when the veil had been removed and the shiver seemed to start inside me and end on the rocks.

The earth had answered me. The earth had *reacted* to me.

I used Kai's scarf to cover my mouth as I desperately tried to breathe without coughing, black spots dancing in my eyes as all my thoughts and fears stormed inside my mind and I still couldn't *breathe.*

Kata had *told* me, she'd told me for *years*—she always thought I had an ability. A power. Like her, but she could control water. What if I could control earth?

Foul sorcery.

No. No, I couldn't possibly. If I could control earth, if I was like Kata, I would be a traitor to my new country. Peace would be broken before it was even *real.*

The scarf helped, and I finally got in a full breath, then another one. A cough came quick on the heels of the third, and the spots burst across my vision again.

Which was worse? Dying here for lack of air, or living to break the peace and betray my new husband with a power I couldn't possibly have?

"Kairos," I said, my voice shaking.

"Stay quiet, Shy," Kai said softly, moving off me and pulling me farther into the alcove.

I nodded, trying to repress my cough as I followed him.

"Are you all right?" he asked quietly, looking up, watching the mountain like it was about to attack.

Was I? "Can Osmost get word to Kata?" I asked.

His eyes met mine, confused and questioning, always seeing more than I wanted them to. Then understanding sparked, and his head jerked up, searching the cliff again. "No, Shalia. I know she always said—I know it's *possible*—but of anyone, you cannot have that power. Not with your husband."

"Kairos, can he get a message to her? I have to see her. I have to . . ." I trailed off, looking up at the cliff. "Kairos, please."

Something clamored closer in the dust, and he huffed out a breath. "Yes," he said. "Don't breathe a word of this, Shalia. Don't even *think* about it."

I nodded, gripping his hand and pulling myself up.

"Shalia!" I heard someone yelling. The clanging noises of steel were becoming quieter, and I saw shapes moving in the clearing dust. Kairos moved away from me as Galen charged through the dust. "You're all right?" Galen asked, touching my chin and turning my head this way and that.

"I'm unharmed," I said. It certainly wasn't the same thing, but it was the only answer I could give.

"Come with me," he said. "The column is broken. I need to get you to safety."

"Where is Calix?" I asked.

"He's coming behind us," he said. "We need to secure you both as quickly as possible."

Kairos let out a low, sharp whistle, and his dark brown horse came trotting back to us, with no sign of mine.

"Take my horse," he said. "I'll be right behind you."

I nodded, swinging onto it. Galen put his foot in the stirrup, and I pulled at the reins. "What are you doing?" I asked.

"Escorting you."

"We'll be faster on two horses," I insisted.

"You're all right to ride on your own?" he asked, surprised. "It's a difficult ride."

I nodded sharply. "I told you, I am unharmed. If the horse can do it, I can."

He found his own horse, turning back to look at me. "Follow me closely. Shout if we are separated by more than the length of a horse," he said.

"I will," I promised.

He led the horses off the road, down the steep, sloping terrain littered with rocks and trees. I held my breath at the sharp pitch, but the horse knew what to do, following behind Galen's until we hit open fields, and the horses ran, not at a full gallop, but a quick canter.

We crossed through fields, and passed small farmhouses, and I wondered why we couldn't stop there. Was there not enough room, or did Galen not trust their loyalty to the king?

"Here," he called, leading me down a path around a field of some sort of tall grain. I saw a large gate guarding a road and, farther in, a sprawling home.

Two guards appeared as we approached, and Galen shouted, "In the name of the king, open the gates!"

The guards didn't hesitate, opening the gates and letting us ride in.

By the time we reached a pretty fountain, a woman was coming out of the house to stand on the steps. She was older, her hair white and still well kept. "Commander," she said, dropping her head to him. "How can I be of service?"

"Forgive the imposition, Domina Naxos," he said, inclining his head to her before he jumped from his horse and came to attend to me. "The king and queen have been attacked. This was the closest place we could come for shelter."

"You are welcome to it, dear boy," she said, turning to a servant and ordering rooms opened, fires lit, food made, and everyone who could tend to an injury made ready. Galen helped me down, letting out a breath when I was on the ground, as if he could relax now that I was secured.

He brought me to the woman. "This is your new queen," he told her. "My queen, this is Domina Naxos. The domina and her late husband were good friends to my grandfather."

"And always to you," she said, leaning forward to kiss his cheek. He warmed to this, and it was the closest to a smile I'd ever seen on his face. She turned to me, bowing and taking my hands to kiss each in turn. "Welcome, my queen. I am sorry for your hardship."

"Thank you for taking us in," I told her. "Has anyone else arrived?" Anxiously, I looked around, but we were the only ones.

"No," she said. "But come. We will see you clean and fed."

Galen nodded me inside, and I followed where she led. She gave us water to wash, and I splashed my face and my hands to clear them of dust. When I was done, Galen took off his black jacket with a grunt, and I saw why. There was a cut on his arm, not deep but still bleeding.

It looked like the work of a sword, not a rock, but it suddenly made me wonder if I had protected my brother to harm someone else's.

But no—the farther I got from that moment, the more I doubted that I had been the one to pull a boulder from the mountain.

Drawing breath, I asked one of the servants for a few bandages. "Sit," I told Galen, gesturing to a stool. "You're hurt."

"And?" he asked, arching one of his sharp eyebrows, but sitting on the stool I directed him to. "Is there something you intend to do about it?"

"Yes," I told him. "You do know I have five brothers quite prone to fighting, don't you?"

He grunted, which I took as a yes.

"They get into many scrapes, which girls are usually required to fix."

"I don't need a woman to tend to my wounds," he said. "I can do it myself."

"Oh, for the Skies," I told him with a sigh. The servant reappeared with the bandages, and I took them from her, dipping a fresh cloth in the water. I reached for his cuff, and he pulled away. "Galen, really," I said. "I'm not going to hurt you."

"My sleeve won't go up that far," he said simply. He tugged his shirt off over his head, and I felt heat flush my face as I focused on his wound.

I took the clean, wet cloth and brushed the debris out of the wound. His jaw went tight, but he didn't flinch, looking ahead as I did it. I snuck glances at his chest. It was similar in size, but so very different from his brother's—full of scars and honed muscles, equally as solid and carved as his face.

"It's not deep," I told him, pressing to stem the blood. "You won't even need stitching."

He nodded. "Thank you."

I smiled at his continued stoniness. "I planned this whole thing," I told him, and his eyes cut to me. "So I could tend to your wound and you'd finally be forced to like me."

I wrapped a length of bandage around his arm as tightly as I could. A muscle in his jaw flared as I tied it. "It needs to be tight," I told him.

"I didn't complain," he answered. "And I don't dislike you."

"Will you answer some questions if I ask you, then?" I sat back, rinsing my hands as he put on his shirt, then washed his face and put on his jacket, all buttoned up again.

"That usually depends on the question," he said.

"What happened today?"

He looked out the window. "I believe the Resistance was after the tax money that Atalo paid us. It was a fortune in gold tri-kings."

The Resistance. Hadn't Kata said that was the name of Rian's cause? He could have been following us since the desert. "Did they take it?"

He nodded. "Yes. Calix will be in a foul mood tonight," he said, his eyes flicking to me like a warning.

"I saw Danae cut a man's throat," I said. "She didn't look afraid. She looked like she knew what she was doing. I've never seen a woman commit violence like that with such ease or ability."

There was a grave expression on his face, and he crossed his arms. "I would ask you to speak to her about that. It's not my information to share."

I nodded, swallowing. What kind of secret did she harbor? "Very well."

"Kairos is here," he said, his watchful eyes on the window. "Do you have any more questions for me?"

"No."

He started toward the door and then halted. "You should tell Calix you were hurt," he said, his eyes on the door and not on me. "I don't know who he'll vent his rage on, but it will be someone, and if he thinks you're injured, it won't be you."

This made my breath stop, but Galen just left the room.

I shook my head. What did that mean? I knew my husband could be short tempered, but the warning made fear curl at the back of my neck.

Moments later, Kairos came to me, eager to wash up. He dipped his hands in the pink-tinged water, and I looked at him, feeling incredibly lost. He sighed heavily, leaning on the table as water dripped from his face. "Shalia, what you said before—" he started.

I shook my head fast. "No, Kai. Not here." I bit my lip, sucking in a breath like with it I could hold so many secrets. "Did Osmost return?"

He nodded. "He's hunting outside."

"How far behind you is the king?"

"Not far," he said. "Apparently the attackers got his money, and he's not happy." I nodded, and he hesitated, forming more words slowly. "The thing before," he said carefully. "What if it happens again?"

"It won't," I assured him, but it was false. I couldn't even consider controlling it, because it wasn't possibly real. Was it? Then I shook my head. "I'm not even certain I did . . . that."

He nodded. "Just be careful. I'll send Osmost out tonight, and I'll let you know as soon as I've heard from Kata."

"What if he doesn't return by morning? They'll be suspicious."

A ghost of a smile appeared on his face. "Of what? My hawk off hunting?"

I shrugged, but my head turned as I heard a horse whinny outside. The carriage was pulling up, and even as a shiver went down my spine, I went out of the room and almost ran for the doorway. The domina was there, bowing to Calix and Danae as they emerged, but Calix smiled when he saw me, motioning me forward.

I went to him and he pulled me into his arms, kissing me. My throat felt tight as so many things pounded in my chest. Galen's strange advice to lie to him, the stolen money that Rian might have taken, and worse, the power that might mean my death. At my husband's hands, no less.

And also, stupidly, the strange look on Calix's face when he asked if I cared for him. I wondered if I could care for him in truth, if that would keep me safe if I was what I feared, if simply caring for him would make him love me.

"Come," I said, pulling back. "You have had such an ordeal, my husband. I will tend to you."

He smiled and kissed me again, pulling me close to his side when he was done. "Thank you, wife," he said. "Galen," he called, seeing him. "Follow us and report. Domina, I will need a bath."

She had never raised her head, but she bowed farther. "Of course, my king. My servants will lead you to a room."

The servants brought us to a different bedroom than I had been in before, with hot water in a basin and clean cloths beside it. Calix sat, and moments later servants brought in a huge basin for his bath and started filling it with bucket after bucket of steaming water.

"Wash me while they fill it, wife," he said, looking at me and the basin on the stand. "Like you did the other night."

Something about the way he said it in front of his brother made it seem shameful, like my attention to him made me weaker and submissive, and heat burned in my cheeks. I took a cloth anyway, dipping it in the water, and I used it to rinse one hand gently.

"Are you going to report, brother?" he snapped.

Galen cleared his throat. "We lost ten men, and—"

"So few?" Calix demanded, sitting straighter. "We lost *ten men* and almost a thousand tri-kings."

"They had the advantage," Galen said. "We couldn't do much on the road. They chose their spot well to attack the gold without much engagement."

"Every man who guarded that gold who is still alive will be executed before I have my dinner," he growled.

"Calix!" I gasped.

His snarl turned toward me. "They should have died to protect it," he snapped. "It's a matter of honor."

"I'm not going to execute my men," Galen said, his voice steely.

"Then I will do it myself."

"Oh, will you?" Galen scoffed. "You will hold the sword, brother?"

"My feet," Calix snapped at me.

I cringed but obeyed him, taking off his boots.

"When you hold the sword, it is I holding the sword," Calix told his brother. "You are my arm. You are my hand. And *that is all*."

"No," Galen returned.

"You have so little care for my queen?" he asked, and I froze. "Keep washing, Shalia."

"I have the highest regard for your queen," Galen said.

"She could have been murdered today. Our peace could have been destroyed. And you won't punish your men for their inadequacies? You may as well spit on my wife and my marriage." I looked to Calix, but he wasn't looking at me, invoking me like I wasn't there at all, just using me to make a point to his brother.

"My men defended her admirably. And they will continue to do so."

"So my wife is more important than my money. Is that what you are saying?" Calix asked. He looked down and saw that I was finished washing his hands and feet. "You may disrobe me, wife, so that I can bathe."

I didn't dare turn toward Galen, but I heard him make some small noise as Calix stood with a smirk on his face. I rose with him to untie his shirt. "You disapprove of the way I treat my wife, brother?"

"I made no such comment."

Calix chuckled. "Execute them, or I will brand them as traitors and their families won't receive a pension," he said. "And they will still be dead."

I pulled Calix's shirt over his head, and my hands shook as I reached for the ties on his lower half. Was this a trick? Surely he didn't want me exposing him to his brother. Had he no modesty?

"I will inspect their bodies as soon as possible."

Galen grunted. "Allow me to give them a good meal, at least. And if I can do it while the others sleep, there will be less dissent from the men."

"Very well. It is Domina Naxos who is paying to host them, not me." Calix cupped my cheek, smiling at me darkly. "Now go, before you embarrass my wife."

I heard Galen's boots on the floor, and the door shut behind him. Only then did I look up to see Galen gone, and at Calix's urging, I helped him remove the rest of his clothes. "You can wash me in the bath, wife. I think I enjoy being taken care of."

I stared at the floor while he got in the steaming water by the fire.

"You look displeased, my love."

"I didn't like that," I said softly. "I wish to care for you, but to do it in front of your brother—it made me feel subservient, Calix. Not like your wife."

He tugged my hand, but I resisted him. "I wished only to show you off," he told me. He tugged harder, and I moved, frightened by the strength of it. "You are queen, and I need you displayed always."

"And you will make a display of those men," I said, my heart aching. "I don't understand why you want more death on such a day."

He pulled my arm until I dropped to my knees beside the bath. "Your heart is soft, and that is good and right, wife. But mine cannot be. More important than love, than grief, more important than anything is power. And to allow them to live would be to sacrifice it, and I cannot do that."

His voice had a hard edge to it, and I nodded, biting my lip.

"Wash me," he ordered.

I did as he asked, and when he was through, I helped him dress and left the room to ask the servants to bring supper.

As the door shut behind me, I saw Kairos, skulking in the darkness. His mouth lifted, and he waggled his eyebrows at me, but said nothing.

I pressed back the urge to cry again, giving him a tiny smile and going to find a servant.

My husband and I ate supper together in silence. Afterward, he stretched and said he was quite tired, and I stood. "Do you mind if I take the food back to the kitchens?" I asked him. "I'm so restless. I think a walk will help."

He looked at the bed like he knew this was a ploy to shirk my duty, but he sighed. "Very well. I'm tired. I won't be awake when you return."

"I won't disturb you," I promised.

I brought the food back to the kitchens, swayed for a moment by the warm fire, but there were too many servants looking at me curiously there. I went out the first door I could find, emerging onto a wide expanse of grass fading into dark night where the lamplight ended. It was so cold outside, and I hugged my arms around myself, feeling the shaky tremors of unshed tears still stoppered inside me. My husband wasn't there, but still I didn't want to let them free.

Walking out to the edge of the light, I drew slow breaths, listening to the night birds rustling in the trees. I wondered if these strange places were governed by the same spirits we had in the desert. The stories I had heard of them mandated that spirits were in everything, everywhere, and they could not be destroyed or created, only remade. But it seemed strange that they could survive here, with no one to respect them or remember them.

But if that were true, wasn't it possible that the powers of the islands could be found somewhere else too? They were not unlike spirits, from what I'd heard.

What would it even mean? I knew some of Kata's power—she could control water, make it do her bidding. She had opened temples one at a time, releasing water, air, fire, and earth, like the breaking of a dam. If I had moved the rock—*if, if*—my element would be earth. I could manipulate the earth?

Despite knowing enough that I desperately wanted to hide such knowledge from my husband, I suddenly felt like I knew nothing about these powers—not really. Kata had said that anyone could have them now, but who *did* have them? Were there no ceremonies, no rites—how could such power just *appear*? I didn't even know how common these powers were. When the powers still lived in the islanders, their people had been legendary—they could build palaces with nothing but their hands; they had the most mighty naval fleet in the world. They could re-form the earth to their will.

I looked down at the ground, dotted with small rocks, covered over with spiky grass. I held my hand out to it, frowning and squinting at it, willing it to *move.*

Nothing happened.

I tried again, feeling utterly foolish as I held my breath and tensed my muscles, acting like I could push the earth with just my will.

Nothing.

Curling my fingers into fists, I walked faster. Of course. I couldn't be an Elementa. It wasn't even possible, much less likely or probable or even *reasonable.*

And looking back to the large building, I was grateful that I was no Elementa. It had to be a lie, a trick, something—I couldn't be *that* and be married to Calix.

I would not survive.

My hands were shivering by the time I came around to the front of the house, drawn by the sound of the burbling fountain. It sounded like the river that tripped through Jitra, but false and confined.

My skin prickled, scraped by the cold, and I nearly turned to go back into the house, but something caught my eye on the dark edge of the courtyard. I could see boots, just the very tips of them, and I walked closer.

My hand flew to my mouth, and I sank weakly to my knees as the tears I had fought for hours came rushing out.

Four men were lying there like they were asleep, their throats cut, their skin gray. I could only guess these were the failed soldiers, the ones my husband ordered killed.

The men *Galen* killed. How could he follow such an order? My husband ordered it so, but Galen was commander, powerful in his own right. And he just killed his men who had done their best.

But Galen hadn't wanted to obey. It was easy to see in the way he defied his brother—I could not imagine what such a task must have cost him. What years of struggling under such orders must have cost him.

"Shalia?"

I turned and saw Galen on his horse, riding closer, his eyes sweeping back and forth like he was searching. "Where is Calix?" he said urgently.

But I couldn't stop crying, covering my mouth to stop from making noise and drawing my husband out here to see my weakness, his softhearted wife.

"Shalia, three hells, stop crying," Galen said. "Where is Calix? Has he seen these men?"

When I raised my head, I saw he was covered in blood, his hair mussed, his uniform ruined. But—I turned back to the bodies, and despite their throats being cut, there was very little blood on the wounds.

The tears shocked out of me, I looked behind him. He had been riding a horse, and on it was a prostrate body. "Great Skies," I breathed.

"Shalia, *has Calix seen this*?" he demanded.

I struggled to stand, coming closer to him, but he shrank away.

"I'm covered in their blood, Shalia," he warned. "You can't touch me."

"He's asleep," I told him, sniffing and wiping my face. "These men—how did they die?" It wasn't here, by his hand—that I was certain of.

Galen swallowed. "In the attack. He won't know these aren't the men who guarded the gold." His eyes watched me carefully. "Unless you tell him."

Another secret, but this one felt more important than the others. It was deceiving my husband, directly undermining his orders.

And yet, not speaking this truth would save the men who were supposed to die—and possibly even Galen. And if there was even a chance I was an Elementa, I would need so much more practice in keeping things from Calix.

I wiped my cheeks again. "I would never."

"You were crying for them?" he asked.

For everything, I thought. "Yes," seemed like a safer answer. "And you," I admitted, lowering my eyes.

"Me."

I dared to look up at him, so pale and covered in blood it was as if he had been the one murdered. "They're your men," I said, my voice catching. "And I knew you didn't want to do what he asked."

His jaw worked, muscles slowly rolling and moving. "Neither did you, it seemed."

Yet he had figured out a way to thwart his brother, and I had knelt at Calix's feet like a dog, obeying him. The thought stung. "I'm happy you didn't have to," I told him honestly.

"I'm the commander of an army, and I hate death," he said, his voice soft.

I drew a breath, bobbing my head. "It's a difficult strength to have, to be sure."

"You think that's strength," he said, and it wasn't a question. As a statement, it made me feel foolish, but I refused to feel ashamed of that.

"Yes," I said, meeting his eyes again.

But he wasn't trying to make me feel foolish. That was clear in his eyes. He appeared young, and lost, and like he wanted to believe my words. He swallowed and his eyes left mine. "You should go," he said. "Thank you for not telling him."

Another secret. I nodded, sniffing again. "Good night, Galen."

He didn't reply, turning away from me and going to pull the other body off his horse.

I paused for a moment. "Galen," I said, trying not to be loud.

He stopped.

"This may be garish, but they need more blood at their throats," I said, and knew even as I said it that helping Galen create his lie was worse than just hiding the truth from my husband. "He'll be able to tell."

Galen looked sharply to the bodies and nodded. "Good night, my queen."

I went back to Calix. I changed into a nightdress the domina had brought before dinner, sliding into bed beside my husband. I jumped when his arm snaked around me, but he didn't fully wake.

It took me a long while to fall asleep, counting my secrets like armor.

Calix woke me before the dawn that came in gray and overcast, and the domina gave me fresh clothes and a new, thicker coat to wear. As we gathered to leave and Calix's attention was elsewhere, I embraced her as I'd seen Galen do. "Thank you," I told her. "Your hospitality has been such a salve on the wounds of yesterday. I am so sorry I have nothing to offer you in return."

Her soft cheeks lifted like there were small apples inside them, and she bent and kissed my hands, then pressed my cheeks with her own hands. "Nonsense. You are most welcome, my queen. May the rest of your reign be more peaceful than this."

I smiled. "Thank you."

"My king," she said, stepping back and bowing to him as he entered the room. His hand slid around my waist, pulling me close to him. "Your queen is graceful and kind."

"Yes," he said, taking my chin and turning my face to him, kissing me in front of her. I tried to draw back, but he wouldn't allow it.

"Why don't you get settled in the carriage, my queen," he said, finally releasing me.

I dropped my head to him, pulling away as Kairos strode into the room, carrying several long, furry animals tied to a branch. "Domina," he said, bowing to her. "A gift for you, for your generosity. I'm told these pelts are very precious."

She laughed, delighted, moving forward. "Oh my. Are these mink? Goodness, I didn't even know we had any on this land."

"My hawk is an accomplished hunter," he explained. "And it goes against our ways to leave a host without a gift."

She laughed again and thanked him, coming to kiss his cheek. He grinned, leading me out to the carriage while the domina took pains to fawn over my husband as well.

Galen was on his horse, looking stiff and tense, his face still pale though he was cleaned of blood. His eyes met mine for an instant, but they flicked away just as quickly.

Kairos helped me into the carriage, and I saw Danae sitting there, waiting for us. Her eyes looked up at me cautiously. "Yesterday," she said. "I know you saw me kill that man."

I sat beside her. "Yes," I said.

"It's best if you don't speak of that to anyone," she said, raising her chin in a way that reminded me of Calix.

"I thought not," I said carefully. "And while I know what I saw, I don't know what it meant."

"Yes, you do," she said, her voice sharp. "Princesses are supposed to be married, and instead, I was trained to be a killer. I became the hidden face in every way that matters," she said bitterly.

"Danae—" I started, but she got up and switched sides of the carriage.

"It's best you don't speak of it in front of Calix," she said, looking out the window.

"He doesn't know?"

"Of course he knows," she said, but she didn't explain further. There were splotches of color on her pale cheeks, and she refused to look at me.

Silenced, I nodded, and Calix entered the carriage, nudging me over more to sit beside me on the seat. "Get on with it," he shouted to the army. "We've lost a lot of time."

I looked at her, and out the window at Galen, and thought of the things both siblings had asked me to keep from their brother. Calix's hand captured my own, and his fingers caught mine, curling them over his, rearranging me around him until he was comfortable. I felt the eyes of this man-made God, my husband, move over me, and I thought of my own secrets too.

Three faces, and two wrapped themselves in lies and shadow so the third wouldn't see the ways in which they defied him.

The Clever Brother

By the end of the fourth day we were closing in on the city, and my husband required both his siblings and me to ride in the carriage, ordering the army to part to let the carriage through so we could move more quickly. He wanted no stops to be made, no delays. It wasn't long before we slanted up a steep road. When the carriage was on flat ground again, I heard a low boom and jumped.

"Gates," Calix explained.

We were in a large courtyard of stone. It was pure white, smooth, and even, unlike anything I had seen, nothing like the rough stone of the desert, worn by sand and wind. The courtyard looked like it was as wide as Jitra itself, standing at the edges of the earth. In the distance on either side of us I saw water, blue and rolling, the whole mass of it captivating my attention.

"Danae, why don't you escort my wife to her rooms. I have preparations to see to," Calix said.

"Let Galen," Danae said, and she got out of the carriage first.

"No," Calix told her.

My eyes went from her to her brothers before I got ready to follow her, feeling shaky.

"Have you ever seen the ocean before?" Galen asked me, following my gaze.

I shook my head.

He nodded sagely. "You'll like your rooms, then."

I turned to look ahead of us. There were three long walkways arching over a pool of water to three separate buildings. They were all the exact same, huge palaces of white stone with smooth walls and sharp corners, a wide square base with a tall tower rising from the center. The entrance to each was an open archway several lengths taller than me, and I could see the guards from where I stood, their armor glinting in the sun, surprisingly pretty with the white stone.

"Very well," Danae said. "Come with me."

My cheeks burned, but when she looked at me, I saw more fear than annoyance in her gaze.

We started up the middle pathway and immediately the wind caught my dress, blowing it back from my legs. I shivered. "It's so cold here," I whispered to her.

"Only compared to the desert," she said with a dismissive wave. "The seamstresses can make you something to keep you warm."

We entered the archway, and the guards all snapped to attention in unison. We didn't have much metal in the desert, and their armor called to me. It was beautiful, and noisy, and strange.

Danae moved quickly, leading me inside. The hallway was wide and airy, light filtering in from somewhere above us in little spots and flickers like the world was dancing around us. The hallway split, and she led me to the right, around what was possibly the base of the tower. We passed through a set of doors that opened without us indicating anything to the guards, and there I gasped.

The room was beautiful. Two archways in front of me, two to my right, all filled with thin panes of glass and leading to balconies on either side. It seemed all I could see was ocean, magnificent and unending.

I went to the balcony directly ahead of me, opening the fragile doors and walking outside. The balcony was larger than I thought, wide and railingless but extending forward to a point like an unnaturally smooth white precipice. I walked forward to the point and found myself suspended far past the edge of the cliff, high above water churning against the rocks below.

A wave of unease hit me, and I stepped away from the edge.

Looking back, my rooms seemed to be only half the width of the building, but there were more doors, more windows, just beyond. I moved toward them as Danae followed me out.

"That leads to Calix's rooms," Danae said. I stopped. "There's a door inside your chamber as well."

I came back to her, unwilling to look into his chambers yet. "We have separate rooms?" I asked.

She shook her head. "No. This is a room for both of you. That . . . is his room. Alone."

Going to the door, I pulled on it, and it didn't open. "It's locked from this side," she said.

He could open it, and I could not. He could sleep with me or alone—all choices I did not have, serving as just another reminder of who held the power in our marriage. I thought of the words of advice my mother and cousin offered on my wedding day, and I wondered if a woman's power was so different here because I was in the Trifectate, or because I was a queen.

She led me inside to a room with a bath and a basin like the one at Vestai Atalo's castle, and beyond that to another room with cushioned seats and a fireplace. "What is this room for?" I asked her.

"Your reception chamber," she told me. "Should you want to see guests."

"Oh," I said, nodding. "Should I do that?"

"You will be expected to receive the court as necessary," she said.

"Danae," I called, stopping her before we went back into the other room. "Why are you angry with me?"

Her small shoulders pushed up with a heavy breath before falling again. "I'm not," she said, turning. "I didn't think you would have to find out about my training, my position. I thought—" She shook her head fiercely. "I don't know what I thought."

"What does it change?" I asked her. Then my eyebrows drew together in consternation. "And you do realize I know very little, yes?"

"You can tell I'm not like you. Not the woman or princess I'm supposed to be. They keep me hidden as much for that as for my position."

"And you are expecting my censure?" I asked her.

She looked at me, her cheeks flushed with color, her chin proud and high. She said nothing.

"You will not receive it."

She drew in a sharp breath, but she did not respond to this. "We should continue," she told me, her voice softer. "I'm sure your attendants have gathered."

"Attendants?"

She led me back into the main room, where four women in white had appeared. They knelt fully down onto their hands and knees. I jumped forward. "Get up," I said quickly, catching one's arm. "You don't have to kneel."

They got up, looking among one another, saying nothing.

"They're *ishru*," Danae told me. I gave her a little shake of my head, not understanding. "Servants," she whispered. "Only they are allowed to serve royalty."

"Why?" I asked, shivering.

"They have no tongues," she said. "So they cannot betray us."

My stomach clenched. "You don't need to kneel to me," I told them. "Ever."

One woman met my eyes and nodded. The others dropped their chins to their chests.

"Calix should return soon. If you ever need anything, Galen and I are close," Danae said, bringing me to the balcony again. She pointed to stone walkways that led over the open air to two other castles. "I'm on the right," she said. "And Galen's is left. The three faces always linked, always separate. Get some rest if you can; I imagine I won't see you until the morning."

I watched her go over the walkway, fearlessly moving forward as the wind blew at her dress. When she was out of sight, I looked to the left.

Galen's and Danae's castles were angled slightly off in either direction, so the points of their balconies faced away, but going closer to my husband's rooms, I could see Galen's balcony.

And he was there. And he was looking over. At me.

And frowning.

I turned away from the dangerous edge, going back to my rooms and telling the guard not to admit anyone without my permission.

I sat on the large bed in my room just to try it—beds were a rare luxury, found only in Jitra. Traveling in the desert, we had rolled pallets and rugs that kept us above the sand, and I found I was quickly becoming used to the indulgence.

Suddenly, I wished that Danae hadn't gone. The ishru were floating like ghosts through the room, but none of them could speak, and no one could tell me what was expected of me now, or how I was meant to get food.

"Do any of you know where my clothing is?" I asked.

One came to me and bowed, not meeting my eyes, and she turned and moved away, so I followed her through a door that led to a narrow staircase and another door.

She opened the door, and I found a room full of fabric, much of it for making dresses like the one I'd been made to wear, but also a row of hooks with more-finished-looking pieces on it. I pulled on a bright blue one with long sleeves that would cover the length of my dress, and it was lined with soft fur from a kind of animal I'd never seen.

For the first time in days, I felt warm, and I shivered with pleasure at the sensation. "Perfect," I murmured.

I returned to the main chamber just as Kairos was coming past my guard. I crossed my arms with a sigh.

"Not happy to see me?" he asked, raising his eyebrows.

"Oh no, Kai, it isn't that. I told my guard earlier not to admit guests without my approval."

"Well, I am your brother, so it shouldn't count, but that is what I'm here about, as it happens." He looked around and whistled with a smile. "Nice room."

He started nosing around the room before he went out to the balcony. "What are you here about?" I called, not understanding.

He came back inside and shut the doors, then raised an eyebrow at the door I'd come from.

"Kai?" I asked again.

"Your protection," he said. "We didn't get a chance to talk during the ride, and I need you to tell me exactly how bad things are."

"Bad?" I asked.

Kairos crossed his arms, his gaze heavy on me. "Tell me how bad it is."

I shook my head. "How bad what is?"

"The way he speaks to you? It isn't exactly hard to imagine him doing worse. The man cannot abide anything outside his control." He watched my face, studying my every reaction. "Either he's harmed you already, or he will."

The only thing I could think of was the pain of our first night of marriage, but even as little as I wanted to mention that to my brother, I was led to believe that was expected. But something else in his words caught my attention. "What do you mean, 'he will'?" I asked.

He gave me a crooked smile. "You know I know things, Shy. And sometimes I see things. And I'm never wrong. So stop denying it and just tell me."

"He hasn't hurt me. I swear it." My throat went dry, and I covered my mouth. "Does that mean he'll find out about . . ." I held up my hands, helpless, unable to say it.

He stared at me for long moments. "Maybe," he said. "But if he threatens you, your kinsmen will stop him. Decisively. King or not."

Shaking my head, I sighed. "You're not kins*men*—you're just one kins*man*. What will you do?" I asked, trying to tease him.

A hint of a smile graced his serious face. "You forget, little sister. I'm not Cael, or Aiden, or even Rian. I don't punch first and ask questions later. I'm the clever brother, and if I need to be, I can be more powerful than the whole clan together."

"There's only one reason I'd need such protection," I told him, looking at my hands. Quieter, I asked, "Have you heard from Kata?"

He drew closer, looking over his shoulder and nodding. "She'll find you. It may take her time, but as soon as she can, she'll come. Has it happened again?"

I shook my head. "No. I think I was imagining things. I had to have imagined it, don't you think? How could someone from the desert have her power?"

His smile became crooked and knowing. "You know I know things, and sometimes I *see* things," he told me again. "Kata says that's some kind of ability between the elements."

My breath stopped. *Kairos* had an ability? "Kai—" I started.

The guard opened the door, and Kai's smile disappeared as Calix came into the room. He raised his eyebrow, looking over Kairos. "You can go," he told Kai.

Kairos kissed my cheek and glared at Calix. "I'll see you in the morning, Shy," he told me.

Calix watched Kairos as he left and then turned back to me. "Come, my love. It is time for you to meet my vestai."

"I thought the presentation was tomorrow."

He nodded. "Yes, but this is a private introduction. It isn't appropriate for them to meet you like commoners."

"So there are more vestai than just Atalo?" I asked.

He took my hand and brought me through the palace to the courtyard outside. There was a carriage waiting there, and he led me into it. "It's a title, for wealthy landowners," he said, sneering. "Men who would fashion themselves king if they could."

The carriage was a silly conveyance, as we only traveled a few minutes before the carriage door opened again.

We were in the courtyard of a white stone building, not unlike the castles but smaller and not nearly as grand. "Where are we?"

"This is the Concilium," Calix said as the guards bowed to us. "The vestai meet here to discuss matters of state."

"Everything in this city seems so new," I marveled, looking up as we began to walk forward.

"It is," Calix said, tugging my hand. "Previous kings of the Trifectate allowed sorcerer pagans to assist in the construction of many of our buildings. Naturally, any vestige of pagan sympathy needed to be dismantled. It's disloyal."

I knew he meant Elementae, and my heart tripped over the memory of the boulder coming down, smashing over the road to protect Kairos.

We walked through the archway and down a long stone hallway. As we passed a break in the stone, I looked in the doorway to a large room with overfilled shelves. "What's that?" I asked.

"Library," he said. "All our historical books. The appropriate ones, of course."

I had heard of books, but I'd never seen them. Paper and ink were not things that could survive for long in the desert; our stories, histories, and legends were written in rock, the eternal places in Jitra that wind and sun couldn't break.

In comparison this room full of quiet paper seemed . . . fragile. Impermanent.

I stopped, curious, but Calix sighed impatiently. "Shalia, I care very little for catering to the whims of the vestai; I would like to get this over with as quickly as possible."

"Yes, of course," I said, and I let him lead me down the hall. Quietly, I asked, "Why do you? Cater to their whims, I mean. You are king."

This seemed to please him, and he looked at me, pausing for a moment to touch my cheek. "Exactly my thoughts," he said. "But they are an old power that challenges my reign every chance they have. I prefer not to give them more opportunity."

We turned a corner, and there was another room off the hallway, but this one made him pause.

He squeezed my hand tighter and walked into the room.

It was small, with a full wall of glass to look out over the ocean that made it seem bigger, endless. The only thing in the room, though, was a large painting with the figure of a woman on it. She was seated, her chin raised, her hair jet black, her green eyes bright, a silvery crown on her head.

Calix was staring at her, and haltingly, he moved forward. The painting rested on a small mantel, and it had three candles beneath it.

He took up a flint to light the candles. As he did, I touched his arm, and he flinched away. "She's your mother," I realized. Danae had said her mother died, but I wasn't sure when it had happened.

He nodded, his throat working.

"When did you lose her?"

"A year before my father," he said, his voice rough and low. I was hesitant to touch him again, but I was standing close to him, so I tried resting my hand on his back. He didn't object, and lit the last candle and put his arm around my waist, staring up at her portrait. "After she died—nothing was the same again."

"How did she die?"

His back rippled with tension, and he shook his head.

"Why is her portrait here?" I whispered. "Why not in the palace?"

He swallowed. "Her father—my grandfather—was the leader of the Concilium until his death, less than a year ago. It was a great comfort to him to have her here."

Gently, slowly, I stroked his back. "We could move it to the palace."

Whatever had opened within him closed, and he pulled away from me. "No."

He took my hand again and brought me out of the room.

Another turn later, we arrived at a huge room with ceilings that soared high above us and a single, long table in the space, not nearly filling it. Men were standing around the room, and they turned as we entered.

"Vestai!" Calix called. "I wish to introduce my bride to you."

Though he seemed to have called to all of them, one man, his black robes layered with a shimmery silver cloth, came forward. He was older than Calix, but one of the youngest in the room—the others were mostly gray old men.

"My queen, I am High Vestai Thessaly," he greeted me, bowing and touching his forehead three times. "Come," he said, offering me a hand.

I took it, and he led me to a large chair at the head of the table. No one else sat, and I felt instantly out of place, watched.

"We are most pleased to welcome you here, my queen," the vestai said. "We have very high hopes for the tremendous benefits of both peace and marriage for our king."

Standing beside me, Calix bristled.

They all stopped, staring at me. Waiting.

I looked to Calix, but he gave me no indication of what I should say to these people who he clearly had to consider—who had, at least at times, been his enemies. "I am grateful for your hope and your welcome," I told him, my voice quiet but strong. "Thank you. And I confess, I find little in the king that needs improvement, by either peace or marriage." I looked at Calix for approval, and he beamed at me.

My chin rose higher, and I smiled at him.

"Such a loving wife," the vestai said, but he sounded disappointed. "Well," he said to me, inclining his head. "It is so important that your nobles can serve you as they ought. To which end, I would like to offer my daughter, Adria, to be your personal handmaiden."

This raised the hairs on the back of my neck. The vestai snapped his fingers and a door opened, and I was sure there was some double meaning in his words—I hadn't seen anyone attend Calix; had he refused his nobles in the past? Perhaps he had good reason to want servants without tongues.

"My honored queen," said a voice breezing into the room. A woman in blue came before me, taller than Danae, but not by much, with hair a lovely light brown color that I'd never seen before. She had a round face and big cheeks that reminded me of a baby.

She bowed so deep she was nearly cowering before me, but there was arrogance there, a calculated knowledge I saw mirrored in her father's smug gaze.

I felt Calix's eyes on me, and I looked to him, his stony face unreadable.

"If my king thinks it proper," I said after a long moment.

"Surely the whole kingdom will breathlessly wait upon you, my love," Calix said. "So why not let Domina Viato be the first?"

The high vestai smiled like he had won some sort of victory.

"So you see," Calix said sharply. "She is soft spoken and beautiful—she will be an excellent queen."

The high vestai met Calix's eyes. "Yes. Now perhaps you can turn your gaze to the problems brewing in the city."

Calix waved a hand. "Tomorrow shall put all your fears to rest, Vestai."

He smiled, but it was thin and tight. "I certainly hope so, my king."

"Yes," Calix said. "The Three-Faced God does not tolerate much doubt."

This made the high vestai's face lose a little color, but neither party retracted their words.

"Excellent," the vestai said. "My queen, I look forward to your presentation tomorrow."

He bowed to me again, and I nodded to him, then looked to the girl still at my feet. "Adria," I said, and she looked up, and though her face was serene, I saw the same smugness of her father in her eyes. "You may attend me beginning tomorrow morning," I told her.

She bowed again, smiling at the floor.

◆

We rode back to the castles in silence. Calix was tense, his movements sharp, and he wouldn't meet my gaze. When we arrived, Calix made an excuse to leave me, and I returned to my chambers. My ishru appeared with food, and I ate a little as they brushed my hair, braided it back, and offered me a garment like the fur-lined one that was only a thin, flimsy fabric that tied in front.

"For bed?" I asked her.

She nodded.

I took off my clothes, trying to slip into it quickly, but they stopped me, washing me with fragrant, warm cloths. Then they pulled the gown on, tying it carefully in front in little bows.

"Thank you," I said, nodding to them.

They disappeared.

With a sigh, I went out onto my balcony. The wind was stronger, kicking the bottom of the robe back. I shivered, returning inside to take the coat I'd worn earlier and wrap it around me again. Then I walked to the point of the balcony and stood, letting the wind ruffle my braid, kiss my face, lick at my clothing. The crash of the waves so far below was hypnotic, and I shut my eyes, leaning into it.

An arm came around my waist, and I yelped, jerking away from the edge. I turned and my husband smiled at me, holding me still. "I scared you?" he asked.

My heart was pounding, and I nodded.

He plucked strands of hair away from my face, and he kept looking at me, taking me in as he drew a deep breath and let it go. "You did well today. I'm looking forward to tomorrow," he told me, letting his finger run down my cheek. "You have no idea the hope that you'll give my people. Our people."

I swallowed, wishing I could calm my heart just by wanting it. "Tell me more of your people," I asked.

He smiled like this pleased him. "Things have been difficult," he confided. "Since my father. Since his reign, and his death. We were torn apart by war with the islanders for much of his reign, and it devastated us. We spent all our money on defenses, ships, weapons. And during a war effort, that is glorious and righteous, but then it ends." His shoulders lifted. "I inherited my country at a time when the people were broken. We had won the war, but at a steep cost. We were weak, and vulnerable. The Saroccans across the sea came and raided Liatos, pillaging and devastating us further."

With a sigh, I slid away from him, sitting on a bench. He followed me, straddling the bench so his legs caged me in and his hands wandered on me, touching my shoulder, my arm, my back. I always thought I had an affectionate family, but I wasn't used to being touched like this—frequently, possessively, in a way that made me unsure if it was a display of warmth or a display of power. "What happened after the Saroccans raided?"

"We had to defend our people. We used the last of our resources to turn them away. That winter, our people starved, and froze, and died. It was my first year as king," he told me, and his hand fell away. "I felt responsible for my people's suffering."

I turned a little toward him. "What did you do?"

His mouth crooked up, and his hand rose. He dragged his thumb over my jaw in a bemused way. "I studied, mostly. My thought was that we needed food before anything else—what good was defending the country if everyone in it starved? I looked at our crops and why they weren't producing reliably. I found ways to irrigate better. We found that there were ways to get more minerals in the ground and grow stronger crops. But then, of course, as we grew the crops, our roads were insufficient, washing away—always more problems. Problems with logical answers, all of them." His eyes drifted over me.

I rubbed my hand on his arm. "You took care of your people," I realized.

He nodded, rustling my hair with his nose. "I fed my people for years. And yet recently, the past year or more, the God is displeased. Droughts cause crops to die; frost sweeps in early to take what we have. We had a tornado decimate half the fields in Kyrikatos." He sighed. "And this insidious abomination of sorcery." He shook his head slowly. "For everything else, I have discovered solutions—ways to fix these problems and heal my people."

"That's why you're looking for that elixir," I said, and my heart suddenly beat faster—I had almost forgotten there was something that took away elemental powers. If I could help him find it—if I could *use* it—I would be safe. "Have your men found anything yet?"

"No," he said. "They're searching the desert, but there are few places to hide something of this nature. I believe it would have to be in the mountains. Can you think of any place that would make sense?"

The lake. But I didn't say it—it was too precious, too complicated to lead him there. If he found the lake, whether or not that contained his elixir, he would have considerable power over the clans. Without that water reserve, our survival would be at the whims of the spirits.

And what if I *didn't* have this power, and the elixir was there? He would have the ability to take Kata's power away from her, and I would be responsible for leaving her powerless before the Trifectate—again.

"There is the cave of our ancestors," I said. "Where we honor our dead. But it's all hard ground—I don't know where anything could be hidden."

He nodded sharply. "I will send word to my quaesitori."

"I will help however I can," I told him. I wasn't sure if I meant it or not, but whether I needed the elixir found or wanted to prevent him from ever finding it, I wanted to know what he knew.

He kissed my neck. "Good," he said.

I asked, "Will you tell me more about tomorrow's ceremony?"

His fingers touched my chin, applying light pressure until I lowered my head a little, ducking to be closer to his mouth. "The Three-Faced God appreciates pageantry," he said. "It's a grand performance. Everything must be perfect. The crowd must be vast and eager; you must be raised up on a stage for all to see." His fingers trailed over my skin. "You must wear the perfect costume to look the part of a queen. And then the play will begin—the trivatis will speak the holy words, a tradition that is both ancient and eternal. And you will dazzle the crowd, and the people will cheer, and they will remember how powerful their king can be."

"Powerful?" I asked.

His fingers ran over my neck, brushing my pulse, his hand spreading out over my throat and moving before I could say anything about the strange gesture. "The Three-Faced God is powerful," he said, bringing his mouth closer to my ear. "And he grants us his power. He wants the people to stand in awe of us, to kneel at our feet and remember that we brought them up from nothing. We stand between them and oblivion."

I shivered, unable to speak, and he pulled my head down and pressed his lips to mine.

Three Silver Branches

The day dawned cool and beautiful. The sun on the water had all the dangerous beauty of a desert mirage, sparkling and twinkling and making the water look like a living thing.

The ishru dressed me in a silvery, shimmering swath of fabric, and an older woman came and adjusted the dress, suiting it better to my frame. She then put a blue dress the color of night sky over my head, laying it along the silver one so it was edged with the bright, metallic color. Dark blue ribbon was next, and she knotted it carefully so that it outlined my breasts, hugged my hips, made me feel somehow taller, if still incredibly exposed.

She snapped her fingers and the ishru brought out another coat, this one a matching blue and lined with white fur, knotted with silver threads that made me ache for the desert.

"The princess advised me that you are used to much warmer climes," she said. "Will this be too warm?"

She slid the coat onto my shoulders, and I looked down. There was a stiff collar around my neck, and this one didn't close but cut away to show the dress underneath. It was the softest thing I'd ever had on my body, and I sighed with pleasure. "This is . . . exquisite," I told her. "Can I have more like these?"

She smiled like a kind old mother and bowed her head. "My queen."

"What's your name?" I asked her.

"Zova, my queen."

I pressed my hand to hers. "Thank you. This is lovely."

She bowed again and dipped away from me. She picked up another stretch of the silver film and let it flutter down over my head, wrapping it back so it wasn't tied but held still.

The guard opened the door to let Adria in, and I scowled at him, steeling myself to deal with her.

She bowed, and I noticed she looked resplendent in a dress of green and gold. "You may stand," I told her. "I dislike people bowing to me."

Her eyebrows rose, and I wondered if this was something she would report to her father. Then she looked me over, her mouth pursing.

"You look very beautiful, my queen," she allowed. She didn't sound very pleased.

"Thank you," I said. "Would you lead me to the presentation?"

She bowed her head. "Yes, my queen," she said, and the guard opened the door as she led me out of the room, down the hall, and to the front of the castle.

In darkness, held back from the wide arch, I could see thousands of people, and the platform, and everything Calix described. The people were noisy like the ocean, moving in the same restless, relentless way.

Adria stopped and I kept moving, seeing Calix coming forward to me. He took my hand, raising it to his lips to kiss, as I struggled to find my breath. "Don't be nervous, my love," he said.

Men stood behind him, all dressed in a version of Calix's clothing, the same style he wore to our wedding. I had seen enough guards to figure this was a military dress of some sort. Yet today he glinted with shiny silver details, a brightly handled sword and a jeweled knife that looked like a treasure from the islands. A crown on his head, three silver branches woven together to form a circle, shimmered in the sun.

A small boy shot through the ranks, tangling in the knees of one of the men as he bent over. I recognized High Vestai Thessaly and went over to him.

"My queen," he greeted me, giving me the formal triple bow. "May I present my son, Aero Thessaly?"

Aero gave me his own version of the triple bow, which wasn't quite as sharp in his small body. "Three blessings," he mumbled quickly, like it should have all been a single word.

"Thank you," I told him, crouching down. "How old are you?"

He held up three chubby little fingers. A fourth started to lift, and he tucked it down with the other hand.

"Oh, you look at least five. Are you very brave?" I asked.

He nodded.

"And very noble, I suspect."

He nodded again.

"Will you—"

"Shalia," Calix said sharply, standing before me and putting his hand in front of my face. I put my hand in his, and he pulled me to my feet. "High Vestai," Calix said, nodding.

Thessaly bowed to him with his hands on his son's shoulders. "Aero, go find your mother," he said. "I'll be there in a moment."

"Adria, you may follow your brother," Calix told her. Calix nodded once to me and guided me away from Thessaly without another word.

The other men began walking forward, progressing by twos down the walkway. We settled into line behind them and I lost sight of Thessaly as my heart tripped faster in my chest.

As we crested the archway, I looked down to see the vast pool beneath us, reflecting the sunlight and flickering like it was on fire. Drummers around the pool pounded out our footsteps, and the crowd fell very silent. I saw Thessaly on a wide platform with two other men behind him, and a beautiful woman holding Aero, with Adria beside her.

The wind went still, and I barely breathed as we marched, dipping down behind the height of the platform before climbing the staircase up to it.

I stepped onto the platform, and the people cheered. My heart swelled as their joyous noise overtook the drums.

Calix stepped forward, and my hands fell to my sides. The people quieted. "My people, we have known war, and fear, and hunger," he said. "We have been in an age of terror and pain. That age is over."

The people cheered for this, and my stomach felt shivery and nervous. Calix waited, collecting their approval.

"Today I give you a queen, born of the desert, foreign to our city, our country, our home. Knotted together in the most eternal of bonds, together, we give you peace." He looked back to me, giving me a brilliant smile that at once felt stunning, and intimate, and utterly new. "Together, we bring you love."

The people cheered at this anew, and I stood silent.

Calix stepped back, moving behind me to gather up the silver filmy material that covered my face. "My people, meet my wife, Shalia!" he yelled, right in my ear, and he stepped forward and took the fabric and pulled.

It was as shocking as when Galen stole my first veil from me, and I gasped and blinked as the force of their cheers hit me like a blast. Women and children and men were jumping, heaving, pushing at the guards, their faces open and eager and screaming their approval. I felt like the rocks at the bottom of the cliff, the force of them churning against me, sweeping me away.

I sensed motion on the platform, and a small man in a black coat with a length and style similar to mine appeared beside me. He held up my crown, a thinner, daintier version of my husband's, and the crowd went quiet again.

"By the might, the power, the right of the Three-Faced God," he boomed, "I crown Shalia of the Desert Peoples the queen of the Bone Lands by holy appointment. She will live in the service of the Three-Faced God, she will reign in the glory of the Three-Faced God, and she will die in honor of the Three-Faced God."

The crown settled on my hair as a sudden panic clutched my heart at those last words.

I looked at my husband, but his expression was unchanged as the people cheered again, louder, wild, pushing forward so I felt a jolt at the platform.

"Calix?" I said, my hand reaching for his as the platform swayed. The guards pushed the people back, rough and forceful, but I didn't find his hand. I looked at him, and his head was turned, his eyes behind me.

I followed his gaze. The pool of water that extended beneath the archways looked strange, like it was forming a white crust.

People screamed, and my focus whipped away from the water to see them pointing behind me. When I looked back to the pool again, it was too late. Huge vines of ice were twining up out of the pool, curling forward like they were reaching for something.

They were reaching for me.

"Calix!" I cried, leaping and straining to get to him. He met my eyes, but it happened so quickly he didn't even get the chance to save me. The ice caught me, freezing, shimmering vines wrapping my feet and pushing me up, up, up into the air as fear strangled a scream in my chest.

Ropes of ice as thick as tree branches formed a cage around me, and then the ropes grew spikes, pushing Galen and Kairos with their hacking swords away.

It was cold inside the cage, and quieter, my own breath magnified, rattling around inside the ice. There were wide gaps between the ice branches that meant I could see out, but in a limited way, the light refracting and bending as it came through the glass-like ice. I was nearly twenty feet above the platform, far enough that if the ice broke, it would be a long way to fall.

The ice wrapping my feet pulsed like there was energy rolling through it, and my fingertips tingled and itched. The air around me felt thick, tangible, like it was full of fine threads that breathed and rushed with energy.

No, not energy—*magic.* Something in the ice was calling to me, making my blood rush and beat, making power thicken around my fingertips.

The ice around my feet loosened, and I gasped, stepping out of it, but the power didn't calm, rushing so fast it made me dizzy. It was an Elementa who was controlling the ice, and being so close to it made my power tremble frighteningly close to the surface. With every terrified heartbeat, my power drummed closer.

There was no denying what I was, not now, not with the feeling so intense beneath my hands. I was Elementa, and in a moment, my husband and his whole court would see me completely unmasked if I couldn't control the threads weaving wildly around my hands.

"We have been in an age of terror and pain!" a voice yelled. "But it is NOT over!"

The voice seemed to move, changing locations in the middle of a word, a syllable, a breath. I tried to track it, but I couldn't see enough around me to even begin to follow the source of the sound.

"You steal our people from their beds!" a new voice shouted.

"Kill them!" I heard Calix shouting at his guards.

"You hunt and kill those of us with power!" This was another voice.

I was breathing in short little gasps, trying to suppress the threads pushing at my fingertips, and Skies Above, it wasn't working.

Now several voices joined in. "You have no power, you have no might, and you have no dominion over the Resistance!"

My eyes roved over the crowd, trying to find who was *doing* this. Everyone was moving, turning, talking, searching, but there was one face staring straight at me.

Unmoving.

Smiling.

Rian winked, and I couldn't tell if he truly saw him or not, but I watched Calix stretch out his hand toward my brother.

Instantly, my control on my power snapped and I felt it rush out, a wave of crushing, numbing relief sweeping through me.

It was as if someone took a hammer to the side of the cliff the castles were built on, and one hard jolt threw my husband to the side, swaying the platform.

The ice around me cracked, and a moment later it shattered, a barrage of sharp crystals that melted as they moved.

I screamed as I fell, dropping toward the ground in the shower of ice shards.

Arms caught me, but the force was too much and we crashed to the ground in a heap. The fall slammed the breath out of my chest, and Galen was under me, gripping me tight, every inch of his body against mine.

I couldn't open my eyes for long moments. I could smell him, like sweat and salt and something I wasn't used to, that I vaguely knew from the ride here as the scent of forest. Green. Free. I was surrounded by his body, safe and sheltered, and I dug my fingers into his chest, trying to claw out a breath.

He touched my face, and I heard him calling my name, his chest heaving so hard that it pushed me up and down. "Shalia!" he said.

I opened my eyes. My hands on him curled tight, and I drew in a hard breath.

Galen held me as he sat up, then managed to get his legs beneath him to bring us to our feet without letting go of me. I stood and my knees sank as if I was standing in sand. He held me close.

I was vaguely aware of him checking me over in his soldier's way, the touches quick and light and impersonal, but my head was buzzing and I was still struggling for deep, even breaths.

"Shalia?" he asked, holding my arms now. "Shalia?"

I nodded belatedly.

It was like all the noise around us rushed back in at once; Calix was yelling and pointing, and people were screaming, trying to rush out of the courtyard, but the gates were closed.

There was a keening sound, and then a terrible crack as the platform buckled.

"Clear the platform!" Galen shouted, and he pulled my hand, rushing to the stairs and tugging me behind him. "Jump!" he shouted at me, and I obeyed him, leaping from the stairs as the platform collapsed in a cloud of dust. His hand in mine anchored me, guiding me close to him.

"Kairos!" I called, seeing him in the rising dust.

Galen let go of my hand. "Get her out of here!" he told Kai.

Kai pushed me in front of him as we ran up the walkway. I felt weak and disoriented, but I kept putting one foot in front of the other, glancing back to see his scimitar drawn and gleaming in the sun.

When we were in the archway, I looked back and saw the madness. The gates were shut, and the guards were trying to control the terrified people. I watched them use their shields like weapons, battering people and pushing them back.

Hurting people.

At the center of it all, my husband was barking orders for the guards to search the crowd by any means necessary, very nearly condoning their brutality, but somewhere in the melee, Rian was there too. Which one of them was more to blame for the people's suffering?

"Shy, come *on*," Kairos growled.

"Rian will be trapped," I told him, my voice hushed.

"Rian wouldn't come into the courtyard without more than one way out," he told me, his eyes flinty. He wasn't surprised. He'd seen Rian too—maybe he'd even known Rian would be there.

I moved forward, and we rushed through the halls. We made it to my bedroom, and Kairos ordered the guard not to let anyone in without his explicit approval. He brought me to the bed, and I sat with a sigh.

"Are you all right?" he asked. His head swept around the room carefully, and he asked, "The shaking—was that you?"

I swallowed and nodded slowly. "But not the rest."

He shook his head. "No. That was the Resistance. From what I can gather, that is the bulk of their forces—recruiting people with elements that need protection. That and some farmers and dissenters."

"But they seemed so organized," I said, drawing my knees up.

"They are," he said. "More than I can give Rian credit for too. Whoever Rian's working with has a strong eye for that sort of thing."

"Why would Rian do this?" I asked, shivering. "He's attacking *me*."

Kai sat beside me on the bed, his shoulder pressed to mine. "No," he said gently. "I think our brother is a damn fool, but I can see, at least, that he was making an effort to do it in a way where you wouldn't get hurt. Except for being dropped from the sky, but at least Galen saw to that. And as far as I can tell, he's doing this to protect people from Calix's injustice. Especially the Elementae."

"Does *Rian* have an ability?" I asked.

He sighed. "Not that I know of. But Rian was in the islands during the massacre—do you remember that? Whatever he saw while he was there, it changed him."

I drew a deep breath, uncomfortable with the idea that there were sides of my brothers I didn't know at all. "I think Calix saw Rian."

Kai's expression turned stormy and dark. "*That* Rian cannot risk. If your husband believes you have anything to do with this—even through Rian—" He stopped abruptly. "Skies," he muttered.

"But I don't," I insisted. "We don't. Right?"

His eyes flicked to me and away. "I don't know if things like 'reason' and 'responsibility' really matter to your husband. If he wants to see a connection, he will."

I shook my head, standing from the bed. It was growing foggy and dark outside, and it felt like this was finding its way inside my mind and smudging what I was certain of. "He wouldn't. He's my husband." I stepped closer to the glass, but looked back at Kai. "What about Kata?" I asked.

He lifted his shoulders. "I haven't heard more." Standing from the bed, he sighed. "I'm going to find Galen. You need your own guard, and I'm assuming he'll agree to it after today."

"Will a guard help if it's my own brother endangering me?" I asked. "If it's my very *hands*?"

He raised an eyebrow. "Yes," he said, coming and kissing my temple before he left me alone again.

The Night the Three-Faced God Walked

I wasn't shaking anymore, but there was an uneasy tremor deep inside me. I lay on the bed, but I couldn't sleep, staring at the ceiling as my heart thudded in my chest.

I stood, pacing about the chamber, walking out onto the balcony in the thickening fog, but there wasn't enough space to walk, and somehow the fog carried the green scent of Galen on it.

How could I be thinking of him now?

"Shy," I heard, and I turned back toward the palace, but no one was there.

"*Shy*," I heard again, and I turned into the heart of the fog.

Warm arms came out of the fog and wrapped around me, and Kata hugged me as the fog around us grew thicker still.

"Kata!" I cried, pressing my face into her neck. So many emotions rushed through me like pebbles tumbling down a slope, and I looped my arms around her shoulders, hugging her tight.

"I have you," she whispered to me. "I have you. You must have been so frightened, but you're safe now."

"Was that you today?" I asked. "With the ice?"

"No," she said. "That was another member of the Resistance. There are many Elementae who have joined us."

"So it was true," I said. "What they were saying about hunting and killing those with power?"

She drew back from our hug. "I told you that, before you were married."

My chest felt tight. "I know," I said.

"And you didn't think it mattered to you," she said softly. "Until now."

For all I spoke of caring for my people, of wanting to lead and save, she was probably right. The weight of this stung, but she put her hand in mine.

I nodded. "I have the power you always thought I did."

"I figured," she said, her mouth tight. "I'm sorry it's not what you wanted."

I looked at our hands. "If we were back in the desert, this would just be one more thing for us to share. One more thing that makes us sisters in the way that birth didn't. And maybe I was stupid," I said, "but I married him. And I'm *here*. And these powers are illegal, and he hates the people who practice them. And I'm *married* to him, Kata."

"You're not stupid," she said fiercely. "You protected your family. I would have done the same if I had the chance."

"Can you fix me?" I asked her. "You can heal—surely you can heal this."

She frowned. "You aren't *broken*. You don't need to be fixed."

"Calix knows of an elixir that can take powers away from Elementae. If we can find that before him, I could drink it. I could use it—"

"No," she said, shaking her head. "Such a thing doesn't exist. There is no elixir. Whatever errand he's on, he won't succeed. These powers are part of you; they are as essential to your body as your blood. They cannot be removed or rejected."

"How can you know? You were so young when you left the islands—you barely know about your own power."

She pulled away from me, crossing her arms. "I know enough! I've never heard of something that can curb elemental powers. Even the genocide didn't destroy them."

"Then close the Earth Aede. You opened it; you must be able to close it."

An indignant huff came out of her. "The powers retreated to the Aedes because of the genocide, Shalia. Like a child who runs and hides when their life is threatened. Like *I* had to hide in the desert after my family was murdered. Like I still hide, because if your husband knew there was still a daughter of the high priestess alive, my life would be forfeit. It is not as simple as opening a box and closing it again. And even if I could—it would remove *all* the Earth powers. You would do that for your own gain?"

"No," I told her, desperate, my hands beginning to shake. "But there has to be a way. I can't control it. It just happens, and I can't stop it. And soon someone will be able to tell that it's *me*." Visions ripped through my mind, of rage on my husband's face, of blood and sharp things meant to punish me for this power I never wanted.

"Stop," she said, and I looked up to her. "You can control it. You have to use it—that's why it's unpredictable now."

"How do I learn to control it? How did you?"

"It's different for me." She held out her hand, and the mist curled to meet it in a thin, swirling plume. "Most of my kind show their gifts very young. My gift never arrived. Not that I could see. And then the night came that they say the Three-Faced God Walked, and I could feel my power. And then the powers of so many other people, rushing to me, overwhelming me. Using me as a conduit," she said. "And—well, you remember when I knew the Aedes needed to be opened again."

My fingers curled around hers. She had been so sick, and I'd never been more scared for her. We brought her to the lake at Jitra, and the water had healed her, but the search consumed her after that. That's when she started to leave, and my parents refused to let me go with her. She left first for weeks, and then for months, and I had carried on without my best friend.

"I know . . ." I rubbed my fingers over her skin in our clasped hands, and she gripped me back, binding us tight, letting me confess my shame. "I never asked about the Night the Three-Faced God Walked. Your nightmares . . . I didn't want to ask. I didn't want to know."

"And I didn't tell you," she said, her voice rough. "Because I love you. Because I've always loved you, and I don't want you to know."

"But I love you too," I told her, "and I want to know what you've suffered."

She nodded, not looking at me but at the water. "I don't remember much. I was eleven. I was a child. I was with my brother when the siege came. People panicked. I was locked in a room with my brother while my mother and sisters went to fight, and my father went to protect them. My mother's gift was legendary. She could rule the oceans.

"I don't know what happened. How it could have been. Rian was there, trying to help the Vis people in the war. My mother and all her court were there, in their full power, in their full glory. How could one man have fought them and won?" She looked at me like I would have an answer.

"I heard they surrounded the islands. He had so many men he just overwhelmed you," I told her.

She shook her head. "It was more than that. They found me and my brother, and my brother started swirling the air into a tornado, trying to protect us. They stabbed him to death."

I took her other hand, desperate to comfort her, desperate to forget what it felt like to watch my brother burn.

She drew in a short, unsteady breath. "And they spent hours hurting me. Trying to make my gifts appear, but they never came. So they bound up anyone who didn't have powers—with Rian tied right beside me—and they said we would watch the unclean people be sacrificed to the God. As if they weren't planning on murdering us too—as if there was any way they would have purposefully left anyone alive to remember."

She was quiet for many long moments. "They were so fast. They built the structure in a day, and it took another day to fill it," she told me. "It didn't look like a man, not at first. It just looked like a cage of sapling and wood. And then they filled it, tying my people inside the structure. He made sure I could see my parents. And they stuffed the empty places with grasses and hay. When night came, they lit it on fire. The people—my people, my *family*—struggled so much, so hard, that the structure moved, filled with hundreds of screams. And then it fell like a man to his knees. And so they called it the Night the Three-Faced God Walked."

She pushed a tear off her face. "When it fell, it shook the ground, and something within me broke. And water came in, so much water that the island flooded and pulled Rian and me away with it. And we survived, because the water was part of me. The water was me." She sniffed. "My gift—it comes from anger. And hate. But yours doesn't," she said, and she looked around us.

Circling our feet, sand was building in small mounds, like an infinitesimally small desert. "I did that?" I asked.

She nodded, wiping another tear. "You're incredibly powerful, Shalia. Your power begins with your love for people," she said. "That's where your greatest strength lies."

I frowned. "But I didn't—before, I could feel threads, like it was a fabric I had to tug on to get it to obey me."

She nodded. "That's common. It helps you focus; as you grow stronger, you may still have a sense of the threads existing—they're the energy of the natural world—but you may not have to manipulate them to use your power."

"But how do I grow stronger? I have to *love* people more?"

She shook her head. "No. You have to hold on to it," she said, her voice rough. She leaned her head on mine, and I wished I could take away the things she had suffered. "Soon it will be easier, but when it's difficult to control, you have to hold that emotion within you. Remember it and treasure it, and it will open your power."

"But what can my power even do?" I asked her. "I don't really understand."

"Anything that is of the earth will do your bidding. In my experience, I can't make water manifest where there is no water, like in the desert. But usually there's water *somewhere*, and earth's presence is endless. Her shoulders lifted. "We're in a palace of rock; there couldn't be a better place to try something."

"Can I grow things?" I asked, suddenly wanting to see ilayi blooms in this foreign land.

She tilted her head. "In a way—if the seed is there, you can give it soil and the right conditions to grow, but you can't grow something out of nothing. And it would be better if you had a fire element to give it heat, and a water element to nourish the soil. The elements are at their most powerful when they work together."

Disappointment filled my chest.

"But remember," she said. "Many things come from the earth. Metals, minerals, crystals, to name a few."

I thought of the gold that Rian had stolen, killing ten men to do it. When did ten—or even one—become the number of lives my brother felt comfortable taking? I wished for the precious metal, curling my hand into a tight fist, willing it to be full of the gold he needed.

With a sigh, I let go, opening my hand.

"Nothing happened," I told her, showing her my empty palm.

She just looked at me, patient. "Don't focus on the earth. Focus first on yourself, on that emotion."

"On love," I repeated, the words rough.

She nodded.

I thought of Rian on my wedding day, my fear and confusion and joy as I saw him in front of me, the first of my family to give me a gift, to give me his hopes for my future. Even when it was a future he wouldn't choose for me. He was the first to put a thread around my neck, and the gold in the foreign coins had a soft shine before the full sun rose.

I felt invisible threads now at my fingertips. Just like the ones my family had given me, these connected me to something greater. I felt it as little pieces of things—flecks, really—pulled up from the soil in the cliffs below, from other rocks, from all around me, rolling and jumping into my hand.

When I opened my eyes, I held a tiny chunk of gold.

My heart pounded as I showed it to Kata, and she nodded, smiling at me. "You see?" she said.

"Show me more," I asked.

Kata guided my practice for a while longer, including bending a silver hair comb, but we soon heard a noise behind us. Without a word, Kata kissed my cheek and walked back into the fog. In seconds, I couldn't see her.

"Shalia?" Kairos called.

I came toward him until I could see him in the fog, still heavy but clearing. He squinted, looking through the fog with a wry smile.

"So many curious secrets, sister," he said. I opened my mouth, but he shook his head. "I don't need to know."

He offered me his arm, and I took it. "Where are we going?"

"To meet your new guard," he said, glancing around. "If you can see them."

He ushered me out of the chamber and up a staircase. In a sort of courtyard around the central tower, more than twenty men were lined up in the hazy glow of the fog.

"These men have all volunteered to create the Saepia, the Queen's Guard," I heard Galen say, and I turned to see him walking toward me, his hands behind his back, making his shoulders seem broader still.

Shoulders that had sheltered me not even an hour ago. Saved me. The thought made me mute as he came closer and stopped several feet away.

He looked me over for a stark moment. "You're not injured," he said.

I nodded, my mouth dry. "Just shaken," I managed to say.

"Which brings us to your new guard," Kairos said.

"Yes," Galen said, clearing his throat. "As I said, these men have volunteered. They are some of my best soldiers."

His eyes, lush and vibrant green, met mine. I hadn't realized his eyes were just as green as Calix's—maybe more so. They were brighter, somehow, such a strange contrast to his carved-rock face.

Galen didn't seem to register my curiosity; he turned away from me and gestured two men forward. They didn't look like the rest; one was thinner, smaller, with a shifty look to him that reminded me of the way that Kairos slid around things, and the other was utterly massive. They wore the same black uniform, but theirs were looser, less fitted. The taller one came to me first. His hair was blond and longer than the rest of his fellows, tied back by a leather string. Two swords hung on his hips, and he had a long, broad weapon strapped to his back that looked as deadly as it did heavy, with a wicked, notched curve like a scimitar, but different.

He knelt to me. "My queen."

"This is Zeph," Galen said, gesturing to the large man.

He stayed kneeling, and the second came forward. He was shorter, and he wore a leather breastplate over his uniform that was lined with small knives, and a sword on his back like Zeph.

"This is Theron. These two will be your personal guards. These are men I have trained myself, and I would trust them with my life," Galen said. "Which is the only way I will trust them with yours."

I glanced at Galen at such words, but he didn't look at me. "Please don't kneel to me," I told them. "I don't like it."

They shared a glance but stood. "We'll be with you night and day, my queen," Zeph promised me. "We do not take today's insult to your person lightly."

I nodded to him. "Thank you."

"They will lead the others," Galen explained to me. "They will be in shifts around you as needed. Some will guard your rooms, whether you're there or not. Others will support Zeph and Theron as needed on the move. Let me introduce you."

He introduced each man in turn, and I did my best to remember their names. They didn't know me, but they all had come, ready to defend me. It was reminiscent of my brothers back home, and I found comfort in the thought.

I felt my power, as if suddenly my heart stretched all the way to my fingertips, and farther still, as if there were a million fine threads that my fingers were stroking against. And in that moment, I was totally aware—of the stone beneath our feet, of the grains of fine sand moving over them, of the steel and silver of the armor and weapons of the men before me.

Breathing to control my power, I looked for my brother. Kairos watched it all in silent consideration. He was changing, my funny brother, and I wasn't sure I liked it—certainly not if the change was because of me.

The men were dismissed, and I felt the gears shifting into place as Zeph and Theron gave orders, sliding twenty feet apart with me in the middle. Just like that, I felt a protective barrier between me and the world, and I could breathe easier.

"Dinner's soon," Galen said, coming to me again.

"Even after today's events?" I asked.

"The court loves nothing more than to gather and spread gossip," he said. "I'm sure it will be a great comfort after such a day."

"Shy," Kairos called. His sly gaze moved between Galen and me, and I felt heat in my face, like his eyes saw something that wasn't there. I hurried over to him, and Kairos followed me back to my chambers without comment, Zeph and Theron a few steps behind him. When I went into my bedroom, Kairos stood at the door, watching me thoughtfully.

"Are you all right, Shy?" he asked softly.

I squeezed his hand. "Yes. Thank you, Kai."

He kissed my cheek. He left with a sigh on his lips, and Zeph stood at the door while Theron gestured down the hallway. "We'll be right outside your door, my queen."

"Thank you," I told them.

That Is Power

When the sky grew dark, Zeph knocked at the door. "The ishru would like to attend to you, my queen," he said.

"They can come in," I told him. "And thank you for asking."

Zeph's mouth twitched as he opened the door. "You shouldn't get in the habit of thanking your servants," he said.

I smiled. "You shouldn't get in the habit of correcting your queen."

He chuckled as he allowed the women in, and they quickly set about attending to me, changing my clothes and brushing my hair to prepare me for dinner. When I was ready to leave, Zeph led me through the halls of the Tri Castles.

The second floor was a huge room with white stone and tall windows. Glittering red fabric draped down the walls to pool on the floor. There were ten steps that led to a higher level against the back wall of the room, with space enough for a single table with four seats all along the back edge, so that those seated would look out over the place.

In the center of the lower part of the room, there was a large pit of fire with an iron shelf around it. Several pots were on the shelf, ostensibly being kept warm for the meal.

Something struck the stone with a resounding crack, and then the noise came again. I jumped.

"The queen!" shouted a voice, and I looked up to the raised level to see the small man in the long black coat striking a staff on the stone.

The rest of the people in the room—a host of nobility in a riot of bright colors and exposed skin—turned and looked at where I stood in the doorway. There was a moment when I didn't move, didn't breathe, staring back at them all in panic.

But then a young man in front bowed to me, and they all followed suit.

I took a breath and stepped forward, skirting around the fire to walk up the staircase. I didn't like having my back to the people, and at the top I turned, just as the small man struck the ground again.

"The king!" he bellowed.

Calix strode through the room as the people bowed, his flinty green eyes on me alone. He mounted the stairs, his back ramrod straight, stopping two steps down. He caught my hand, his fingers sliding up my palm to thread through my fingers. Flipping my hand over, he pressed his lips against my pulse, and I wondered if he could feel it pounding back against his mouth.

"Where have you been all day?" I asked softly.

He met my gaze but didn't answer. He climbed the remaining stairs but kept my hand captive, drawing me around the table. Pulling back the chair, he led me into it by my hand. I sat, and he took the chair beside me.

"Calix?" I asked.

He didn't look at me.

The man struck the floor once, and everyone slowly took their seats. Danae and Galen appeared, together, and the man struck the floor again to announce them. They climbed the stairs without hesitation, and Galen helped Danae into her chair beside me before going to sit beyond Calix.

I touched her hand. "Are you all right?" I asked. "I didn't see you this afternoon."

She glanced at me and away, like the flicker of fire. "Fine. I should be asking you."

My shoulders lifted. "Between your two brothers, I was well looked after. Where were you?"

"Hidden. We all have our roles in the service of the Three-Faced God." She sighed, moving her eyes carefully toward Calix. "And I've been searching the city since."

"For those people?" I asked.

"The Resistance," she said, and now her careful eyes were watching me. "Your brother's cause."

"You cannot believe my brother would be involved in something that would put me at risk," I said. Despite speaking to Kata, *I* still couldn't believe it.

"No," she said. "But they are growing stronger. And both my brothers must take action to quell such insurgence."

"And I support them," I said, raising my chin. I would never stand against Rian, but I didn't like thinking of him stirring up violence against innocent people, even if he believed it was for a greater good.

Then again, I didn't want to have to make my loyalties clear to either my brother or my husband.

Her eyes met mine. "Good. I'm sorry I wasn't standing with you today. You must have been frightened."

I nodded. "But I'm safe."

Danae nodded.

The lids of the pots were all lifted, and an army of servants climbed the stairs to our table, offering the food to us. I couldn't recognize a single thing; it didn't look like meat or vegetables at all. There were liquids and things floating in the liquid, and it smelled foreign and strange.

Calix pointed, and servants placed dishes in front of me. The smell hit me and turned my stomach.

"What is this?" I asked Danae in a whisper.

"Fish," she said, using a spoon to lift a chunk of something white.

My stomach clenched.

She gave me a small smile and passed the bread in my direction.

Tearing some of it off, I gave her a grateful nod.

My guards followed us back to our rooms, staying outside my door as we entered. Calix drew a breath and let it out slowly, his hands on his hips. I turned to him, wondering if I was meant to touch him as he so often touched me, if that would break the icy silence he'd given me all through dinner.

Before I decided, I said, "You never told me where you've been today." Too clearly, I remembered the feeling of reaching for his hand and never getting it.

He put his hands on my shoulders, but instead of pulling me closer, he pushed me aside. "Busy," he said. "I don't know if you noticed, but we came under attack today."

His rejection burned through me. "Of course I noticed," I said. "I could have *died*."

His face turned to mine, angry and stormy. "That's what I thought too, Shalia. That everything we are fighting for could have been undone in a moment. But I saw him. I'm sure of it."

"Saw who?" I asked, but I knew already.

"Rian," he snarled. "The brother who I *assumed* would never act out against his sweet little sister. So it remains that either he is disloyal and a sorry excuse for a man or you knew exactly what he planned. You *agreed* to risk yourself to tear my kingdom down."

My dread was overtaken by anger. "You think I *knew*?" I demanded. "I have never been more frightened in my life, and when I tried to reach for you, to get to you, you did nothing. You were so concerned with your hate that you could not spare a thought for me. And it was your brother, not you, who defended me."

"He's my *commander*—that's his thrice-damned job!" he shouted at me.

"And you are my husband," I returned, my voice quiet but clear. "I was scared, and I wanted *you*."

"Not your brother?" he growled, moving closer to me. "What do you know of his rebellion, Shalia? What haven't you told me?"

"*Nothing*," I insisted, backing away from him.

"You're *lying*," he said, his face twisting.

"I know only that it was part of the reason you married me," I said, stopping and raising my chin, drawing a breath, and meeting his eyes. "Nothing else."

He stopped advancing; his eyes narrowed and focused on me, calculating, assessing. "I have a spy in his camp, you know. I know Rian's not the leader—Tassos says the leader's true identity is a closely guarded secret. You know who it is, don't you?" he asked.

A spy? I made a note of the name, though I wasn't sure if I could give such information to Rian. But if Calix had a spy in Rian's camp, he needed to know. Didn't he?

Calix's voice had lost the fury of a moment before, but I was still trembling, and I shook my head. "No. I don't, and you *know* I don't or you never would have married me," I insisted. I crossed my arms. "I don't know how you can even ask me this, Calix."

He turned, waving one arm as he shook his head. "You do not understand what they did today. What this sorcery—what people *seeing* this sorcery—represents."

"You told me of this prophecy, but I don't understand why you are blind to everything but hate when you are confronted with them. You have spent so much time caring for your people and solving their problems, but you forget it all when you encounter these powers."

"You're the one who is blind!" he roared, and I stepped back from him. He lunged forward, shaking his fist at me. "This sorcery will play tricks on your mind, wife. It seeks to destroy, to overpower. It wants my throne and my life, and it will do whatever it can to steal them from me."

He was wild, but for the first time, I felt like he was showing me the cause of his hate. "Calix," I said gently. "I don't understand."

He drew in a breath, turning abruptly away from me and walking to the balcony doors. He stopped with his fingers on the handle. "It's all a trick," he said, his voice rough. "First the trivatis who gave me that prophecy. Then *her*."

Slowly, I came toward him. I put my hand on his shoulder, but he moved away. "Who, Calix?"

He turned to me, seizing my arms and pushing me until the back of my knees hit our bed. "Calix?" I questioned.

His touch was hard on my skin, and he shook me.

"Calix, stop," I pleaded.

"Are you deceiving me?" he growled. "I loved her, and she tricked me. She wanted my throne. She deceived me. Are you deceiving me?" he demanded.

I couldn't help the fear trembling through me. "I'm not deceiving you," I told him.

I leaned forward carefully, and he brought his arms around me, lifting me up and kissing my lips.

A lie, sealed with a kiss, to stop a conversation that it seemed neither of us wanted to have.

That morning I woke early, close in my husband's arms. He was still asleep, and I wanted to get up—perhaps I could walk someplace, after being trapped so long in a castle and in the carriage before that—but I didn't want to upset him after whatever precarious peace we had achieved last night.

He had mentioned so many things—the prophecy, a spy in Rian's camp, a trivatis, this girl who once had so much sway over his heart. It must have been the girl he told me he loved who had died—but did she have powers? Could he have ever loved an Elementa girl and act the way he did toward their kind?

My kind.

I'm not deceiving you, I'd told him. Now the lie rang like a bell inside my mind, the sound bouncing back and forth, unending.

Growing impatient, I nudged my husband's foot. He drew a deep breath and rolled over, and I elbowed his back.

"Wife?" he groaned, shifting.

I sighed like I was still asleep. "Hm?"

"Ugh. Good morning," he grunted.

I yawned and sat up, drawing the nightclothes around my shoulders. "Good morning."

He looked out the window. "It's early."

"I couldn't sleep much, thinking of yesterday," I told him. "You never told me what you will do in the wake of the attack."

He stretched. "My army was hunting them through the night, but I don't know if they'll find anything. These sorcerers—this *Resistance*—hide in plain sight. Among neighbors and friends who cover for them, if they know at all."

"And what of this elixir that you're searching for? Have your men found it in the desert?"

An edge of suspicion came to his eyes. "Not yet. They're trying to re-create it in the south," he said. "But so far they have had little success."

"So what can we do to comfort the people?" I asked him. "There was so much fear in the courtyard yesterday."

"Fear," he mused. "Yes. People should be afraid, shouldn't they?" He sat up. "Perhaps that's the key to this whole thing. If we make people afraid of their neighbors—if we teach them how insidious and deceitful these people are—they will cease harboring them."

"Calix," I said, shaking my head, "I meant that there is already *enough* fear. Surely it's not a good idea to encourage more."

"Fear is healthy," he said with a dismissive wave. "No, this is an excellent idea. But how best to show them that they should be afraid?"

"You cannot tell me it was easy to see children clinging to their mothers in fear," I said.

"Where are the ishru?" Calix shouted toward the door as he stood from the bed.

The door opened, and Zeph bowed his head to me as the women in white filtered in like wraiths. They bowed to Calix, and then stood and nodded to me.

Calix stopped. "What is the meaning of this?" he demanded. "Why would you not *bow* to your queen?"

The ishru all dropped to their hands and knees, and I jumped from the bed as Calix towered over one. "Calix," I told him, coming by his side. "I told them not to. I don't like it."

"Don't *like* it?" he demanded.

"Yes," I said. "I don't want them bowing to me. I don't want you making people humble themselves before me."

He squared his shoulders off against mine. "And what would happen if the Concilium saw that a slave no longer needed to bow to a queen? Or to my other vestai? I was crowned king as a child, Shalia, and they will always see me as a child. I can barely retain the respect that I have clawed from them, and it sounds foolish and small, but something so simple as a slave failing to show proper deference could threaten my position as king. And your new *attendant* will be watching you always, ready to report these infractions to her father. How the Thessalys would relish hearing that a slave doesn't bow to a king." He shook his head. "Ruling cannot be about emotion, my sweet. It has to be about power and control. Always."

"True power does not force others to make themselves smaller," I told him.

Anger simmered in his eyes. "No, wife. You're wrong."

My eyes met his. How could he truly believe that?

"Apologize to me for your foolishness."

My mouth opened in shock. "It's what I believe, Calix," I told him.

He stepped closer to me, and I stepped back. "You are my wife. You will believe what I tell you to believe. Apologize."

My eyes burned. "Calix," I said, shaking my head.

He stepped forward, and as I stepped back again, there was a sick feeling inside me I recognized as fear. He didn't just want his people afraid—he wanted me afraid. And I was. "I'm sorry," I whispered.

"For what?" he demanded.

"For my foolishness," I said.

He nodded once, leaning his head closer to mine. "So you see," he murmured. "That is power."

The ishru dressed me, and when I was done, Calix was waiting in the chamber, straightening his own clothes as he dismissed the servants. "Lovely," he said, his eyes brushing over me. "You are right, wife. We must look to the children of this nation, first and always. I would like you to go to the Erudium today and allay their fears. Coddle the children and convince them that they were right to be afraid, but we will protect them. Tell them to tell their praeceptae and parents if they see sorcery." He shook his head. "No—tell them that *only with their help* can we protect them." He nodded, a smug smile on his face.

"What is the Erudium?" I asked.

"A temple of learning," he told me. "Where our young men are educated and our young women are groomed."

"Groomed," I repeated.

"Yes," he said. "Taught in the arts that will serve them as wives and mothers. Sewing, how to fix their hair, that sort of thing.

We've seen the dangers of overeducating women in other countries—we do not make such mistakes in the Trifectate."

I remembered my father laughing and saying that he would rather spend more time educating his daughters, because they were the true leaders in every home, and to educate them was to educate a whole family at once.

My head fell at the memory. "What will you do?" I asked.

"Instruct the vestai to spread word of the same throughout their lands," he said. "With one difference—that they will receive a tax credit for every Elementa that they produce. It's brilliant—my vestai swear their first loyalty to their overflowing coffers, and it will keep them busy and happy, *and* quash the Resistance."

I gasped. "Calix!"

He came and kissed my cheek with a bright smile. "You inspired the idea, my love. Thank you." His hand slid over my chin, drawing it to him and pressing his mouth to mine. "You are good for my kingdom, wife."

Irredeemable

When I left the room, Adria was outside, and she bowed to me. I no longer had the will to ask her to stop, so I merely sighed, and straightened my back. "You will show me to this Erudium?" I asked.

"Yes, my lady. And your guard?"

"Stays with her," Zeph said.

"Very well," she said with her sly smile. "This way." She led me to the courtyard, and a waiting carriage.

I drew a breath. "Is this building somewhere in the Tri City?" I asked.

She looked warily at Zeph. "Yes."

"Then we will walk there."

"But—" she gasped. "We cannot walk there."

"You will lead the way," I told her. "Or I will tell the king you refused to take me."

She huffed, looking at her thin silk shoes like they would melt away, and walked down the wide causeway. "It isn't close. And they're expecting us quite soon. In fact we should have been there already. An absence that will not go unnoticed, I'm sure."

I glanced at Zeph, and he glowered at her in return.

She looked at me, pausing as she walked. "I don't mean to be disrespectful; I know that you haven't been here before, and I just want to make sure you know of our ways," she told me. "I am your attendant, after all, and no one wishes to displease the king."

I recoiled a little, unsure if this was meant as a threat or some kind of bait to get me to speak ill of my husband. "We will *walk*," was all I said to her.

She bowed to me. "Of course, my queen."

As Adria, Zeph, and I left the Tri Castles, the recognition from people was instant—even in their clothes, my skin was so different from anyone's in the Bone Lands. A few had a warm yellow tone to their skin, but nothing like my and Kairos's rich brown. Still, not many people were in the streets, and those who were there barely raised their eyes to me as they moved quickly past.

We passed a large building with a low rumbling noise coming from it that shook the ground a little, and Zeph nodded to a man in uniform as we walked by. "What's that?" I asked.

"A grain mill," he told me. He pointed to a long wall that ran out behind the building as far as I could see. "Grain gets sent on the road, and men grind the grain to make flour."

I nodded once, and as we walked farther, we saw long lines of weary-looking women and children standing at the back of the mill. I frowned, looking at Zeph.

He raised his shoulders. "They are waiting for their grain allowance."

"Is there not enough grain?" I asked. "The fields looked so healthy on our way down here."

"There's enough grain," he said. "But not the men to grind it."

"Where are the men?" I asked.

"Serving as soldiers," Adria said, cutting a glare to Zeph. "Or building ships and armor in the communes. Skilled men are sent away."

"And why can the women not work?" I asked, looking over the lines. The women were thin and bedraggled, clutching their children.

Adria looked like she had bitten something sour. "Oh no. Women cannot *work*."

"Why not?"

She shook her head. "Well, first of all, it would surely interfere with childbirth."

I looked at the mill thoughtfully. Grinding grain could not be so much more difficult than carrying tents, and women did that up until they gave birth in the desert. "When they are close, perhaps, but not while they are with child."

"But it's . . . unsuitable. The Three-Faced God does not like women to be so . . . active. Like walking," she added, raising her chin.

Unsuitable. Perhaps this was what Danae had meant when she said she wasn't the princess she was supposed to be. We walked past, but the sight of the mill stayed long in my mind as we approached our destination.

The Erudium was in the center of town, past the factories and far from the water and the docks. It was the very heart of the city. New, like most of the city, it was massive, white and square and tall, with giant swaths of white fabric that dragged my eyes upward.

Uniformed men stood guard out front, like this place held all the treasures of the kingdom.

They let us in, and I watched as the Erudium guards all lined up behind Zeph. Adria breezed in, and I followed her. She led me into a wide, deep room that reminded me of a place in Jitra that had been formed by rock and used for public speeches. This was man-made, the rings where people could sit or stand perfectly spaced, growing ever wider as they rose up.

The room was full of children. Women, not dressed like the women of court but in sturdier red garments that covered more skin and had many cloth ties, stood along the aisles, perfect end pieces to the rows of children.

No one so much as twitched as I was led forward, down a staircase to a platform. A chair on it was set off to the side, and Adria gestured for me to sit.

As my bottom touched the chair, the entire crowd stood up, chins raised, chests pushed forward, and they sang.

Three Faces of the God
To watch over and protect me
Three Faces of the God
To see all the good that's in me

I will be powerful, righteous, and true
I will stand tall for my country
The Bone Lands will rise anew
And my brothers and sisters will be free

In one motion, they all sat down and stared at me.

I stared back, my heart beating faster.

"My queen?" Adria murmured behind me.

I turned.

"I believe the king told them you would address them. Explain what happened yesterday," she told me.

I nodded and stood.

They all stood with me.

"Sit," I said, and they immediately sat.

"How many of you were in the castles yesterday?" I asked. Slowly, about twenty of the hundred or so children in the room raised their hands. One of them was Aero, and he smiled when I looked at him.

"I'm sure it was frightening," I said, and several heads nodded. "They were trying to scare you."

"I wasn't scared!" shouted a boy, standing up. "I only wished for a sword in my hand to gut them like fish!"

The children cheered at this, and I waited for them to quiet. "*I* was frightened," I told him, and this brought total silence to the room. "I wasn't sure if they meant to kill me. I wasn't sure if I would die the day I became your queen."

"Who are they?" came another voice. "Who are the Resistance?"

I opened my mouth, but no sound came. I knew what my husband wanted me to say—what I *had* to say. But they said "Resistance," and I heard "Rian." If we spoke of Elementae, I would hear my own name.

"I don't know," I told the child. "Perhaps the king, in his wisdom, knows more than I do. I don't know who they are. But I know that where they go, violence will follow. And you must . . ." My voice lost its surety. "You must . . ."

"You must defend yourselves and your families from evil."

My head rose as everyone turned to look behind them. Up at the top of the amphitheater, Galen started to come down the steps, his eyes on me for a long moment before they swept over the room.

"You are the nation's every hope," he said as he descended. "And you must be the ones to tell your parents or your praeceptae if you see someone using elemental magic. You must know what to look for—anything that seems out of place, or strange, or unnatural. You must trust your instincts on this—you are trained men and women of the Trifectate, and you know right from wrong."

He came to me, bowing over my hand before kissing it and returning to his audience. He clasped his hands behind his back.

"Your queen was threatened yesterday," he told them, glaring at them like they were responsible. "Who among you will defend her?"

Every boy leaped to his feet, shouting.

"Women, will you not defend your queen?" he asked.

"They're just girls!" one boy shouted.

"When our nation is strong, we are all strong!" Galen shouted. "When our nation is defended, our queen is defended! How will you defend her?" he asked, pointing to an older girl up front.

"By trusting my instincts?" she said.

"Yes!" he shouted. "Keep your eyes open! Trust your instincts!"

The girls stood now too, and everyone clapped and shouted excitedly at him. Galen surveyed them sternly, not seeming to enjoy their praise, and as young as he was, I could see the military commander in him.

"Now," he said, "while I'm here, I wish to examine our future recruits." He nodded to one of the standing women, who clapped her hands and ordered the children to the training grounds. They began filing out, and Galen turned to me. "Forgive the intrusion," he said, bowing his head.

"It was welcome," I said. "I didn't really know what to say."

He shook his head. "Calix has always been totally at ease before a crowd. It took me far longer to feel comfortable speaking to others." His mouth pursed thoughtfully. "And still most of what I do is shouting."

I looked down. "That," I agreed softly. "And you managed to say what he wanted without it sounding so very hateful."

"Keeping an eye on your surroundings and trusting your own understanding is usually good advice for our recruits. I figured it applied here. Truly, I don't think there's much for them to observe, so I don't see the harm in it."

"There's harm in rewarding turning on one another," I told him.

His eyes cut to me, and then behind me, where I was sure Adria still stood. "You should stay for training," he told me flatly. "I'm sure the boys will enjoy fighting for your praise."

"More fighting," I said, my voice barely more than a sigh.

The corner of his mouth turned up the smallest bit. "Less blood with the children, usually." He offered me his arm, and I caught my breath as I put my hand on him. He lowered his arm a little, pulling me closer as we walked forward. "Adria is not to be trusted," he told me softly. "I don't mean to rebuke you, but you must watch your words around her."

It was the same as the ishru—my husband would not be defied, would not be diminished, and certainly not by his wife.

You will believe what I tell you to believe, he had said to me. My gaze dropped to the floor, and I felt Galen's eyes on me, but I didn't look up.

He left us at the side of an arena with the rest of the girls and went to advise the boys as they practiced fighting. The girls all watched, straight backed and silent. Adria matched their posture perfectly. I noticed one girl, seated in the back with no one around her, her hair short at her neck while every other girl had long braids.

"They cut the hair of willful, unruly girls," Adria said, following my gaze. "So no one will marry her."

"What does her hair have to do with marriage?"

"There are contests," Zeph explained, clearing his throat. "The Consecutio. The boys prove their lessons in physical combat. When they win a contest, they are allowed two privileges—to join the army, and the choice of a wife."

"Wife—they're *children*," I said, looking to him.

"Elena—the one with short hair—has seventeen years," Adria told me. Her eyes flicked over me. "The same as you, my queen."

I looked back at her, surprised. She looked like a child to me. When people saw me, did they see a queen, or a girl in a silver crown?

"The boys are not given much to judge the women with," Zeph told me. "The hair—it warns of an unsuitable match."

"You both went through this?" I asked them.

Zeph nodded, and Adria raised her chin. "Of course," she said. "I was one of the finest pupils. I was chosen when I was fourteen."

"You're married?" I asked her.

She took a breath and held it, her body showing the tension of it, but she nodded. "Yes."

"Zeph?" I asked.

His mouth twitched. "I didn't exactly win a contest—but I wouldn't have chosen a wife that way. I am not married, my queen."

"Boys have the option to refuse?" I asked.

"As I said, it is a privilege, not a requirement."

"So girls can also refuse?"

Adria's mouth fell. "No," she said. "We should attend to the practice, my queen."

"So what do you mean, you didn't win a contest?" I asked Zeph, ignoring her advice. "You're in the army."

"Yes," he said, grinning. "And that is why I am the stuff of legends."

"Oh, please," Adria said. "*You* are just a brute."

He chuckled.

I knew I shouldn't take her bait, but Adria's comment was still on my mind. "You wanted to refuse your match?" I asked her.

She stiffened. "He . . . wasn't the one I was expecting to choose me," she said carefully. "I was in love with someone else," she admitted, her voice breath-soft as she looked away from me.

But Zeph made a huff of disbelief.

I looked to him, and Adria shook her head sadly. "Do not mock me," she said, but the command had the tone of begging.

"You didn't love him," Zeph said. "You thought you would *get* him; there's a difference."

"Who?" I asked, looking between them.

"The commander," Zeph said, and she looked to him, betrayed at the information as her face filled with color.

"How *could* you?" she snapped. "You're a terrible bully, Zeph, you always have been." She shook her head. "Besides, Galen knew—he *knew* what my father wanted for us. That was the plan, and I would have thought he would have had more consideration in refusing the wishes of the high vestai."

Zeph shrugged. "There was no contract."

Adria shook her head bitterly. "I don't want to discuss this any longer."

If only feelings were dictated by a contract, I wanted to tell her, but it couldn't be said. Not to her, not in this court, perhaps not ever. "I'm sure Galen must have simply missed his opportunity with you, Adria. Especially since I know that my husband and I both have great respect for your father and his wishes. I can only imagine my husband must have taken him to task—privately—for such a slight."

Her chin rose a little higher. "I suppose so, my queen."

"Besides," I told her with a smile, "these military men are all the same. They need clear, direct orders, or else they're completely helpless. Isn't that right, Zeph?"

He bowed his head. "My queen is wise beyond contradiction," he said with a smile.

Adria nodded. "Quite so, my queen." She met my eyes, a begrudging gratitude in her gaze, and it felt like a small measure of kinship between us.

After the boys finished their training, Galen offered to escort us back to the Tri Castles. When we got outside, he caught sight of one horse, and he turned sharply to the young man standing beside it.

"Where is the queen's carriage?" he asked the groom.

"We didn't take one," Zeph told him.

"We *walked*," Adria huffed. Galen looked to her, and she looked away from him.

Galen frowned. "You are aware you were attacked yesterday, my queen?"

I raised my chin. "Are you not confident in the abilities of your Saepia to protect me, Commander? I rather thought that was the point."

"The point was *not* to use them to take unnecessary risks."

"Precisely!" Adria said.

"Domina Viato," Galen said. "You can take my horse back to the Tri Castles, and I will escort the queen."

"But—" she protested, looking to me.

"I will manage without your services," I told her. "And thank you for your assistance today. Now I know not to cut my hair."

She smiled. "I would not recommend it. It was my pleasure, my queen. Shall I wait to attend to you at the Tri Castles?"

"No need. Thank you," I told her.

She stood and mounted the horse, and Galen looked thoroughly confused as she rode out of sight. "You were thinking of cutting your hair?" he asked, walking down the steps.

I walked with him with a grin, and Zeph lumbered behind us. "No, of course not."

Confused, Galen looked to Zeph, who shrugged.

I waited a moment, then opened my mouth and drew a breath. "Galen, may I ask you a question?"

He thought for a moment. "I can't guarantee I'll answer it, but yes, you may ask."

"Calix mentioned a few strange things to me last night. One was something he's mentioned before about a prophecy and now a trivatis. Do you know what that means?"

Slowly, Galen nodded. "Yes. There was a trivatis my mother favored—a holy man," he explained at my look. "Like the man who crowned you. This trivatis received visions, he claimed from the Three-Faced God, and my mother put a lot of faith in them. Just before she died, he had a vision that Calix would meet his death at the hands of an Elementa. Calix called his powers sorcery and convinced my father to put him to death. That was the start of the powers being illegal in this country."

"*Calix* started that?" I asked. "But I thought it was your father who hated the Elementae."

"No," he said, shaking his head. "My father was at war with them. They were a powerful enemy, and we were losing the war. He hated the Vis Islands, but not the Elementae specifically." His shoulders rose. "When we heard the prophecy, my father thought it meant Calix would die in the war. It made him fight harder, but no, I don't believe he ever hated them the way Calix does. He feared them."

"Then why did he *murder* them?" I asked hotly. "You expect me to believe it was just a war dispute, and he wiped out an entire race? That was an act of hate."

"*Shalia*," he said firmly, stopping in the road. "You have to stop. Stop talking like this, stop questioning these things. You won't like the answers or the consequences."

"The answers?" My thoughts started rushing faster. Calix hated the Elementae. Murdering them, burning them alive, while the only remaining child of their leader had to watch—these were acts of hate. If their father hadn't been the one who hated the Elementae— "No," I breathed, shaking my head. I staggered back. Everything Kata said—it had been Calix who had done that to her? "No. Calix—Calix couldn't be responsible for the islands. It was your father. Everyone knows that."

His eyes were locked on mine, holding me as sure as a physical touch. "Everyone knows what he wants them to know," he said. "And that's it."

"No." I pulled away from him. "No. How could that be? He wasn't even *king*."

Galen nodded slowly. "Do you know much of what happened before?"

"The war?" I asked. "Some."

"The islanders were incredibly powerful. The gifts they had—they could control the natural world. And for a long time, they were content. They ruled the seas; they were the wealthiest country in the known world. But they didn't have much land, and the high priestess decided she wanted more. She wanted the Trifectate."

I shook my head. "It wasn't so simple. Your father was threatening her, setting up trade embargoes—" I sighed. "War is never so simple as a single person's greed."

His eyes were on me for a long time. "No," he said. "And to be very honest, I don't know what changed. Calix wanted peace. He spent months convincing my father that he could end this war with the islanders peacefully, if only he could negotiate. I think there was even talk of a marriage. Father granted him a fleet of new ships to negotiate peace, but within days, Calix had murdered every one of them he could find. And when he came back, he told everyone my father had issued the order. He convinced everyone my father was insane. And then Calix became king."

"That makes no *sense*," I said, shaking my head. I started walking faster, like the motion could push my mind to work faster. "How could he lie so completely? How could he petition for peace and then turn around and commit genocide?"

"Something changed," Galen said. "I've just never known what it was. And he won't tell me. At this point, I'm not sure it matters."

"Of course it *matters*," I snapped at him.

"Why?" he demanded, keeping pace with me. "Is there *anything* that you could discover about those days that would change what happened? That would lessen the things he did?"

"I don't know!" I returned. "How do you live with it? Knowing what he's done?"

"Because he was eighteen. And as far as I can tell, scared and foolish. It was a terrible act, but he's been a good king for years. He's protected me whenever I needed it."

"He's a murderer," I snapped back.

Galen stopped, his face flat, and I turned in a fury to meet his gaze. "So am I," he said.

This drew a sharp breath into my chest.

"Me too," Zeph called brightly from a few feet away, though he didn't sound ashamed like Galen did. I scowled at him.

"You're supposed to pretend you can't hear us, Zeph," Galen told him.

"Right," he said, nodding.

Galen's throat worked. "Does taking a life make a man irredeemable in your eyes, Shalia?"

"There's a difference between taking a life and a *genocide*."

He shook his head. "There shouldn't be. A life is a life."

"I don't think Calix would agree with you," I told him. "And *that's* the difference."

Galen's eyes swept around us as he grimaced. "It's getting dark," he said. "We need to get back to the castles."

I looked up at them, looming ahead of us in the distance. The thought of Calix kissing me, touching me—it turned my stomach. Those hands had tortured my dearest friend. They'd tied her up to watch her family burn, and Rian beside her.

"Shalia."

I shook my head. "I *can't*."

"One decision doesn't make a man a monster," he said. "You choose your fate with every decision. And he's listening to you. So help him make better decisions."

My eyes closed. I wanted to be more to a man than just something to improve him, but this was my fate. This marriage had been my choice, and there was no turning back.

"You should tell him," Galen said. "That you know. See what he says about it."

I opened my eyes, surprised. "Telling him I know does not seem wise."

"Everyone wants to know they can be loved even in consideration of their most monstrous parts," he said.

I didn't voice it as we walked forward, but there was a flaw in Galen's logic: it would require me to love my husband, and I wasn't sure I could do that.

Seemingly to spite the churning recesses of my mind, it was a peaceful walk. The sun began its slow dive below the edge of the world, sending out lovely, desperate colors as it clung to its last moment. As we neared the castles, it made the three white structures look like some kind of deity indeed must live there, shrouded in the most beautiful colors of the world. As we rose on the Royal Causeway, the colors caught on the moving, shifting surface of the ocean.

I stopped, staring at it. "Skies Above," I breathed.

We were high enough on the rise of the causeway that I could look out over the low parts of the city, and I could see people moving in the streets, and the winding lines still trailing from the grain mill. The place was long closed, yet they stayed there, waiting for food.

I looked back to the beauty of the Three Castles. Perhaps Galen was right—perhaps the past couldn't possibly matter. Perhaps it was only this, the things that I could change for the future, helping to create a day when more people would live than die. Maybe that's all I could ever do. Maybe it was enough.

Call to Service

Galen escorted me into the castle and to the large hall, but kissed my hand and told me he couldn't stay for the meal. He lingered for a long moment like he wanted to say something else, but then he turned and left.

I went into the hall alone; Calix wasn't there, and Danae and I sat on the raised dais. I saw Kairos, and when our eyes met, I looked to the hallway and back to him, and he nodded once, raising his wine to me.

"Are you well?" I asked Danae. Her posture was straight and careful, her muscles tense like she was waiting for something.

She leaned back, but she still seemed watchful. "Yes. Court makes me . . . edgy."

I nodded, taking a bite of stew that thankfully didn't seem to have fish in it.

Her eyes swept over me. "And you? How are you finding the City of Three?"

My shoulders lifted, unsure how to answer the question. There were so many things crowding my mind—I needed to ask

Calix about his past, and I could only imagine it would be an ugly conversation. But I also wanted to do something about the grain mill that I had seen, and the nagging feeling that I could be doing far more as queen. "Foreign, of course. But there are problems that plague all people."

"Oh?" she asked, turning slightly toward me.

"Hunger," I said. "Safety. The need to protect your children. Everyone does it in different ways, but the Tri people and the clans are not so different."

Her eyebrows lifted. "Are we not?"

"We know hunger well," I told her. "Not as much recently—my brother Aiden has become a tremendously skilled hunter, and it seems he could always make food appear for us—but as a nomadic people, we have few steady sources of food and water. The people here face hunger on a larger scale, of course."

Danae propped her chin in her palm and covered her mouth with her fingers, but she nodded. "Yes."

"I wonder if I can help," I told her softly. "I wonder if I could ask Calix to allow the women to work in the mill. To work to feed their families."

She was very still for long moments, and then her eyes shifted over me, and she rubbed her mouth before dropping her hands into her lap. "It is an excellent thought," she said. "But it would not be Calix's decision. The Three-Faced God must make such a declaration." Her eyes met mine.

"How . . . how do I get a God to make a declaration?" I asked. "Is that something *you* can do?"

Her mouth twisted into something that was too bitter to be a smile. "No, I cannot. Calix feels he alone is the true conduit for the God's voice. But the call of the Three-Faced God—particularly a call to service—is very, very powerful," she said, raising her chin.

Drawing a breath, I nodded. "How do these calls to service usually present themselves?" I asked her.

She waved a hand. "They can come in many ways. Dreams, visions—but the most powerful is in response to prayer. Asking the God for an answer."

I nodded. "And he will listen?" I asked.

"The God?" she asked, and her smile lifted with amusement. "Or Calix?"

"Who is more important?"

"Calix," she said, looking forward. "And I cannot know his mind, but yes. He likes solutions—if it solves a problem, he may listen."

Curling my hands around the arms of the chair, I sat up straighter, feeling hope rush through me. I could do this. I could be the queen they needed, and in finding peace for this country, protect Rian and Kairos and all the desert clans.

As soon as I stood at the end of the meal, Kairos appeared, bowing to the dais. "Sister," he greeted me. "Let me escort you back to your chambers."

I smiled. "Of course," I said, and took his offered arm. "Good night, Danae."

"Good night, my queen."

Kairos led me down the steps and out of the hall, and Zeph was waiting. He inclined his head and let us go several feet in front of him, but I still didn't dare tell Kairos of what Calix had let slip the night before until we were truly alone. Kairos filled my nervous silence with chatter and, when we got to my chamber, led me out onto the balcony as Zeph shut the door behind us.

"Now," Kairos said, glancing around us on the empty balcony. "What did you want to tell me?"

I leaned closer to him. "The king said that he has a spy in Rian's ranks. His name is Tassos."

"He told you his *name*?" Kairos asked, narrowing his eyes.

"Yes," I said. "It was an accident. We were arguing."

Kairos shook his head slowly. "No, I don't think it was, little sister. The king is far too calculating to tell you something like that by accident. He's testing you. Trying to see if you'll tell Rian. Or perhaps if I will."

"But doesn't Rian need to know there's a spy in his camp?"

Kairos crossed his arms. "I would hope Rian always assumes there's a spy in his camp and acts accordingly. It's what I would do. And it's the only way they keep the leader so well protected."

I watched my brother. "Is the leader Kata?" I breathed.

He considered it but shook his head. "Doubtful. Whoever the leader is, they are exceedingly careful. Kata shares Rian's reckless streak, in my opinion."

"Do you know who it is?"

His eyes flicked to me and away, and I gasped. "No, I'm not certain," he said quickly. "I have my suspicions. But I can't share them, especially since they're unconfirmed. And not with you."

That stung, but I thought of my husband questioning me the night before, and I nodded. "I understand." And I did. I couldn't tell Kairos that Calix had been the one to kill the islanders, and Kairos couldn't share this with me. Not only were we fighting to keep each other safe, but marriage had also fractured my loyalty. "You should probably go, before my husband returns."

Kairos nodded with a sigh, kissing the top of my head before going back into my chamber and out.

Calix didn't return soon. I spent a long time on the balcony, thinking about my conversations with Galen and then Danae.

Calix had been the one to murder the islanders. He had killed Kata's family, and he nearly killed Rian, who had been in the islands during the massacre.

I wanted to confront him about it. I wanted to tell him I knew, to demand an explanation.

But more than that, I wanted to do something *good.* I wanted to do something meaningful, and I knew that if I could just make him see that it was an easy solution, I could get him to agree with me about the mill.

The sound of the door closing drew my attention, and I saw Calix, smiling at me. "I was trying to surprise you," he said.

I didn't stand from the bench, the one I liked, closest to the edge so I could see out over the strange and moving water. He came to me, sitting on it, tugging my chin to him, but I pulled away.

"Wife?" he asked.

I shook my head, still unsure, still hesitating between what I wanted to say.

"Galen said things went well at the Erudium."

"Yes," I said quietly.

"You should go back there tomorrow. It's a good place for you to be seen."

"No," I said, and then shook my head again, but this time I had made my decision. "I saw the grain mill, and the women and children waiting for food behind it. It's wrong," I said, looking at him. "Those women who stand in line for days—this is not the life they want."

He opened his mouth with a scowl, but I remembered what Danae had told me.

"They want to serve the God," I continued. "They want to serve their country. The God has been trying to show us what he wants—he wants women to feed their families and serve. And I believe he wants me to lead them to it."

Calix watched me suspiciously. "You wish to pound grain?" he asked.

I looked at my hands. "If I must. But I believe the Three-Faced God wants me to serve by helping women serve their country."

"So you want women to work."

"Yes."

"And the Three-Faced God told you this?" he asked, his eyes narrowing.

I drew a breath. "I can't claim to know," I said. "But this idea came to me when I thought of how I might serve."

"But you don't believe in the Three-Faced God."

This stopped me. I didn't; could I lie outright about such a thing? "How else could I come by such an idea?" I asked, my voice hushed.

He scowled, standing. "I suppose that's true. The women work in the factories—and we pay them?"

"Paying the women would mean they have money to spend. And money for tax," I added.

"Hm. The labor will not interfere with raising families," he insisted.

"The children are meant to be at the Erudium anyway."

"But if a woman is with child, she will not work," he said.

It seemed a small concession. "Of course not."

He drew a slow breath. "Very well, wife."

He walked inside, but I stayed on the balcony longer, looking out over the wild sea. I felt numb from the horror I had discovered, but I knew this was progress—this was something my mother would be proud of.

But now I knew the terrible price of the crown on my head, and I couldn't forget that. And if I did, I feared it would mean sacrificing my humanity.

Salvation

Calix didn't wear his uniform and declined a carriage as we walked out of the Three Castles. Both our guards and Adria flanked behind us—some of the men obvious, in uniform and formation—and others not, hidden and watching. The morning was gray and cool, the clouds overhead making shapes in the air that my people believed could watch our actions. Calix held my hand in his as we walked down the causeway, and for a moment, I imagined what we looked like—a young couple, hand in hand. Simple.

But nothing was simple. He had selected my dress for the morning; he had orchestrated the whole event to be another display, another showing. He had selected how many guards were attending to us and where they would be, and it was easy for him. Immense calculations he did without thinking.

We walked down the causeway, easily strolling the short distance to the grain mill. The few people in the streets followed us, watching, like we were a spectacle, a dog that had learned to walk on its hind legs. Calix tugged my hand, bringing me into the guarded entrance of the grain mill. The men standing watch sprang to attention, opening gates without a word from my husband.

Even before we entered the building, I felt the threads trembling just beyond my fingers, vibrating in time with the rumbling beneath my feet.

Stone, I realized. They must be using stone to grind the grain, and the force of it called to me.

My palm grew sweaty in Calix's, but I didn't pull away. I drew a slow breath, asking my power not to react. I remembered Kata's warnings about having less control if I didn't practice it, but I couldn't do anything with my power here. Not with Calix—with *everyone*—watching.

When we entered, the low rumble stopped. There were fewer than ten men working at large stone stations in a room that had space for more than a hundred. The men stared at us, and there was noise and movement as someone rushed from a room above, skittering down a stone staircase on the far wall.

"My king! My queen!" he bleated as he came close. He was a round, balding man with bright red in his cheeks. He bowed, and then bowed again, and again.

"Stop," Calix said, holding up a hand. The man straightened a little and backed away. "Come with me. All of you," Calix ordered, waving his hand once to the others in the room. They looked at one another—wondering, worried—but Calix moved on, my hand still trapped in his. He went through a door and down a long stone hallway where light flooded in at the end. As we grew closer to the light, I could see the ragged lines of people waiting in the back.

We appeared, and again, everything froze. A moment later, the people who had waited so long for their grain fell back, afraid, desperate to get out of the reach or the sight of the king. The three people who were parceling out small bags of grain looked bewildered, and then they tumbled out of their chairs to bow before my husband and me. The people in lines took to this too, and everyone dropped to their knees.

"No," Calix shouted, rushing down the steps to an old woman who couldn't bend enough to kneel. He touched her shoulder and called a guard over to help her as he came back up the steps. "You do not need to humble yourselves further. The Three-Faced God has seen your humility, your dedication, and your fears. On this day, the Three-Faced God has seen fit to save you."

Was that it? It seemed another game of power—servants refusing to bow to him diminished his power, but here, with his pageant graciousness, the refusal to let an old woman bow made him seem greater than he was.

The woman was weak and frail, and the guard knelt on one knee so she could sit on the other, and she wavered against him. I went down the stairs to her, looking at Calix. "My king," I called softly. Calix looked at me. "This woman needs food and water. Desperately."

Something like pleasure flashed across his face, but he turned to the overseer. "Food," he ordered. "And water. All you have and can procure. *Now*."

The overseer ran, and Calix nodded at a guard, who trotted after him.

"You will be well," Calix told her, and she nodded against the guard's chest.

"The Three-Faced God knows you wish nothing more than to serve your families, your country, your God," Calix said. "But how can you do that without food for your children? Is not nourishment one of the greatest things a woman is called to give?"

There were murmurs and nodding.

"We are a strong people. A prideful people, and to beg for grain—it breaks us," Calix said, pressing his hand over his heart like he knew anything of hunger. "The Three-Faced God has called for women to work—here, if you're willing—to feed their families, to provide grain and food for their countrymen. I ask not for your humiliation but for your work. Who of you is willing to work, for your pride and for your families?"

The women and children were silent, stunned and frightened. The guard came back with water, offering it to the old woman as I looked out, my breath caught in my chest. Calix's face folded into a deep glower as no one moved.

"I am, my king," I called, stepping forward.

Calix raised an eyebrow, but his face lightened. "My queen—you want for nothing. Surely you do not need to be pounding grain," he said, but it wasn't reproachful—he was still using his loud voice, his voice that spoke of pageantry and stagecraft.

"I want for my people," I told him, my voice quiet. "I want to serve the Three-Faced God."

"I will," said another voice. "If—if it pleases my king and my God." I turned around, and another woman raised her hand. Some spoke, some nodded. More women agreed.

Calix held out his hand to me, beckoning me, and I walked up the stairs to him. He caught my hand and drew me close, bringing my knuckles up to his mouth to kiss. "My love, I will leave these people in your capable hands. The Three-Faced God is most pleased with your care."

I nodded, and Calix released my hand to stare at me for a moment, almost as if he cared for me in the way he claimed. And then his hands slid around my waist and he tugged me closer, kissing me. My body was stiff, unyielding, not expecting such a display and unable to adapt before he let go of me. People were clapping behind us as he pulled me to his side, waving and smiling at them.

And then he let me go, and he made his way through the mill, and several guards followed him. I took a breath and turned to the overseer. "Very well," I said. "Show us how to grind grain."

The stations were all large, flat circular stones that were in stacks of two and as wide across as my outstretched arms. They had a basket beneath and a hole in the top stone, and the overseer and the more practiced men showed us how to pour grain in the hole in the top and then turn the top stone with a handle. The grain was ground between the two stones, and came out the edges into the basket. The stones rumbled as they turned, and soon the floor was trembling, shuddering with the effort, in a way that felt almost joyous.

The overseer also showed us curved stones with a shaped rock where women could make the flour even more fine, something he had ceased to do when there weren't enough men.

Quickly the women organized themselves, some porting grain and moving baskets, some turning stones, some packing it up when it was finished. Zeph and Adria both helped, the former far too delighted with the idea of pounding grain by hand, and the latter thoroughly distraught with the idea of her hands potentially revealing that she had done physical labor.

I took my place at the second stage of grinding, my hands eager to touch the stone. I closed my eyes as I learned the motion of it, and running one stone over another felt like plucking the strings of an instrument. I felt the different hums deep in my bones, and when no one could hear me over the unyielding noise of grinding, I hummed back.

But it wasn't just the imaginary strings of a nonexistent instrument. There were strings there, tightly packed in the stone, vibrating with noise and life at my touch. My power was alive and strong, rushing around me as all the stones scraped against one another.

The stone I was holding grew warm under my fingers, pushing against my hand, and I could feel the slight unevenness of it, the places where the curve of the stone didn't meet the curve of the bowl in perfect alignment, and it felt like a snag, a grating that was scratching inside my ears. Glancing around, I focused on the stone, revising the shape of it like a blacksmith would sharpen a blade, pressing it to sit perfectly in the bowl.

I moved the stone around the new curve, and it seemed like music, like playing my fingers across the threads had created a low, thrilling tune that resonated deep in my bones and shivered up my spine with delight.

With each sweep and turn of the stone, the pleasure of it washed over me again—this was a stunning gift, to be able to take the rough and uneven and perfect it, to improve what nature had given us. In my hands, every motion felt like hope.

"My queen?"

I dropped the rock with a gasp. One of the women was there, nervous to ask me a question about distributing the grain, and I stepped away from the stone to help her, the warmth of it still making my fingers tingle.

Fool. What was I thinking, using my power like that? It was hidden and small, but even the smallest suggestion of magic would get me killed with sure and swift finality. Even though Calix had left us to our task, how many minutes would the greedy overseer wait to turn me in if he suspected my power? How quickly would the Saepia guard betray their newborn loyalty to me?

Shivering, I took up the cart full of bags of flour and wheeled it down the long hallway. There were still many more people there than could work in the mill, and I helped the men in the back hand it out as quickly as we could, far enough from the moving pieces of stone that the trembling power inside me was more like a murmur than a roar. Just before we ran out, Zeph came with his giant arms full of more bags.

By the time the overseer rang a bell to signal the day was done, the sky was blushing dark. The line had been cut in half, and it seemed a small thing, but with a few days' work, there would be no line.

Adria came to join me outside, looking at her hands, worrying a bit of skin between her finger and thumb. "I think I'm getting a blister," she said.

"You'll know if you get a blister," I told her with a deep sigh. "We should start walking. Zeph?"

"Here, my queen," he said, emerging from the mill with a mighty stretch that caused mysterious parts of his anatomy to crack and pop. He gave a monstrous yawn that sounded like some kind of animal call and then smiled. "I like milling."

"Of course you like milling—it isn't *difficult* for you," Adria whined.

His shoulders lifted. "If I'm being honest, not much is difficult for me."

"Hiding is probably difficult for you," I told him with a smile.

"And you probably sink like a stone in the water," Adria said, crossing her arms.

"I'm an excellent swimmer," he said defensively.

"You must have been hit by a tree branch or two riding on a horse," I said. "You're so very tall."

His brows knit together. "Occasionally."

"What do you do when you have a wound?" Adria asked, a hint of a smile on her face. "There's no way you could hold a needle with your giant, calloused hands."

"I rub some dirt in it and move on with my life," he grunted. "I don't like this conversation anymore."

Adria snorted. "You started it."

Calix and I arrived separately to dinner, but neither Danae nor Galen appeared for the meal. Calix took my hand as soon as I sat, kissing it, smiling at me. "How was your day of labor, my love?" he asked.

I smiled back, though it didn't feel as real as I wished. "Difficult," I said. "There was much work to be done, but they all took to it. We fed everyone who needed food."

"Fantastic," he said. "Quite an endearing display."

I nodded. "Your people love you, Calix," I told him.

His smile grew thin. "And yet this Resistance continues. They rebel. They don't trust my rule."

"No," I assured him. "It's just difficult to look past a hungry belly."

His thumb pushed over my fingers. "Hmm," he said, looking forward. "This worked well, but the more ideas you have, the more I will think you are displeased with my reign."

And there it was, the reproach I had been waiting for since the day began. I walked along the edge of a knife with him, balancing between being a queen and a traitor.

I squeezed his hand. "Never, my king."

But no matter what he said, my actions at the mill were real. I was helping, and changing things for the fate of our people. This was the road to peace, without bloodshed or death. And his words could not chase that from my heart.

That night, I woke with a gasp to darkness. "Enter," Calix called, and I twisted, realizing it was still night, and there must be someone at the door.

A jarring flare of light burst into the room as a guard entered our chamber with a torch in hand. I scrambled to cover myself, and Calix snarled, "Turn away!" to the offending guard.

The man spun before he could even take a full breath, and Calix moved from the bed, finding my coat and handing it to me. I slid into it, clutching it closed. "What is going on?" I asked him.

"Report," Calix snapped, scowling as he found his own clothing.

"The quaesitori sent urgent word for you, my king," the guard said.

"Bring it to me," he said, and the guard came closer, holding out a folded page.

Calix took it, opening it and reading the contents while the guard stood there.

"Guards!" Calix shouted. Theron appeared in the doorway, bowing, awaiting orders. "Make ready to leave within the hour. Notify my council as well." Calix glanced at me, and then at the guard with the torch. "And gouge out his eyes."

"My—my king!" he pleaded. I looked to Calix, confused. Surely—Calix couldn't mean—

"Be grateful I don't demand your life for defiling the queen," Calix said. "You are dismissed."

The guard ran out of the room, and Theron grimly watched him go before leaving as well, closing the door.

"Calix," I begged, getting out of bed. "Calix, please, you cannot take that man's eyes. I am not *defiled*. He didn't harm me in any way."

My coat had parted, and he stopped and stared at me, and the narrow piece of flesh exposed by the gap. He shook his head slowly. "No man could see you in such a state and not covet you, my love. It was a mistake not to kill him—but you make me lenient."

"But you called him into the room!"

Calix's eyes narrowed. "And did I also tell him to stare upon your naked body? No. You would have him stare at you? Wasn't it you who said that a *desert man* would never let another covet his wife?" He stepped closer to me, sliding his hands under the coat. "You cannot question me like this, Shalia. I am your king. And though I am pleased you waited until we were alone to do it, it needs to stop. Do you understand me?"

I shivered, casting my eyes down from his hard gaze. "Where are you going?" I asked.

"South," he said, drawing away from me and pulling his clothing on. "My quaesitori believe they have a breakthrough."

"What do you mean?"

"They think they can re-create the elixir," he told me. "I must go see the results immediately."

My heart jumped. "I will come with you."

"No," he said sternly.

"Calix," I insisted. "You have trusted me with this from the beginning. Why would you not do so now?"

"It is gruesome work," he told me, his eyes narrowing.

I came closer to him. "My place is by your side," I said.

His hands caught me, pulling me to him. "What of the mills?" he asked.

"The mills will run in my absence. I will have Adria see it done."

His mouth was hard, but he nodded. "Very well."

In less than an hour and well before the light of day, we were led through the halls of the castle, coming out into the cool dark of the courtyard.

"What is the meaning of this?" Calix grunted.

I peered around him to see Kairos on the walkway, turning to smile at us. "Good morning."

"What are you doing here?"

He shrugged. "Seemed like an excellent time for a walk. Where are you two off to?"

"The south," I said, and Calix squeezed my hand hard.

"It's business of state," Calix snapped. "You can either remain here or return to the desert, but you cannot accompany us."

Kairos grinned. "Surely if it's safe enough for my sister, it's safe enough for me."

"Kairos," I said, stepping in front of my husband and meeting Kairos's eyes. "The king said you cannot come."

His eyes searched my face. "Very well," he said. "Watch the skies, little sister."

He kissed my cheek, sliding past me. I watched him go before Calix hurried me along, and it took several long minutes to realize that Osmost was not on his shoulder.

"Did you tell him we were leaving?" Calix demanded.

"No," I said, turning to my husband.

"Your brother is outlasting his welcome," he told me gruffly. He brought me to the carriage that was waiting for us and offered his hand to help me inside.

I sat on one cushioned bench, and a moment later he sat beside me in the darkness, his arm sliding around my tense shoulders. I sat forward, and his arm fell away from me.

"Wife?" he asked.

"It means a great deal to me that Kairos is here. You know that. You don't need to threaten him."

He shifted a little. "I did not threaten him."

"'Outlasting his welcome'?" I repeated. "You—you just gouged out the eyes of a man for less."

"I'm sure his eyes haven't been gouged out just yet."

I shook my head, though it was dark enough that he couldn't see. "I cannot watch you be so casually cruel with an easy heart, Calix. I can't."

There was a long silence in which I could feel my heart beating, the risk of displeasing my husband rushing in my veins.

Then he sighed heavily. "He can stay a little longer," he allowed. I felt his hand cover my stomach, his touch possessive, caging me. "After all, hopefully he will be an uncle soon enough." His lips brushed over my temple, his body curling around me. "I'm not cruel, Shalia."

"You *terrorize people*," I whispered to him.

"Sometimes I have to," he said. "A ruler cannot be emotional about life—every day I have to choose a path that will save the most lives. But I will never be able to save every life. It is a terrible burden." He was silent a long while. "Is this just about the guard, Shalia?"

"Who did maiming that guard protect?" I asked, avoiding his question, certain I did not want to confront him about his past and what I knew here, in such an enclosed space.

"Him," Calix said. "I was protecting *his* life. Every time he glanced at you, I would see it in his eyes—his memory, his desire. And before long, he would force my hand. Men are animals of nature, my love. I could see his heart like I see my own."

I shook my head, anger making me resolute. "Perhaps that has made you a good king, Calix, but I cannot think such ruthlessness will make you a good father."

"The only ruthlessness my children will ever see is the swift death of anyone who tries to hurt them. Or you." His hand tightened on my stomach, gripping me until I made a noise, and he sucked in a breath. "Forgive me, my sweet, forgive me," he murmured close to my ear, his fingers skimming over me. "The thought—I don't know what I would do if I were to fail as a father. The thought chills me. But I have to trust that this is your purpose—to show me what it means to love, so that I can love our children. I can't wait for the day you carry my child, Shalia. It is my every hope."

"It's so very important to you," I whispered, looking toward him.

"A man is nothing—his legacy nothing, his lifetime nothing—until he has someone to continue on in his stead. All I achieve is useless without you."

Warmth curled around my heart as the carriage moved, rolling gently into motion to carry us south. "I want to have many children," I admitted to him.

His mouth kissed my cheek, slipping closer to my lips, and it made the warmth travel to my bones. "I will give them to you. I will give them all to you." His fingers spread on my belly, like he was willing life into being there.

I covered his hand.

"A son to start," he whispered. "My heir. I will grow him up in my image and teach him how to rule. Then perhaps a little sister, someone for him to protect and care for. A girl with your beautiful face. And then another girl—she'll be the mischievous one."

I leaned my head on his shoulder, touching his fingers on my stomach, wanting to believe this man was more real than the vengeful ruler who blinded a guard for a moment's mistake. The warmth of his hand was soothing. "Will she?" I asked. "We'll have to watch out for her."

"Zeno will watch out for her," he said.

"Zeno?"

"Our son," he said. "And then we'll need another boy—Zeno will need someone to command the armies."

"Was it so with you?" I asked. "Did you three know the roles you would play at birth?"

"Mostly," he said. "I would be king, of course. For Galen, he could either vie for the military or the trivatii—a religious appointment."

"And Danae?"

"She is the hidden face," he said. "She has always been unpredictable."

"And did your father teach you in such a way?"

He was silent for a long while, and I was about to speak, say something else. "There's another piece of the vision," he told me softly. "The one that foretold my death. There was a book full of his visions that was discovered after his death. In it, he said I would not see my first child born into this world."

I tried to pull back from him, but he held me tight. "What?" I asked. "Why didn't you tell me that before?"

"It's not true," he said softly. "It can't be. And you will be my way to prove that. We will have many children together. We have to."

"What do you mean, we have to?"

There was another stretch of quiet. "The Concilium of Vestai knows of this prophecy also. They trapped my father—either we were the Three-Faced God incarnate, as he claimed, and I could thwart such a prophecy, or we weren't, and that made him a liar and our reign invalid. If I don't pass my crown on to a son or daughter, it will fall to the Concilium. And I can't imagine they'll allow my siblings to survive such a shift in power."

I gripped his hand. "Do Galen and Danae know this?"

"Yes," he said softly.

Pale light peeked into the carriage, and the gray haze lit his face enough for me to see deep worry etched there. "We'll have many children, Calix. I promise."

Then he drew me closer, holding my hand on his heart. "You are my salvation, Shalia," he whispered to me.

Watch the Skies

It was a short carriage ride to an ocean port. The sky was dark, full of ropy, bulbous clouds that were barely catching the light of the coming dawn, and the wind was picking up as guards ushered us down a long wooden pier. Theron walked in front of me, getting into what I assumed was a boat despite never having been near a body of water larger than the lake at Jitra until recently. It was long and wide and staffed with men at oars. I hesitated at the edge of the pier, glancing at Calix, but he was speaking to a guard.

Unsure, I looked back to Theron, and he nodded sharply, holding out his hands. Sucking in a breath, I put my hands in his.

"Jump here," he said, tapping a raised board with his feet.

I closed my eyes and obeyed. My feet hit something solid and I wobbled, my knees going weak, but Theron held me until I was steady and opened my eyes. He smirked at me.

"Well done, my queen."

I huffed at him, but he pointed me forward, and I pried my fingers away from him slowly.

The boat was a living thing. It rocked under my feet, and I gasped, tipping forward to find something to grab onto. Theron came to me, offering his arm, and I gripped it. "Sit, my queen," he said, pointing to some kind of narrow wooden bench in the center.

I nodded, sinking down. My husband stepped on the boat and it pitched again, and I yelped, gripping the wood.

Calix sat beside me, chuckling. "We must work on your sea legs, wife!" he said, patting my knee.

The wind blew through me, but I couldn't figure out how to hug my coat tight around me and hold on to the bench at the same time. I shivered, but I refused to let go of the bench.

Theron sat on the left side of me, and he blocked some of the wind, but then the oarsmen pushed away from the pier and the boat lurched again with the effort. I kept from crying out, but fear shot through me and I found my fingers on the bench shaking with the effort to hold on.

Calix stood, shifting the boat again, moving closer to the pointed front of it.

I could feel Theron's eyes on me, but I couldn't even look at him. He coughed. "The boat is very safe, my queen," he said. He spread his hands, explaining, "It's a wide, low boat. It means it's difficult to tip over."

I managed to nod.

"We will only be on the water for a few hours," he said. "This is the fastest way to Liatos, the southernmost of the Bone Lands."

I shivered at the thought, and a fierce wind rushed under my clothes.

"Let me see if I can find something warmer in your things," he told me, standing.

He moved, and I shuddered at the rocking of the boat and a sharp gust of wind. My husband sat down again beside me, and I clutched his arm.

"Oh, my sweet," he chuckled. "The ocean is nothing to be frightened of. We have conquered it the same way we have conquered the land. You!" he said, shouting at Theron, his voice close to my ear. "Sit. You are disturbing the queen."

Theron scowled but obeyed before he could find me something warmer. I shivered, and Calix put his arm around me.

It was warm and comforting, and as the boat rocked and moved, I wondered if this was what marriage was meant to be—slowly finding ways to need each other and comfort each other. Perhaps this was how it had been for my parents at the start—perhaps love was something that grew, not something that was determined by who removed my veil.

But then I thought of the man who even now was probably having his eyes taken away. I was capable of caring about Calix, I knew that was true. I could live with him and I would love our children with every bit of my heart. But as I shuddered against the cold, I sent a dark wish out over the sea that I would never grow to love my husband.

The skies grew dangerous with heavy, rain-filled clouds as a new shore came into sight. Even the smudge on the horizon was an incredible relief to me.

Calix stood, going to the front again and shouting orders at the oarsmen. Two rocky jetties came out into the ocean, curling around the harbor to allow for only a narrow passage that no more than a single boat could go through at a time.

The rock walls were thick and rough, with huge columns jutting above them to support a narrow ledge. I could see guards walking the length of it, illuminated along the way with bowls full of fire, and at uneven intervals, I saw something trailing from the ledge, swaying in the wind like a banner.

As the boat slid through the narrow passage, I saw that the banners were bodies.

I gasped, covering my mouth, looking at Theron. He leaned closer to me. "Punishment," he said. "For disobedience in the communes."

There must have been thirty bodies hanging along the length of the wall. From what I could see, some had been there for a very long time. In some places there was an empty rope, moving in the breeze, and I imagined there had been bodies there, swinging until the wind broke the ropes and let them fall onto the rocks.

I stared as long as I could. It felt like the only way to honor them.

The oarsmen brought us deep into the wide harbor. It looked like a bustling city; there were many ships in the harbor, more still at a complicated network of floating piers and docks. The boat brought us swiftly to a dock with no other boats on it. Soldiers were flooding down the planks, and they all fell into place at the precise moment that the boat sidled up alongside the dock. Calix made a gesture that I thought meant for me to stand, and I did, on stiff and shaky legs.

Calix moved with confidence, stepping on the side of the boat and grabbing a soldier's hand to jump onto the dock. The boat pitched hard and I yelped, my legs twisting weakly underneath me. Theron caught me, pushing me up off the boat and into Calix's arms.

The motion was too much, and I gripped his arm for a long moment, trying to steady myself. Even though I could see the dock was still and unmoving, I felt like the ground was shifting and rocking beneath me.

"You'll be unsteady for a while. Come," Calix said, tucking my hand in his arm, leading me down the walkway with a tug. My legs were weak and watery, and I found myself clinging to his arm, and my husband never looked so pleased.

The army led us to a horse, which I mounted to sit in front of Calix, and as we rode slowly through the city, I saw the people first. There were long lines of men walking in slow, even paces, like a ghostly version of the soldiers' march. These men wore torn clothes that all had a chalky white on them. They were emaciated, their bodies looking bent and stooped, if not entirely broken. And they were marching down into the ground.

When the road turned again, I saw where they went. The ground was hollowed out, hundreds of feet deep, a stone cavern that was filled with men and the unfinished bones of a huge warship.

A crack and a boom sounded, so loud I jumped, but no one else reacted. Everyone just kept on working, blind to the others around them, and I wondered if nothing had actually happened, or if it simply didn't matter.

"We have the best shipbuilders in the world," Calix told me, his voice in my ear. "Our workers have unparalleled skill and dedication. The results are extraordinary."

I nodded, struck mute by the sight of it. As the road turned again, I could see two more stone caverns, and yet somehow, my eyes caught on a pair of very worn men's shoes, askew and abandoned by the side of the road.

The city was laid out in a tight, confined grid. It seemed that there were enclosures, their walls high and impenetrable, and around each large enclosure were spaces where only the soldiers could go. Above it all, I saw a tall tower, and Calix went on straight, heading toward a hill above the flat area extending out from the bay.

There was a grand palace set in the hills, white stone like the Tri City but low and wide, with looming white gates that stood open for our approach. Calix rode slowly through the guarded gates and into a wide expanse of garden that stood before the palace itself, full of archways and breezy courtyards.

He called a servant over and helped me down into the man's arms before dismounting behind me. "Welcome to the Summer Palace, my love," he told me. "This was a favorite retreat of my mother's, and the current home of the quaesitori's inquest."

A man in a long black coat came out and bowed, which made his hair flop over his face. "My king, welcome. My queen. We have much to show you."

"Excellent," Calix said, his arm around my back. "There is no time to lose. Show us your work, Quaesitor."

The man bowed again, and then turned, leading us into the palace as his coat flapped out behind him. He led us through a long room paneled with ornate wood, and into a room that must have been, at one point, a grand reception chamber. It shone, panels of metal and mirrors lining the walls to make the whole place glitter. There were two chairs set in the center and, in front of them, a table with liquids and glass containers upon it.

Calix's arms left me the moment we neared the table. "Is this it?" he asked, picking up a glass bowl with a liquid so dark red it looked black until the liquid moved.

It looked like blood.

"No," the quaesitor said, going to a stoppered glass bottle. "This is."

This liquid was dark green, and Calix frowned. "It didn't look like this the first time."

"In my experience, we can never replicate nature's exact formula," he said. "Something is always different, even in a small measure, but the result is the same."

Calix nodded sharply. "Show me." He took my hand, kissing it and drawing me over to the chairs. I sat beside him, holding on to his hand, nervous as the quaesitor walked out of the room.

When he returned, it was with three guards, two women, and a young man, and my eyes jumped to Calix, but he was impassive. They looked tortured—there were bruises and cuts on their skin, and their eyes were sunken and smudged with darkness. The smaller woman was limping hard—her leg looked like it had been broken and never healed properly.

"Calix?" I breathed, but he held up a hand and didn't look at me.

"What is the risk?" he asked the quaesitor.

"Minimal, my king. We have done frequent studies about how weak they need to be to prevent being a threat, while still being strong enough to make their powers present in some small way. It is quite an exact balance."

Calix nodded sharply.

The man was first. Barely older than Kairos, he let himself be led, and the quaesitor directed him to a spot in the room. The young man stopped there, and the quaesitor took up another bowl.

"Water, my king," he said, and poured it out in front of the man. To the young man, he said, "Do it."

I held my breath as the young man raised his hand, and slowly the water lifted, trembling a little, betraying the weakness of either the man or his ability. I gasped, looking to my husband.

But instead of anger, there was a hungry greed on Calix's face.

"And now," the quaesitor said, reaching for the bottle. He unstoppered it, holding it out toward the young man expectantly.

The water stayed aloft, and the young man looked at the quaesitor, unsure of himself.

The quaesitor tilted his head and splashed some of the green liquid on the young man. He gasped, recoiling, and the water fell.

Calix pushed forward in his seat. "Raise the water again," he ordered the young man.

The green liquid seemed to have only scared him; he was unharmed, but he shook his head. "I can't," I heard him whisper.

"Can't or won't?" Calix asked, standing from his chair. "Motivate him, Quaesitor."

The Elementa man hurriedly held up his hand, and it shook visibly, but nothing happened.

"You see?" the quaesitor crowed.

The young man looked at me, and I felt the threads push up at my hands and skin, choking my throat, demanding I do something.

I shoved them away, trembling. I would not be exposed, not here, not now, not *ever*. Not if this was the result.

Not unless I knew that elixir worked, and I could get some for myself.

"Again!" Calix shouted, clasping his hands behind his back.

A girl was brought forward, the one with the bad leg, and her lip curled in fury as they pushed her. "Don't *touch* me," she snarled, but her eyes were locked on my husband.

"Stay back, my king," the quaesitor said. "She was part of the Resistance."

"I *am* part of the Resistance," she corrected. "And you just put me in a room with the king."

She raised her hand, and Calix made a choked noise.

"Calix?" I cried, jumping from my chair. I ran to his side as his face flushed darker and his hand clawed at his throat.

The quaesitor threw the liquid on her, and nothing happened.

She laughed. "You will die by an Elementa hand," she snarled. "Isn't that your fa—"

Calix dropped, and so did she. The guard behind her withdrew his sword from her chest with a disgusting crack. I stared at her in shock—she had landed on her knees, and she held there for a moment as blood bloomed on her chest, and she looked at me.

But then she fell, crumpling to the floor, and the spell was broken.

Shaking hard, I reached for Calix, who was gasping and coughing. I touched his face, but he sat up and pushed me. I fell back onto my hands as he stood, wiping spittle from his face as he went to the guard who had killed her and yanked a knife out of his belt.

The girl was dead, unmoving and quiet, and still Calix launched on her, stabbing her over and over and over again.

"Calix!" I sobbed, covering my mouth and trying to push away as her blood caught on my skirt and her body was mangled beyond recognition.

Calix threw down the blood-drenched blade and strode over to the quaesitor, grabbing the front of his black coat and dragging his face close. "Your *elixir* couldn't stop an *insect*! You think this is a game?" he snarled. "You think I am *joking* about this? Next time you come to me with imperfect results I will take your head—do you understand me?"

"Yes, yes, my king!" the man cried.

"Get this scum out of my sight!" he roared, shoving the quaesitor toward the Elementae.

A loud sob escaped me, and I covered my mouth as my husband seemed to notice me. "Stop crying!" he roared. "Get up!"

I struggled to my feet, and as soon as I did, he grabbed my arm, dragging me into the hall with blood-drenched fingers. He stormed through the hallways, flinging open a door and pounding down a dark stone staircase echoing with chains and distant cries.

"Who else is with the Resistance?" he bellowed. I tugged against his wrist, too frightened to cry, too aware of the rocks around me that wanted to answer my fear with power. It felt like nausea, my body desperate to give in and desperate to resist in the same awful moment.

The quaesitori down here skittered to open more doors, and Calix yanked my wrist, turning me to face him. "You think I'm cruel, wife? You think I'm cruel because I try to eliminate enemies who try to murder me? They work on *your brother's command*!" he roared at me.

"You're hurting me," I whimpered, trying to pull away.

He let me go, and I stumbled back against the rock as he turned to face the quaesitori. "Execute them," he snapped.

"My king, it will destroy the validity of our information—" one protested.

"Your information is already *invalid*," he snarled. "Now. So my wife can see."

I screamed as they slit the throat of one middle-aged man, and I didn't wait to see another. I turned and fled back the way I'd come, my heart pounding.

I kept running until I hit the open garden. A section of the garden was built around a large boulder, and the moment I fell against it, I felt stronger, and the revulsion brewing in my stomach eased.

Then I hated myself, that I could breathe easily again after watching those people murdered before me.

And worse, the fear that shook every bone and every bit of me wasn't for them. I saw my face in their stead as I relived the murders I had just witnessed. My face, streaked with blood. My body, feeling the pierce and crunch of the blade that I was supposed to be able to control.

If I couldn't get rid of this power, it would be my fate.

And if I couldn't sway his heart, it would be the fate of hundreds of others.

It was a long while before Calix emerged. I had struggled to my feet and thought better of it, sitting down again on a bench and looking at the closed gates. As little as I wanted to, I knew I had to wait for him. I had to compose myself and put my fear behind me. I had to convince him to see the madness of his actions.

Then he appeared. He looked at me and moved past without touching me. A soldier brought his horse, and he waved it away, cutting a sharp look to me. "You like to walk, don't you?" he snapped.

I nodded, silent, and he waited for me to step beside him before he started walking at a punishing pace. I kept up with him.

"Thrice-damned incompetent fools," he said after a long while. "If their work weren't so important, I'd kill the lot of them."

"So they will be punished," I said. "Put on trial for imprisoning people like that. That's what they're doing, isn't it?"

He stopped, wheeling on me. "Who? The quaesitori? They aren't imprisoning people; they're imprisoning traitors and sorcerers."

"Who are people!"

"They are *not* people," he growled. "You saw what they can do. They're dangerous, and this could lead us to controlling them." He shook his head at me, disbelieving. "I thought you understood why this work is so important!"

"I understand why you might want to find this elixir," I told him. "I want to help you do that. But you are *torturing* people!"

He jerked away from me. "We aren't *torturing* them. We just use their blood and their abilities."

"That isn't all you do!" I cried. I was shaking, and I felt hysterical, dangerous, uncontrolled. "You killed them, and you killed them all years ago! You—you—all this, it's because of you!"

"What did you say?" he snarled at me.

"You did it," I told him. "You killed the islanders. I knew, when you told me you were tricked, something wasn't right—you killed them, and it wasn't just in the past. You're still *killing them*."

"Yes!" he shouted at me. "Is that what you wanted to hear?"

I turned around, wildly looking for a way out of there. All I saw were white stone walls and the guards standing farther away than usual. How could I leave this place?

He grasped my arms, and I shrieked at the unexpected contact. "You know nothing about that day, Shalia! I was the one who was betrayed, not her. I can't change what happened, but what I did—I acted out of emotion, and that has never happened again."

He had just stabbed a dead woman more than twenty times because of the depth of his hate, but he was too wild, his hands too tight, and I couldn't say the words.

"I was secretly engaged to Amandana. We were going to marry and stop the war. But your brother was there, and she decided she'd rather have a desert man. So I put the elixir on every weapon we had, and for the first time, they couldn't stop our arrows. They couldn't control our swords. I broke the islands, and I made them all pay for her cruelty."

He was shaking me, his eyes boring into mine, and I couldn't catch my breath. Rian had something to do with this? Rian had been in the islands, offering aid, but—

Calix pushed me away and shouted, "Water!" at one of the guards, who came trotting up with a skin. He handed it to Calix, who gave it to me. "Drink," he growled. "Before you faint."

I did as he commanded with trembling hands, and Calix stalked around me, restless and scowling.

"The elixir," I breathed. "You used it before?"

He nodded.

"How did you get it?"

"The trivatis who made the prophecy. He found it in Sarocca and offered it as a way to protect me."

And you killed him for it.

"I never intended to use it. I was bringing it to the islands—to Amandana—as a show of faith."

"Who was Amandana?" I asked. I knew I had heard the name before, but I didn't think he had said it—it felt like it was from a very distant memory.

"The daughter of the high priestess," he grunted, and I felt the blood drain from my head.

Kata's sister. Calix had been engaged to Kata's sister—which was why he thought he'd seen Amandana the night of our wedding. But if she was Kata's sister, that meant—

"She was an Elementa," he said, nearly under his breath, just as I thought it. "Fire."

I shook my head slowly as the pieces fell into place. His hatred for Elementae, it all came from a broken heart?

"No," I said, shaking my head. "How could you possibly go from loving her to treating Elementae like *that*?" I asked.

Red flushed high in his face, and his gaze on me burned. "It is *because* of that. *That* is the reason for all of this. And don't you *dare* speak to me again of this, or I swear to the Three-Faced God, I will make you regret it," he snarled.

We stared at each other for long moments as his ugly threat settled between us, his breath ragged and unchecked, his eyes wild.

"Do *you* regret it?" I asked him, my throat working. "You said you can't change what you did. Do you even want to? Because what I saw today—I think you would do it all over again if you could." My voice got quieter and quieter as I spoke, and I risked a glance at his furious face before looking away from him.

"I *refuse* to regret," he growled at me, his voice low and hard. "And it wasn't enough. You *saw* what that sorceress did today. What she said to me! An Elementa will cause my death, and the Resistance is rounding them up like sheep. Both the Resistance and all sorcerers need to be cut down before they have the chance."

I nodded slowly, and I knew why I had waited so long to confront him about what I knew. I could never learn to live with what he had done, or accept it.

"Shalia," he growled, and I saw his hand reaching for me.

I ducked away from his touch. I couldn't even look at him. I felt ill.

"*Wife*," he snarled. "You will—"

"My king!" I heard, and I looked down the wide road to see a figure on a horse and several soldiers behind him. Even from this distance, I knew it was Galen, and Calix cursed as he stopped again.

Galen was upon us in moments, swinging down from his horse easily. "My king," he said, bowing his head.

"Brother," Calix grunted.

"Why would you leave the Tri City without my protection?" Galen asked, his eyes rushing over Calix, stained with blood, and the blood streaked on my arms and skirts.

"Do not think to question me, Commander," Calix snapped, but his eyes cut to me and I felt pinned by his gaze. "Do your men not inform you? I assumed that, as you have not previously seemed wildly incompetent, you would be close behind, and I had urgent business to attend to."

Galen looked to me, and I crossed my arms around myself, turning away from his gaze. "And your business—" Galen asked.

"Concluded," Calix said sharply.

Galen dropped his head to Calix. "Yes, my king. Would you prefer to return to the Tri City now or in the morning?" he asked.

"The morning," he said, taking the reins to the horse. "Escort my queen back to the Summer Palace, and we will have a meal."

"No," I said, and everyone looked at me. "I won't go back there."

"It is my palace. Where else do you suggest we go?" Calix sneered at me. Then his head moved, and he looked toward the tall tower looming up above the center of the city. "Fine. Galen, escort her to the Oculus."

Galen's eyes shifted toward the tower, like he barely dared to look at it. "You wish to take the queen to the Oculus?" he asked.

"Without further delay, Commander. I will join you shortly." Calix mounted Galen's horse and wheeled it around, going back toward the Summer Palace.

A soldier dismounted and offered Galen his horse, but he waved it off. "The queen prefers walking," he said, and this sounded resigned. "Three of you follow the king; the rest fall back."

Galen nodded to someone, and I turned, seeing Theron ten paces behind us. He nodded back to his commander.

Galen waited for me to start moving, and he clasped his hands behind his back and fell into step with me. I kept my eyes pinned to the ground, watching my feet shuffle quickly over the gray stone. Galen led us down the wide avenue, and when we turned between two white stone walls, he asked, "What happened?"

I shook my head, but suddenly tears welled up in my eyes. I kept my face down, and they fell from my eyes unchecked. I didn't dare look up to see if Galen noticed or not.

"Did he hurt you?" he asked, his voice soft.

I shook my head, though perhaps that was a lie.

"Did he hurt someone else?"

I halted, and suddenly the tears were sobs and I couldn't hold them back.

"Wait," he murmured, pressing a hand to my back and urging me forward. He brought me to the spire, ordering guards away from us. He opened the door and urged me inside, and it was instantly dark, and cool, and secluded. I felt Galen's arms come around me, tight and comforting, pressing me into the shelter of his shoulders, his neck, his arms. He whispered, "Go ahead. No one can see."

I don't know how long we stayed like that, wrapped in darkness and something forbidden, though I wasn't sure if he shouldn't be touching me or I shouldn't be crying—perhaps it was both.

As the tears slowed, Galen's hand was following the path of my hair down my back, his head pressed against mine, and it was so gentle. It made my heart warm and full in a way that I hadn't felt in a long time, and while I could feel the threads, they weren't desperate and demanding like at the coronation.

"You're ruining your reputation as a tough soldier," I said.

He laughed, the sound a rumble against my chest, and I suddenly deeply regretted not being able to see his face. He smiled so rarely—seemed *happy* so rarely—that it seemed like a terrible thing to have missed what he looked like laughing.

"It's all an illusion," he told me.

I sniffed, pulling back from him and wiping my face. My whole face felt swollen and sore, and I shook my head. "I'm so sorry. I didn't mean for you to have to do that."

"I didn't have to," he said. His hand lingered on my arm for a moment, and I could sense his eyes on me, but I didn't look up.

His hand fell away from me, and he opened the door again with a sharp flood of light. "Theron," he said, and turned back to me. "Are you ready to go up?" he asked.

I nodded. An endless staircase curved along the wall of the tower. In the center, a wide basket rested on the ground with ropes that disappeared upward.

Galen flipped open a door on the side of the basket, holding it for me. Without being given an order, Theron started trotting up the stairs.

"My queen," Galen said, and I stepped into the basket.

Galen got in before shutting the door. It was very close; our legs were pressed together, and the only way my whole body wasn't mashed against my husband's brother was by leaning backward, gripping the edge of the basket.

I gasped as the basket lifted, twisting hard once it was in the air. I was unsure if I could reach for him now that I wasn't crying, if his arms around me had been a desperate act or something that would become part of our friendship.

The motion was swift but uneven, and I wondered what poor soul was hauling us up on the other end of the rope. We moved up through the middle of the tower, quickly passing Theron as we rose.

The basket stopped, and Galen unlatched the door, motioning that I should go first. We were in the top, the broad square perched on the narrow tower. The room we entered was filled with sunlight, and I could see the distant mountains through the windows. Awed, I went closer to them, opening a wooden door that led onto a balcony.

"Shalia, you shouldn't go—" Galen warned.

My breath caught, but it was not for the natural beauty of this place.

The enclosures—there were hundreds of them, filling the valley between the oculus and the mountains with endless gray squares.

More, maybe. Some were larger, with long buildings in the center. They seemed an endless block of stone, with no grass, no space, no air. In many of the enclosures, as if prompted by a clock striking a certain hour, long lines of people were being led from one building to another. They were all moving slowly, evenly, like the shipbuilders. They had no fight, because they had nothing—no choices, no chances, no hope. Just stone and guards, and one building and then the next.

"Slaves," I said, turning to Galen as he came out to the balcony.

"I didn't want you to see this," he said, his voice soft.

"You . . . they're all slaves."

"Calix won't call them that," he said, his back straight and body tense. "They are laborers. Very skilled laborers for the most part."

"So they can leave? You pay them?" I demanded.

"According to my brother, they serve the Three-Faced God. What higher purpose is there?" He passed a hand over the view, his voice bitter. "We feed them. We clothe them and house them—we go to great expense to see they are taken care of. He believes that is a fair wage."

"How can he do this?" I asked. "How can he do any of these things?"

"Calix believes stratification is a natural part of civilized society. There must be soil so the tree can take root. There must be a working class to drive industry."

"Slave labor is not the same thing!" I cried. "And those bodies hanging in the harbor. And these quaesitori?" I asked. "And the islands. How long will this list become before you believe he's a monster, Galen?"

I looked at him, and he was tense and still beside me. "Do you?" he asked.

"Yes," I said, resting my head in my palms.

"Maybe he is," he said softly. "You spoke to him about the islands?"

"Yes," I said. "He admitted it. I thought I could accept it." I shook my head. "I thought—maybe, in time—but I can't. I won't. Not after today."

"What happened today?" he asked again.

"I realized that he hasn't changed. It would be one thing if he regretted it. He doesn't. He says he refuses to regret."

Galen nodded. "He's a king. If he were to admit a mistake, his enemies would use it against him. He was such a young king—he didn't have the luxury of being wrong."

"That doesn't make him *right*," I told him.

"No," he agreed. "It doesn't. But it does make it complicated. If he had been overthrown, we would have been killed. All of us. People nearly succeeded several times, but Calix—he held strong. He learned to be inflexible."

"And where did he learn to hate?" I demanded, glaring at him. "Because you don't hate the way he does. Danae doesn't. How can you defend him?"

"He's my brother," Galen said, bristling. "Sometimes he's been a bad king in order to protect his siblings, and sometimes he's been a great king and sacrificed our needs for the many. I don't envy him any of the choices he has had to make." Galen's jaw worked. "How can you even ask me such a question? You would never condemn your brother, and I would never ask you to."

I thought of Rian, taking lives when I hadn't thought he was capable of it. That, at least, I did understand. But I couldn't will myself to bring Rian into this argument, so I stayed silent.

"He does what he believes is right," he continued, issuing a heavy sigh. "I saw what Calix did with you in the mills. And the quaesitori—they developed an irrigation system to get water to crops in droughts," he said. "That arguably changed the nation. And they developed an incendiary powder from a yellow mineral found in the mountains and *sugar*, of all things, and that's been able to save hundreds of men from breaking their backs in the mines."

"Incendiary powder?" I asked. "I don't even know what that means."

"It can catch fire," he said. "But instead of burning like oil, it bursts—particularly when it's contained rather than out in the open."

"And that *saves* lives?" I asked.

"Mining is hard work. If we can save a single hour of manual labor, it's a great gift." His shoulders lifted. "But I also see the danger in that substance. Calix wants to fit it onto ships to allow us to disable our enemies without engaging them on the water."

"But that *prison*," I said, shuddering. "I cannot reconcile what they're doing there."

"What prison?" he asked, his sharp face creasing with displeasure.

"You didn't know?" I asked, shaking my head. "The Summer Palace is home to Elementae who are being used for his *inquest*." I thought of the bruises and all the blood, and I couldn't form any more words.

His gaze shot out over the enclosures, fixing on the palace in the hills like he could see right through the walls. "I will look into that."

I shook my head. "How is that different from this?" I asked, sweeping my hand out. "They are slaves for a different service."

His eyes met mine. "It is," he said.

I wasn't sure what his promise to "look into that" would yield, but it did ease my mind a little. "Thank you," I said softly.

"What will you do?" he asked.

"Do?" I repeated bitterly. "What do *you* do?"

"I make his reign secure," he told me. "I make it so that he doesn't have to make such terrible choices anymore."

"And you lessen the impact when he does," I said. "Like with those men guarding the gold."

A muscle flared in his jaw, but he nodded, looking away from me.

I sighed. "Maybe I can't fix him, or change him. But I can change the world that our children inherit. My children won't learn to hate. They will learn to rule with grace and wisdom, and they will change this country when they do."

"That's a beautiful vision," he said, his voice rough and soft. "I will defend them with my life." He swallowed, the action moving his throat. "You must be hungry," he said. "I'll call for some food to be sent up."

With a sigh, I nodded. He turned away from me. Curious, I followed the pathway to the edge, chasing the pink splash of light that heralded the sunset. Finding that the balcony actually turned the corner, I rounded it. There was another door to another room, and this part faced the water, the glorious sun just starting to make the sky glow above the horizon.

The water looked peaceful and distant, but the view was marred by the deep scars in the earth for the shipbuilding dry docks. From the Oculus I could see there were gates that barely restrained the ocean tide; I could only imagine the fury of the ocean as those gates were lifted.

It made me think of Kata and her gifts and, inescapably, about my own.

I heard a shrieking call and turned to see Osmost, flapping his wings to slow down and land on the railing beside me. "What are you doing here?" I murmured, smiling at the bird. He sidled closer to me, and I petted his head slowly. We were used to each other, but Osmost had always made it very clear that he was still a wild animal, and I had the scars to prove that.

Watch the skies, Kairos had told me. I shook my head with a smile—he had sent his hawk to watch after me when he couldn't. And this Oculus closely resembled a human bird's nest, so Osmost was fairly delighted.

I dug my fingers into his feathers, scratching the base of his wings, and he raised them a little, making a fond clicking noise at me. I could see the town that Galen mentioned—the only place around the wide harbor with structures that weren't made of stone, sweet little buildings that looked like they had been there forever. Off one of the docks, it looked like people—maybe even children—were running down, jumping high, and splashing into the water.

I sighed, leaning on the railing. It was nice to know there was a little happiness in this bleak city.

Osmost's head cocked, and his wings fluffed once before he leaped back from the balcony, diving low and out of sight. Galen rounded the corner a moment later, not coming close to me. "You should eat," he said. "My men brought some food for you."

"What about Calix?" I asked, turning to him.

"He never has a good sense of time when he's with the quaesitori," he said. "He may be a while. But I've had the men clear the barracks—you can sleep here."

This made me feel foolish for having demanded a different location than the Summer Palace, though I know he didn't mean it that way. "I'm sorry to displace your men," I said.

"You are their queen," he said, his face nearly hinting at a smile. "They'd jump off the balcony for you, so this is a small request."

"Still," I said, and walked toward him, going into the room, where a tray of food sat on a table covered with maps.

Theron stopped when we entered the room, a chicken leg sticking out of his mouth. He hurriedly pulled the bone out and dropped it onto a plate as Galen snorted. "Has the queen stopped feeding you?" Galen asked.

I smiled at him as I sat, and he looked to Galen. "No," Theron said, "but the king was quite fixed in his attention, and I don't believe the queen has eaten all day. Which also, incidentally, means I haven't eaten all day."

"Then we shall remedy that," Galen said, also pulling a chair over as Theron sat back in his own, going to work again on the poor chicken. I took a piece of chicken, though I attempted to eat it slightly more delicately than Theron. There were also bread and fruits and cheeses, and Galen poured us wine.

"Are we leaving tonight?" Theron asked Galen.

"No, I believe the king wants to go in the morning," Galen replied. "I've sent word to Zeph and the rest of the Saepia. They should be here by then to properly escort the queen."

Theron nodded.

I leaned back, looking to Theron with a smile. "Speaking of Zeph," I said. "Why don't you have one of those giant sword things?"

Theron huffed. "It is *not* a giant sword. It's a khopesh, and frankly, I'm hurt, my queen. I thought you, in your infinite wisdom, would have seen the limitations of such an unwieldy weapon. Knives, however, are suitable for any occasion."

He gestured to his knife-lined breastplate, where at least twenty thin, deadly stilettos gleamed back at me. I laughed. "I think the point of such a weapon is that it frightens enough people that it's rarely used," I returned. "And I like it because it resembles a scimitar."

"Ah," Galen cut in. "But the curve is for an entirely different purpose. Did you notice the notch behind the curve?"

I shook my head, and he gestured with his fingers, showing a little hook right before the long blade curved outward.

"Here," he said. "It's meant to snare people and swords so he can slice through them with it."

"No," Theron interjected, pointing a finger at Galen. "It ends up just trapping people so he has to use something *else.* And the big oaf isn't fast enough for that."

I laughed. "I'm sure you could learn to use it too."

"It's too heavy for him," Galen said with a smile.

Theron tossed down his piece of bread. "Three hells. It's an inferior weapon; when will people *understand* that?"

I ate a piece of cheese, laughing happily to glimpse the boys inside the tough warrior men.

Before long, it was dark and Calix still hadn't returned. Galen left us to go check in on him, and I felt tired enough that I went to the empty barracks room in the tower. There was another door out to the balcony there, and I curled up under two blankets, staring at the moon, which looked like she was waiting just outside for me.

Sailing in the Dark Sky

There was blood in my dreams.

That was the only thing I was aware of as I woke with a scream, the world bursting and shattering around me.

"Get down!" Theron yelled, pulling me off the bed and throwing a blanket over my body on the stone floor. A moment later he was beside me, his arm covering my head.

Glass and rough debris pressed against my body, and my panicked breath was unnaturally loud in the space created by Theron's arm. "What's happening?" I cried.

There was a horrible noise above us, and a jerking, tearing motion rocked the floor. I screamed, curling tighter against the rubble.

"There's a thrice-damned *ship* flying through the air!" Theron yelled.

Something gave way, and another shower of stone, wood, and glass hit us. Something struck my leg, and I cried out, but the sound was swallowed by a low keening groan as the bunks started to tip over.

Theron was so much faster than I was. By the time I saw the beds moving, he had already grabbed me, shoving me out into the middle of the room. Jagged fragments scratched at my skin, but Theron crawled out right before all the beds tipped and collapsed.

"Where's Calix?" I wailed.

"Not back," he said. He looked at the door, totally blocked by beds, and then raised his eyes.

I saw where the noises were coming from. A ship's anchor tore its way through the roof, wrenching the whole tower with it.

Theron hauled me to my feet, pushing me forward. "We need to get outside!" he roared. The glass and rubble cut into my feet as we ran for the balcony.

We halted when a series of loud, booming cracks sounded out.

"Down!" Theron yelled, pushing me to the ground inside the balcony doorway. I huddled against the wood, and he braced us both in the frame.

The tower lurched and rocked as one final, shuddering boom rang, and I looked up to see nothing but sky. Several long heartbeats later, I heard screams and a loud crash as the roof must have fallen to the ground below.

Soldiers ran out to the balcony, lighting arrows on fire and shooting them. I followed one to see what Theron had meant—there, barely visible, was a ship, sailing in the dark sky. There were still beads of water dripping from the hull, and the black sails were indistinguishable from the night around us. It was moving fast, coming back toward the tower.

One of the flaming arrows struck the sail, and I could see with alarming clarity as the big anchor came back around, swinging on a long rope to strike underneath the lip of the wide square that formed the top of the Oculus.

The top of the tower rocked hard to the side, and Theron grabbed me, slamming us against the wall as the square lifted up fast. A soldier beside us lost his footing, and he cried out. As the floor rose, he seemed to move in slow motion, his arms wheeling backward. "Here!" I yelled, holding my hand out from the protection of Theron's body.

The soldier met my eyes, but my hand was nowhere near close enough.

And then gravity took him, and he rushed down the balcony floor. I saw him hit the rail and flip off the edge into the night, and I couldn't breathe.

The tower gave a rumbling protest as the stone beneath us tipped more. A loud groaning noise vibrated through our feet as the floor jerked and slid, and I could see the rope attached to the flying ship drawn taut.

Theron untied a belt from his waist and wrapped the thick piece of leather around us both, tying it tight. "The top of the tower is about to fall," he told me, meeting my eyes. "We have to get off the tower."

"*What?*" I screamed, whipping my head around. The stairs were blocked, the whole floor was tilted up—if we moved off this wall, there was nowhere to go but open air.

"I need you to follow my orders without questioning them, my queen," he told me. "Can you do that?"

The floor shuddered and wrenched, and I nodded frantically.

"Grab the breastplate as tight as you can. Do *not* let go of me," he roared. I wrapped my fists around his breastplate, careful to avoid the pointy ends of the knives.

He turned and leaped onto the balcony rail, wind whipping hard around us and almost knocking him off. The white stone enclosures below us were faint and small and dim in the darkness, and I shook my head wildly.

"No," I cried. "No, no—"

But he jumped off the edge.

I couldn't close my eyes. I couldn't breathe as fear swamped through my lungs, much less scream or thrash or fight. Everything solid fell away, and we were still rising, rising, a tiny bit, and then the feeling changed.

We were falling.

Air rushed around me and we turned, too fast for my eyes to follow.

Theron somehow managed to catch the rope, and the sharp stop flung us around so hard my fists slipped free from him.

I flapped backward, but the leather around my waist jerked and held, digging in deep to my skin. Theron's face swam above me, and behind that, the dark, looming ship that we now seemed to be attached to.

Theron grunted but gave no other protest, and I grabbed onto him again, my hands shaking, clinging hard. The city looked like a toy below us. My breath was too stuck in my lungs to even manage a scream.

Our weight on the rope dragged the anchor free from the Oculus, but it didn't swing back in a natural motion. It hovered in the air for a moment, and then started rising upward. I looked to the boat above us, and the fire on the sail went out, dousing the illumination.

As the anchor drew close to the ship, Theron swung a little and caught the edge of the deck with his hands, letting the rope free as he ordered, "Grab the railing. Quick!"

I obeyed, wedged between him and the wood.

"Untie yourself from my waist," he said.

"No!"

"Quickly, or we'll both fall," he said.

Trembling, I broke the knot with clumsy fingers. I could feel his arms shaking with the effort to hold us.

"Go over the rail," he said.

I nodded, scrabbling for purchase with my feet, catching on his knee. He groaned, but I pushed up a little to jump over the rail of the massive, impossibly floating ship. A second later he was up and beside me, his feet hitting the deck and his arms out as he shoved me behind him. "Don't, she's the queen!" he cried.

I gasped. There was a tall boy there, pointing a crossbow at Theron's chest.

"You're not," he said, and I saw his finger curl over the trigger.

Osmost shrieked, flying in talons-first to hit the crossbow away as the bolt flew harmlessly over the edge.

"Damn bird!" the boy yelled, readying another arrow.

"Bast!" another voice cut in.

The boy lowered the bow as a girl climbed the steps to the front deck. I could see other people behind them, but they all looked young—barely older than I was, if even that.

This girl wore dark clothing, with rings and strange designs in chalky white—*salt*, I realized. That's what had been all over the shipbuilders. Her dark hair was coiled like a head of snakes, and it was lighter on top from the sun.

But nothing shocked me nearly as much as Osmost swooping in, his wings outstretched, to rest on her shoulder.

"Hello again," she said to him, and he clicked at her.

"You—you know my brother?" I asked, coming out from behind Theron.

She raised an eyebrow. "Your brother is a hawk?" she asked.

"No. The hawk is Osmost."

"Osmost," she said, looking at him again. He ducked a little, and she scratched his chin. "I only know the bird. But I'm guessing you're the Tri Queen." She turned to glare at the boy. "And we don't kill queens on this ship."

"Who are you?" I asked.

"Aspasia!" someone shouted.

I looked behind her to see a young girl, holding her hands out at her sides and shaking.

Aspasia took off down the stairs before the young girl even got a chance to say, "I'm losing it."

Aspasia nodded, standing in front of the girl and holding her palms up in the same position. "I'm with you."

"You're tired," the girl cried, sniffling back tears. "I can't hold this much longer and neither can you."

"You're Elementae," I breathed, coming down the stairs like their power pulled me closer.

Aspasia snapped a glare in my direction. "How else do you suggest we fly a ship in the air?"

A different boy was behind the young girl. "Take deep breaths," he said, putting his hands on her shoulders. "It's not much longer. Just hold on." He looked up at Aspasia.

The Bast boy came down to the deck as well. "We have to get out to open water. And we can't take them with us."

"We can't just leave Dara there," the other boy protested. "You know what they'll do to her."

Aspasia's arms were trembling, and the concentration and frustration showed on her face.

"It's her or all of us," Bast said.

"Vote," Aspasia said. "Quickly."

"Save Dara," Bast called. Of the ten or so children on the deck, only Aspasia and three others raised their hands.

"I'm sorry," Aspasia said to the boy. "We have to leave, now."

"We're not leaving her!" growled the other boy. "You can't do this! We'd go back for any of you!"

Sweat beaded on Aspasia's face. "Come on," she urged the girl. "Let's go."

The girl whined, and a tear shot down her cheek, but she nodded. The boat wheeled, pitching violently to the side before it sailed out toward the harbor, faster than I imagined it could.

"My queen," Theron murmured to me. "When I say, jump."

I nodded without further explanation. Especially since I was very sure that I didn't want to know what that entailed.

As soon as we cleared the land, Theron surged forward, pushing the two girls so they stumbled. The boat dropped like a stone, and Theron yelled, "*Jump!*" at me as he pushed off one boy, then another child.

I didn't look back. I just ran for the edge, and I jumped.

The water was as black as the night, shining and moving like a demon below me. I braced for the fall into it, but for long seconds, it didn't come.

I felt the threads. Even though there was no earth around me, there was nothing for them to hold on to, I felt them surrounding me.

Just before I hit the water, I knew why—the Elementa on the boat had broken my fall. It wasn't my power I felt; it was hers. So different, but made from the same forces. I wondered if, with that touch, she knew what I was too.

I hit the water, and the cold slammed against my body, covering me and taking me in, stealing my thought and my breath as I fell deeper into the arms of whatever spirits governed the sea.

The power I'd felt—her power—was gone, severed the moment I hit the water. If Theron was near, I couldn't see him. My brothers, my family were flung far from me, and neither my husband nor his valiant brother were here to save me.

I was alone, and the water was crushing me.

My lungs burned, and I kicked my legs, trying to figure out how to find the surface when everything was dark around me like I was blind. I hadn't been practicing using my element—not like I should have. I had used this power helplessly to save Kairos and Rian, but I had never believed I would need it to save myself.

I had been so frightened of my own power that I had forfeited my best means of survival.

Clawing at the ocean around me, I fought. I refused to believe it was too late. I was desert born. I was Elementa. I was powerful beyond my own understanding, and I would not be defeated by this.

This wasn't like the lake in the desert. This water burned with salt, and it was so deep and vast and dark that I seemed to be weightless, and I twisted, unsure if I was up or down or where the air was. I fought the urge to breathe in water and called my power to my hands.

I could feel rocks, bright threads far below me. That meant the air was up, and I pushed as hard as I could.

I broke the surface with a wild, gasping breath as Theron struck the water, swamping me with a wave that brought me under again. I kicked and fought, panicked, breaking the surface again. I couldn't keep my body aloft, though, and I started sinking.

"Hold on," Theron gasped, hooking his arm under mine. He drew me back against his chest, lying flat in the water and using one arm to swim as his legs kicked, keeping us afloat.

A light shone on us, and a moment later, a boat appeared. Galen abandoned his oars, other men steadying the boat while Galen pulled me up and out of the water, leaving me in the bottom to cough and gulp for breath. Theron was next, pushing up over the side as Galen grabbed his clothing and heaved him the rest of the way.

Soldiers covered us in blankets and their cloaks, and as I shivered, I knelt by Theron. "Are you all right?" I asked.

"My queen," he gasped, still catching his breath. "That is the question I need to ask you."

Relieved, I wrapped my arms around him, feeling shuddering sobs that were some mixture of the cold, my tears, and my utter gratitude rack my chest. "You saved my life," I told him.

"And he will be very generously rewarded for that," Galen said, hauling back on his oars. There were two other men rowing in the boat, and Theron and I were wedged between their seats. "Are either of you hurt?" Galen asked, looking down at us as he pulled back again.

"The queen was injured when the tower was attacked," Theron said, still panting for breath.

"Just scratches, I think," I said, shaking my head at Galen.

His eyes met mine, his scowl softening a little in a way that made him look . . . worried. He was worried about me. He swallowed and looked away. "A quaesitor is waiting to see to your needs. I'm sure you have all kinds of cuts and bruises," he said, his eyes flickering back over me.

"I'm well," I said, huddling under the blankets and shivering for warmth.

"And you?" Galen asked Theron.

"It will take more than falling from the sky to hurt me," he said.

Galen snorted. "The quaesitor will check you also, my friend."

Theron's hand flopped up from the boat and then fell again. "Bah," he said. "If something needs stitching, I'll let you know."

Galen gave a sharp nod, drawing in a deep breath like he hadn't for a while.

"Was this the Resistance?" Theron asked.

Galen shook his head. "No. We don't believe so. They were stealing workers—it's possible they're foreign slavers with powers. We've heard reports of people disappearing from the communes, but we never knew how they were doing it. Now we do."

"Damn sorcerers," Theron muttered.

My eyes flew wide to him, but I didn't say anything.

"Did you see who they were?" Galen asked.

"No," I said before Theron opened his mouth. Even if I trusted Galen with such information, I refused to arm my husband with information to help him track a ship full of children.

Theron looked at me. "No," he repeated. "We never made it on deck."

Galen nodded, and we all stayed silent while they rowed us back to shore.

There were soldiers waiting for us at the dock, but Calix wasn't among them, and I looked to Galen. "Where's Calix? Was he hurt?"

His face went grim as the oarsmen grabbed the dock, looping ropes around little metal bars. He stood, helping me to stand as well. "He's occupied," he told me. "But safe. We need to make sure you're all right."

Galen helped me from the boat, and Theron behind me. "Theron, go rest," Galen ordered.

He shook his head. "I won't leave the queen unattended."

"I'll stay with her. Zeph will be here with more guards soon anyway."

Theron nodded, putting his hand on his side and wincing. "Keep an eye on those quaesitori," he said solemnly.

Galen chuckled. "Yes, soldier."

Theron nodded again and sighed, like he could finally relax without me to protect. Galen led me toward the communes, to one of the first buildings that had men running in and out of it. I could see the Oculus, now no more than a spire—the whole top had fallen off.

This building seemed to be the primary military space, and a wide hall that was probably used for meals had been cleared, with sheets serving to section areas off. We walked through it briefly, only to go out another door, but I saw so many men wounded or dying.

Beyond that, there was a long hallway of sleeping quarters, barracks like the one we had been in when all this started, and then giving way to what I guessed were officers' quarters. Galen led me into one, and a quaesitor dressed in black robes was there, poring over a tray of instruments. I gasped.

He turned, bowing to me. It was not the same man from earlier, but it didn't change how little I wanted to be in this room. "Fear not, my queen. My art is not intended to harm you."

Galen put his arms behind his back, looking at me.

I stayed still, not believing him. Whether he knew it or not, his *art* was certainly intended to harm people like me.

"Please remove the blankets and your clothing, my queen," the quaesitor said.

"No," I said immediately.

"I need to examine you," the quaesitor said. "It will be difficult if you are clothed."

"No," I repeated again, raising my chin. "I don't want your ministrations. I saw what your work involves."

"Shalia," Galen said gently. "I'm not going anywhere. We need to be sure you aren't injured."

"I'm *fine*."

"Many people don't feel the pain of their injuries immediately," he told me. "You need to be checked."

My hands were shaking badly. "Not by him. I won't, Galen," I swore. I cast about, pointing at a small mirror. "Give me a moment, and I will check myself with the mirror."

"My queen, people fear only what they do not know. I promise I will not do you harm."

Galen's eyes snagged on my outstretched, shaking hand, and I saw muscles in his jaw tense and flare. "Very well. Leave us, Quaesitor."

The man sighed, but he left, leaving his tools behind.

"I will wait outside," Galen told me. "If something needs attention, knock on the door and I will help you."

He left, and I heaved a breath as the door shut. The longer I stayed still, the shakier and weaker my body felt, and I sat on the bed. There was a pile of things—a blanket, a sheet, a pair of pants, a long shirt, and a stiff black coat. With a shiver, I took my clothes off, using the mirror to check the places I could not see. There was an angry scratch on my leg, and I found poultice and bandages in the quaesitor's belongings and applied them. There was another wound high up on my side. I applied the poultice, but it fell off before I could get the bandage on.

Frustration curling through me, I pulled on the pants and the shirt, going to the door and knocking. Galen entered and his eyes ran over me. "Well?" he asked.

"Where is Calix?" I demanded.

He looked away. "Not here."

"Then get him!" I demanded. "I need my husband, and I will not accept the help of those—those—*murderers*," I told him.

"You're wounded?" he realized.

"I need *Calix*, Galen. Please."

He drew a deep breath and nodded sharply. "I'll bring him to you, then."

I closed the door and went back to the bed, sitting, wrapping myself in the blanket as I shivered with cold.

It was a long while before the door opened again, and when it did, Calix strode in, shutting it sharply behind him. I looked up at him, and he put his hands on his hips, staring at me. "What is it, wife?"

The shivering gave way to shaking. "*What is it?*" I repeated.

"Yes. What could you possibly want from your evil, cruel husband?"

My gaze fell to the ground as I shook my head. "Skies," I said. "I was worried about you. I thought, perhaps, you'd be worried about me too."

"Yes," he clipped out. "Galen said you're hurt. Was that some gambit to get me here so you could reproach me again?"

"I can't dress the wound," I told him bitterly. "But clearly I should have asked someone else to do it instead of you. You seemed rather particular about people seeing me undressed, but I suppose I shouldn't have bothered you."

"Where is it?" he demanded.

I pushed the blanket off, pulling the shirt up to reveal it. "There are bandages and poultice over there," I said, and looked at his face.

His jaw was working and rolling, and his face was flushed with color, like he was fighting against himself. He went stiffly to the table, taking the supplies he needed.

He sat beside me, and I flinched when he touched the poultice to the wound. Quickly, he covered the wound with the bandage, wrapping it around me to keep it in place.

"Done," he said quietly, tugging the shirt down over it.

I didn't move, facing away from him, unsure of what to do.

"Of course I was worried about you," he said, the words low and sharp. "I saw the Oculus fall and I thought you had died still hating me."

"You weren't with me," I whispered.

"You didn't want me with you," he sneered.

I pulled away from him so I could wrap myself in the blanket instead. "Fine. I'm sorry I bothered you."

"Three hells, Shalia," he snapped, standing. "I can't stand you looking at me and thinking I'm some kind of monster."

I looked at him as he paced about the small room. "Then release those people. In your prison. Let them go."

"How can you say that? You were nearly murdered by some pirates navigating a ship *in the air*. You think that's not sorcery? If I had the elixir, you would have never been in danger. Now, more than ever, I will do everything I can to prevent this infection from spreading."

"Then focus your efforts on the desert. Consult that book you told me of, with the visions. See if there is more information in there." And perhaps I could find a way to examine it as well, and discover what secrets it held of the desert, and this elixir, before my husband did something I would regret.

"Impossible," he said, waving his hand. "The book was destroyed."

"Destroyed?"

"Yes," he said. "Along with the trivatis who had the visions in the first place. His visions were sorcery. But I'm sending Danae to the desert to uncover its secrets. If anyone can find this elixir, it will be her."

"Then stop persecuting people here."

"I *cannot*," he snapped. "We caught one of the pirates, and she will be made an example of when we're through interrogating her."

"Why?"

"So my people see that we respond to such sorcery *decisively*. They killed almost a hundred soldiers, and more workers besides—she cannot be allowed to live."

I shuddered as I realized why he had been so occupied, and what it meant that he was interrogating her. If the others on that ship were any indication, she was probably just a girl and they were torturing her.

But I knew he needed a better reason to spare her. "So you would have your people see that one woman caused so much destruction? You would be aggrandizing the very power you're trying to stop."

He glared at me, and my heart pounded. "You think I should, what, let her go? She committed treason, and she will answer for her crimes."

"Fine," I said, standing too. "But privately. Don't make a spectacle of it. Give her a fair trial and help the country move on."

He came to me, staring at me for many moments before sliding his hand over my cheek. "It's a good suggestion. And what about you, wife? What spectacle, what trial do you need to move on?" His fingers stroked my skin. "I can't ask you to forget what you know of me. But can you stop hating me? Or will you keep turning to my brother, crying in his arms?"

My breath caught.

He laughed, his hand still on my face. "You thought I wouldn't find out?"

"There's nothing to find out, Calix. I was upset, and he was there when I didn't have my own brother to comfort me."

Even as I said it, the idea of comparing Galen and Kairos felt false. However I thought of Galen, it wasn't like my brother.

I took Calix's hand from my face, holding it. "I need to know you still have compassion, Calix. I need to know you're still a good man, despite everything I know of the past. Stop torturing the Elementae, and that will go a long way in proving it to me."

"I don't have to, you know," he told me, his voice soft and his face close. "It changes little, whether you hate me or not. We'll still be married, you will still be my queen and mother of my children."

I looked away from him. I knew that too. My threats, such as they were, were hollow and empty.

"But I don't want that, Shalia. I don't want our children to have parents who hate each other. I want your care, and I want your esteem." A hopeful breath filled my chest as I met his eyes. "I can't let them go completely—their powers are illegal and confirmed. But I will halt the experiments on them. Does that please you?"

"And you won't experiment on any others?" I asked warily.

"No," he said.

My fingers curled around his, and I nodded. "Yes. That pleases me a great deal, Calix."

"Good," he told me, moving forward for a kiss. I accepted it, hugging him and instantly missing the gentle comfort of Galen's embrace.

"I'm sure you're tired," he told me, pulling back and holding my hands. "But I want you out of this city as soon as possible. The rest of your Saepia have arrived; I'd like for you to leave with them now, and I'll follow as soon as my business here is done."

"I don't think I could weather another boat," I told him honestly.

He nodded. "I'll get a carriage to take you the land route. The trip will take a few days."

"That's all right," I said. "I'd prefer it. Galen will stay here with you, I assume?"

His hands on mine tightened. "I know that there were other things at play, and bigger issues between us, but hearing of you in his arms—it burned me, wife."

"Calix, nothing—"

"It's not a discussion," he told me. "There is work he can do here for a few weeks, or longer. He will stay here, and we will return to the Tri Castles. And I will not hear his name on your lips again. Are you ready to leave?"

I nodded, and he let one of my hands go to bring me to the door, opening it. Galen was outside, his arms crossed, watching the door from the other side of the hall.

"Is everything ready?" Calix asked.

Galen bowed his head. "The Saepia are prepared to escort the queen."

"We need a carriage."

Galen gave a nod. "It will take a few moments to procure."

"Good. Meet me immediately upon her departure. I'll leave you here, wife," Calix told me, catching my chin and kissing me again. He paused for a moment, and pressed another kiss to my mouth before letting me go.

"Be safe," I told him.

"You too."

He let go of me, and Galen gestured me back toward the large hall.

Galen glanced at me once, but I looked away. Calix was already punishing him for comforting me, and I did not want to make an issue of it or to add anything more to his sentence.

I first noticed Zeph's arrival when I saw men practically jumping to clear a path for him. He was stone faced as he strode through the hall, a giant of a man making everyone else seem little. He came to kneel to me.

"Oh, Zeph, you know I hate that," I reminded him.

He stood, scowling down on me. "Yes," he said. "And when we are not in front of half the army, I will give you a very stately hug instead."

"Easy, soldier," Galen told him, raising an eyebrow.

He crossed his arms. "Don't tell me 'easy.' Theron will have bragging rights for far too long because of this night."

I smiled. "I'll see what I can do to endanger my life when you are on duty."

Zeph nodded, satisfied. "We're leaving this damn city?" he asked.

"As soon as possible."

They led me outside the hall and into the cool night, and once the door was closed, Zeph caught me up in a hug that lifted me straight off the ground.

I laughed, hugging him back. "I'm all right, Zeph."

He put me down with a sigh. "From the stories I've heard already, I'm not sure how that possibly can be. But I am grateful for it."

"As am I," said a voice behind him. My heart cracked the moment I saw him, even before I noticed Osmost wheeling above, and I started running toward him. Kairos took big, lunging steps to get to me, pulling me into a tight hug. "Great Skies," was the only thing he muttered into my hair as he clutched me.

Tears pressed behind my eyes, but I was hugging him so hard it didn't really matter if they fell or not—they wouldn't ever be seen, ever be betrayed, always hidden between us.

He let me go, looking at my cuts. "You should try not to get in so much mortal danger," he told me.

I laughed. "You should try to be as useful as your hawk."

He raised an eyebrow. "Don't encourage him; his feathers are plenty fluffed out already."

"Looks like we were both late to the fight," Zeph said ruefully, nodding to Kairos as he let me go and Osmost landed on his shoulder.

"No, I infallibly appear when I'm needed most," Kairos told him. "*You* were late."

Zeph growled at this like an unhappy dog.

"Where's the hero of the hour?" Kairos asked. "I hear Theron fought off an army of sorcerers for my sister."

"Three hells, that didn't happen, did it?" Zeph grumped. "All I get to do is take her for walks."

"Skies, stop wishing more danger on my head," I told him. "I thought Theron was resting. Will he join us?"

Galen nodded. "I'll let him rest a while longer and send him to catch you on horse," he told me. "If it pleases the queen."

I looked at the ruin of the tower, where I had almost lost my life. "Yes. Let's go back to the Tri City."

I wasn't so tired that I accepted the carriage, and without Calix there to protest, we all left on horseback. Our pace was fairly easy and gentle, so Theron could catch up to us by the end of the first day.

On the second day, Kairos and I rode close together, talking quietly while Zeph and Theron and the other guards drifted behind us, and I told him of everything I had seen in the communes and the Summer Palace.

"Do you think he'll really stop experimenting on them?" Kairos asked me.

I drew a breath slowly. "I don't know. Can Rian find out?"

He sighed. "I'll get word to him. Do you think you'll want to know the answer?"

No. Yes. I had no real answer—which was worse: to realize that my husband lied to me, or to never know that he did?

"What about this elixir?" Kairos asked.

"It's real," I told him. "He's seen it before. He used it to attack the islands. I have to talk to Kata again."

He nodded, glancing at my guards. "I'll make it happen."

"Thank you," I told him. "Did you ever tell Rian of that spy in his camp?" I asked, looking behind me to measure the distance of the guards.

"Tassos?" Kairos said. "I found out who he is. He's not well-placed enough to be a threat, and besides, Rian seems to suspect that the Tri Crown has put several spies into the Resistance. They won't learn anything of value."

I nodded.

"And you must forget such things, little sister. The less you know of Rian's cause, the safer you'll be."

"Yes," I said. "Safety is so clearly part of my daily life already."

Kairos gave me a wry look, but didn't respond, and we rode on in silence.

The next day, we entered the City of Three, and people were waiting for us, shouting and throwing flowers in front of our horses, the delicate blooms bright and whole for a moment before the horses crushed them beneath our weight.

Give Up

When we reached the Tri Castles and dismounted, I stretched with a yawn, smiling. “Zeph or Theron, could we go to the mill? I’d like to see how things are faring in my absence.”

Zeph nodded. “I’ll escort you, my queen.”

“Would you like to come, Kai?”

“Not unless you need me,” he said, dismounting and kissing my cheek. Osmost yelled but didn’t come down from the skies. “I will see you tonight.”

Nodding, I glanced around for Adria. She wasn’t there, and I didn’t feel like I should have to call her to attend to me, so I didn’t.

“You don’t wish to rest, my queen?” Zeph asked.

I stretched my arms out and yawned. “Skies, no. I’m desperate for a walk. I only wish the mill was farther away.”

He grinned. “You’re a very strange queen.”

I knew this wasn’t a rebuke, so I smiled and shrugged.

The stone underfoot, the fresh air in my lungs—it felt good. It wasn’t enough to shake the darkness of the days in the communes from my heart, but it felt good.

When we reached the mill, the ground rumbled and vibrated beneath my feet. Walking out to the back, I saw the lines moving fast, growing shorter. My effort was helping. It was doing something.

I went inside, and to my surprise, I didn't see only the plain linen and cotton dresses. I saw blue and pink and silver silks, shiny hair, and soft, silly slippers.

The pounding stopped as the women saw me. It was Domina Thessaly, and Adria beside her, who first came over to me. They came forward and bowed, and the rest of the women bowed behind them.

"My queen," Domina Thessaly said. "Welcome."

"What is going on here?" I asked her.

She looked over her shoulder. "The women of the court would like to help ease the suffering of our people."

My breath caught. It wasn't a joke, or something they were doing to mock me. I could see it on their faces—they wanted to help. Or at the very least, they wanted to be seen helping. Which for my purposes was much the same thing.

"Thank you," I told them, pressing my hand to my heart. I inclined my head to them, and I heard them all rush to bow at the gesture. "By all means," I said. "Let us continue."

My heart swelled with emotion, and I felt threads running near my fingertips. I struggled to breathe slowly, trying not to disrupt them, and it occurred to me that I had to practice my abilities, or happiness here would be a very dangerous thing indeed.

The next morning, I had the luxury of waking alone, but instead of a husband, I found a note on the floor by the balcony. *Kairos told me. Meet me in the garden.*

I tossed the note into the fire, calling the ishru to dress me and leaving the chamber as fast as I could.

Zeph was waiting outside my door, and I smiled. "Morning, my queen," he greeted me.

"Good morning. Zeph, can you take me to this garden I've heard so much about?"

"The Royal Garden?" he asked.

"I believe so."

He gestured forward. "Right this way, my queen."

He led me through the castle, and then out the courtyard and down a sloping road that curled under the castle, pointing out the army's barracks and training grounds and a road that he said led to a small beach under the cliff.

When we arrived at a thick green hedge, two guards stood by a break in it. They bowed to me.

"Why is this garden guarded?" I asked them.

"It was a favorite retreat of the former queen," Zeph told me softly. "Ever since her death, the king has kept it as she wanted it."

"The king was married before?" I asked, and then realized my error. "His mother," I murmured. "Who cares for it?"

"There are gardeners, my queen," one of the guards said, dropping his head to me.

"Are they currently at work?" I asked, panic striking me.

"No, my queen. We can keep them out, if you wish."

"Yes," I said. "And, Zeph, would you mind staying here? The garden is guarded anyway, and I should like a little time alone, I think." This must have been why Kata suggested such a place. She would have known I could be here unguarded.

He hesitated, then nodded. "Yes, my queen. I will remain here. If you need me, shout."

I turned and took a deep breath, and went into the garden.

The two thick green hedges continued on inside, forming a wide pathway. It turned, and still the walkway continued. It turned again, and there it opened, onto a wide square with roses and dense beds of flowers with a stone bench in the center. I left the square, following the hedge on the other side of it to another walkway. This one turned twice and led to a large fountain.

The next room in the hedges had a line of three trees, so large and leafy that they shaded the whole space between the hedge, and their roots grew up knotted from the ground. A long, narrow fountain burbled with a bench near it, birds dashing to and fro.

"Shy," whispered Rian, appearing from around the hedge.

I ran to him, hugging him tight. "Rian!" I yelped softly. "I thought it was Kata who sent the note."

"It was," he told me. "I just wanted to come with her." His arms pulled tighter on me. "I heard about the communes. You could have been killed. You know that wasn't the Resistance, don't you?"

"I know. I heard they were pirate traders. And I'm safe," I assured him, hugging him back. "It is so good to see you. But my guards are right outside. What if they catch you?"

"We're safe in here," he told me.

"How do you know?"

He grinned. "This isn't my first time in the garden, Shy."

I stepped back from him. "Who else do you meet in here? Where is Kata?"

He lifted a shoulder, glancing around. "She's coming. I have an informant in the castle."

"*Who?*"

His head tilted. "Come now, you know I can't tell you that. It's important the king never suspects you know as much as you do."

"Did Kairos tell you about the Summer Palace?" I asked.

His face turned grim. "Yes. I'll find out if he's still experimenting on people. I can only imagine how frightening that was for you, Shy, but you know he kills these people, yes? Sometimes with a farce of a trial. Sometimes it's towns taking justice into their own hands and burning people, or hanging them."

I looked at my hands. "He wants everyone to hate Elementae as much as he does."

He sighed. "Is Kata right? You're an Elementa?"

I raised my eyes. My oldest brother, my hidden ally in this hostile place. I nodded slowly.

"Skies, Shalia," he breathed, rubbing his forehead. "We need to get you out of there. We have an opportunity while he's away."

Hope fluttered up in my chest, but it didn't last. "Rian, I can't. I can't leave. He'll come for me—he'll come to the desert and make our family pay."

He stood from the bench. "You can't stay. He will murder you, Shy. He'll make a spectacle of your death."

"I can control it," I told him. "There's a reason I have this power. I know that now. I'll practice. I won't let it get out of control."

"To hide it for the rest of your life?" he said bitterly. "This power is incredible. In other countries it's *worshiped*. You want to pretend that it doesn't exist while you have a family with him? You want to teach your children to hate what you truly are? What Kata is?"

"*No*," I said, standing too. "My children will not learn his kind of hate."

"How can you prevent it?" he said. "Unless you stand against him."

I shut my eyes. "It is so easy for you to say, Rian. You weren't there when Torrin came back to be burned in the sands. You didn't have to see the cost of rebellion and war. You weren't there when Calix ordered more men dead because you stole his coin."

"And *you* weren't there when he started all of this, when he killed Kata's people, and he would have killed her and me both if she hadn't stopped him."

I drew in a breath. "No. I wasn't there. But why were you, Rian?"

"To help!" he said. "The Vis sent word to the desert for aid. And I took our men and answered the call."

I drew a breath. I didn't believe that Rian had somehow transgressed with Kata's sister, did I? "What about Amandana?" I asked.

His head tilted, surprised, but he didn't look ashamed or angry. "Amandana? Kata's sister?"

"Calix said he was supposed to marry her, but he saw you with her instead. That she betrayed him."

He frowned, shaking his head. "Amandana?" he repeated. "She and I were friends, in a way. She and I were together before the battle, but not . . . not in the way you're suggesting, little sister. I don't know what he saw, but she didn't betray him with me."

Was that true? Did Calix wage a war on misinformation, or would we never truly know about those days?

With a heavy sigh, I rubbed my forehead. "Rian, I'm worried you are blind to the price that everyone else around you is paying. There are innocent lives being lost in your Resistance."

His eyes were heavy as he looked at me. "No, I'm not blind to that, little sister."

"Then *stop*. Give up the Resistance. Let me work for peace."

"First, it isn't mine to give up. Perhaps some see me as the figurehead, but I'm not the leader of the Resistance, Shy. And second, how?" he said gently. "With women working in mills? By asking him to stop torturing a few prisoners? There are hundreds being killed. There are thousands of slaves. And now his hate is spreading, and those suspected of having powers are being killed like animals."

I shuddered, remembering how Calix refused to call the Elementae people. Remembering how quickly his heart turned from Amandana.

"You're not talking about peace. You're talking about ducking your head in the sand, and if you don't see it, it doesn't exist," Rian continued.

"I chose this," I told him hotly. "So that others wouldn't die in my stead. I'm not leaving."

"Very well," he said. "Then I should go. I can't risk your being connected to my activities in the city."

"But you'll look into the people at the Summer Palace?" I asked.

He nodded, but he didn't leave. "Kata said something about an elixir. A magical liquid to cancel out the elements. If she finds it, do you want it for yourself?" he asked me. "To take away your gifts?"

I sighed. "I did," I said. "Maybe I still do. But more than that, I don't want my husband to control it. I want to decide who has that power."

He came to me, hugging me tight. "If you ever need me, tell Kairos. Osmost can find me just about anywhere. And if you need to flee, I will find a way to get you out. Understand? You're not alone in that palace."

I hugged him tight. "Please be careful."

"He won't be," Kata said, and I pulled back to see her. "But I'll be cleaning up behind him, so he'll be fine."

I laughed, and Rian let me go, going deeper into the hedge, leaving me and Kata alone.

"So you believe the elixir's real," she told me, replacing Rian and hugging me tight.

"It is real," I told her. "Sit down."

She pulled back from me. "What?"

"It is real, because Calix used it before," I told her softly. "When he attacked the islands. It wasn't on his father's orders; it was on his."

She drifted to the bench, ashen. She looked past me for a long time, her gaze not seeing me, as if she was replaying all that she knew about that day. "Why would he do that?" she asked. She looked up at me. "He hated us so much?"

I sat beside her, twining our fingers together. "No," I said. "He was in love with your sister. Amandana."

She looked stricken at her name.

"He thought they were going to marry. For peace. And when he came to the islands, he found out she was with someone else. He thought she tricked him. He said she was with Rian."

She didn't say anything.

"Kata," I said, tugging her hand.

"She *told* me," Kata breathed. "She told me she was going to marry. She told me he'd come for her any day now. And everything would be different when he did. *He's* the one she loved?"

I felt a tremble run through her, and I turned. Droplets of water were rising from the ground slowly, drawing the moisture away from the soil like the earth was crying into the air. "Kata," I said again.

She pulled away from me. "That sick, cowardly *bastard*. And he used this elixir to do it? To kill her?" Her eyes whipped to me. "He's going to do it again. She trusted him, and he killed her for it. It won't be any different with you."

My hands scrabbled to hold on to hers. "Kata, no. Kata, *Kata*, he won't."

"If he knows what you are? He'll kill you."

I caught her hands tight. "He won't get the chance. I will never trust him."

This seemed to calm her a little, and she breathed, nodding.

"But there was a trivatis who had visions," I told her urgently. "He wrote them in a book. The book said there was more of the elixir in the desert, in a sacred place. Calix destroyed the book, but it's the only clue he has to go on. He's sending Danae to find it, but you know the lake, at least better than she does. I think it's submerged somewhere in there. You'll be able to find it where she can't. And you have to do it before her."

She nodded, and then stopped. "A book?" she repeated. "It was meant to be burned, right?"

"I don't know, but that sounds like a good way to destroy a book."

"We have it," she said. "I think the Resistance has it."

"How is that possible?" I asked.

"Because. The Resistance has all sorts of things the king wishes didn't exist, and one of those is a large cache of books that were supposed to be burned. One of our faithful saved them."

"But this was *years* ago," I said. "Before the islands."

She nodded. "And this girl held on to them. I can't be sure, but I suspect we have that book." She met my eyes. "Maybe we have a clue he doesn't."

I clutched her hands. "Then find it. And get the elixir before Danae does."

"What about you?" she asked. "You almost died."

"But I didn't," I told her. "Because of my power. I won't deny it again, I swear it. I'll practice as often as I'm able."

"Good," she said. "When I come back, I'll bring news of your family."

The breath rushed out of my lungs as I thought of her hugging my mother, joking with my brothers, playing tricks with water to delight Catryn. "Skies," I said, nodding and fighting back the swell of emotion I felt at the thought. "I'll look forward to that."

She hugged me fiercely. "You should go," she told me. "I don't want your guard suspicious."

I nodded, burying my face against her neck, and it struck me how lucky I was. Rian told me I wasn't alone in the castle, and though often it felt like it, he was right. There were people in the world who I trusted beyond every shadow of doubt, and Kata was one of them. "I love you," I breathed into her hair.

"I love you too," she said.

Hero

My husband returned later that day, but true to his promise, Galen did not. Then word came that the Resistance had attacked the Summer Palace, and Calix demanded Galen not return until they figured out how the Resistance had discovered their operations there. Smugly, in private, he told me it would be months before I saw Galen again, and I didn't like the ache that created in my chest.

I took a walk one morning, and Kairos was waiting in the courtyard. "Morning, sister," Kairos called, and Osmost clacked out some version of the same.

Zeph sighed beside me.

"Morning," I called, smiling.

"Well, if you insist, I will join you on your walk," he told me. "Where are we headed?"

"I was heading to the Royal Garden."

"Very well," he said. "Zeph, I can escort her back to her chambers if you wish."

"Just don't leave the palace without me," he said, waving us forward.

I laughed, shaking my head as I joined Kairos, and Zeph turned around. "Can I revise our destination?" Kai asked.

I glanced back at the castle thoughtfully. "As long as we don't leave the palace."

"We won't."

"Then certainly."

"Good," he said, offering his arm in the Trifectate way. I took it. "Osmost brought a letter from home," he told me softly.

"He did?"

He nodded. "From Mother and Father. Cael is to be married to a d'Skorpios girl," he said.

"Soon?" I asked. Traditionally, desert weddings were very fast—it was only mine that had been planned so far in advance.

His mouth turned down a little. "It's probably already happened."

My heart ached. I didn't like to think of them living their lives when I couldn't be there with them. "Oh," I said softly.

"And Aiden is living in Jitra. Courting some Tri girl over the land bridge," he said to me. "Can you imagine?"

I shook my head. "I can't imagine the land bridge as a thoroughfare instead of a boundary," I told him softly. "What else?"

He shook his head, and I nodded. There was so much more, of course, and I mourned the small things I would never hear about because they couldn't be communicated in a precious, secret letter.

"Have you heard from Rian? We all heard that they raided the Summer Palace."

He looked at me. "He said he didn't find any prisoners."

I drew a breath, nodding. "That doesn't really mean Calix kept his word, of course."

"No."

"But it's something," I allowed.

Kairos lifted a shoulder, and I understood. He would never approve of Calix or this marriage, and even if I needed to cling to the hope that my husband still had a shred of humanity left, he didn't.

"But that's not why I came here today," he said.

"It isn't?"

"No," he said. "You need to practice."

We had just discussed our brother's treason and a secret letter from my family, and yet at the thought of someone overhearing about my ability, I looked around us. There was no one in sight, except guards in the courtyard we were leaving behind to go down the road past the garden.

"No one can hear," he whispered. "And no one can know. But you still need to do it."

Nervously, I nodded.

Up ahead, I could see the entrance to the garden, with guards standing there, and they bowed to us as we walked past, not speaking.

Kairos led me farther, under a stone archway. "That leads out from the castle to a walkway in the cliffs," he said. "We'll go there next time."

The path was growing steeper, and we walked down to another stone arch with a heavy iron gate in it, and yet another guard. "My queen," he greeted me, bowing.

Kairos nodded, and I asked the guard, "Please unlock the gate."

He obeyed, and we walked out past a small dock with two oared crafts and onto a long, rocky beach that lay in the shadow of the massive cliff the castles stood on.

Far down the beach, Kairos stopped me. "Here will work," he told me.

"What am I supposed to do?" I asked.

"Use your gift," he said. "Use it the way you were always meant to. Use it so it won't control you."

It wasn't the same as the desert, but I took my soft slippers off to dig my feet into the cold gray sand and I felt the threads leaping against my hands at the touch of so much stone. We were up on the dry part of the beach, and yet I felt the tide as if it were rushing over my skin, dragging on the rocks, taking smaller bits of sand, and curling it into the gentle, rolling wave in this protected cove.

With a deep breath, I stretched out farther along the threads, to the distant rocks that the violent ocean gnashed against.

"You don't need to reshape the earth," Kairos told me, following my gaze with a smile. "See what small things you can do."

I pulled the silver comb out of my pocket and held it up, curling one tine at a time and straightening them out. "I've been doing this," I told him.

He nodded. "Rake the sand," he said, pointing down.

I followed where he pointed and looked at the bands of color. There was a dark line that didn't feel like rock—perhaps it was a shell of some kind, ground up into the sand. There was glittery white, and that was rich and vibrant against my hands. The thick bands of wet gray were heavier, like they were sleeping and didn't have any interest in being woken.

Sweeping my hand, I watched as the white rock pulled against itself, forming a blob and sliding up the beach.

Smiling, I left it there, and then nudged at the gray sand. It was almost like it sighed against my power, and it let me move it, scooping it up the beach to join the small pile with the white sand.

I saw a series of small stones in the surf, and experimentally I pushed against them. My power felt like it ended by trying to pass through the water, but I remembered being submerged in the communes, and I knew it wasn't quite so simple.

I reached my power along the sand, under the water, and I connected with the small rocks.

First one, then two, and three, they leaped out of the water. I caught the first and second, and with a grin, Kairos caught the third before it hit my hand. "Good," he told me.

Laughing, I sprayed him with sand.

It seemed like I was getting stronger. My power wasn't wrestling me for control—it was there for me to use, in small, secret ways, and despite not having the power himself, Kairos was as good a teacher as he had always been with weapons, or fighting, or even teaching Catryn how to win an argument.

I spent my days at the mill or at the Erudium, where they wanted me to preside over their Consecutio, the day of contests when boys would claim they were men and fight to be eligible to join the army and pick brides.

I heard of the Resistance, in murmurs and mentions that weren't meant for my ears. Actions here and there in the country;

stealing money or crops, distributing it to the people. Protecting the Elementae, and building an army of them.

Calix and I had settled into being married over the past few months. I couldn't love him, knowing what he'd done, but we were peaceful together, and it felt like enough to build our future on. I had bled once, right after I returned from the communes, and though I tried to explain that my cycles had never been very regular, he didn't speak to me for days. I dreaded the day that my blood would return, and wondered if it was something he could frighten out of me.

For the most part, I walked. Sometimes in the Royal Garden, sometimes on the cliff walkway that was secluded and lovely and made entirely of stone, which Kairos urged me to manipulate. When we went out in the city, I pressed my attendants to walk farther each day, but I still felt like something was being lost, like I would never be able to return to the long days of walking in the desert.

Yet now walking served a new purpose. I had not forgotten those moments beneath the water—this power was part of me, and if nothing else, I needed to know how to use it. It might be my damnation, but it might also be my salvation, and I wouldn't know which until it was far too late.

As Theron, Adria, and I left the mill one day, Adria turned to me. She had ceased to complain so much about walking, and I wondered sometimes, in moments like this, if I could ever come to consider her a friend.

"Ismene is with child," she told me.

"Who is Ismene?"

"Domina Abydos," she told me. "Her husband's father is one of the higher vestai beneath my father." She sighed. "I hate her."

I laughed. "That's a little stark."

"I do," she said, shrugging. "We were the same year in the Erudium. She was married after me, and yet that little show-off has a baby, and I will never have one. And of course, her mother is acting like the Three-Faced God blessed her specifically." She rolled her eyes. "She's requested an audience with you. Must I allow it?"

I smiled, but my smile faded. "I suppose so. But will you never have a child?"

Her head turned down. "No. As soon as I married, the king sent my husband to the south and demanded I stay here. My father is the most powerful vestai, and the king doesn't want me having a child before you do. It would threaten his reign."

I watched her. "And if I have a baby?" I asked.

Her shoulders lifted. "I hold little hope. I can't presume to imagine what it will take for the king to feel secure in his legacy."

Stepping closer to her, I threaded my fingers through hers and held her hand tight. "Then no, she can't have an audience with me."

Her fingers squeezed mine, and she gave me a small smile.

I turned forward, saw people on the Royal Causeway ahead of us, and my breath caught; I was not sure why there were so many there.

Theron saw it too and put his hand on my arm. "Stay close, my queen," he told me.

I tucked close to him and pulled Adria against me, keeping our fingers together.

The guards were blocking off the road, so when they saw Theron with me they let us through to walk in the open center of the causeway. People started screaming and crying at us in delirious excitement when they saw me and realized who I was, and I flinched.

"Come quickly," Theron said, walking behind me, sweeping his eyes over the crowd as we hurried up the hill.

We crested the hill and saw what the fuss was. A military regiment had returned, and people were cheering. The soldiers were off their horses, and I could see hands waving at the crowds but nothing else.

Theron growled at the stableboys to get the horses out of the way, but I just led him and Adria to skirt around them. That was when I saw Galen, and my breath caught, halting me for a moment.

I started moving again, quicker, admonishing myself. I was simply surprised—it had been months since he'd been at the palace, and I hadn't expected to see him. That was all.

The people began cheering louder again, and Galen looked in my direction. Our eyes met and I felt it, every pulse of blood in my body, the million fine strings at my fingertips.

I didn't dare move. The threads were *alive*, stronger than I'd ever felt, sparking with heat and light and lightning. I'd been using my ability in small ways here and there, trying to learn to control it in secret, but I hadn't ever felt my power like this, so bright in my hands.

Adria made a noise, and I jolted forward, walking toward my husband's brother with my chin raised, trying to summon the cold and the stillness I'd known while he was gone.

He came to me and knelt, dropping his head, and everyone quieted to hear our exchange. "My queen," he said.

I nodded to him. "Commander. You've defended us well, but we are happy to welcome you home."

"Thank you, my queen."

"You must rise," I told him. "As our valiant hero."

The people burst into cheers at this proclamation, and I started to move away as they quieted.

He stood, calling out to me. "My queen, I've heard you've been busy here, as well." I looked back at him, and his eyes made me flush. He took a step closer. "Feeding our people. Protecting our women. Perhaps it is you who should be called a hero," he said.

"Don't be silly," I denied, but he caught my hand and kissed it.

For something that Calix did so often and made me feel nothing, the radiating heat of his lips on my skin took me utterly by surprise.

Warmth rushed over me, and before I could tamp the feeling down, the heat burned out of my skin and over the threads. The threads burst, and all around us the white stone squares of the courtyard suddenly shattered beneath our feet, dissolving into sand.

Adria screamed. I fell back, pulling away from Galen as I landed in the sand.

"My queen!" Theron called, pulling me behind him like it was an attack.

When my eyes found Galen, his sword was drawn, turning as he shouted orders to defend the queen. Theron hurried me inside, and I saw Calix standing on the step, his face twisted in a dark snarl.

Calix met my gaze, and the threads, and the power at my fingertips, vanished. I didn't look back to the courtyard.

I couldn't leave my room. I knew that Calix would come, and avoiding him would only make it worse. He knew—he'd seen what I was, I was sure of it. What I could do.

But I still couldn't leave. I stayed on the balcony until the sun set. And then I came in from the balcony, sitting on the floor, holding myself tight and shaking. I skipped dinner, waiting for Calix to return.

The door didn't open until very late. I was sitting on the bed, wrapped in a coat with my arms twined tight around my body. I had stopped shaking, but there was still something shivering deep within me.

"Wife?" he asked. I looked up, and his face was folded in a frown. "Why are you still awake?"

My heart started pounding again. "Today . . . ," I tried, but my courage failed me.

There was a knock on the door before I could finish my sentence, and Calix called out for it to open.

Theron opened it. "Princess Danae?" he asked.

"Yes," Calix said, his face lightening.

Danae came in and went to her brother. "I just returned," she said. "You wanted an immediate report."

He drew in a sharp breath. "You found it," he said, his eyes gleaming.

Danae shook her head. "We couldn't find it. We found a lake. The quaesitori need further instructions if you want them to search other caverns." She looked to me. "Shalia, we need your help."

I hesitated. "It's sacred to us," I told her. "But it wasn't there?"

She shook her head.

"Calix, what else do you remember of the vision?" I asked. "Perhaps there's something we missed."

He shook his head. "No. The vision spoke of a sacred body, a desert lake. It could not be describing anything else."

"Why didn't you tell me this, Calix?" I asked him.

He didn't meet my gaze. "Why didn't you tell us about the lake?" he said. He turned to Danae. "Were you able to drain it?"

"*Drain* it?" I gasped.

He shot a glare at me.

"No," she said. "It's not possible; there's nowhere for the water to go. And we mapped much of the bottom, but there are crags and outlets that we can't get into."

"Then take more men," he said. "Take the yellow powder and burst it open."

She shook her head. "That is neither safe nor possible, Calix. You can't burn the powder underwater, and it's as likely to collapse the whole place as to reveal the elixir."

"You need an Elementa," I told him, placing my hand on his arm. "Surely they would be able to feel something that interrupts their powers, or test that it's there?"

He scoffed, pulling away from my hand. "Why would one of them ever help me?"

"There are many people who don't seem to enjoy their powers," Danae said. "If you paid them well, offered them an opportunity to get rid of it—I could find someone who would help."

He looked between us. "Very clever. I find I like you two working together."

I smiled at Danae, but it was false. There was an Elementa in pursuit of the elixir already, and perhaps Kata had little opportunity while Danae and the quaesitori were near, but if it could be found, she would have it in hand already.

And if it couldn't . . . I didn't know how my husband would react to that.

"There's more," Danae said, and the smile died on my mouth. "You should come to the courtyard."

Calix nodded sharply, striding toward the door without hesitation. I wasn't sure if I was meant to follow, if I was part of the intended "you," but after a moment, I followed them.

The courtyard was nearly restored. Half of it was filled with new white stone to cover what had been lost, but the work had halted, and the gate hung open to reveal three smears of blood. Uniformed guards were dragging three bodies inside, and they stopped when they reached Galen, who was standing in the courtyard.

I covered my mouth. They were dead, their throats slit. Executed.

"Three of my soldiers," Galen said, his face hard as he glared at Calix. "Tassos, Arius, and *Magan*." He stressed the last name, and I didn't understand why.

"Tassos?" I asked, looking at Calix. The spy from Rian's camp? Danae, too, seemed to recognize one of the names.

"Calix, we need to discuss this," Galen said. "Now."

"Get rid of them," Calix ordered. "We can discuss this in my chambers."

Galen nodded and turned to issue orders to his men. I couldn't look away, watching as the guards carried the bodies back toward the garrison until Danae turned me away from the scene, leading me back into the castle.

No one said anything more until we were all back in our rooms, and Danae sat me beside the fireplace. I felt ill and too hot.

"Magan, Calix?" Galen snapped, his hands on his hips. "Tell me, Danae, which of those names was familiar to you?" he asked.

Danae stood. "Calix told me he had a spy in the Resistance named Arius," she said.

I gasped, and Galen looked to me. "Your *wife*?" he growled, pointing to me as he glared at Calix.

Calix shrugged. "You cannot break an enemy unless you understand the enemy," he replied.

I blinked rapidly. "I don't understand what's going *on*," I insisted.

Galen turned to me, the anger fading from his gaze but the tension remaining. "You knew one of the names, didn't you?" he said. I looked from him to Calix, not wanting to betray something I shouldn't. "My guess is Calix told you that Tassos was a spy inside the Resistance. And he told me the spy's name was Magan, and he told Danae the spy's name was Arius."

I shook my head. "Why?"

"Because he had three spies," Danae clarified. "And if one of them was revealed, it would mean that we were feeding information to the Resistance. Meanwhile, the other two would be safe. However, in this instance, the Resistance seemed to have discovered all three at once and sent us a message. This is a low move, even for you, Calix," Danae said, crossing her arms and turning away from us.

I looked at Calix. "Is that true?" I asked. Kairos had warned me of such, but it wasn't just me whom he'd distrusted—it was his siblings as well.

"Do *not* look at me like that," he growled at me. "Like I have betrayed you in some fashion. I needed to be sure of your loyalty to me and not to your damn brother."

"And were you worried about my loyalty, brother?" Danae said. She wouldn't meet his eyes, and she sounded heartbroken.

"All I knew was that we needed more information and you hadn't delivered that yet," Calix snapped at her. "You all have failed spectacularly at your jobs, and I took action. We are attacked at every turn, and my commander cannot counter it, and my spy cannot anticipate it."

I looked up at him. "And your wife?" I asked softly. "What job have I failed at?"

He strode closer, leaning over me and pushing his hand against my womb. "You have failed at your only purpose, *wife*. Where is my child?" he growled. I felt fear rising in my throat, but refused to look away from him. "Why is your womb still cold? That is your sole value, and you cannot manage it."

"Calix!" snapped Galen, but Calix didn't tear his gaze from me, and I returned it, pressed back against the chair.

"That Abydos girl is expecting, and I have dogs that display more robust signs of intelligence. Clearly conceiving can't be that hard, can it?"

"Why must you vent your rage on me, Calix?" I asked him. "None of this is my fault."

"But Tassos is still dead, isn't he?" he said. "Perhaps that *is* your fault."

My heart pounded. "I never told anyone about that," I lied.

"The only way all three could have died at once is if we were not responsible," Galen said. "Calix, you know that. Stop threatening your wife."

Calix straightened up. I looked to Galen, grateful, and despite how mild his words had sounded, his chest was rising and falling rapidly, and his face was etched with tightly leashed fury. He crossed his arms on his chest, the knuckles white as he gripped his bicep.

"Then give me a solution," Calix demanded. "We need reliable information about the Resistance. All we know is that Rian is *not* the head that we can cut off. Today's attack will give the vestai even more arrows to cast at my reign. *Do something*," he snapped.

Attack. I felt dizzy and tired and my head hurt. As Galen and Danae argued with their brother, I went out to the balcony, forgotten. The cold air helped, but I still did not want to return to the room and risk confessing that I was the traitor they were looking for, that I was responsible for the "attack." All because I couldn't help the way I felt when Galen touched me.

Instead, they would use this as a reason to continue to hunt my brother, another crime to attribute to his cause. And I would let them, the silent, coward queen.

No More Fish

The next morning I woke alone. It was late in the morning already, and still I felt exhausted, the events of the day before weighing heavily on me. I woke and dressed and found Theron outside my door, but Adria was absent.

"Where is she?" I asked Theron, confused. "It's late."

"I'll send someone to fetch her, my queen."

I nodded. "She can meet us at the Erudium; they want me to approve of something for the Consecutio."

"Yes, my queen." He sent another guard off to find her, but we hadn't even reached the gates before the guard returned.

"Report," Theron told him as the guard bowed.

"My queen, Domina Viato is with the king in the Great Hall."

That couldn't possibly be good news. "On what business?"

"I don't know, my queen. The High Vestai Thessaly is with her."

I shot a look to Theron, and he nodded. We turned back around, going into the castle to the hall where we had court dinners every night. Calix still sat on the raised platform, Galen standing off his left shoulder, but now Thessaly and Adria were at the bottom of the stairs.

Buried in a throng of people straining to hear, the trivatis still saw me and slammed his staff on the stone to announce me, interrupting the proceedings and flushing heat to my face.

"Wife," Calix said, standing. "Come join us."

The people parted for me, and I climbed the stairs slowly, taking his hand. He kissed it, a shadow of Galen's action the day before, and it embarrassed me to remember the storm of emotions I'd felt at such a simple touch. I couldn't look at Galen.

Calix directed me to sit beside him, and he sat down. "I believe you were insulting my honor and prowess as king," Calix reminded Thessaly.

Thessaly's face was mottled with anger, and for her part, Adria looked uncomfortable beside him. "Do not belittle my concerns, my king. My daughter could have died yesterday, and you do nothing."

My back straightened. Died? When? She had been with me all day. Surely—*oh*. He meant in the courtyard, when the stone exploded into sand. Something they all thought was an attack.

I saw Kairos, standing in the crowd of people, and his eyes met mine with a smile and a slight nod.

"And the fact that you are so cavalier not only about my daughter's safety, but about the queen's safety as well, is a blatant act of disrespect to the tenets of the Three-Faced God. Are our women not holy vessels? Are they not in need of protection and guidance? And yet this Resistance strikes at your very heart and you do nothing. I demand a response! I demand satisfaction!" he bellowed, and the words seemed to echo on the stone walls.

Calix's face was a dark scowl.

"My king, might I offer a thought?" Galen asked, stepping forward.

"Yes, Commander," Calix said.

"I was in the courtyard yesterday," Galen said, turning to look at Thessaly, his face stern and disapproving and his hands clasped behind his back. "Neither the queen nor your daughter suffered any kind of injury. Indeed, half the army was there to protect them as necessary, and no action was needed. While I acknowledge your legitimate concern, let us not overestimate the nature of the events."

"Quite," Calix agreed, propping his elbow on the arm of the chair.

"But it does not remove the seriousness of the situation," Thessaly insisted. "If the Resistance can strike at us in the Three Castles, we are not safe anywhere. They have sorcerers on their side, and clearly, they can use this destructive power anywhere and anytime they wish."

This caused a cascade of murmurs and voices to rush through the hall, and Calix watched it all, not quelling it.

"What will you do, my king?" Thessaly asked.

Calix leaned forward. "What is it you wish me to do, Thessaly? Or in your rage, have you just considered how to hurl accusations without a mind toward solutions?"

Thessaly's gaze turned to me. "They say Rian d'Dragyn is the leader of this Resistance," Thessaly said. "Perhaps you need to use the leverage you purchased and send a message."

I gasped, and Adria's head whipped to her father, but Calix chuckled. "You think attacking my wife is wise, Thessaly? She is the most holy of holy vessels. Besides, you are betraying your ignorance of the matter. Rian d'Dragyn is not the leader of the Resistance. So other than dangerous misinformation and egregious insult to my wife, what do you bring me for a solution?"

Thessaly's gaze flicked between me and my husband. "I do not have a solution, my king, because I am not the Three-Faced God incarnate. Where is your solution?"

Calix paused, a hint of a smile on his face, his gaze narrowed on Thessaly, appreciating the moment. "You do not have a solution because it is beyond your capability to judge, High Vestai," he told him. "You and your daughter are here as fearmongers, but my people are not taken in by such antics." He paused again, rubbing his mouth thoughtfully. "The God relies on his people to stand against such injustice and sin. Going forward, any of my people who have information about the Resistance or a sorcerer in their midst will be rewarded in coin," he said. Again, murmurs and gasps rose through the hall. "And my commander shall act accordingly. We will not submit to fear; instead we shall let true justice be our guide."

My gaze shot to Kairos. Rian had to be warned about this—he and all his organization would be at risk. Kairos nodded at me, turning and leaving the hall.

Thessaly started to say something, but Calix stood.

"Everyone is dismissed!" he shouted.

The guards sprang into action, shepherding people out of the hall, and Calix sat back down to watch them leave. Galen didn't move, and so I stayed still, watching as Adria gave me a forlorn look over her shoulder.

The moment the doors shut behind them, Calix sighed. "I don't want to hear it, brother."

"Clearly," Galen said stiffly. "Not an hour ago you agreed that plan would tear the city apart. And now you've just publicly enacted it, without consulting me."

Calix stood, turning to his brother. "Because I'm *king.* I don't need to consult you. I swear, I will find a reason to divorce that man's tongue from his head. Using his daughter as a way to come at me—and my *wife.*"

"But, Calix, people will be falsifying information for money," I told him. "Instead of peace, you're going to have civil unrest."

Calix glared at me. "He's not wrong, you know. Think of what a reaction I would have if I flung your lifeless body off the battlements for your brother to see."

My stomach turned that he could even threaten such a thing so easily—and moments after he had defended me. "Don't speak to me of Rian. He left the desert when I was a child for this Resistance. I lost him *years* ago. And I have left my family behind for peace between our peoples. In spite of him."

"Good," he snapped. "But still. He needs to remember that we have you, and I will do with you what I want to stop him. They will collect information in the courtyard. You will be there, for everyone to see. For everyone to be reminded where my queen stands."

"As you wish," I said, raising my chin. "But if I'm going to be there, the rest of the women of the court will be with me." He opened his mouth, yet I continued. "And we're going to give away as much food as we can purchase or spare. I won't have our people desperate *and* hungry."

"Fine," he snapped. "Whatever you see fit." His gaze flicked to Galen. "See that the queen does as she's told."

Galen didn't respond. I stood from my chair and walked slowly down the stairs. Galen followed.

"Wife," Calix snarled, and I turned. "Don't forget to wear your crown."

I swallowed. "As you wish, Calix."

Galen and Theron trailed me in silence back to my chambers, where the ishru helped affix the crown to my hair. It was light, but I still felt the awkward weight of it on my brow, blotting out my face and my skin and my family until all they would see were three silver branches.

Once the orders had been given to the palace cooks, storekeepers, and women of the court, we assembled in the courtyard. Adria was there, looking small and ashamed, her mother by her side with her arm around her.

I waved Galen and Theron away from me. I was here, and I didn't need them by my side in a courtyard that was full of guards. The women of the court all watched as I approached Adria.

"Go," I ordered them. "See that everything is set up to feed our people."

The women scattered at this, still looking over their shoulders to see how I would react to Adria. Domina Thessaly didn't say anything, but she was looking at me with such worry on her face.

"How could you do that?" I asked Adria, my voice quiet and low enough that the others couldn't hear. I kept my face as even as I could, but I couldn't help looking at her with an accusation in my heart.

"I didn't want to," Adria told me miserably. "I didn't know he would say those things about you. He doesn't really believe them, I swear it."

My throat worked and my chin rose higher. Calix would rebuke her, loudly call out her disloyalty, and dismiss her from service. He would use this excuse to get what he had always wanted.

And in that moment, I saw the temptation of it. I could taste how sweet the words spoken with anger would be in my mouth.

I thought of Calix making me apologize to him months ago, leaning his face close to mine and saying, *That is power*.

"My queen, please—" Adria continued.

"Stop," I said, holding up my hand. I would never believe in Calix's brand of power. "I'm sorry that I was so concerned with myself yesterday that I didn't consider how you were faring. I cannot hold you responsible for your father's actions. Do you wish to keep attending to me?"

She looked up at me, surprised. "Yes, my queen."

"Good," I said. "Then let us focus on our people, and their needs. We have so much to do, and no time for any petty thoughts."

I held out my hand to her, and she took it, squeezing it with a grateful look. I brought her over to the table where women were cutting and arranging bread, and let her stand beside me.

I felt the weight of someone else's eyes, and I looked up and across the courtyard to find Galen's warm gaze following me. He gave a judicious nod when our eyes met and turned away, calling for the gates to be opened.

◆

Hundreds of people came to inform on their friends and neighbors. The bread disappeared, and more bread, cured meat, and cheese replaced it.

Kairos came, working beside us and teasing the women, laughing with the guards, another d'Dragyn conspicuously in the king's courtyard, doing his bidding, showing where we stood. But Osmost wasn't on his shoulder, and I was certain that the hawk was carrying a warning to the one d'Dragyn we were supposedly standing against.

"I think you should sit," Kai said. It was late afternoon, and the line was only growing longer, with more people for us to offer food to as they waited to tell their tales for a coin.

Adria nodded at this. "You do look tired," she said. "And I thought you rather liked hard work."

"I do," I told her. "So I will continue."

"You haven't eaten," she said.

"Why don't you rest, and I'll get you something to eat," Kairos said.

"I'm not hungry," I told him. "And I don't really understand your concern."

"I don't think it would do very well for the queen to faint in the middle of all this," Kairos told me, raising an eyebrow.

Perhaps he had something he needed to tell me? "Very well," I told him, and he led me over to a stool. The moment I sat, I sighed heavily. I *was* tired. I pressed my hand to my stomach—it seemed a sad reflection on how little I did every day that a few hours on my feet handing out bread could exhaust me.

The cook was bringing out a huge vat of stew, and Kai waited for her to set it up before requesting a bowl. I couldn't hear what was said, but I saw the cook smile and angle her spoon at Kairos until he laughed. My brother, ever the charmer.

He brought it over to me, but I smelled it a foot away and stood up. He halted, looking at me curiously. "Skies, that's the fish, isn't it?" I asked.

He looked at it. "Yes. Has it offended you? I think it already lost its head, but I'm sure we can cook up some kind of revenge." He grinned. "Cook up?" he repeated with a wink.

I backed away, but it was like the smell was a thick, physical presence in my nostrils, clawing down my throat.

"*Oh*," I cried, and barely made it to the edge of the courtyard, the grassy patch that led down toward the garden and the ocean, before my stomach wretched up its meager contents.

Kairos was beside me, twisting my hair back and holding my crown steady. "Very well," he said. "No more fish."

My stomach heaved again, but nothing came up. "Water!" he called, and I heard someone offer it to him.

I straightened up, and he let my hair go to rub my back, passing me a skin of water. I drank a little, but it made my stomach feel tight and angry, and I passed it back to him, shaking my head.

I turned around. Adria and Kairos were there, but the guards had formed a blockade around us, their backs to me, affording me some strange level of privacy. "Here," Adria offered, handing me a piece of bread. "Try that. My mother said that's all she could eat with Aero."

I didn't take it. "Aero?" I repeated.

Skies Above, she thought I was with child. But I couldn't be—I had last bled—

Months ago, I realized.

I had been exhausted for days. My mother had been so tired with Gavan, especially for the first few months.

My head was pounding. "Skies," I breathed. "I think I need to sit for a minute."

"Yes, we established that," Kai told me. "Theron, bring that stool here."

A moment later it materialized, and I sat. Kairos stayed right beside me, handing me first the water and then the bread. "Try to eat something," he said. "And then we'll get you back to your chambers to rest."

I nodded, nibbling at the bread. I looked up. "What a scene this must be causing," I said, shaking my head.

"I think it's the best sort of scene," Adria said with a smile. "The king will be beside himself. My queen, you're with child!"

People heard her, and the murmuring voices around us started to pitch to yells.

I searched the soldiers' backs, thinking of Galen. It was difficult to tell, but I was nearly certain he wasn't one of the men standing there. Admonishing myself, I shut my eyes. I was expecting his brother's child—I couldn't think of Galen anymore. Not that I ever truly could.

When I finished the piece of bread, I stood, and Kairos put his arm around me. "Easy," he told me.

I flapped my hand. "Skies, Mother could walk for days in the hot sun when her belly was heavy with child," I told him. "I'm fine, I just needed a moment to rest. Please let us pass," I said to the guards.

"My queen—" Adria started.

The guards separated, and I instantly felt the weight of hundreds of eyes upon me.

I took a deep breath, smiling at the gathered crowds, and they leaped forward, shouting, calling my name and offering me congratulations, blessings, praise of the God.

I jumped back, and the guards immediately fended them off.

"You're going to start a riot," Galen told me. He put his arm on my back, steering me up the walkway as Kairos and Theron blocked people from following us.

"Thank you," I told him, glancing back over my shoulder to see people pushing at the guards for my attention—and more than that, the line of informants that stretched down the road and into the city itself. "Where's Calix now?" I asked.

"In the tower," he told me, glancing up. "I'll call for him."

"Nonsense," I said. "Take me to him?"

"It's a few flights of stairs," he warned.

I waved my hand. "This is important."

Galen led me inside to the central tower of the main castle. I'd never been in it before; I'd been told there were battlements and barracks, that it was largely a soldiers' post, not unlike the Oculus in the communes. "So it's true, then?" he asked. "You're with child?"

We started up a staircase with a soldier always in sight. "I believe so," I told him.

His face was stern. "Almost as if he threatened it into existence."

I raised my chin as we turned up another stair. "Yes, well, none of that matters now," I told him.

"It doesn't?" he asked. His voice was low, careful, but he said, "I could have killed him for saying those things to you."

This made fire burn in my cheeks, but I ignored it. "All along, he has wanted a child. A child will make him more powerful with the vestai, it will prove the prophecy wrong, and I know he hopes that it will at least quell some of the violence from the Resistance."

"He said it himself: Rian d'Dragyn isn't the leader of the Resistance," Galen told me, turning another corner. "Why should it matter?"

"If it didn't matter, why did he marry me?" I returned. "Once he knows about the baby, he'll stop all this information gathering that's threatening to turn the city against itself. It isn't necessary, and it actively threatens the peace."

He stopped me. "Shalia, what if he doesn't want peace?" he asked.

"He *does*," I insisted. "That's what all of this has been for. That's why I married him. Perhaps it would not serve your purposes, *Commander*, but Calix believes in peace."

He blinked, leaning away from me. I sighed. That wasn't fair. Galen wasn't some kind of warmonger—from what I could tell, he spent far more of his time trying to lessen the harm of Calix's orders. I opened my mouth to say so, but he said, "Peace is a noble goal. But there is a difference between peace and submission."

I started up the stairs again. Of *course* there was a difference. Calix wanted peace—we had discussed it many times. In his worst moments, he acted out of fear and anger, but he wanted peace. And this child would be a balm to those fears—this child would give him the ability to act for peace alone.

We didn't say anything further, even as I felt Galen's watchful gaze on me. We crested a platform, and Galen headed toward a door that was flanked by guards.

The guards opened the door when they saw us, revealing Calix bent over a table layered with maps and documents. He straightened with a frown. "Wife?" he asked. "What's wrong?"

"Nothing," I said, smiling. "I have good news, actually."

His eyebrows rose. "I like good news."

"I couldn't eat fish," I told him. He looked confused. "Not that I've ever been fond of it, but when I smelled it, I felt so ill that I was sick, and I've been so tired lately, and it's been several months since I bled—"

He strode around the table, catching me in his arms with a bright smile. "You're with child? Are you sure?"

I laughed. "I think so. As sure as I can be, I suppose."

He kissed me. "Oh, wife, this is the most incredible news," he said, holding me tight to him. I closed my eyes for a moment, letting warmth rush through me.

"There was nearly a riot in the courtyard when they realized why she was ill," Galen told him.

Calix kissed my temple. "Of course there was! Our people need this hope. Galen, we'll have to plan a grand tour—the whole country will want to see my wife carrying my son!" Galen nodded to him, and Calix stroked my cheek. "Does that please you, wife?"

"I'm happy to do whatever you two think is best," I told him.

He kissed me once more and let me go, pointing to Galen. "We'll need a whole chest full of jewels," he said. "And clothing and furs—whatever my wife desires. It will be a glorious spectacle."

Galen nodded. "I'll see that it's done."

"Make sure the whole court knows by tonight," Calix said.

"That won't be a problem; every woman in the court has already heard," Galen said.

"Calix, what about the informants?" I asked. He turned to me, confused. "You'll stop collecting information now, won't you?"

He crossed his arms. "Well, no," he said. I looked at Galen, but he avoided my gaze. "I cannot just reverse an order I gave this morning. Not only would it be damaging to my reign, it would be disrespectful to Thessaly. This was an answer he called for. It isn't as simple as stopping."

"But you won't act on it," I insisted. "You won't do anything with the information you collect, right? Whether it's persecuting the Elementae or targeting the Resistance—you don't need to do that anymore."

His gaze narrowed. "You think I'm *persecuting* them?"

"Calix," I said, coming closer to him and tugging his hand. "This child proves that you'll have an heir, and the prophecy is merely the prattle of some misguided fool. I just want to make sure you're not resorting to violence when you don't have to. Not when we're starting a new age of peace."

He drew a long breath, but his fingers entwined with mine and he lifted my hand for a kiss. "How can I argue with that?" he said. "Very well. We won't act on the information. We'll keep collecting it for a few days, if only so people can have their coin."

I nodded, but it didn't feel right, not after Calix's rabid need to get information on the Resistance. In agreeing, he was silencing my concerns, but could I trust him not to act on the information?

He pulled me close for another kiss. "Why don't you go rest?" he said. "I'm sure dinner will be a theater of supplicants tonight, so you may want to prepare for it."

I shrugged—I was tired. "Very well," I told him.

"I'll escort you," Galen offered.

"No, Galen, we have far too much to do," Calix said. "Unless you need an escort, my love?"

I shook my head, even as Galen frowned at his brother. I was only halfway down the staircases when I heard voices and saw Kairos making a guard bend with laughter.

Grinning, I joined them. "Oh, Kairos," I said, shaking my head.

He chuckled, putting an arm around my shoulders and kissing my cheek. He nodded to the guard and led me away. "How did he take it? Is he building a white stone sculpture in your image?"

I elbowed him. "He's very happy."

"And you, little sister?" he asked. "Are you happy?"

I smiled. "Of course. I can't wait to be a mother." A sudden realization made joy bubble up inside me. "And we'll have to bring the baby to the desert to be blessed. Kai, we'll get to see everyone."

"See them?" he scoffed. "Father's going to be so smitten with his grandbaby he'll probably give up the desert altogether. The whole d'Dragyn clan will have to leave the desert for the Trifectate."

I laughed happily at the vision—that was truly what peace meant. Not just the day when my brothers would stop dying at my husband's sword, but the day when they would all be welcomed in the Tri City. When everyone gathered around my child, working together to make a better world so that he or she could inhabit it.

"And when we go to the desert," he said, hugging my shoulders gleefully, "the clans will celebrate until the mountains shake."

Foolishness

Absolutely not," Calix said. Rather than attend court dinner, Calix insisted we stay in our reception chamber so that the court could come to us. "Go to the desert? With my unborn child? No. Never."

"It's tradition," I told him. "The baby needs to be blessed in the desert, or it won't be healthy and strong. I could even show you the lake, and we could look for the elixir."

He waved his hand. "Foolishness. Trifectate babies are perfectly healthy without setting foot in the desert. It's unnecessary."

"It's necessary to *me*," I told him. "The whole clan gathers, and there are songs and dances. Light and love. I want my family to bless the baby, Calix. I want that for my child."

"Your family is here," he told me. "Now, we must speak of more important things. I'm sure we should wait for the tour until your belly grows—everyone will want to see my child growing in truth." His hand covered my stomach, warm and gentle. "I wonder how long that will be."

"Not long," I said. "I haven't bled for more than two months."

He nodded, pleased. "Excellent. We will tour you around the country as soon as arrangements can be made."

"What about the Consecutio? They are eager for us to attend."

He lifted an unrepentant shoulder. "They will manage their disappointment. It's not nearly as important as allowing the country to fawn over you." He kissed my forehead. "My precious wife," he said. He grinned. "Wait until you see the jewels I've commissioned!"

I shook my head. "I don't need any of that. I just want to go to the desert, Calix. Let my family come and bless the child. It will be good luck." I tugged his hand. "Please. We needn't go into the desert; they could all gather in Jitra and meet us."

He kissed me again. "No," he said, smiling at me.

Zeph opened the door. "My queen, there are vestai who wish to pay their respects," he told me.

"Send them in!" Calix crowed.

Two men entered, bowing low. "My queen, we came to offer gifts for you and your child," one said. He handed me a basket of strange, brightly colored fruit. "These were brought from my estates in the south," he told me. "Only the most delicious food for the future king."

Calix beamed at this.

"A necklace, my queen," said the other man, holding a stone as green as Galen's eyes on a leather cord. Calix took it in delight, lifting it from the tiny wooden chest it was in to string it around my neck.

"Lovely," Calix told me. "A stunning jewel for my own priceless gem. Vestai, you please me."

They bowed at this. "Thank you, my king!"

Calix grinned as they heaped honors upon him. I smiled and sat there while courtiers kept coming with gifts that seemed to have materialized out of the air. Or maybe not—maybe they had all been waiting for this, for the child who would change everything.

While courtiers fawned over Calix far more than they did me, I took a moment to go out to the balcony. The wind was strong, and I found myself staring at the narrow bridges that connected the castle to Galen and Danae. I couldn't see any activity at Danae's castle, but I wasn't sure if she had left to return to the desert yet.

When I turned to the other bridge, Galen was standing on his balcony.

Glancing over my shoulder to see Calix still quite occupied, I went toward Galen's side. The bridge reminded me of the one I was married upon at Jitra; it was white stone and a little wider, but it didn't have sides or handholds of any kind. Taking a breath, I stepped up onto it, walking a few feet forward.

The wind pushed me so hard I swayed, and I froze, looking down the hundreds of feet to the churning ocean water.

"Shalia!" Galen called, seeing me. He didn't hesitate, striding across the bridge, his hand meeting my waist and gently pushing me back. "It's not safe up here. Certainly not in your condition."

I stepped onto the balcony, and his hands left me as he glanced at the large windows. "You must be aching to remind me you were right," I told him. "About the information. That he doesn't want peace at all—he wants submission."

"Maybe I wasn't," he said, but his eyes moved away from mine. "He said he won't pursue the information."

"But he still has it," I said. "It seems like a very careful distinction."

"You are queen," he told me. "Your life is full of careful distinctions."

It almost felt like an encouragement, and my mouth lifted a little. "You'll be an uncle," I said, looking at him.

His shoulders curled forward a little, his head inclined, and when he looked at me, it was with such sharp pain that I felt it inside my chest. "Yes," he said.

"Galen," I breathed, raising my hand toward him, but there was nothing I could say, or do.

"I should just leave," he told me, his voice soft, the wind pulling the sound away as it ruffled through his dark hair. "But I can't just leave. I can't leave you here with him. I can't leave the city to his caprices."

My mouth was dry. "Galen," I whispered.

He stepped forward and kissed my cheek, his mouth hovering there, warming my skin, making my whole body tingle and throb. "I have nothing, Shalia, nothing of worth to make promises. And maybe I can't even keep such a promise, but I will protect you and your children. I'll protect you until I die."

In my heart, I knew what he was speaking of. I knew why he should leave, why I shouldn't say his name, or touch him, or fight with him. Like the power I wanted to hide, the way he made me feel hovered just beneath the surface, stronger for having never seen the light. "I don't want protection."

He pulled away and his green eyes met mine. "That's all I have. That's all I am."

I stared at him so long my world drowned in green. "That's not all you are, Galen."

The corner of his mouth turned up, but the ghost of a smile held no amusement. "You don't really know me."

I crossed my arms around myself, nodded. "Good," I said, shutting my eyes.

"Good?" he asked, his voice too close.

I kept my eyes closed, desperate to open them, to move closer, to run my fingers over the scars on his face. "Yes. It's easier to think that I don't know who you are at all, that I'm imagining this."

"Maybe I'll try that," he said, his voice low and heavy. He was still two steps away, but I felt him, everywhere, close to me, hovering just beyond my skin, calling my power up and making it shiver to be unleashed.

"Ha-ha!" Calix shouted, and I jumped, turning as he closed the balcony door behind him. "Galen, are you hoarding my wife?" he said, striding up to me and putting his arms around me from behind. His hands fanned over my stomach, his lips touched my cheek, and I shut my eyes rather than look at Galen while Calix touched me.

"Forgive me, brother."

"Most of the court is lined up to see us, wife. Galen, come in and take note of who isn't there."

"I'll stay out here," I told them. "A few minutes longer."

Calix kissed my hand. "Are you all right?"

I nodded. "I feel a little ill. The fresh air helps."

He kissed my mouth, nodding and relinquishing my hand. I watched them walk in together, and I turned away, looking for solace and finding only the endlessness of blue sea.

The World Spun Upside Down

I didn't sleep well that night. I woke early, hiding the comb in my pocket, eager to go to the garden and practice my power. I bent every tooth of the comb forward and back, even focusing enough to lift the comb off my hand, but it wasn't enough. In the garden, I moved the stone bench, I raked my power through the ground and tore up small rocks, large rocks, tiny flecks of minerals. It was never enough.

I had everything I had been hoping for—a child, and a tenuous grasp on peace that was slowly becoming stronger. My husband would finally lay down his arms.

My power still felt desperate, something wild that was artificially pinned down and aching to be freed, and it never felt more wild and desperate than when I was with Galen, when he looked at me and touched me and said the things that I spent hours turning over in my mind.

I was so close to everything I wanted, and it felt like I would never possibly be happy. I walked the garden twice over, but I still couldn't shake the feeling.

◆

Zeph and Theron both came with me to the Erudium that day, and when Adria and I walked outside the castle, I saw a carriage waiting for me.

"We will walk," I said, directing an imperious stare at Adria.

"It wasn't me," she said quickly.

"My lady, the news of your condition has spread throughout the city. The people are overjoyed for you, and I just want to ensure your safety. Crowds can be dangerous," Zeph told me.

I lifted my head. "Then you will protect me as you so ably do, but I will not take a carriage."

"My lady—" Zeph started.

"Zeph," I interrupted, stepping closer to him and speaking softly. "The carriage makes me ill," I admitted. "And my stomach is uneasy already."

"Oh," he said. He crossed his arms over his big chest. "Hm. How about a horse, then?"

I nodded. "A horse I can manage."

"Theron!" he shouted. "Horses!"

Both guards fussed over me as I mounted the horse, as if I would suddenly tumble from the creature's back and shatter like an egg. I scowled at them both, and they mounted their own horses when they were satisfied I was safe. It was a wonder it didn't take them tying me to the saddle.

"Theron will go first," Zeph told me. "And I'll be behind you and Adria. You must keep going, no matter what, and keep pace with him. Yes?"

I nodded. "Yes."

He nodded once. "Good. After you, my queen."

Theron started riding, and I followed him at a quick canter. The guards opened the gates, and my heart soared as I saw flowers lining the walkway, and then people at the bottom of the slope. At the sight of me they started cheering, and people started pressing in toward us. I didn't even know where people were coming from, but it seemed they were multiplying.

"Faster!" I heard Zeph say behind me, and Theron sped up. The people parted for us, and we sailed through. They blurred around me, hands waving and reaching out for me. I felt them touching me, and spurred my horse.

The crowd thinned away from the castle, but it never dissolved completely. When we arrived at the Erudium, the children were all gathered on the front steps, and they cheered and clapped for me.

People from the city flooded in behind us, and the young men sprang into action, running into a formation to block the others so I could come in. I dismounted, and the children rushed around me, pulling at me and hugging and touching me.

"Back!" Zeph growled, sweeping an arm out to clear the children. They gasped and leaped out of the way. "Is this how the Erudium conducts itself?"

This seemed to mean something to the children, and they all went back to the steps, standing in formation to welcome me. "We have a very special day planned for you, Tri Queen," the praecepta told me. She gestured me forward, and I drew my back up straight, going inside.

When we left, we faced a smaller crowd, still calling to me, waving at me, praising and blessing me and my baby, but not so many that I was frightened. Zeph didn't even insist we ride fast or in any formation, but he and Theron stayed by my side, watchful.

Our route to the Tri Castles wound mostly along the coast, where the road was wide, and it seemed to be traveled more by merchants and wealthy women than the common people, but there was a small stretch where the road narrowed and went by the edge of the Maze, a tight warren of houses in the center of the city. We had just turned the corner where the road shrank, and we could hear shouts and yelling coming from an alley.

"My queen, we should—" Zeph started.

"Theron, would you see what's going on?" I asked him. A scream rang out, and I paled. "Theron, please! Zeph can stay with me."

Zeph nodded his agreement, drawing his sword and circling his horse in front of me and Adria as Theron dismounted and entered the alley. I watched him for a moment, and when I blinked in the sun, I couldn't see him anymore. Adria made a whimpering noise.

The ground shivered, and I clasped my hands, for a moment thinking I had caused it. As soon as I realized it wasn't me, I looked at Zeph.

"Ride!" he roared at me.

I jerked the reins to the side, and my horse jumped into action, only to rear and stop so short I nearly fell as black uniforms flooded to one side and a river of commoners came in from the other. I heard Adria scream and tried to wheel around to look for her, but an arm wrapped around my waist, and I screamed, too, as I was pulled from the saddle.

"My queen!" Zeph shouted in my ear, and I stopped yelling. He dragged me back against a building, crowding me behind him and yanking Adria's wrist. He tossed her behind me and turned, sword drawn, ready to defend me.

But they weren't there for me. The horses bolted, and I could see the fighting. The uniformed Trifectate soldiers were hammering the common men, and it was brutal and bloody.

"What's going on?" Adria yelled, crying on my back.

"Stay down!" Zeph yelled.

My stomach dropped. The wind kicked up, and the soldiers fought harder, cutting down the commoners and executing them in the streets. I watched one soldier not far from us slash a man's throat. The man dropped as a river of blood poured out of his wound, and his eyes searched upward, looking for something. An answer, maybe.

The soldier lunged and impaled a man on his sword, running him cleanly through until the red-stained blade came out the other side. He jerked it out again, but his victim wasn't dead. The man lurched forward with a knife in his hand, and the soldier hacked at his arm. The heavy sword bit deeply and something cracked; the soldier had a hard time pulling his blade free.

When he did, blood sprang up like the world had spun upside down, catching in the wind and bursting in a red spray.

I didn't realize I was crying until Adria put her arms around my shoulders, hugging me from behind, and when I felt a shudder, it wasn't her.

The soldier left the man to fall to his knees in his own blood and moved on to his next victim. This man had two knives, and he was fighting valiantly. He was fast, but his back was turned and he didn't see the soldier coming.

The man turned, and my heart stopped. No matter how little I had seen it in recent years, I would never fail to recognize my brother's face.

"Rian!" I screamed before I could help it. "Rian! *Rian! Rian!*"

Zeph whipped around and covered my mouth.

I didn't even feel the threads this time—it was too fast, like a tide swamping me, and my love for my brother—my fear at seeing him threatened—took over. I curled my fist, and the dirt of the road sprang up, whipping around Rian to slam into the soldier. More and more dirt and rocks and mud welled up like a wave, and in seconds the soldier was flat on his back like he had been buried in the middle of the road.

Rian stopped for one moment and met my eyes, and then he turned back and kept fighting.

The rush of power left me, and the last thing I was aware of was hands, or arms, or something trying to hold me upright, and failing.

Dragon of the Desert

My queen."

Waking felt the way a chick in a shell must; there was a world outside I was aware of, but I saw only darkness until I could pierce through.

"My queen." Zeph's voice helped.

I blinked, and the world was moving sideways. It took me a moment to realize he was carrying me, and we were moving, but the effect on my stomach was the same. "Please, put me down," I begged him, and he obeyed.

Falling to my knees, I vomited into grass on the side of the road. Adria caught my hair and twisted it away, and I saw her pale, tearstained face.

We were close to the beginning of the Royal Causeway. I tried to stand, but my stomach wrenched again and I fell down, vomiting and shaking. When I was done, I leaned against her, and to my shock, she put her arms around me.

"My queen—" Zeph said, not finishing his sentence.

I nodded, using his hand to struggle to my feet. "Yes. Where's Theron?"

"He didn't come back," Zeph told me. My breath caught. "Yet, my queen. We must get you to the castle."

"Only if you go back to look for him the second we arrive," I said.

"I can't leave you unattended, my lady."

"For Theron, you can," I told him.

"Let's get you back, and we'll discuss it. May I carry you?" he asked.

Shaking my head, I walked, Adria to one side and Zeph to the other. I felt dizzy, though, and incredibly weak, and within a few steps Zeph picked me up anyway and started striding so fast Adria nearly had to run to keep up. For once, she didn't complain.

The closed gates opened for us and snapped shut behind us again. Adria stopped in the courtyard, but Zeph kept on going, walking fast to my chambers. He shouted for someone to fetch Kairos. "There are few men I trust to watch over you," he said. "Your brother is certainly one."

With a sigh, I nodded, and in moments I was back in my room, laid upon my bed. A fleet of ishru came in, wetting cloths in cool water and wiping my face and neck and hands. Zeph turned away as they opened my robes to check if I was cut or bleeding.

They covered me up, and moments later Kairos arrived, rushing to me. I heard Osmost shrieking outside. "Go," Kairos told Zeph. "I know why you called me."

Zeph nodded sharply and left, and Kairos sat on the bed, taking my hand.

The moment the door closed I gripped it. "Kai, Rian—Rian was there; you have to make sure he's not hurt!"

He shook his head. "No. Not now. I have to stay right here with you and watch over my niece since you're clearly not thinking of her."

I put my free hand on my stomach, staring at the ceiling, trying to breathe evenly. "We were caught in some kind of skirmish, and Zeph pulled us to the side." Kairos squeezed my hand, and it made my mouth tremble. "They killed so many people, Kai," I whispered. "There was so much blood—and then Rian—Rian was just—and they were going to—"

I couldn't take a deep breath, couldn't breathe properly at all, and Kairos pulled me up, sliding me closer and hugging me tight. He rubbed my back and held me, whispering to me. "Hush, sister. Hush, you can't upset yourself like this. You have to calm down and protect that sweet girl in there," he told me.

Hiccuping and taking a stunted breath, I asked, "You think my child's a girl?"

He nodded against my head. "A tiny little princess."

"Is this a sense, or are you making this up?" I asked him.

"A little of both," he said, and I heard the smile in his voice.

"I used my power," I whispered to him. "I didn't mean to. Someone was going to kill Rian, and it just . . . happened."

He pulled back a little, meeting my eyes, dark and serious. "Don't ever tell anyone that, Shy."

"I know."

"No," he said, shaking his head. "You don't. Something isn't right. Something awful is going to happen, and I can't see it. But I feel like your husband will do it, and I feel like you will pay the price. And whatever it is, it's . . . awful. Unimaginable."

Shivers of cold ran over me. "What kind of awful?"

"I don't know," he said, his mouth tilting up. "'Unimaginable' means I can't quite picture it."

I touched my head to his, wishing he could share the vision—or feeling, or sense, or whatever it was—with me. "We'll be all right, Kai. We're together. We'll be fine."

He hugged me tight. "I hope so, Shy."

I drifted off after a while, gripping Kairos's hand in mine, and I woke when he tried to pry it away. "I'm not going anywhere," he snapped, but the words weren't for me, and my heart sped up.

Sitting up quickly, I felt dizzy but still stood from the bed. There were soldiers in the bedroom, and Calix was with them, and Zeph and Theron were nowhere to be seen.

"Seize him, then," Calix ordered the soldiers, and I grabbed Kai's arm as the men in black uniforms came toward us.

"Calix, no, what are you doing?" I screamed. They grabbed Kai, but they wouldn't touch me, wouldn't separate us.

Calix stormed up to us and pried my hands off him until I cried out, pushing me back so I stumbled and fell.

"Don't touch her!" Kairos roared, throwing off one of his captors and punching another.

They cracked a sword hilt over his head. "No!" I shrieked, struggling to my feet. "What are you doing?"

I tried to run past Calix, but he raised his arm and cracked the back of his hand squarely across my face. The blow was blinding, so hard and fast that I was on the floor without remembering how I got there, pain bursting over and over in my face. Blood dripped onto the floor, and I wasn't sure where it was from.

Everything had stopped. The only thing I could hear was Calix, breathing hard, his face in a snarl as he looked down at me. Kairos had stopped fighting, but he had murder in his eyes, staring at my husband.

"You disloyal desert *bitch*," Calix spat. "You know what we found when we chased down the information we collected? Rian d'Dragyn. Little wonder you didn't want me to act on it. You thought you could *trick* me?" he growled. He stared at me, cowering at his feet, and then turned to look at Kairos. "You and Kairos must have been in league with Rian this entire time. Going behind my back, feeding him information—you both will tell me everything you know of the Resistance. Take him and question him," he ordered.

"Make no mistake," Kairos said, his voice a dark and deadly snarl. "I will repay every wrong you inflict on my sister. I am a Dragon of the desert, and nothing will slake my thirst for vengeance."

"I'm fine, Kairos," I lied, shaking to say it. "I'm fine. Please just go with them."

Kairos didn't even acknowledge my words, and they pushed him out of my chamber.

Calix paced, and I shifted slowly to curl against the wall, still huddled on the ground. "You saw him," he accused. "You had to know he was here."

I shook my head. "You promised me," I told him. "You promised me you wouldn't hurt our people. You were executing them in the streets."

"I lied," he said. "And I'm glad I did. Now we will see what else you're deceiving me about," he said, grabbing my chin and forcing me to look at him.

I pulled away from him, shrinking in a tight ball, protecting my head with my knees.

"Have you lost your mind?"

Danae's voice was clear, and I knew it was her, but I didn't raise my head.

"Her *brother*—" Calix started.

"Did you hit her?" Danae asked, and the voice sounded closer. "You struck the mother of your child? Your wife?"

"She betrayed me!" he roared, and I recoiled, curling tighter. "Rian is in the city—she had to have known about it! She's been helping him all this time. For all I know she's lying about the child too! To manipulate me!"

"Three hells," Danae snapped. "Rian d'Dragyn has been in the city since Father died. She had nothing to do with his being here, and it doesn't sound like you have any proof that she's helping him with *anything*. She isn't lying, and she isn't deceiving you."

There was a long pause. "I want Rian d'Dragyn dead."

I raised my head at this, but Calix wasn't looking at me. He was looking at Danae. Issuing the order.

"Then it will be done." She looked at me. "But you let your temper get the better of you, Calix, and you could have killed your wife and child. And you're *wrong*. I will kill him only when you find a way to make this right with your wife."

"Kai-Kairos," I stammered, looking at her.

Danae frowned. "Kairos? Is he all right?"

"My men are questioning him. Which they will continue to do," Calix snapped. "He may still know something."

"I will stop them, Shalia," she told me.

I nodded, and Calix turned toward me. I cringed.

He sighed. "I was wrong," he said. "Get up."

"Leave," I told him, staring at my knees.

"Shalia," he said, coming closer.

"Please," I said, huddled against the wall, shutting my eyes and wishing it would change what I found when I opened them. "Please leave."

I knew he was angry, but I didn't care. I didn't look up or move, either, so I suppose that belied my bravery.

"Go," Danae said. "You release her brother, and I will take care of her."

I jumped when I heard the door shut. I felt her shadow on me and heard her moving nearby, but I didn't look up until I felt her hand touch my foot.

She was sitting in front of me on the ground, leaning against the wall in the same way I was, reaching out to me. She sighed when I looked up, then stood, getting one of the damp cloths the ishru had left. She knelt down, touching the cloth to my face, and I winced. It came away bloody, and I stared at it.

"There's a cut on your cheek," she said softly. "And it looks like your mouth was bleeding a little too."

She cleaned it, slowly and gently, and I just looked at her, silent.

"You're younger than me—did you know that?" she asked. I shook my head a tiny bit. She nodded. "By more than a year. It's strange. You seem so wise, you know. You're very self-possessed. Strong. And I thought, when he married you, that the better parts of him would prevail." She sighed, rocking back.

"This doesn't surprise you," I said.

"Calix can be very cruel," she told me, lifting her shoulder and not looking at me. "But he can also be protective, and sweet, and loving, when he's not so very afraid."

My eyes shut as my head throbbed. "Will you really kill Rian?" I asked.

She put down the cloth, and the pounding pain in my cheek seemed to get worse. "That's what I do, Shalia. Calix tells me to kill someone, and I do. I don't stop until they're dead."

Anger made me glare at her. "You have a choice. You don't have to do what he says. Danae, *don't* do what he says," I told her. "Please."

She sighed. "Calix never wanted this for me, you know," she said. "I just—after my parents died, there were many attempts on us, particularly on me because I was very young and weak then. It got to the point that I was frightened to go places alone. I thought I was being followed. And then someone poisoned us all, and I almost died. I was sent to live in safety, away from court." She leaned against the wall again, watching me. "And I didn't want to be helpless. I wanted to be more than a rabbit in a snare."

I pressed the cloth to my lip, trying to be calm, trying not to notice the blood building up on the white cloth. "He doesn't deserve your devotion," I told her bitterly.

"He does," she said. "Maybe he doesn't deserve yours, but he deserves mine." She looked away from me. "And I don't want to know of a day when he doesn't, because I won't be welcome here. I won't be welcome anywhere in the Trifectate," she told me. "So I have to be useful. But with any luck, Rian's left the city already."

"If Calix accepted you as you are, everyone else would," I said.

She gave a dry, sad laugh. "Calix doesn't mind that I'm a spy, or an assassin, or whatever else I must be to serve the God. But he'll never forgive finding me kissing another girl when I was thirteen," she told me, shaking her head. "That's too much to ask."

"He loves you," I said. "Why would he care who you kiss?"

Her stare was flat, defiant. "The girl was found below the cliffs the next morning, so I think he cares." She shrugged, and I could only imagine how painful the memory was for her. "You don't seem shocked. Is such a thing common in the desert?"

I pulled the cloth away, dabbing at my cheek again and looking at it. More red, new patterns. "There's a different ceremony if you choose someone of your own sex. Because you can't have children of your own, you can choose a clan and travel with them. It's not common, but it's not strange."

Danae was quiet for many long moments. "In the Trifectate, people like me are meant to be sacrificed to the Three-Faced God. Like the Elementae."

I reached forward and took her hand. She squeezed mine tight.

"Is it throbbing?" she asked, looking at my cheek.

I nodded. "I can't stay here, Danae." Tears pushed up behind my eyes, and the pressure made the pain worse. "I can't *be* here."

She met my eyes, full of warning. "You can't leave, Shalia."

Pulling my hand from hers, I shook my head. "Please. I have to. I can't stay here. Not right now. The tour—why can't I just go to a city now and wave a bit or whatever it is he wishes me to do?"

"They'll see the bruise, Shalia. As bad as things are, they'll be worse if people know that Calix hit you."

A shiver racked my body thinking of Kairos's words. "Will you find Kairos? I don't believe Calix that they'll release him."

"Yes. But, Shalia, you can't—"

"The rebels," I told her. "He can use me as part of his ridiculous reasoning to tear his people apart. Tell them I was injured by the rebels. But I will leave in the morning."

She stood with a sigh. "Well, he'll agree to that."

"I don't give a damn if he agrees," I told her. She extended a hand to help me up, but I shook my head.

She held out her palm for a moment longer, and let it drop. "I know. But, Shalia, if you leave him, if you go to the desert, 'cruel' will not begin to describe the things he will do to your people."

I shuddered. "Yes, I know." She walked to the door, and I watched her. "Danae," I said, and she stopped. "Thank you. For your help, and your honesty. I appreciate both more than you know."

She met my gaze. "I trust you, Shalia. And that's not a simple thing in this court."

She left, and I stayed frozen.

Binding

I slept curled against the wall. When I woke to the first blush of dawn, I asked the ishru to pack things for me and opened the door. Zeph, Theron, and Kairos all stood there in the same clothes from the day before, looking haggard and tired.

"Great Skies," Kai breathed, touching my chin and turning my face a little. I pushed away from him. I hadn't looked at it yet—I didn't want to look at it. Zeph and Theron looked mournful, and Zeph opened his mouth, but I held up a hand.

"You should have slept," I told them. "We're leaving as soon as we can."

Zeph straightened. "Where?" he asked.

"I don't know. Pick a city that my husband wanted me to tour—it doesn't matter. As long as it isn't here."

"Your guard—"

"Take whatever men you need. I'm sure you can figure that out quickly."

Zeph nodded, and when he turned, I saw Adria standing there, her face pale. "You're leaving?" she said, and then a second later her eyes fell on my face. "My queen," she said, her voice soft and urgent. "I heard—I *know* you didn't get that bruise on our way home yesterday."

My eyes widened. I hadn't thought of her—the one person who would notice, and know. "Adria—" I started, but I had no idea what else to say.

Kairos took a step forward, standing between us, his hand on his scimitar's hilt.

"I won't tell," she said quickly, looking between us. Her eyes met mine, deep with meaning, and she continued. "If you don't want me to. It's the sort of thing my father would be very interested in hearing, because of how it might build sentiment against your husband among the vestai. So I won't tell—unless you want me to."

I shook my head. That didn't seem like a solution. "I don't know what I want. But I'd prefer if you didn't tell. You should go, Adria. I don't think it would be for the best if Calix saw you now."

She drew a deep breath and nodded.

"Shy," Kairos said, and I turned to him as she walked away.

Tears filled my eyes as I looked him over. "You're all right?" I asked. "They didn't hurt you?"

"Not badly."

I covered my mouth.

"Shy, I'm fine. You're not," he said. His voice dropped. "If we're leaving, we should head north. To the desert."

I shook my head. "First we leave. Then we'll discuss what to do next."

His mouth folded down, but he nodded. "Very well."

The ishru packed in a flurry while I dressed, and from the small room where my clothes were, I heard voices raised. My heart tightened, and I finished dressing, winding a length of purple fabric around my head to make a hood—for as long as I could, I wanted to hide my face, and hide the marks that my husband had put there.

I opened the door to find my brother leaning casually in the doorframe, facing out, his arms crossed over his chest, standing between me and the rest of the room.

"Kai?" I whispered.

"The queen does not wish to—" Zeph was saying, but Calix tried to push past him and Theron.

"I will cut off your hands if you keep me from my wife," Calix snarled.

"Don't do that," Kairos murmured, even before I moved around him, fury rising within me.

"I have had *enough* of your threats," I yelled at Calix, standing well behind Zeph and Theron where I could see him without being close to him. Kairos crossed in front of me like a cat, noting the distance, his hands inching near his scimitar. He was wearing the second one now, something desert men usually only did in war. "How dare you fault these men for protecting me when *you* assaulted me?"

"Shalia, I need to speak to you without them here," he told me.

Shame and anger made my throat thick around my words. "Why?" I asked. "You don't think they know what you did?"

"Shalia, you have to see, it's not my fault. It's your family, your damn brother, they come between us at every turn!"

Kairos crossed his arms. "Which brother would that be?" he asked.

"Both of you," Calix snarled back at him.

Kairos smiled. "There are more where we came from, you know. All sorts of brothers getting in your way. Imagine what my littlest sister could do."

Calix's eyes narrowed on him.

"Is that what you think?" I whispered, trembling. "You believe that my *family* made you strike me? Made you hate the Elementae, made you gouge the eyes out of that guard, made you—you are *cruel*, Calix," I cried. "You're *cruel*. My family had nothing to do with that. You would rather demean and maim and . . . and kill people than truly work for peace."

"No?" he asked. "Rian has undermined me at every turn. It was *him*, you know. Him who stole her from me. He has always sought to steal what's mine. But you, my wife—I love you despite these things. I love you and our child more than *anything*, and I was a fool to be blinded by your brother's treachery. Please don't go. Please let me make this up to you."

I was trembling, but I shook my head.

"You're weak, and tired," he said. "You're not in any condition to be traveling."

"I can't *look* at you," I told him, my voice full of steel and ice. Even the light movement of my cheek burned. "I can't stay here. I can't listen to you and these awful things anymore. I can't keep crying because my face is swollen and sore, and I just want to stop hurting so much, Calix."

He didn't say anything, and I looked to Zeph. "Please," I said. "We should leave."

He nodded once, and he and Theron shifted so Zeph could lead me out and Theron could block Calix.

"Shalia!" Calix shouted, and I flinched away from him. He looked shocked by this, but Kairos put his arm around me, blocking my view of my husband, and shepherded me out.

By the time I reached the courtyard, ten guards, my brother, and my belongings were waiting for me. A saddled horse stood, flicking his tail restlessly, and I hesitated as I got close. Usually I didn't have any problem getting into the saddle, but I felt weak and shaky still; I didn't think my muscles would hold.

"Here," Galen said, appearing from behind me. I jumped, and he glanced at my face and the purple cloth that covered it, but he looked away before he could have truly seen beneath the hood. He knitted his fingers together and held them out.

My heart beat faster as I watched him, but he didn't lift his eyes to me, just staring at my foot, which wasn't moving toward his hand.

He cleared his throat, and I raised my foot, putting it into his hands.

I grabbed the saddle and he pushed me up, raising me high and fast so I could mount the horse. "Thank you," I said, my heart racing.

He nodded sharply and went toward another horse.

Kairos saw Calix before I did, and he moved his horse between me and the wide entrance to the castle. Osmost leaped off Kairos's shoulder to take to the sky, like he was as ready to defend me as my brother was.

Standing in the archway in his black clothing, Calix looked small and insignificant, like an insect. But I couldn't help the shiver within me.

"I will give you two days, wife," he called. "If you don't return before that, I will bring you back."

"It will take longer," Galen said, walking toward him, standing at the bottom of the walkway. "We're going to Trizala."

I blinked, looking at him. He was coming with us?

Calix came slowly down the walkway, and I felt every step closer to me like a growing threat. "Pick another city."

"She'll like Trizala," Galen said. "We'll be back in three days at the earliest."

Calix glared at his brother. "Fine."

"Oh, and, Calix?" Galen said, closing the several feet between them. Calix looked at him, and Galen drew his arm back, launching his fist into his brother's jaw. Calix stumbled back and Galen turned away, shaking out his fist as he went to his horse and mounted it.

Calix straightened and watched me as he wiped blood from his mouth. "I love you, wife. Don't forget that."

I turned away.

Galen called for the gates to be opened, and he led us out, guards ahead of me and behind, and Zeph and Theron both exhausted on either side of me.

We rode through the city, Galen keeping a slow pace as we passed a few people, who all shied away from the sight of so many men. It wasn't long before the cluster of the city faded into farmland, and the road was wider, and we still rode slowly.

"Is there a reason we're going so slow?" I asked Zeph. Osmost was making lazy circles in the sky, searching for prey, lacking a challenge.

Zeph's jaw rolled a bit. "I believe out of concern for your health, my queen."

I pushed my shoulders back. "Then if it's out of concern for me, we can go much, much faster," I told him.

"My queen—" he started, but I wheeled my horse to the side of the column and spurred the stallion onward.

Every jarring hammer of the horse's hooves felt like power, like strength, like something solid and whole. My heart beat stronger with the effort, and I craved it just to remember what it felt like to have my heart race with something other than fear.

My horse thundered past Galen at the start of the column, and I didn't look at him as I went charging onward. My horse seemed desperate to run, as desperate to stretch his legs as I was to feel that freedom, and he kept on, strong and powerful.

I heard another horse, and I turned to see Galen riding hard to catch me, a stormy look on his face. I turned forward, urging my horse on faster, delaying his angry lecture as long as I could.

Galen's horse was bigger, and faster, and he caught up to me. I expected him to take the reins from me, to yell at me to stop—something. It never came, and he rode beside me, galloping along the country road until I was heaving for breath, my chest burning for air, my muscles bright and sore, like I was finally alive. Finally awake.

I kept on, even as it hurt and burned, even as I felt every harsh breath like it was fanning the pain in my cheek, my blood rushing doubly hard there.

I only slowed when Galen fell behind. I drew the reins of my horse gently, and he eased out of his gallop. Galen caught up, coming astride me as my horse began to walk. "Three hells," he said, smiling at me as he panted hard.

Emotions flooded in with that one rare smile. My heart was still pounding; it rushed with something hot and dizzying. But like a physical reminder of the things that kept us apart, when I tried to smile back, the pain forced the look from my face.

My hood had blown back, and he saw how I couldn't smile, and his eyes rested on my cheek. I broke his gaze, looking behind us to where Zeph and Theron were ahead of the others, but still struggling to catch up. I tugged the hood back up, making sure it covered my face.

"I didn't know you could ride like that," Galen said, facing forward.

"I'm not terribly good at it," I told him.

Another smile came to his face, and I wanted to pluck this off, treasure it, collect his smiles from him. "I've never met a woman who wanted to ride so damn fast," he said with a laugh.

"I can't stand sitting about," I told him.

"Which must be why you walk," he said, nodding.

"I walk for an hour each day. Maybe even less," I told him. "In the desert, we'd walk for whole days in the hot sun. To go somewhere. For food, water, shelter. For a purpose. There's no purpose here."

He was watching me. I could feel it, but I didn't turn to him. "It's half the reason I like fighting," he said. "The practice. Hours a day, moving, hitting, running. Sweating until your heart is pounding," he said, placing his hand on his chest. I couldn't help it—I looked at the hand, his broad chest rising under it.

I nodded.

"Court is a little useless," he admitted.

"I thought I would have a purpose," I confessed. "I wanted being queen to be about something more than just being his wife. And I understood, when I arrived, that perhaps I could have that, but only if I fought for it. I'm not afraid of that."

He glanced at me. "You've done tremendous things, Shalia."

I shook my head. "That is not the word for them. I've done things—things I am proud of—but I don't know that they've made any difference. I keep waiting for the sands to shift, and I thought that this child would be the change we needed. And then he lied to me, and killed yet more people, and did this."

He stayed silent, listening to me.

"Maybe I was wrong."

His eyebrow rose. "About what?"

About telling Rian that his Resistance was foolish. About trying to change Calix. About believing that this country could be saved through peace. I sighed. At least that last one was safe enough to be repeated. "About believing peace is even possible."

His mouth pursed, and he nodded. "I spent a lot of time reading as a child," he told me. I tried to imagine the battle-hard warrior with his broken nose in a book. "Histories, mostly. Of war, and such." His shoulders lifted. "I was meant to be the military commander from a very young age. It seemed wise. But there have been many rebellions, followed by many wars. In the history of our country, and others. The Trifectate started as a rebellion of a small group of people who were thought at the time to be religious fanatics. When there is a rebellion, no party comes out unscathed. The whole country bears a scar so deep that no one in that generation comes out the victor, not truly. They've lost so much, even if they won the conflict, that it ceases to matter. Perhaps the next—perhaps the children the survivors sire will have the chance to know prosperity in their lifetime."

He was silent for a long time, our horses gently clopping along in tandem.

"I know every man in the army. They've all crossed my path at least once. If I choose to believe that peace is impossible, I have to be willing to see every one of those men die." He looked at me, and the green was bright, catching the light of the sun. "Your costs are different, but no less high."

My hands settled on my stomach, and I thought of all the people I would watch Calix endanger over the life of our marriage. I thought, too, of the people who he would punish if I never returned to the Tri City. Either way there was blood. I shut my eyes.

"Why is it so important to go to the desert?" Galen asked. "With the baby, I mean."

I felt my cheeks flush. "I'm surprised that Calix took it seriously enough to mention it. He dismissed it when I brought it up."

He stayed silent, his stony face impassive, and I wondered if Calix had passed it on the same way.

"It's a blessing," I said after a moment. "The clans—we're nomadic people. We travel the desert for weeks, months at a time. But when there's a new clan member, they need to know the way back to Jitra. They need to be able to find their feet, and find their heart. So we journey to Jitra, and before they're even born, they're blessed in the water there. With all the clan around, so they will know family, and home, and love. No matter where sands and stone take them, they will know these things."

He cleared his throat and nodded. "That would be a beautiful thing to give to any child."

I sighed. "He won't consider it. He knows it's important to me, and he won't consider it."

His mouth opened, and it closed again, and he squinted into the distance. Several moments later, he didn't turn to me, but he asked, "Do you love him?"

Heat rushed to my face, but I wasn't sure why. It seemed like such an easy question, but it wasn't a simple answer. "Sometimes I think I cursed myself," I admitted. "I saw Calix, in Jitra, before the wedding, and he was handsome. I wished . . ." My embarrassment, my foolishness choked my words. "I wished for him. For him to be my husband. Because I thought it was that easy—I would marry a handsome king and love him. Why would I not? I've never met a married couple who were not at least tremendous friends, if not deeply in love. And I thought it would feel powerful, and overwhelming, like a sandstorm." I flushed, thinking of the jolt in the earth when Galen removed my veil. "And then I understood that I had only a sheltered young girl's idea of love, and more likely, love is something that grows between two people. And there are moments when he's kind to me, or thoughtful, and I feel something like hope—but I hate those moments more than any other, because they mean that I am beginning to mistake the absence of cruelty for love."

His throat worked, and he looked down and back up again. "You know the difference," he said. "You can't possibly care about people the way you do and not understand what it means to be truly loved in return."

I laughed, embarrassed but warmed by his words. "I don't know. But I do believe that my parents are very lucky. They love each other so very much."

"Was their marriage arranged?" he asked.

"Of sorts," I said. "My father was about to become the leader of d'Dragyn, and he wanted to marry. There were only so many suitable women across d'Falcos or d'Skorpios, and my mother was the sister of the man who would become the Falcon."

"So the position is passed from father to son?" he asked.

"No," I said. "Well, in a manner. The clan leader will groom someone for the position; often it is a child of theirs, but not always. The clan leader must be the strongest, the most fit to lead. It doesn't happen often, but if need be, the leader will select someone outside his family." I smiled. "So I suppose you could say their marriage was arranged."

"So was there ever someone else?" Galen asked, and his mouth teased at a smile.

"For my parents?" I asked, horrified. "*No.* They loved each other from the start."

He laughed, and it was unexpected. "For you," he said. "Surely you can't have grown up thinking you'd marry Calix. What plans did you have for your life?"

"I thought I'd be just like my mother," I admitted. "There's a d'Skorpios boy around my age, Alekso. He was being groomed, and my brothers had met him and said he would be a good leader. I figured that was all there was to it—he would be my husband, and as soon as he removed my veil we would fall wildly in love and have seven children." Even I had to laugh at how that sounded now, and Galen chuckled with me. The laugh stung my cheek, and I sobered. "How life has changed in a few short months," I said.

But he had caught the bit of information I had accidentally betrayed. "Your *husband* is meant to remove the veil?" he asked.

Blood rushed into my face, pounding beneath the bruise. "Yes," I said, glancing at him.

He met my eyes. "No one told us that."

"They wouldn't have," I said. "Certainly not after it happened. The unveiling is supposed to be a spiritual connection—a binding. Some higher power. It's supposed to be the husband who unveils his wife, revealing her to him. The start of their life together. The forging of their bond." I gave him a sad smile.

"And I unveiled you," he said, his voice low. "Not my brother."

His eyes met mine. They looked bright and unnaturally green, regarding me in a way that made my skin tingle and shiver, the sensation as delicious as it was dangerous. I tore my eyes away from him. "I shouldn't have told you that."

"No," he said, and I glanced back to him. He was gazing ahead, sitting straighter, with a ghost of a smug smile on his face. "I'm glad you did."

Trizala

With another stretch of breathless galloping in the afternoon, we made Trizala well after nightfall; I almost regretted my fast rides that brought us to this strange new city without the light to see by.

Galen said we were getting close when the road rose steeply, the horses slowly climbing switchbacks cut into a mountain. It was dark, and the growing height made me uneasy, but Galen seemed confident and sure, and I followed close behind him.

After another turn, Galen stopped as we faced a wall, a stone gate bridged right over the road.

"Open the gate for the Trifectate Queen!" he bellowed.

"Open the gate!" someone called back.

Without us seeing how, the gate slowly rose until we could pass easily with our horses, and Galen ducked his head and rode into the dark shadow. I followed him, holding my breath.

A torch illuminated the dark area, and the man holding it bowed. Galen nodded to him without saying anything, and rode on.

The city was built into the mountain, houses balanced along the road, which continued in switchbacks up the mountain. As we continued higher, the houses were more elaborate and huge, carved into the rock itself.

"It's like Jitra," I marveled. "I never knew there was another city like this."

Galen turned around, one side of his mouth winging upward. "I thought you'd like it. I figured you'd feel safe here."

He turned around front, and it took me a moment to spur my horse to follow him. Perhaps I was just starved for affection, but his thoughtfulness touched my heart.

We kept going until we crested the mountain. At the top, there was a great flat space carved out between the mountains, and it was lit with a hundred torches. People were gathered there, a man who I guessed was a vestai and his family, and I dismounted, taking in the grand spectacle of it. Peering off the edge into the night, I could only get a rough sense of the sweep and beauty of this view; it felt like a rich, dark mystery, full of promise.

"Definitely crafted by Elementae," Kairos said, coming up behind me. "Maybe you're *not* the first Elementa from the desert, you know. Jitra would make a lot more sense."

I looked at the rocks. "Maybe," I whispered back.

He put his hands on my shoulders. "How are you feeling?"

Leaning against him, I smiled the small bit that my bruise would allow. "Free," I told him.

Like a good brother, he didn't remind me that was a lie, even as his hawk wheeled around us and dove for something in the dark, the only creature here that was really free to do as he pleased. Kairos just rubbed warmth into my shoulders and stood behind me.

◆

Vestai Nikan brought us to his stronghold, tucked into the mountains. The rooms were all carved stone, cool and dark, and walking into them, I felt my power bubbling around me. Not triggered or pulled, nothing to do with me—just preexisting and natural.

Zeph and Theron went into my chamber while I waited in the hall. Galen stood across from me, close enough that our feet were nearly touching, and Kai wandered up and down the hall, restless, looking at everything.

"What will we do here?" I asked, glancing around. "In my rush to leave, I hadn't thought what I would actually be doing."

"Whatever you wish," Galen told me. "I would recommend addressing the people at some point. Vestai Nikan is planning a feast in your honor tomorrow night."

I nodded. "Thank you," I told him.

Galen didn't look at me. "Of course." Zeph emerged and nodded, Theron coming out a moment behind him. "Secure?" Galen asked.

"Yes, sir. My queen," Zeph said, gesturing me into the room.

"You're not going to stay here, are you?" I asked them.

"Kairos and I will sleep next door," Galen told me. "But yes, they will absolutely stay here."

"They haven't slept, and they've been riding all day. Can't one of the others stay here?" I asked.

"Theron will sleep and I'll watch over you, my queen," Zeph told me. "I'll be fine waiting until tomorrow."

"But you won't be sharp," Kairos said. "I'll stay the night, and then I'll sleep during the day tomorrow while Shy performs whatever queenly duties she must."

Zeph frowned.

"Very well," Galen said. "Just for tonight."

Kairos stepped closer to my door, and the muscles of Zeph's arms tightened. "My queen," he said, looking at the ground. "I won't offer you an apology. I don't deserve your forgiveness, and you shouldn't give it to me. But please know that I will regret failing you for the rest of my days," he said.

"There's nothing to forgive," I told him. "You couldn't have changed anything that happened yesterday."

"My queen—" Theron started.

I held up a hand. "I grew up with six brothers. Five of whom were older than me."

"I'm aware," Kairos said drily.

I gave him a look. "I understand that I'm bruised, and that you all care very much about my safety and my health. You care about chivalry and what a woman may or may not deserve. And I treasure that. Your concern means a great deal to me. But your guilt isn't about me, or my body, or my pain. It's about Calix, and it's about you seeing me as a thing that needs to be protected, like I shattered when he h-hit me."

They all looked at me as my voice failed me for a moment, and I pressed my lips together, trying to stop more unwanted emotions from rushing out.

"I don't want to feel broken. I don't want to give him that power. Calix did not—and will never—break me. So don't apologize, and if you must feel guilty, then share that with someone other than me. Do you understand?"

They all nodded grimly.

"I hope this is the last we have to discuss it," I told them.

Zeph nodded, nudging the others away. He, at least, understood when he was dismissed.

Galen glanced at me and turned away, following my guards. Kairos slipped inside my room before I could shut the door.

I shut it behind him with a sigh. He went to the windows, gazing out into the darkness, looking at the windows themselves. "Well," he said. "We should be able to get pretty far before they realize you're gone." He turned back to me. "If we're leaving."

Drawing a breath, I shook my head slowly. "We can't leave, Kairos. Or I can't leave. But I think you should go back to the desert."

He snorted. "Like hell," he said. "Why would I ever leave you alone after all that's happened?"

"Because he won't hurt me the way he'll hurt you," I said, squeezing my hands together, trying to stop the trembles that came anyway.

"I swore a promise," he said, crossing his arms. "I'll make him regret what he's done to you."

"No," I said, looking at him. "*No*. This," I said, fingering the bruise on my face, "is a distraction. Yesterday Calix proved that he's not interested in peace. Maybe he's interested in submission; maybe he wants war. Maybe he doesn't care. But I still want peace, Kairos."

He lifted his shoulders. "How can you get it if he doesn't want it?"

"That's what I need to figure out. But it is not so simple as running back to the desert—or anywhere—when he still has men there. We cannot risk more lives." I looked out the window, into the dark that was dotted with torchlight in a strange pattern. "The greater question is whether peace can ever be achieved with Calix as king."

He drew a long breath. "Rian believes it can't."

I tucked my hands around myself, rubbing warmth into my arms. "And if I believe that, then it would make sense to join Rian. To help the Resistance."

Kairos's eyes flicked to the wall, reminding me that my guards were likely next door, not to mention my husband's brother. "Have you considered other options?"

I looked to him. "Such as?"

"Waiting until your child is born, and then removing Calix."

I shuddered, shaking my head.

He looked at me, and he appeared so much older suddenly. "None of these options will let him live, Shalia. If he lives, then there will be no peace."

I thought of Galen, of seeing every face of every soldier and choosing their deaths and calling it peace.

"Besides, you may not have that long," Kairos said. "Your power is growing stronger. It seems like it's harder for you to control it. If he ever sees it, baby or not, your choices—if not your life—will be taken away."

I nodded. "I know."

"The desert can repel the Trifectate men who are there. It would only take a note from Osmost, and it would be done. We could run right now."

I shook my head. "No. It's rash, and it's risky. Besides, Galen and the Saepia will pay the price for it. I won't bring that on their heads after all they've done for me. I need more time to think. That's why we came here," I told him.

His mouth drew tight, but he didn't disagree with me. "Very well."

"Do you know if Rian is safe?" I asked.

He shook his head. "No. But we would have heard by now if he wasn't."

I sighed. "I suppose."

He came forward and kissed my cheek. "Good night, Shy."

After everything that happened, it wasn't my husband hitting me that haunted my dreams. It was the attack in the Tri City, seeing the soldier hack into the man's arm without cutting it off completely. A gaping wound with a geyser of blood.

In my dream it sprayed all over me, hot and soaking my hair, my skin, my clothes.

I woke up with a scream, and Kairos was in the room before I was fully awake, his double swords unsheathed and ready. Shaking my head, I told him, "A dream."

"I'll stay in here until you fall asleep," he told me.

I shook my head. "That may be a while." I got out of the bed, pulling one of my thickest coats around me. "It's colder up here, isn't it?"

He nodded, and I went to the small basin of water. I dipped my hands in it, splashing water carefully on my face. I looked up and my reflection stared back at me, my brown cheek stained purple and black, the area around the cut swollen and red.

"It feels fake," I told him. "The way it looks—this isn't my face."

Kairos's lip curled. "Wait until you see how colorful bruises can look on his pale skin."

"You can't hit the king, Kai."

"Galen got to," he grunted.

"Calix isn't your brother."

"Brother by marriage."

"Besides," I told him, with as much of a smile as I could muster, "you were never the brother who hit back. You were the one to put a scorpion in a bedroll."

He looked at me, calculating and dangerous. "Yes," he said. "So just imagine what your husband has earned."

I looked at him. "Perhaps I'm the scorpion in that situation."

"You're a daughter of the desert, Shalia. You have always had the ability to pierce and sting."

"It's getting close to dawn; do you want to take a walk with me?"

He grunted. "No. I'm exhausted. But I will if you want to."

I nodded. "I won't tax you. I just want to see the world outside."

He went and opened the door. "After you, Shy."

I walked through the door, and we went down the hallway side by side. The hallway led to a huge room and the platform at the top of the city beyond that, and the areas were deserted. "Maybe it's earlier than I thought," I murmured to him.

"It definitely is," he grumbled.

We went outside, and a wind immediately whipped around us. It was still dark, in the shadow of the mountain, but at the edge of the world a pale blue light spread over the sky, and I had my first look at the deep valley and the city we had come up through. The city dropped sharply downward into green grass coating the bottom of the valley, cresting up into gray-blue mountains and trees, rolling out like the ocean made green and immobile.

Kai stood beside me, looking out. "I need to say something, and I don't know what to say about it," Kai said, pushing out a breath. With his hands clasped behind his back, he looked so much like Father that it stole my breath for a moment. "I want to ask if I should be worried about Galen. He chose this place to comfort you, and that . . . means something, Shalia."

I opened my mouth to speak, but he shook his head.

"And then I thought, maybe I should speak to him—play the big brother like Cael or Rian would. Threaten him, accuse him, poke his chest or something. Or maybe speak to you and warn you of the way he looks at you. But I think you know, don't you?"

My mouth was dry, but as I glanced down, heat didn't just fill my cheeks—I felt it rush around my chest and heart, and flutter in my stomach. Yes, I knew what Kairos meant. I nodded.

"And you look at him too."

Slower now, I nodded again. I still wasn't sure what it meant, but yes, I had looked at Galen in the same manner he'd looked at me.

"And that's as far as it's gone."

Nod.

He sighed. "I should do all those things. But instead I'll just say that I want you to be happy, and I want you to be safe. Unfortunately, I don't know that you can have both at the same time right now."

I looked down. "I don't know that I can have either, Kai."

He put his arm around me. "One day. One day."

Leaning against him, I watched as the sky grew brighter, slowly illuminating the mountain around us. Soaked in new light, I felt the threads against my hands, tingling and strong.

I pulled away from Kairos, going to the back of the flattened platform. There was an outcrop in the rocks maybe fifty feet up, and I desperately wanted to climb.

I put my hands to the rock, searching for a handhold, and it felt warm, like it moved against me to feel my touch. The threads were weaving together, tight and substantial enough to be fabric.

"Shalia," Kairos said, grabbing my waist. "Do I need to remind you you're with child?"

I slapped his hands, and he let me go. "I don't think I could hurt myself here if I tried," I told him, gazing up rather wondrously at the rock. "I feel . . . tied to it somehow."

He lifted an eyebrow, watching me go. The climb was quick and easy—everywhere I put my hand or foot, the rock responded, giving me a hold on it.

"Shy!" Kairos protested.

I stopped, glancing down at him. I looked at the space between us curiously.

"I wonder," I said softly. I curled the threads around my fingers and tugged through them gently.

The rock shook a little, and Kai shouted my name again, but the mountain was already moving. Small pieces falling and breaking, pushing back and jutting forward, as the stone shifted and changed beneath me—until a perfect staircase was cut into the mountain face, connecting me and my brother.

I was breathing heavily, stunned and a little winded.

"Great Skies," Kairos murmured, stepping up tentatively.

The staircase went all the way to the outcrop. I climbed the stairs, sitting on the flat rock while Kairos came up behind me. He squatted down. "That was incredible," he said. "I've known what Kata was for a long time, but I never saw her use her power like that."

I sighed, feeling the weariness in my bones. "Honestly, it was a little more exhausting than I expected."

"Stay up here. I'll get you something to drink," he told me.

I nodded.

He went down the stairs quickly, trotting inside.

Rolling my shoulders, I rubbed my neck a little. It helped my discomfort, my weakness, but as that eased, there was something else. My power was humming, tense, alive—and insistent.

Curling the threads around my fingers, I felt a tightness to it, like the threads had all been interwoven to form a dense, strong fabric. Following it upward with my gaze, I saw a small opening in the rock.

Osmost screamed and sailed past my head, landing on the lip of the opening. He stood there and shook his wings out at me, calling me forward.

Slowly, I got to my feet. Rather than climb this time, I called up a set of stairs first—narrow and steep, but leading straight to the mouth. Drawing a deep breath and feeling the rocks buzzing back at me, I started up the steps.

I was breathing hard by the time I reached the lip. There was an arch carved out of the rock and it went straight through, leaving a small chamber within. The carving was too smooth and perfect to have been made by man or nature—it was an Elementae dwelling.

The threads felt thickened, pulsing with life and energy and making my breath rush faster. The wind swept through the open space powerfully, and I felt like it was trying to push me away. I pressed on against it, seeing two bowls on pedestals the height of my waist on either side of the room. One, I could see from several paces away, was full of fire, still burning, despite the wind and the fact that there was no evidence of a way someone other than me had been there—or could have even breached such a place.

I went toward the other bowl. It was full of liquid, but it was too shadowed and still to tell what it was.

"Water," I realized, walking toward the middle of the space. I could see for miles in either direction, out into the bluish darkness of uninhabitable mountains and back over the lightening blush of the valley. The wind pushed at my skirts and my hair, cooling my skin. "Wind. Fire. *Earth.*"

The second I stepped in the center, the nexus of the four elements, the threads around me snapped. I felt my power like a growing thing, rising from the rock and weaving through my skin. The rush—the power—was unlike anything I had ever known, like it was wrapping me and seeping into me at the same moment.

Like this place was the source. Like it was the fount of my power.

Drawing a deep breath, I pulled myself out of the center, and it was only then that I noticed the dark stain where I had stood. It was old, months old at least. Perhaps because of my awareness of this place, I knew what it was without explaining it—blood. And more than that, I suspected I knew who it belonged to.

Kata had been here. This was the Earth Aede. This was the place she had visited, the place where my power had retreated when harm had been done to it, when my husband sought to wipe it from the face of the earth. It had been waiting for Kata to come and align it with the other elements, waiting to be free.

Without knowing it, Galen had brought me to the source of my strength. The source of my power.

I held up my hands. This power coursing through me was eternal, indestructible, but I was not. I only had a finite amount of time with this gift, and I was wasting it, watching as others with my power were tortured, experimented upon, hunted, and killed.

I would not stand idly by anymore.

My heart beating hard, rushing my blood fast and powerfully through my veins, making me both shiver and feel superhuman in the same intoxicating moment, I went back to the mouth of the cave and looked out.

My hands rested over my stomach. I couldn't feel her in there yet, but I knew in that moment she would never be raised by Calix. Maybe I would have to wait until she was born, or maybe Kairos and I could find a way to stand with the Resistance before then, but I would not let her come into a world where she watched her mother stand passively to the side.

I was trembling with the frightening clarity of my thoughts, but slowly I walked down the stairs back to the outcrop Kairos had left me on. With barely a thought, the staircase to the site shifted and faded back into rock, and pressing my hand to my heart, I sat down on the outcrop.

It was only moments later that Zeph, Theron, and two other guards came racing out, Galen shouting orders at them to search the city.

"What's going on?" I called.

Galen halted, spinning around and taking long moments before looking up enough to see my perch.

"What in three hells are you doing!" he roared, his hands on his hips.

I folded my hands in my lap. "I couldn't sleep. I came out here."

I saw Zeph lean in, and from the scowl that Galen returned to him, I wondered if Zeph had previously offered a similar explanation.

"What's going on?" I asked. "What are you looking for?"

"*You*," he said crossly. "You weren't there, your brother wasn't there, I thought you . . ." He trailed off.

"Ran away?" Kairos asked, coming from another exit with a skin of liquid. Osmost swooped and landed on his shoulder, and he walked past Galen without looking concerned. "I tried to convince her to."

This made Galen's glare worse. "Well, what on earth are you doing up there?" he demanded. "You're climbing? In your condition?"

Kairos raised an eyebrow as he stepped onto the stairs.

I saw color in Galen's cheeks. "Oh, hells," Galen said, turning away. "Do whatever you want."

Zeph chuckled.

Kairos climbed up and handed me the skin. "It's some kind of juice they make from flowers," he told me.

"Thank you," I said as he sat beside me, letting his legs hang off the edge. "Why don't you all come up here?" I called. "The sun will rise any minute."

Zeph and Theron seemed to take this as an order from me and immediately started trotting up the staircase. Galen crossed his arms and drew a long breath, making his chest rise under his arms. He looked up at me, and even at such a distance, meeting his eyes hit me hard.

I wondered if he would come with me if I joined the Resistance.

He let out the breath and climbed the stairs.

Zeph and Theron crested the outcrop, and Zeph sprawled out on the rock beside me, while Theron stood behind us. Galen was slow climbing the stairs, and I turned to see where he was. He was stopped, a few stairs below the top, and he was looking at all of us, at the rock, at the sky. His throat worked, and his eyes skittered around again as he took another step.

Was he scared of heights? Surely calling attention to it wouldn't soothe his pride. I met his gaze, questioning, and his throat bobbed again, but he came to the top of the stairs, and stood beside Theron. Galen clasped his hands behind his back, and we all waited in silence as the blue blushed to pink, then to a bright orange, then the whole sky burned with the raging color and light that matched my traitorous heart, and the true, full beauty of Trizala was revealed.

Control

The vestai's wife took us on a tour of the city that lasted most of the day. With little sleep and after the exertions of the day and night before, my strength wasn't what it should have been. It worked to my advantage, though, when I was allowed to rest and their people came to greet me, bringing me babies and children to kiss like it was a blessing.

I kept my purple hood off. Everyone asked me the questions with or without it, and after the first time or two of issuing the lie, Galen answered for me, telling curious folk that the Resistance had staged a rebellious act and soldiers had had to put it down while I was caught in the middle of it. I was grateful. The words turned to ash on my tongue.

That afternoon, I ate a little and promptly vomited it back up. Thoroughly exhausted, I went to lie down in my chamber, not expecting to sleep.

My baby seemed to have other ideas, however, and I woke to Galen gently shaking my shoulder. The big windows showed nothing but darkness, and I yawned.

"I missed the sunset," I said.

His eyebrows pulled together. "You fell asleep," he told me.

Sitting up in the bed, I saw he had a plate of food in one hand. "What's that?"

"The vestai's wife made these," he said, pointing to pale, hard-looking squares. "They're baked ground grains. She said they were the only thing she could eat when she was in her first few months with her sons."

I took one, biting into the crisp edge. It didn't have much flavor at all, and I could see why they would be easy to stomach. I nodded, taking another bite.

"We shouldn't have ridden like that yesterday," he said. "That was irresponsible of me."

"No," I said, shaking my head. "I needed that far more than I needed not to."

"Still."

I finished the first and took another crisp square.

"Why didn't you leave?" he asked me, not looking at me. "This morning, when I thought you were gone—I was a little relieved," he admitted, his voice soft.

"Relieved?" I repeated. My heart lurched in my chest, thinking of my bold thoughts this morning.

He was looking at the stone walls. "That you weren't going back to him."

I shook my head. "There are too many people at risk," I told him. "I have to go back." *For now. Until I can figure out how to leave him safely.*

He glanced at me, then away, opening his mouth.

"Are you afraid of heights?" I asked quickly, spitting out crumbs to try to speak before he could.

He looked at me, offended and confused. "What? No."

"You can tell me if you are. This morning, on the rock, you looked . . ." *Scared.* "Uneasy."

His head whipped away from me. "I'm not afraid of heights," he snapped, going closer to the window.

"What was it, then?" I asked. "It's all right if you are."

"Three hells, Shalia, I'm not afraid of *heights*," he growled. "I think I'm a little afraid of *you*."

My eyes blinked wide at this.

He looked at me, leaning against the window ledge and crossing his arms. "You just—you don't realize what you do. Zeph and Theron—they're hardened killers, but they're puppies for you. And Kairos loves you. You just—you make people love you, Shalia. And I'm not talking about—about other sorts of love. It just looked—it felt—it looked like a family. Like a family is supposed to feel."

I pushed the food away, putting my legs off the side of the bed slowly, like he was an animal and might spook. Things tumbled through my mind, about his sister, his brother, his father. "Family frightens you," I said softly.

"No," he said, shaking his head, resolutely looking at the ground. "Wanting family frightens me."

I stood, staying close to the bed. "Why?"

A dark red color flushed through his cheeks, even as the muscles in his jaw rolled and bunched. "I've committed a lot of sins in the name of family," he said, his voice low and harsh, like the sound was caught in his throat.

"But it's different, isn't it?" I asked.

He looked at me, and I felt like I was standing too close to him suddenly, because there was something open and raw in his eyes. "Wanting a woman?" he asked. "Children? It's different."

Imagining him with some other woman and with some other children felt different—and sharp—too. "But still frightening."

His eyes shut, and every muscle in his face looked tense. "Yes. I can't want that, Shalia."

I waited. I knew I didn't have to say the word for him to know that I was waiting to hear *why*.

His throat worked, and his voice was rougher when he spoke. "I'm no good at caring about people." His eyes opened, and the openness there betrayed something new, a wound inside him that he'd never let me see before.

My skin prickled a warning, but I stepped closer. My heart ached for him, for his loneliness, for his pain. I reached for his hand, to reassure him with a touch like I would my brothers, but I couldn't. It would be different, and *more*. I cleared my throat and let my hand fall, trying to sound steady and strong. "I think you're wrong. But your believing that matters much more."

For long heartbeats, I looked at him, and he stared into my eyes. His mouth opened and closed, and whatever more there was to say, neither of us could find the words to say it.

I stepped back. "I assume you came to get me for the feast?" I asked.

He nodded.

"Give me a moment to change."

He stood still for a moment, then bowed his head and left.

The feast was served on a wide platform at the top of the mountain, a beautiful scene lit by flickering torchlight. The vestai's wife was kind enough to make a few more items she thought I could stomach, and I ate my first full meal in days by virtue of it. When musicians started to play, the city folk immediately jumped up to dance. Within moments I saw a pretty girl teaching Kairos the dance.

It wasn't terribly hard—it seemed like a slightly slower version of the dances we did in the desert. There was a lot of jumping and swinging, but instead of a group, this was done with just two people, turning each other around while you held on to your partner.

"Does the queen know our dances?" Vestai Nikan asked, bowing in front of me.

"I don't," I told him.

"May I have the honor of teaching you?" he said, straightening up and extending his hand.

"Be gentle, Niki!" his wife warned.

"Yes, please!" I said with a careful smile that didn't push my cheeks up as I put my hand in his.

He led my hand to his hip, and he put his on my opposite hip so we could hold on to each other. He was gentle and quite respectful, but as we danced I saw how this could be so thrilling, to hold your love tight and whirl around under the stars.

One of the vestai's teenage sons stole me from his father, and he held me much tighter and closer, so our bodies were pressed side by side as we turned and jumped. He smiled wolfishly, holding me closer still as the dance went on.

The musicians paused for a moment, and we stopped jumping. I pulled away from the vestai's son, thanking him for the dance. He stepped forward like he meant to ask me for another as the musicians started again, but I found a new hand on my hip.

"My turn, Niko," Galen told the young man. The boy scoffed, but he bowed out.

I shivered as Galen's hand took a firmer hold of my hip. "This might be a terrible idea," I whispered to him.

He nodded, but his eyes were locked on mine. I barely felt the motion as we began to dance, until the first jump brought us closer, his hard chest and side supporting me. He swung me faster, and a nervous, happy laugh bubbled out of me.

As the dance sped up, I forgot to be so conscious of him and we just danced together. He was good at it, fast and strong, and as he spun me around, I tilted back to look up at the stars, glittering overhead.

He pulled me back up as the dance ended, and we were face-to-face, chest-to-chest, breathing hard.

My eyes dropped, and I couldn't stop staring at his lips, the way his breath rasped out over them, making his bottom lip shiver the tiniest amount.

Kiss him.

I pulled back sharply. I'd never consciously wanted to kiss someone in my whole entire life. As soon as it occurred to me, I couldn't stop thinking it, and the idea alone caused my stomach to twist in a lovely, nervous way that made my whole body warm.

Trying to make it look like I wasn't running away from him completely, I went back to the vestai and his wife, and within a moment made my excuses. I shook my hands, my traitorous hands, going to the far side of the platform. The vestai's wife had shown us a cave that morning, and I went there, thinking that if I ran into Galen on the way to my room, I would—I would—I didn't know.

I couldn't possibly find out.

The cave was sharply colder, lit by a few torches. I took a deep breath for the first time since my dance with Galen began. I stared at the walls; I had wanted to come back here because it reminded me so much of Jitra, and I found myself running my fingers over the walls, trying to draw on my family to calm my racing heart, my traitorous mind.

"Shalia," Galen called, and I shut my eyes, not turning around.

"You shouldn't have followed me," I whispered.

"I know," he said, and it was so low it was nearly a growl.

I turned around and felt my power rush around my hands. He was so handsome, and the way he looked at me—no one had ever looked at me like that. Made me feel the things he could. "Why did you?" I breathed. "Why did you come here at all?"

"I lied before," he said. His throat worked. "It's not that I'm not good at caring about people. I care so damn much I feel like I'm going to snap in half. People are no good at caring about me," he said. "Except you."

Heat flooded through me, and I stepped closer to him. Taller than his brother, taller than me, he was the perfect height for me to tilt my mouth up to him.

And I did. I didn't think, I just moved, closing the gap between us. For a second we hovered close, and I felt heat radiating out from his mouth, brushing over mine and making me shiver with want. Our lips touched, and my heart felt like it burst in my chest.

His mouth covered me, his lips damp as they slid over mine, matching and twisting until it felt like something was sealed between the two of us. His tongue touched mine, and lightning burst through my body, making my limbs jerk against him. My hands crawled over his chest, touching and feeling, memorizing.

He made a sound into my mouth, his arms clasping around my lower back, pulling me up and against him in a way that felt like it revealed what we were meant for. Every bit of his body that was against mine was like a thunderstorm, hot and damp and sparking. His arms unclasped to touch me, his hands running along my sides that suddenly felt so sensitive and ticklish that I was twisting against him, holding on to his shoulders like an anchor.

His hands came up to span my shoulders, holding me strong and close, and he broke our kiss, his mouth dropping to my neck.

I gasped, fisting my hands in his uniform jacket. I heard him chuckle as he kissed me again, right along the pulse in my throat.

"I don't—" I whimpered.

He stopped, pulling back. "Don't what?" he panted.

"Don't know how—is it *supposed* to feel like this?" I asked.

"Does it feel good?" he asked.

I nodded, pressing my face against his head. He kissed my neck again, and warmth jolted through my skin.

"Then yes," he told me. His arms changed, coming around me gently and rubbing like he was hugging me, really holding me as he kissed my neck.

I dug my fingers into his hair, and he leaned up, kissing me again. He shuffled back until he was against the wall, holding me tight against him, and his tongue dipped deeply into my mouth. When Calix did that, it always felt like an attack, but this was different. Shyly, I pushed my tongue forward along his, and he groaned.

A powerful shiver ran through me at the noise he made.

My hands moved, eager to touch him, pushing off his jacket and feeling the heat of his skin rising through his shirt. He tugged my coat off one shoulder, and instead of cold, my bare skin felt electric and alive.

I pushed at his shirt, wanting his skin, wanting to make him feel as uncontained as he made me feel. My coat dropped off me as I found his hem, sliding my hands underneath, up along his chest.

He shivered as our mouths broke apart. He blinked, looking at my face, stroking my hair back. "You're so beautiful," he breathed over my lips.

Feeling dizzy, I pushed his shirt up higher, pressing a kiss to the bare skin over his heart. I looked up at him, and his hands went tighter on me. "You're—" I started, but something bright caught my eye.

Turning, I gasped, shrinking back from him.

The cave had changed. Crystals were jutting out of the walls, bright and glittering; one torch was now fused to the wall, covered over by square purple rocks.

The torchlight twisted and moved, and new colors caught my eye. There was a swirl of blue veins dancing over glittering white quartz, a line of jagged, angular dark charcoal spikes. The floor was covered over with green, crystals that were as lush and vibrant as the color of his eyes. It was everywhere, like a physical manifestation of how much he made me feel.

Embarrassed and frightened, I covered my mouth, trembling. I looked at Galen, and he was taking it all in.

"Shalia," he said, his chest still heaving for breath. His hands balled into fists as he looked at me. "Oh, God, Shalia."

"I can . . . explain," I breathed.

"No," he said, shaking his head. "No, you cannot explain this. Do you understand? You can't say the words that would explain this. Not to me, not to *anyone*."

I just stared at him.

"Not to *anyone*!" he roared. He turned and started kicking a crystal, chipping bits of it off, then snapping it, leaving rough, broken shards.

"Stop!" I cried, not daring to step toward him. "You'll hurt yourself!"

He wheeled around. "Me? *Me?* Shalia," he said, his voice softening. He came back to me, and I gasped, but his hands slid over my neck, cupping my face. "Shalia, if Calix ever finds this out—"

I nodded, the feel of his hands on me making calm and warmth rush through me. "I know."

"You *don't*," he insisted. "Do you have any idea what we found when we went into the Summer Palace?" I pulled out of his grasp, but he didn't stop, eager to torment me with his words. "I found bodies of—" Galen halted, swallowing, his jaw tense. "He made a device to transfer blood into another living thing, and he tried it on animals, birds. Humans. A girl. Until she ran out. Until she had no more blood left. He's the one who *devised* these tortures."

I was shaking, hard enough that a crystal I was leaning against cut my arm. "Don't tell me these things," I whimpered.

He came closer to me and touched my cheek. "Shalia, you have to leave. You have to run. He won't just kill you. He'll torture you, and then he'll use your death to make a point. You have to go."

"I can't," I whispered. "I will not just *run away.*"

His forehead touched mine, so lightly. "Please."

"I can't!" I snapped at him, pulling away. "You know I can't. He will come after my family. He will break peace with the desert."

"Let him!" Galen cried. "They can fight for themselves! They have before!"

"I'm having his *child*!" I yelled. "If I run, he would never just let me go. Never. He would hunt me, and find me, and punish everyone involved, including the whole of the desert. And I will not see my family die in the process."

"And what about *you*?" he demanded.

"No," I snapped. "What about *you*? You're the commander of his armies, Galen. You command every sword he has at his disposal, and you would have me run! Subverting his evil acts is not the same as changing his soul! What line must he cross for you to stop defending him?"

He stepped back, bracing his hands on his hips. "If he ever raised a hand to you in front of me, I would *kill* him. I don't think I could stop myself," he said, lifting his eyes to meet mine. They looked dark, and dangerous, and they struck something deep within me. "Is that what you want? Do you want me to kill my brother?"

My mouth opened; "yes" hovered on my lips. It would be easy. I was sure he could do it, and perhaps, if I asked him, he would. I covered my mouth with my fingers. "No," I said. "I would never ask that of you."

"But it would be better, wouldn't it?" he said. "If Calix were just to die. Everyone's life would be better, wouldn't it?"

My eyes moved over him. "Is that what you want?" I asked, my voice going soft.

His jaw tightened, and he nodded. "I've imagined it."

"But you haven't done it."

He drew a deep breath. "He's my brother. And more than that, I just—I don't believe that more violence will help anything. Killing him would destabilize everything—the crown would fall to the vestai, and they would make thrice-damned short work of starting a civil war over which one of them deserves the most power."

"His death would not be the end of the violence," I finished.

He swallowed. "No. It would be the start of war. And worse . . . I can't say I'm not responsible, Shalia."

My blood ran cold, and I feared another horrible admission from his mouth.

He looked at me. "He became who he is to *save* me. And Danae. There were threats, and attempts—one nearly succeeded. One of the vestai poisoned all three of us, and it nearly killed Danae. I was sick for weeks. When my brother found out who was responsible, he didn't hesitate. He killed him, in cold blood, with no trial, with no delay." Galen's eyes shone with pain as he stared at me, as if he was willing me to condemn him. "I was relieved, Shalia. I was grateful. That I was safe, that my sister was safe. Whatever he has become, it's partially my fault. And I owe it to him to bring him back from this. Whether I like it or not, I cannot give up on him." His head dropped. "But seeing that bruise on your face—this is the closest I've ever come in my whole life to it. For him to hit you when he claims to love you—to blame it on your *family*—perhaps that is the line. Perhaps he is too far gone. And perhaps I am a coward because I refuse to see it and act."

I stepped closer to him, putting my fingers above his elbows. His skin shivered under my touch. "Don't say that. It's not your fault. It's the same as blaming it on my family—he will act as he wishes and he will find an explanation for it later. That doesn't mean you're to blame."

He didn't say anything, but his arms opened, twining around me, pulling me tight against him, and I hugged him, his hands in fists on my back.

"There's still hope," I whispered. "Maybe he doesn't want peace, but I do. You do. We can change him, Galen. We can be stronger than his hate. This baby can be stronger than his hate."

"Shalia," he said into my hair. "You don't understand. You can't go back to the Tri City. He can never discover this, and we'll never have another opportunity to get you away from him."

My shoulders lifted, tugging away from him. "No. He has men in the desert; it's too much of a risk."

"Shalia—"

"You cannot tell me to run when you decide to stay and fight! You cannot tell me to sacrifice my family when you're trying to protect yours!"

"That's *not* the same thing!" he shouted, shaking his head. "He will *hurt* you! *Physically* hurt you, Shalia!"

"He already has!" I yelled, pointing at my face.

"This is worse!" he roared. "And you're not just risking yourself—you're risking your child!"

"I can control my power!" I yelled back.

He flung his arms wide. "This doesn't look like control!"

I shook my head, walking for the mouth of the cave. "Believe me, the things that trigger my power won't be a problem anymore. And they never were with Calix anyway."

He caught my arm, and I pulled away. "Trigger?" he asked. "What things?"

He reached for my arm again, and I stopped. "You will *not* touch me when I don't want to be touched. Do you understand that? Maybe I can't stop your brother—and maybe for that, I'm a coward too—but you will *not* touch me."

Galen stood still for a moment, and at the look in his eyes, I doubted everything I said. He looked cut open, and vulnerable, and I wanted so badly to be the one to protect him for once. To cover that vulnerability and show him he deserved to be loved.

But I wouldn't. Not now, not if it meant running while he stood and fought. I strode for the mouth, where I saw Theron and Zeph guarding the entrance. Where they could most likely hear everything. And even if they hadn't, I'm sure they had their guesses, or they would have come inside.

Shame burned on my face, and I nearly ran back to my chamber. Theron followed close behind, and Zeph stepped in front of Galen.

He didn't dare yell after me with people so near, but I could feel his anger and reproach on my back. I didn't care.

I knew that his anger would keep me safe—without his touch, without the stolen looks that irrepressibly opened my heart to his, I wouldn't lose control of my power again. Nothing else called my power up so forcefully.

And yet it felt like the fragile thing between us had shattered, and of all the horrible things that had happened in the previous days, it was the most devastating.

It would keep me safe, and it broke my heart.

An Anthill

We returned to the City of Three long after dark on the third day. I had wanted to defy my husband's mandate, but after fighting with Galen, I didn't have it in me. We rode the whole day long, and by the time we returned, I could barely hold myself upright and my stomach was tight in knots at the thought of seeing Calix.

The Royal Causeway was lined with guards holding torches, and it made me shiver. Calix must have ordered them there to wait for me, like a burning sign of his displeasure, a display of his power.

At the beginning of the causeway, I stopped, causing all the guards and men around me to stop as well. I dismounted, slipping from the horse, drawing new breath when my feet struck the ground.

Kairos jumped off his own horse without a word and stood by me, half a step back. I started walking, and he walked with me, Osmost happily chirping out clicks from his shoulder.

"Shalia," Galen called. "What are you doing?"

"We are Dragon," Kairos said. "We are desert born. And our feet will never fail us."

"Three hells," I heard him mutter. "You really think it's wise to remind him of that right now?"

Maybe it wasn't wise, but this, with my feet on the ground, walking forward, this was how I knew my own strength. I knew the power in my feet, my legs, my muscles, my body. And the only thing I wanted when I saw my husband again, the husband I couldn't leave, the man who terrified me and fathered my child, was to feel my own strength and know it wasn't something he could take away.

If the guards stayed on their horses, they didn't pass us. I could feel Galen's steps not far behind me, and I continued up the steep rise of the causeway.

We crested the courtyard, and I released a breath I'd been holding. Calix wasn't there, even though I was certain his guards reported that I had returned. It made the hair rise on the back of my neck, wondering what kind of confrontation awaited me.

Galen took my horse and ordered Zeph and Theron to follow me back to my room. We went in silence, Zeph moving ahead to open the door for me.

I walked over the threshold and halted.

"My queen?" Zeph asked, peering around me.

There were flower petals in a thick layer on the floor. The doors were open and the breeze ruffled the top layer of petals so they twisted and skittered over the others. They were beautiful, white and pinks and purples, and a few brushed over my feet.

Zeph turned to the guard who had stood there during the day. "Who entered the queen's chamber?" he demanded.

"Just the king," the guard said.

Zeph frowned, but I stepped forward, wading through the flower petals. A few were blowing outside, like they were leading me that way. "Calix?" I called.

I saw something on the balcony. Sliding my feet through the petals and letting them rush over my skin, I went out. Flower petals tumbled around a table with two chairs, more flowers, and a man with his back to me.

For a few moments I had the foolish hope that this whole life was different, that all the awful things that had come before were erased, and the husband who stood there to greet me was Galen, my brave and handsome defender, a man who would never give up even when it seemed utterly bleak.

Calix turned and smiled at me, and something inside me broke a little more.

I stopped, and Calix came to me, sliding his hand on my hip and kissing my cheek. I turned away.

He sighed and stepped back. "I know you're angry with me, my love."

"I'm not angry," I told him. "I'm bruised, and betrayed, and furious. I'm confused and wondering if you're even the kind of man I can allow near my child."

His throat worked. "Don't joke about that, Shalia."

"Calix, you *struck* me," I told him. "Why would I let you do that to our child? Or let our child see you do such to me?"

"I'm sorry, Shalia. That's why I did all this," he said, sweeping his arms out over the table. "To show you I'm sorry. What I did—it won't happen again. Never."

Chills ran over me, and I knew the words I was about to say would anger him, but they had to be said. "Another promise. I don't *believe* you, Calix," I told him.

He stepped forward, but I skittered back. "Shalia," he said with a sigh. "I know. I know you can't trust my words right now, but I will make it right with you. This child is everything to me. *You* are everything to me, and the thought that you have been away from me—*hating* me for what I did to you—I've been sick. I can't bear to think that I could lose you."

There was bitterness on my tongue. "You can't lose me. You *know* that I can't leave you or turn from you. This whole apology is yet another show, another *act*—" I halted.

"My love," he murmured, coming close to me and rubbing my arms, chafing warmth into my cold skin.

I pulled away from him, feeling sick at his touch.

"Shalia," he said. "Please."

"I don't want you to touch me right now, Calix," I whispered.

He stepped away, shaking his head. "Punish me all you like, my love. I more than deserve it."

A wild hiccup rose in my chest. "Punish you?" I repeated. "Calix, I feel *sick* when you touch me. Because I'm afraid of you, and ashamed, and terrified for our child. And I can't just pretend that away."

"Striking you—letting my temper overrule my judgment—that was a grave mistake. It will never happen again. And I will spend the rest of my life making it up to you, Shalia. I promise you that." He sighed, walking closer, and I cringed, but he went into the room.

I drew a shaky breath, trying to calm my heart, but it was short lived. He reappeared a moment later, putting a coat around my shoulders. "You're cold, love."

His fingers lingered long enough for me to shudder, but he pulled away before I could open my mouth. I slipped my arms into the sleeves of the coat, turning around. "Thank you."

He stepped back. "Come. The cooks have prepared a special meal for us, and I want to prove to you that I do care for you. You're my wife and the mother of my child, and that means something to me."

I looked at the table, crossing my arms. "How will you do that, Calix?"

He glanced around. "All of this is for you, my love. All of it."

"And it's a lovely gesture. But it proves nothing."

He reached toward my hand, but I pulled away, shaking my head.

"I know I was wrong to say that your family was the reason . . . well. I was wrong. I know now, that as long as you have family on this earth, you'll love them as much as I want you to love me. It's only natural, and more than that, it's part of why I think you will be an amazing mother. And, well, I wanted to wait to surprise you, but I did hear you when you told me how important it was to you to go to the desert. I know there are many problems between us, and chief among them is that you think I don't hear you, and I don't listen to you. But I do, my love. So I think we should go to Jitra. If it means so much to you to have the baby blessed by your clan, they can gather there and bless him, yes?"

I blinked, looking up at him. "What?"

He nodded, his mouth twitching toward a smile. "Would that please you?"

My mother, pressing her hands to my stomach and smiling at me. My father, glowering at Calix and protecting me. My brothers, standing beside me always. Catryn, crawling into my bed to sleep curled against me. Little Gavan, hearing that he would be an uncle. All of us, dancing until the cavern shook to welcome my baby with joy.

I couldn't breathe, covering my heart, relief racking me so hard it felt like pain. Calix stepped forward and halted. "It doesn't please you," he said.

"It does," I told him. "It does, it does." Drawing in a slow breath, I looked at him and nodded. "Thank you, Calix. This means the world to me."

"I know," he said. "I want to give you the world. I want to make you happy, Shalia, and I'll give you all the time you need until you're happy with me. So, will you please eat dinner with me?"

I drew a shaky breath, but I nodded. I still didn't want his hands on me, I still didn't trust him, but it was certainly a start.

When I woke early and alone, Zeph was at my door to take me for a walk.

Kairos was waiting for me at the cliff walk, and I smiled, shaking my head. "How do you know when I'll be here?" I asked, delighted.

He kissed my uninjured cheek. "My sister. Always with the silly questions," he said. "Zeph?"

Zeph sat on the step and waved us forward, relaxing in a beam of weak morning sun like a gigantic cat.

The path was just wide enough for us to walk side by side. "How are you feeling?" he asked.

My shoulders lifted. "I slept well. I just feel . . . worn. Tired."

"You weren't eating much in Trizala."

I touched my stomach. "I don't quite understand why some things make me ill and others don't."

"We will find things you can eat. My niece will be well fed," he said, nodding once.

I smiled. "It won't always be like this. I remember Mother was usually terribly ill for the first few months, and then she was very healthy."

"Did you have problems with him last night?" Kairos asked, glancing back toward the castle.

"No," I said. "I told him I don't want him near me. He said he would respect that, for now."

"You did?" he asked, his eyebrows shooting up.

I nodded. "I can't stand the thought of him right now, much less the idea of him touching me, kissing me." I shuddered.

"With someone like him, that's a dangerous choice," he told me.

"At this point, it isn't something I can choose differently." I sighed.

"You weren't at dinner last night," Kairos said. "I heard Calix made some sort of gesture for you."

"The court knows of that?" I asked. "They know what he . . . was making up for?"

"No," Kai said. "They were all whispering that he was showering you with presents, that he's so madly in love with you."

I crossed my arms, remembering the chill of the night before. "He's allowing me to go to the desert for the blessing."

Kairos grunted. "Allowing you."

My shoulders shrugged up. "It's an opportunity, Kai."

His eyebrow arched, questioning.

I stopped on the path, taking a deep breath and looking at him. "I won't see my daughter raised here," I told him. "We need to speak to Rian and figure out the best plan to get away from here. To leave without hiding, without endangering the desert."

His chest swelled with a deep breath. "You want to fight."

I nodded.

He let the breath out. "Good. I'll contact Kata, and Rian. We'll figure out a plan."

I sighed. "I confess, the thought of seeing Mother, and Father, and everyone again is soothing to me."

He looked me over and nodded. "I know. It's strange being away from them for so long, isn't it? And it's only been a few months."

"If that isn't the right opportunity for me to leave, I want you to stay with the clans," I told him.

He chuckled. "Not a chance. No matter what, our brothers will know of his treatment of you, and you will have a new, desert-born Saepia. I would write to them of it already, but they would invade the damn city."

The thought felt warmer than my coat. To have family around again, to feel protected and safe—I'd grown up itching to get away from the protection of my brothers, and now it was all I wanted. "They can't come. They have their own lives, Kai. You know that."

He put his arm around me. "And they would leave everything to defend their sister. Even Gavan will try to come."

I nodded. "A few more weeks, then. We can last a few more weeks, can't we?"

He kissed my temple. "You can last through anything, sister. Don't ever think otherwise. You're much stronger than he is."

I covered his hand on my shoulder. "At least now we know what that awful feeling you had was about," I told him. "Certainly things can't get much worse than they are."

He didn't move.

"Kai?" I asked, turning to him. "It was about Calix hitting me, wasn't it?"

He shook his head. "No," he said. "If anything, the feeling has grown worse. And I can't explain it, but it's not simply about you or me; we are at the crux of it, but it's like an anthill. There is a center, and something dark is streaming away from that center. Growing over the earth."

My mouth fell into a grim line. I shook my head. "No. We will make it a few more weeks, and get to the desert, and all will be well."

He didn't lie to me. He didn't say anything.

Yellow Powder

The procession to Jitra was slow. It was far slower than our first trip from the desert—what had been a four-day journey to the City of Three took us more than a week.

Everywhere we went, people lined the roads, desperate to see us, to touch me, to throw flowers at my feet. We seemed to go out of our way to stop at several castles and cities—mostly so I could be fed only to retch my food back up, but also so that the army could go ahead of us and ensure the safety of our route.

My husband was in a startlingly good mood. In the weeks since he'd struck me, Calix was considerate, kind, nearly affectionate with me, and still respectful of the distance I asked him to keep. He oversaw all the preparations for our journey with a zeal that disarmed me.

"Maybe there's hope," I told Kairos on the fourth day. We were riding together, the carriage just ahead, and Galen and my guards on horses behind us.

"He was attentive to you at dinner," Kairos allowed. "That doesn't mean he's a different man, Shalia."

"I know," I told him. "I know that. But it gives me hope that he *could* be. That isn't so wrong, is it?"

He looked at me fondly, but it made me feel foolish. "No. It isn't wrong. But does it mean that we won't be leaving in the desert? All the arrangements have been made."

I sighed. "I don't know. Every time I imagine it, I feel uneasy. I think Kata's plan to wait until after the baby is born is smarter, but we will never have so many men as we do in the desert. I feel like the moment I see Mother and Father, I'll know what to do."

He nodded. "They're ready to eject the Trifectate. They can do that after we leave, if you prefer."

He looked weary. "You aren't sleeping well?" I asked.

He shook his head. "No. I thought it would be better once we left the capital, but the feeling grows far worse. When I do sleep, I dream of being buried alive. Being choked on dirt and earth and ash."

Shivers ran over me. "You don't think—my power—"

"No," he said quickly. "No, the whole thing—it tastes of hate. And hate is not something in your heart, Shalia. Certainly not in your gift."

"What can we do?" I asked him. "How can we stop it?"

He shook his head. "I don't know. I'm hoping the visions will show me how to stop it, but I can't control them. I can't make them show me anything."

I nudged my horse closer to his so I could take his hand. "And trying means you're not sleeping."

His shoulders lifted, and he squeezed his hand in mine. "I have to try."

He let my hand go. "I wish we would move faster. I'm so desperate just to *be* there. It seems so long since we've been home," I said.

Kairos's smile was weak. "We're nomadic, Shalia. We don't really have a home."

I grinned at him. "You know what I mean. Family. The whole clan gathered to celebrate."

He nodded. "It will be wonderful."

His expression fell quickly, though, and I could tell he was weary to the point of pain. Whatever these visions were, they were taking an awful toll on him.

By the seventh day, we were climbing higher into the mountains, and the air was growing dry and warm. We had eaten at the castle we'd stayed at during the night, but barely an hour into the ride my stomach twisted hard.

"Oh," I yelped, dropping from my horse fast enough that I almost fell, voiding my stomach on the side of the road. The dirt was packed hard, and the mess splashed onto my dress and coat, and I even got a little in my hair.

"Shy?" Kairos said, helping me up.

I was staring at my hair. "I can't—I thought we would make the desert by nightfall." I felt suddenly and stupidly close to tears. "I don't want them to see me with vomit in my hair. And on my *dress*," I told him. "I hate being sick all the time."

"I know," he told me, putting his arm around my back.

"Ugh," I said, bending over as I retched again. There wasn't much more to come up, but it hurt, my body trying hard to expel things that weren't there.

"My love?" I heard Calix ask behind me. "Are you all right?"

"She will be in a moment," Kairos said, braiding my hair fast away from my face.

My stomach heaved again, and I straightened afterward, nodding. I rinsed my mouth with some water, staying close to Kairos like I might fall over. "I want to walk for a little while," I told Calix.

"Love, you look like you're about to pass out as it is," he told me gently. "You should ride in the carriage."

I clutched my stomach at the thought. "No, I think that will make it worse."

He sighed, but nodded. "Very well." He turned and shouted orders to his guards, that we would travel only as fast as I was walking. He kissed my temple, but he didn't stay beside me, going instead to his carriage, calling one of his quaesitori to ride with him. Kairos stayed off his horse, and Galen and Zeph appeared behind me.

"Shouldn't you be riding?" I asked, glancing at them.

Zeph stretched. "I feel like a walk. Don't you, Commander?"

"Damned relief, if you ask me," Galen said.

I shook my head, but smiled at them.

"Besides, I protect the Princess-in-Progress," Zeph said, looking at my belly.

I covered the bump with my hands. "We don't know it's a girl," I said, casting a wary glance at the carriage ahead. I didn't think my husband would be pleased at the thought. "And that is not a real title."

"It should be," Zeph insisted.

"I'm very excited to see Zeph as the Baby Guard," Kairos said. "I've never seen him frightened of something."

Zeph looked offended. "I'm excellent with children," he grumbled.

"You look like you're excellent at eating children," Kairos told him.

Galen laughed at this. "Children, maybe. But a baby? I can't think you'd have any idea what to do with it."

Zeph cast around as if taking on challengers. "I will be a formidable Baby Guard. This is not up for debate. And besides, the baby is a part of the queen, and I protect the queen. And I'm good at that, so I'll be good at protecting the baby."

I giggled. "I have no doubt, Zeph. You'll probably be the first to give her a sword."

Zeph lit up at this, but Galen shook his head. "Now, wait a moment, no sharp objects until she's at least . . . thirteen."

Laughing, I smiled at Galen. It felt forbidden and strange—we hadn't been alone since Trizala, and though I thought of our kiss constantly, the pain from the argument that followed seemed more real, a heavy weight in my chest. Being able to speak with him and laugh with him now when it had happened so rarely since Trizala felt suddenly intimate. "Thirteen?" I asked. "That's a little specific."

He crossed his arms. "Well, I want her to know how to wield a weapon before boys start coming around."

Kairos smiled. "What boys? They'll have to go through all of us and half the Dragyn clan to get to her."

Galen smiled and nodded at Kairos. "I like that line of thought."

"Great Skies," I said, shaking my head. "You all know so little. This girl will have you all in knots before she's a year."

"When you say 'Great Skies,'" Galen asked, lacing his arms behind his back and stepping closer to me, "is that a god?"

I felt the threads shiver closer to my fingers at the nearness of him. "We don't have gods," I told him. "We have spirits. But we consider the sky to be a sort of deity, I suppose. There are people who can tell the future in the clouds, and we live and die by what we see above us. Our lives are very dependent on the weather and climate."

He nodded. "Do you pray to the skies?"

"We talk to the skies. Thank the skies for bounties—when we go to the desert, the ceremony to bless the baby is asking the skies for good fortune."

"Does the sky ever respond?"

I laughed at this. "Of course! We speak to the sky, and the sky always speaks back in his own way. Rain, sun, clouds, lightning—these are the sky's way of talking."

Galen glanced up. "What is the sky saying now?"

There were few clouds, a gentle heat, and a bright, round sun. "The sky wants us to get to the desert," I told him. "He's making it easy for us."

He smiled. "It's strange to think that you don't have a god to judge your actions. To pass down edicts."

My shoulders lifted. "The sky is something far beyond my understanding. If something must judge, or dictate—to me, that seems little more than a powerful man, doesn't it?" My eyes strayed dangerously close to the carriage with Calix in it.

"Maybe," he said, and his eyes followed mine.

I drew in a deep breath. My head was throbbing; my whole body ached from retching so often.

"You're in pain?" he asked, turning toward me a little.

"Just my head," I told him. "As thrilling as it must seem, voiding my stomach every other time I eat isn't very pleasant."

"And here I was so jealous," he said, brushing my hair off my face. His hand settled on my shoulder, reaching under my braid to rub my neck.

"Oh," I murmured, leaning into his touch, ignoring the danger of his skin on mine because of the relief it brought me. "Keep doing that. That helps."

"When we were in Trizala," he said, taking advantage of the closeness to speak quietly to me, "and you said your power is triggered by something—what is it?"

He was so close, and the others had drifted back. Whether it was his hand on my neck or the words or what they called up inside me, warmth rushed through my skin. "That's not fair," I told him. "Bargaining a neck rub for information."

His big hand was warm, spanning over my neck and softening my muscles. "I'm quite ruthless."

My eyes met his for a tantalizing second before I pulled away, and losing his hand on my neck seemed to shoot nausea to my stomach. "I can't, Galen. Not here, not ever."

He sighed, but stepped closer and resumed gently rubbing my skin. "Why?"

"*You* said we can't talk about it."

"No one can hear," he whispered. Without moving much, I saw Zeph and Kairos laughing, almost five paces back, and no one else near us. "Every day I think about the haunting things you say. That you've been imagining things between us. That something—something we did or said or felt in that cave triggers what you can do. What is it, Shalia?"

Anger bubbled up inside me, and I pulled away again, turning to face him. "No, Galen. You can't do this. *We* can't do this. And you already know—or you suspect, at least," I hissed, trying to keep my voice down. "You want to hear me say that I care about you? Will that make it easier when I have your brother's child?

When he ceases to honor the fact that I don't want him to touch me? Will that *help*?"

Galen looked stunned. Then he looked away, shaking his head like he was trying to clear it. I looked over my shoulder and caught Kairos's watchful gaze, but kept walking. "Wait," Galen said. "There are many, many things in what you just said. Your power is triggered by l—" He stopped, and didn't say that word. "Caring? About people?"

I nodded.

"When I returned home from the south and met you in the courtyard, the stones fell apart into sand. Was that you?"

My face burned with heat. I nodded.

"It happened almost the moment I kissed your hand," he said.

I had hoped he would never put that together. "Galen," I said, shaking my head in warning. It wasn't wise to *think* about that, much less discuss it.

He looked ahead, a strange expression on his handsome face, his chest rising and falling faster than was merited by our walk. "And he hasn't—he hasn't touched you?" His eyes slid to me at this, running over me like a physical touch.

I crossed my arms. "I thought my guards reported to you."

Color bloomed on his cheeks. "Not about that."

"No," I said, looking down. "Not since he struck me."

He nodded. "That's a good reason."

Chewing my lip for a moment, I hesitated to add, "There are many reasons."

He looked to me in question.

"I just can't stand the thought of him touching me," I whispered. "Not after . . . Trizala."

"He took that surprisingly well," Galen said.

I shrugged my shoulders. "He wanted a baby, and now he has one. Besides, he's trying to prove to me that he actually cares about me." I shook my head. "I don't believe him."

I couldn't look at him, even though I felt his eyes on me. "I can't imagine anyone not caring for you," he told me in a soft, gentle murmur.

I tried to laugh, but it didn't quite come out that way.

"Here," he said, passing me water. "You should drink more."

I nodded, taking a sip. I passed it back to him, rubbing my own neck.

He watched my hand. "I'm sorry," he said, soft. "I shouldn't have brought any of this up."

"No," I told him with a sigh. "You shouldn't have."

"I feel like my whole life, I'm desperately trying to hide who I am. And with you, I think you just see it. Or it seems that way." His shoulder lifted. "I can't help myself."

I nodded. "I wish it were different. You deserve to have someone who sees you."

"You do too," he said. "You deserve someone who loves you."

Pulling my coat tighter, I looked at the ground and walked a little faster.

We didn't make the desert by nightfall. We stopped at Vestai Atalo's castle, and he and his wife made a great fuss over me, saying their bedroom with the stars in the ceiling must have given us a child so soon.

We returned to the room with the bathing chamber, and Calix ordered the servants to draw a bath for me. When I slipped into the water, he ordered them out. "May I come in?" Calix asked from the doorway.

I looked at him. He was watching my body through the water, and I felt exposed. "Calix," I murmured, covering myself, looking away from him.

"I just want to talk. Is that all right?" he asked.

I considered for a moment, then nodded.

He came in, sitting beside the bath. "Do you remember the first night we spent here?" he asked.

I nodded again.

"You washed my feet for me," he said. "No one had done something so simple and selfless like that for me in a very long time. I never wanted to love you, Shalia, not after everything with Amandana. But that night, I started to care for you."

I stared at the surface of the water.

"I did an awful thing to you, Shalia. But I did it because I thought you were just like her. I thought you were deceiving me. But it occurs to me, we haven't had much opportunity for the truth between us."

My eyes shifted over to him, surprised. "No," I agreed.

"Is there anything you want to tell me?" he asked, meeting my gaze. "Confess to me?"

I hugged my knees in the water. He couldn't possibly know, could he? I had so many secrets, but no—I couldn't trust him with any of them. "No, Calix," I said softly. "Is there anything you want to tell me?"

A muscle in his jaw twitched. "Danae took a sorcerer to the lake," he said. "They still couldn't find it. I need to know if you will support me damaging the lake—draining it, or blasting around it to find what's hidden."

I frowned. "If you find some indication that the elixir is there, we can discuss the means to retrieve it. But damaging the lake isn't just about the elixir—it's the water reserve for the desert," I told him. "That would be incredibly dangerous for the clans."

He heaved out a heavy sigh, but he nodded. "Maybe we can come up with a way around that. Alternative water stores, or something."

I reached for his hand. "We'll figure it out. But, Calix, what if it's not there? What if you can't find it, and you have no way to defend yourself against the Elementae?"

His face pinched into a deep scowl. "We have to keep looking for it."

"But if you can't find it, Calix. What then?"

"This feels like a trick, wife. If we can't find the elixir, we need to start eliminating this threat before it grows more powerful. But I don't think that's what you want me to say."

"Perhaps you should consider protecting them," I told him. "Working with them. Rather than try so hard to eradicate them, consider how they might benefit your reign. It would remove all the power the Resistance has. It would defend us. It would achieve peace without death."

He stood, shaking his head. "That defies everything I believe, wife. Have you forgotten one of them will *kill* me?"

"Maybe *because* you try to eradicate them," I told him. "And you have an heir now—it seems the prophecy is far more complicated than you believe. I just . . . I want you to consider it."

He paced in the room, shaking his head as he went, and I felt fear gather within me. Then he stopped abruptly. "You don't believe in the God," he told me, staring at me. "That's the real problem here. You've never believed in the God, so you will never see me as his vessel, his voice, his arm. You put all your faith in the desert, in their way of thinking. But tomorrow you'll see—you aren't one of them anymore, wife. You're mine. This is where you belong. This is the only loyalty."

Stunned silent, I stared at him, my mouth open but still.

"Rest," he snapped. "I'll see you in the morning."

We left the next morning, and I was dressed in my new, more modest clothing. Even Calix decided against the carriage and opted for a horse instead, and we rode proudly. Much of the army had gone on ahead, and as we neared the land bridge preceding the pass, we saw them lining the road.

I frowned. "Why aren't they in Jitra?" I asked Calix.

He glanced at them. "The same reason as always. Clans don't allow soldiers in Jitra. They can go into the pass and to the southern edge of the city, but not inside. Your family is very proud, very strong. And the desert is difficult to breach when they are fortressed inside. Which is, of course, why peace between us was so necessary." His eyes flicked to me. "But I don't want to spoil the day."

"You needn't lie about wanting peace. I know all you wanted was the elixir."

Turning my head to look at him, his gaze was sharp and assessing. "Yes," he said. "But you are hardly one to criticize me for being calculating."

"*Calculating?*" I repeated. "How so?"

There was something raw in his eyes. "I gave you a chance last night, to explain. I know you've been communicating with your family. Asking them to hide you from me—to *steal* you from me."

I shook my head. Had he discovered Kairos's plans? "Calix, I never asked them—"

But he continued. "And then you even admit that you don't believe in my greatest cause. You don't want to find the elixir. You want me to *welcome* those sorcerers into my kingdom."

"Calix, stop," I said. "Please. I'm not leaving you, and I didn't say those things last night to upset you. It was just an idea. Please, I don't want to fight about this today."

He drew a breath, looking forward, and slowly let it out. "Finding that elixir—eradicating the sorcerers—is the most important thing, wife. More important than anything else."

We were nearing the land bridge, and I could see the mouth of the pass ahead. "I know, Calix. I—" I started, but I stopped. Just within the pass, I saw my mother and father, my father standing tall with a torch in his hand, waiting for us. My mother pressed against his side, and even from here, it looked like she was crying happily at the sight of me. My tall brothers beamed, and Catryn was struggling to hold Gavan from running forward.

My breath caught. "How did they . . . ?" I asked.

Calix looked at me. "I had my soldiers tell them we were arriving, if they wanted to greet you here."

Filled with joy and gratitude, I smiled at him. "Thank you, Calix. Truly," I told him, and I dismounted.

I saw soldiers, maybe ten or so, walking out, walking away from my family.

I noticed a yellow powder on a man's boots as he jogged past me.

Gavan distracted me, though, breaking free from Catryn to run ahead.

Galen came from behind us, hard faced and riding forward to the entrance to the pass.

A moment before Galen got there, I saw Calix smile, a dark, evil expression.

And then the world exploded.

He Knows

I was on the ground. My head was ringing, but I didn't feel any pain. I struggled to my feet, and someone touched me. Kairos. His mouth was moving.

Shalia. Shalia. I saw him mouth my name. "*Shalia!*" he yelled.

Shaking my head, I nodded. "I'm fine. I'm fine," I said, turning sharply. We couldn't see anything but a thick reddish cloud of dust and ash.

I couldn't think of anything else. We ran forward, and my feet were strong and sure, even as my head was foggy and thick.

My feet will never fail me.

I saw Galen first. His horse was writhing on the ground, and he had been thrown. Galen was groaning and starting to move, and I didn't wait to see if he was all right. I didn't care.

The boy's arm was the next thing I saw. It was at a strange angle, a layer of dirt on it, and stretched out like he was reaching for me still. Like all he wanted was to get to me.

Before I knew what I was doing, I slid to my knees and pushed the rock off his small body with my power, and it rushed away from him. "Gav?" I whispered. I pulled his body to me, and it was leaden and still. His back was covered with blood, misshapen where the big rock had hit him. I turned him over and pulled him against me. "Gavan!" I yelled. "Gavan!"

He didn't move. His face was scraped and bloody, his nose broken. His eyes were open, but they couldn't see me.

"I'll find the others," Galen said.

I hadn't known he was near me, and just as soon, he disappeared into the dust.

The others.

I wiped desperately at the dirt on Gavan's face, trying to pull it off. There was too much of it, and my hands were trembling. Why wasn't he moving? Why couldn't he just *move*?

"Gavan!" I cried, shaking him.

"Shalia!" Kairos yelled. "Someone could still be alive!"

Alive. Gavan was dead. I knew that, but—but—

I stood, feeling sick and dizzy, pushing forward into the cloud that shrouded my family.

I saw Kairos, crouched and throwing rocks off a small body. I saw her hair. "Catryn!" I screamed.

Kairos looked up at me. "Find the others!" he said, his eyes wild, his chest heaving.

Nodding, I ran into the smoke.

Galen was pushing a large boulder that was near the start of the pass. All around me, I felt the threads, angry and pulsing, curling around my fingertips and squeezing. I pushed the boulder off with my power like it was a pebble, sending it flying into the crevasse under the land bridge, and Galen turned and looked at me for a moment before dashing in. As soon as I could see the rocks, I moved them out of my way, and in moments, we had uncovered a tangled mass of bodies: my father, my brothers, my whole family.

I dove forward, but Galen shook his head at me, going to each one and carefully checking them.

When he reached the last one, he closed his eyes for a moment, and picked up my mother's body.

"What are you doing!" Kairos roared, trying to climb over rocks to get to him. "Don't touch her! Don't you *touch* her!"

Galen stood tall with her broken body in his arms. "She's dead, Kairos. Let me get your family out of here."

She's dead.

Galen took a step, and the movement suddenly seemed sideways to me, twisted wrong.

I am a daughter of the desert.

The world took a vicious spin, and then Kairos's arms were around me. "Shalia!" he yelled. "Shalia!"

Something hurt. *I am a daughter of the desert, and my feet will never fail me.*

Lightning crashed somewhere around us, and the moment froze, the light illuminating the dust in a distended vision. In the flash I saw Catryn, the moment she had been born. I had been the first to hold her, secreted away in the caves below Jitra, where the fires were stoked high to fill the cave with heat and smoke so the spirits of our ancestors could walk among us and greet the baby. I brought Catryn, the tiny thing who hadn't cried yet, to my mother.

When we touched, the three women of our clan, I felt something. Something otherworldly and powerful, filling my body. Filling the space.

And then the flash of light ended, and the smoke was full of nothing but the dead.

"Kairos, help me up," I said, but something was wrong. My arms weren't moving. The words sounded foreign and misshapen, even to my ears. Everything was wrong. The threads around me felt like they were strangling me, bloated thick and grotesque, tugging the world at odd angles.

There was pain. My power was turning on me, clawing at my throat, wrapping around my hips, and causing a deep ache that made me cry out.

"Shalia, you're bleeding," Kairos told me, and his eyes were stark, wide open and wet.

Bleeding? No. No—they were bleeding. They had stopped bleeding, because without a beating heart they would never bleed again.

I am a daughter of the desert, and my feet will never fail me. I couldn't feel Kai's hands on me. I felt weightless, ungrounded, like I couldn't tell the sky from the stones.

"Shalia!" he screamed at me, and my heart burst at the terror plain on his face.

The threads pulsed, rippling with anger, with hurt, with fury. The pulse came into my hands, touched my fingertips, and pushed.

My power ripped out of me. It felt like retching, like my body was fighting my mind for control and my mind was losing badly. I saw rocks, from pebbles to boulders, rising up into the air and beginning to swirl around me.

I felt the ground beneath my feet, and I tried desperately to focus. Kairos wasn't touching me anymore. He was on the ground, his hands curled around his face. Dirt was thickening the curtain of moving rock, responding to me, waiting patiently for my command.

I gave my mind over to my power. I rushed out along the rocks, along the land bridge, along the pass. It wasn't as simple as seeing, but where the rocks and dust existed, I could *feel.* The pass was blocked by rocks, but not gone completely. The mountains still stood.

I reached out farther until I could feel Jitra.

What was left of Jitra. I could feel the wounds in the earth where the caved-out rock had broken, where heavy stone collapsed on yielding bodies. I pulled it off. I could feel the heartbeats where people were clustered together, holding one another tight, praying for safety.

And all that stood between them and my husband's yellow powder were a few rocks in the pass.

I saw soldiers at the edge of my vision, through the rotating cloud of boulders that encircled me, and suddenly I knew what to do. The desert would not be at risk. The desert would not fall, and whatever treasures my people protected, Calix would never touch them.

A scream tore out of me as I reached for the land bridge. Breaking, snapping, tearing the rocks to pieces like a twig over my knee. My work was rough and crude, but all I wanted was to cut the desert off from the Bone Lands, to collapse the pass into the mountains it came from.

The land bridge broke in the center first, and with its support gone, the rocks began shearing off in huge, heavy boulders. My power clawed at them, crashing them down one after the other until the land bridge was nearly gone, a jagged mouth of teeth laughing at Calix's audacity, his hate, his mortality.

My work faltered, and it took several seconds for me to feel the pain.

Something was burning in my shoulder, and my power was slipping from my hands. I twisted, looking at my shoulder to see the shaft of an arrow sticking out strangely behind me.

My flying boulders tumbled down into the crevasse, and a crack formed in the ground near my feet. The moving dirt and rocks wobbled in their pattern, flying out, evading my grasp.

My knees went weak, and I fell, and suddenly all the rocks dropped to the ground with me. It was then that I saw the blood Kairos must have seen, seeping down my skirts.

My baby. My daughter.

A new scream came out of me, frightened and trembling and wild, shaking my lungs and my hands and my skin. Then I saw boots striding toward me, and then another set.

I looked up and saw my husband, still a distance away while his soldiers closed in on me.

My hands trembled and I realized, *He knows.*

The soldiers grabbed me and pulled me up, and I thrashed against their hands. Their grips didn't even tighten as I fought, and I realized I could barely control my limbs. I had nothing left.

I cast around, searching for Kairos in the clouds of dust. I heard Osmost shrieking over the shouts of the soldiers, but I couldn't see my brother.

"Kai!" I screamed. "Kai! Kai!"

I heard a roar, and I looked over to see Zeph fighting off at least seven of Calix's men. I couldn't see Theron. Zeph drove his elbow into the face of one man, and the guard dropped so fast I wondered if Zeph had killed him. Galen jumped in between them, tackling Zeph down to the ground. Zeph fought him, but it wasn't like he fought the guards. Galen said something to him, and my big protector stopped.

Both men looked at me, and I shook my head. "Help me!" I screamed. "Please, help me!"

Galen's eyes met mine for a long moment. He was filthy, his handsome face covered in dirt and dust, making his green eyes stand out more. He looked devastated.

But he wasn't moving. He kept Zeph pinned, and even Zeph had stopped fighting. Galen never moved. He didn't even have the decency to turn his face from mine.

"You coward!" I shrieked. "You damned coward!"

A hand struck my cheek, and I turned forward to see my husband. He grabbed my chin. "Did you really think that my own brother would betray me?" he snapped. "For *you*?" His words were so forceful that spittle landed on my face. I flinched, but his fingers were gripping me too hard to move. "I swear to the Three-Faced God," he growled at me, "if our child still lives, I will tear it out of you, and then I will wipe your existence from this earth. Never will a queen of the Trifectate be a filthy sorceress."

Calix pointed to a carriage, and my heart seized. He wouldn't take me back to the City of Three. If I went into that carriage, I would never leave his grasp alive—I was sure of it.

I called for my power, waiting for the threads to curl around my hands as the men pushed me farther. I made my hands into fists, bursting the pain from the arrow in my shoulder. I shook my fingers out.

Nothing.

I remembered Kata's advice, and I tried to call up my memories of Gavan rubbing his face into my stomach.

Gavan's tiny arm covered in blood and dirt.

Catryn, not far from him, twisted and broken.

My baby. *My baby. My baby.*

The guards shoved me into the carriage and brought rope to tie me to the floor. I curled around my knees.

I had no power left.

Missing

By the time they pulled me from the carriage, it had been long enough that my body disdained the movement. My skin was thick with dirt; blood crusted in places that made it feel like I was tearing a new wound open when I moved. It felt like the arrowhead shot into my shoulder hadn't been removed, even though they snapped the shaft off. Every muscle ached and cried, and I could hardly stand on my own two feet. Long enough in the carriage, long enough with my despair, and my feet almost failed me.

It was a whole new heartbreak when my body was already crowded with others.

I knew by the smell of the air that we were near the mountains. We were on a narrow path covered by dense forest, and in front of us a sheer rock face loomed with a small door in it. The door opened, and torchlight flickered, the only light I had to see by.

A single guard took me now, carrying me in his arms. I curled my fingers, searching for the threads, but they were still gone.

Without a way to fight back, I let myself be carried.

He took me into a long hallway that burrowed neatly into the rock. I couldn't tell how long he walked; all that caught my gaze were the moving, jumping shadows of the light on the ceiling of the tunnel.

I heard metal clinking and moving, a low, dark sound somewhere ahead.

A high-pitched scream rang out, strangled and disembodied, sliding over the walls like a ghost. The guard's hands tightened on me, but he didn't stop or show any other reaction.

The tunnel widened, and the jumping shadows on the ceiling receded from me.

"There," I heard Calix say. The guard turned and moved into an open room. The rock here was gray, not like the warm red of Jitra, and the light on it made everything look wet and slick. There was a huge stone altar in the center of the round room, hooks hanging above it with lanterns swinging, illuminating the girl who was lying on top of it.

She wore a dirty dress that might have been blue to start with, and part of her hair was cut off, revealing wounds that had been stitched up on her head. One arm was splayed out, and her skin was an indecipherable mass of bruising, blood, and cuts. Blood puddled beneath her on the ground.

I stopped looking at her long enough to notice six or more doors around the circle where the girl was.

One guard strode ahead of us to open a door directly behind the girl's head, and the guard holding me walked in and put me gently down on a hard bench with a pillow and a thin, small blanket.

"Get the quaesitori," Calix said, standing in the doorway.

The guard left without a word, and I didn't move, glancing at Calix before staring at the wall.

"Comfortable?" Calix snarled.

I shifted my hips a little, but it hurt, and I stopped moving.

"You're going to die in here," Calix told me. "But not before I discover all your secrets. You are the first sorceress who can command the earth that I've ever seen. And before you die, I will know everything there is to know."

"You are your own end," I whispered. "You have struck out against the desert. Against your *queen*. Your people will revolt, and they will unseat you. They will kill you."

"Really?" he snarled. "They never seemed to mind before."

I stared at the wall. I wanted to ask him what he meant, but he wanted to tell me. He wanted to gloat about his sick deeds, and I wouldn't play into such desires, even now, when I had nothing.

"My king," someone murmured, and Calix stepped aside. A man in black robes came into the room, and his eyes swept over me, slow and assessing. "I will examine her, my king."

"I'll stay," Calix said, not leaving the open doorway.

"My queen," the man said, dragging a stool to the bed. "Could you lie on your back?"

"If you think I'll let you touch me, you're mad," I snapped.

"I mean only to see if your baby is alive," he said. "I've been well trained in such arts."

My body shook, but that *if*—*if* my baby was alive—made me put aside my fears and indignity. I lay flat on my back, and he put his hands under my skirt. I wanted to shut my eyes, but instead I looked at Calix, tears coming out of my eyes as the man told me my body had ruptured and the baby couldn't survive like that. When he took his hands away, I shut my eyes, curling toward the wall.

"Very well," Calix said. "Dress her shoulder. Feed her something. She will need her strength for later."

I shut my eyes and must have slept for a while, but it never felt like sleep. It felt just like being awake, the same numbness, the same pain, only that I was in darkness.

But I woke with a start, jumping to the door. There was a tiny grate that was too high for me to see out of, but I could hear a girl—the same girl? I had no way of knowing—wailing in pain.

"Again, Dara!" I heard a male voice yell. She cried out again, and it trailed off into piteous sobs. *Dara.* The girl from the ship on the communes, the girl whom my husband promised to try fairly. A girl he'd clearly been experimenting on for as long as he promised me he hadn't.

"Again!" The answering scream was different, more raw, like she had reached a new level of pain.

"*Again!*"

I fell back from the door as, instead of a scream, a ball of fire rose up in the chamber, blazing fast and extinguishing.

"Write that down," I heard a man murmur.

I couldn't sleep the rest of the night. The screams ended not long after that, but there were still grunts, shuffles, noises that haunted me.

Six doors, at least. I wondered how many of us he had to torture. I wondered where my brothers were, mourning without me. I wondered if anyone was able to burn the bodies of my family so they could return to the Skies.

I wondered how I was supposed to return a child to the Skies when there was nothing to burn.

Hours later, a guard opened my door. "Come," he said, and gave me a cloth and a chip of soap. There were other women coming out of their cells, and one young man who, for a wild moment, I thought was my brother Aiden.

It wasn't, of course. I would never see Aiden's face again, and imagining him into this hell didn't change that.

The guards led us deeper into the rock. I heard the rushing water before I saw it, and they led us into an underground river. The others didn't need to be told what to do. They took off their clothes, putting them in neat piles, and waded into the water.

Slowly, I followed their example, glancing at their bodies without trying to be rude. I saw scars before I could really look at faces; long, thin lines from a whip, or maybe a knife. Long, deep wounds that were crusted with blood. Missing hair, missing fingers, missing eyes.

My skin could barely feel the cold as I stepped into the water. The river was moving fast enough that it plucked painfully at the things crusted to my skin, peeling the day before away without my consent.

"You're the queen," one said, looking at me. She was small, everything about her tiny, with dark hair that was long and knotted. She covered herself up, like suddenly *this* made our nudity inappropriate. "What—what are you—you're the *queen*," she said again.

A taller, older woman touched the girl's shoulder, and I saw her hand was missing two fingers, raw red stumps where they used to be. "And just the same as us, it seems. I'm Iona," she said softly to me.

"Shalia," I murmured.

She nodded grimly. "Do you have the natural powers?" she asked.

I nodded. "Earth," I told her. "You?"

She swallowed. "Water," she said, running her hands into the river.

"You haven't healed yourself?" I whispered, looking at her hand.

The younger girl looked up at Iona, and Iona looked confused. "Heal?" she breathed.

"I know someone with your power," I said. "She can heal people through it."

"I'm not very strong," she said, shaking her head.

"Wash!" the guards bellowed at us.

The women flinched, turning to scrape their bodies with the soap. The young man was already finished, climbing out of the water to take his cloth and dry off, then slowly put his clothes on. He was ashen and weak.

I scrubbed slowly at the dirt, ash, dust, and blood that was all that remained of my family. The river took it, folding every little piece of horror into its waters until I had none left, until my body was frozen and clean. I didn't want to be clean. I didn't want to ever move on from the last moment when the world was safe, when my family was smiling, when my baby was alive.

Blood still wept out of my body, and the river stole it from me.

The Trail of Smoke

When they brought us back to the central chamber, the table in the middle was empty, and everyone else was pushed back into their rooms except for me.

Calix came from down a shadowed hallway. He took a breath and nodded to me.

"Bring her."

I pulled back, but the guards grabbed me, dragging me forward as I fought and twisted and flailed. They brought chains out, and they shackled my wrists and yanked until I was on my feet, standing away from the table, unable to go far. I tugged against my bonds as my heart pounded, making every inch of me panic and hurt.

"Stop," Calix growled, coming over to me.

I shook my head, sucking in breath too fast through my nose, the sound high and reedy.

"I won't hurt you," Calix told me.

I could hardly catch my breath, but I shouted, "You're going to *kill* me!"

His throat worked. "Eventually. It doesn't have to hurt. I don't want to see you in pain. I just need you to show us your power, and I will end all this. Do you understand?"

Flexing my hands, reaching for my power, I shook my head. "It's gone, Calix. I don't have it anymore. I can't feel it!"

He laughed, leaning closer to me. "I understand. I once thought that myself—there was even a girl I tested long, long ago who claimed she didn't have powers. I believed her, and I didn't test as hard as I should have. Since then, I know better. I've tested many people with your foul magic, and I can always, always make it present. It just takes a tremendous amount of persuasion." His hand stroked my face. "I'll help you show your power, I swear. And once we can study it properly, your death will be swift."

I tried to kick him, and missed, and he sighed.

"I know I was angry yesterday, Shalia. You have always been able to make me lose my temper. But I truly don't want you to suffer. It's not necessary."

"You killed my *whole family*," I whispered.

"Yes," he said. "They posed a problem. I needed to shift the lake, and I needed you to know you couldn't leave me. I know you were trying to. Do you deny it?"

"My *family* wanted me to run," I told him. "And I hadn't decided anything."

"Does it matter?" he asked with a dry laugh. "You betrayed me. You deceived me. All that time, I told you what she did to me before. And you did the very same thing."

Three quaesitori entered the room, setting up small tables with paper on them, sitting down.

"Now, I have a theory about you," Calix said to me. "There are only two possibilities to get the power to respond to us. One is to have your body protect you in the event of your near death or tremendous pain."

Skies protect me. Please—ancestors of mine that have returned to the Skies, returned to the earth, please protect me.

"But for you, I believe there is another option. This is to exploit your compassion, my love. You are soft hearted, and I have known this from the first. I believe you will be more positively motivated by the pain of others than pain you might experience yourself. Do you understand?"

The pain of others. I shook my head, vicious and fast. "Calix, please, I don't—"

"Do you understand?" he asked.

My eyes skittered around to the doors.

"Shalia!" he roared.

"Yes," I said.

"Good," he said, and waved to the guards.

They brought the smallest girl out from her cell. She was shivering, staring at the table as they led her over to it. She didn't fight as they strapped her down. "I can do it," she said. "You saw me before. You don't need to hurt me again; I can do it."

Calix stayed back, across the room from me, while the quaesitori came forward. The one who had inspected my body touched her face gently. "You did well yesterday," he told her, and this seemed to calm her a little. "Today you just get comfortable; we won't hurt you this time."

She seemed to believe this, and I watched Calix as he glanced down the darkened hall. He looked back to the quaesitori and nodded.

They finished tying her down, and one of them stroked a knife over the crook of her arm. She flinched, and blood flowed out instantly, collecting in a bowl beneath her.

"That's it," the quaesitor said gently. He smiled at her, and she smiled back.

"Calix," I called, my voice low.

He heard and walked over to me. "Care to show me something?" he asked, smiling.

"Leave her alone."

She shifted on the table. She was looking at me, growing unsure.

"I have a purpose for her," Calix said. "A dual purpose to motivate you. You don't want her to die, do you?" he asked.

"Of course I don't."

"Then save her, Shalia. You tore down the bridge to the desert—you can save one little girl, can't you?"

I shut my eyes. "I don't have my power anymore, Calix. I can't show you what isn't there."

"Then I will continue my work, and you will watch," he told me. "Open your eyes."

I didn't respond, and he pushed me, enough that my weak knees gave out and my body jerked down on the chains, cutting my wrists. I cried out, pushing my feet underneath me. "My feet will never fail me," I murmured.

"What was that?" he asked.

I opened my eyes, looking at him. "I am a daughter of the desert, and my feet will never fail me."

He pushed me again, and he laughed as I fell again. "Well, they seem to fail you a little bit, my dear."

The girl whimpered. She was pale now, and the amount of blood in the bowl was growing.

"She controls air," Calix told me. "I have found many powers of water, and air, and a few of fire. You're the first earth. I wonder if that is the limit of these powers, or if there are more." He looked at me like he expected me to answer and shrugged. "No matter. I'll discover eventually."

"You are a monster," I whispered, shaking my head as I looked at the girl. "She's not even a person to you anymore. She's an insect whose wings you tear off."

"I am a *god*," he growled at me. "And this—unlocking the secrets of this damnation—will not only please the God but it will prevent my enemies from coming for me. I will stop them all, Shalia. I will have all the power, and no one will question my reign again."

"You are *making* your enemies," I told him. "And losing your soul in the process. You don't see what you've done? You killed our—*you* are making your own prophecy come true. Your god will never forgive the torture of innocents. Do you think Danae will, when she finds out? What about your mother? She would be *ashamed—*"

"Do not mention my mother with your filthy mouth!" he roared, and everyone in the room jumped. "You know nothing about her!" he screamed, hurling his finger at me but not touching me.

The sounds of harsh, fast breathing filled the room, and I turned back to the girl. Her skin was disturbingly pale, and she was breathing hard, sweat breaking out on her gray forehead.

"Calix, she's dying," I told him. "Stop!"

"What?" she whined. She looked to the quaesitori, and blood kept flowing out of her arm, dripping into the bowl. "No! No, please!"

Tears rushed out of me as I reached for my power, but it wasn't there. I tried to think of my family and Galen, but every good memory was stained with heartbreak, and I couldn't call my power to my hands.

No one moved, and within moments her confusion and anxiety melted away. Her eyes went half lidded, and her breathing was still too rapid, like a tiny, frightened animal.

"Calix, stop," I begged.

He turned to me, wiping tears from my cheeks. "Your power, not your tears, will save her life, Shalia."

Her body went limp, and still several minutes passed before the blood stopped dripping.

Calix lifted his shoulders. "Too late, it seems." He pointed to the blood, and one of the quaesitori picked the bowl up and brought it down the hallway. Two guards came forward and took her body away.

Calix followed the quaesitori down the hallway, and I was left there, chained and staring at the table where they had murdered a girl without thought or care, like blowing out a candle just to see the trail of smoke it would leave.

Alive

The next time the guards let us go down to the river to bathe, I could barely hold myself up. I stumbled, and Iona caught me, wrapping her arm around my waist and pulling my arm around her neck.

The contact rushed through me, and I looked at her. "Did you feel that?" I asked her.

She nodded.

"Has that happened before?" I whispered.

She shook her head.

As we walked, I felt stronger, her healing power just like Kata's. The cuts on my wrist scabbed over, and she held her hand forward. The redness in the stumps was gone. "*Healing?*" she whispered.

I showed her my wrist. "Yes. If you can control your powers," I whispered, "and heal some of us to do the same, we might be able to get out of here."

She pulled out from under my arm. "Don't say that. They'll hear you."

"Iona—"

"No," she said vehemently. "I can't. Don't ever ask me to."

I wanted to change her mind, to convince her that her power could save us all. But I knew I couldn't guarantee her safety. How could I justify her risk? So I said, "Very well. But thank you, for what you did."

She moved farther from me, putting her head down.

As we took our clothes off and went into the water, I cleaned myself and saw no new blood coming from me.

I went still in the river, shivering and staring at the cloth, without any red stripes on it. "No," I gasped, and cleaned harder. Still, no new blood came from me, and I slipped to my knees in the shallow water, clutching the cloth to me.

I felt the weight of stares on me, but I didn't pay attention until Iona knelt in front of me. I was rocking now, moving back and forth, trying to find some way to breathe around the horrible, huge pain in my chest. Iona touched my arm, and with the rush of healing, something broke inside me.

Curling around my knees until I almost drowned myself, I sobbed. She was gone. Nothing was left of her, not even a little trail of blood between my legs.

I had lost my daughter, my family, my whole heart. My faith, and my way.

The guards didn't take me from my room for a long time, and I had no way of knowing how much time had passed. They fed us, but either the intervals were irregular or I was losing my understanding of time. There were no new screams. There were murmured words about how the blood hadn't worked, and the quaesitori suggesting solutions that I barely understood, something about the freshness of the blood, a way to bind vein to vein.

The next time the guards took me to bathe, I didn't see Calix anywhere. I hadn't heard his voice either, and as they sent me back to my cell untouched, I wondered if he had left.

They stopped feeding me and gave me only water. I had no idea how many days passed, only that my power didn't return and they didn't hurt me. Locked in my cell, I heard Dara as they continued to test her, making her scream until the room blazed full of light and fire.

One morning Iona came to me while we were bathing, catching my hand in her own. My body drank in her power, giving me strength where I had none. "I can't heal the others," she whispered to me. "I've tried. You pull it from me, but I don't know how to do it on my own." She met my eyes. "But he said—he said you took down a mountain. Is that true?"

I shook my head. "In a way. But I can't even feel my power anymore. It's not just that I'm hurt; it's gone."

She jumped away from me, looking at her hand and frowning, then shaking it.

"What is it?" I asked.

She looked at her hand for a moment more. "I don't know. When I was touching you, something . . . jumped. Do you know what that is?"

I felt broken, and weary, and empty. "No," I told her. "I know almost nothing about these powers."

"But—"

"If I knew, my family wouldn't be dead. My *baby* wouldn't be—" I halted, shaking my head. I moved away from her. "I don't know anything about these powers, Iona."

She sighed, and left me alone.

When we returned to the room, Calix walked in, and my heart stopped when I saw Danae behind him. "Danae!" I screamed. The guards grabbed me when I tried to run to her, but she turned to me.

"Shalia," she said, her throat working. She glanced back at Calix, and then walked over to me. "Three Faces, you're thin," she said. She glared at the guard holding me back but didn't order him to release me.

"Danae, please," I said. "Tell him to let me go. Please!"

She nodded. "I'll try, Shalia. But I have a chance," she said, looking impossibly sad, "to help him. I need to help him so I can help you too. Do you understand?"

"No!" I cried. "Danae, please! Please!"

Regret filled her eyes. "I'm sorry for all that you've suffered. I still think of you as my sister, you must know that."

I slumped against the bonds of my guard. "Please," I cried. "Don't leave me here, Danae. Please."

She turned away, and Calix put his arm around her, pulling her farther from me.

I was left alone in my cell, and this time I couldn't hear anything.

The next morning Iona nearly ran over to me while we walked to the river. She clasped her hand in mine, and I felt the immediate rush of power. "They killed her," she breathed.

"Danae!" I gasped.

"No," she said, looking forward at the others. "Dara. The fire power."

I looked around. Iona was right; she was missing.

"You have to heal yourself," Iona told me. "You have to heal yourself and get us out of here. Yours is the only power that could do it."

"I told you—"

She squeezed my hand, and her face looked panicked. "I don't *care.* He's right, you know—I've been here for God only knows how long and everyone presents their powers in the end. The power is always there—it's always in you, it's always inalienable. You have to find a way to get it back. You have to save us before we all die here."

"Iona—" I started.

She gasped, cutting me off and holding up our hands. "There it is again. Concentrate—you must be able to feel it too."

"Wait," I told her, and we took off our clothes to go into the river. Once there, we locked hands again, and her power felt even stronger. I could feel it, like the threads of my power, but instead it was one single thread that slipped between our hands and connected us. Following it, I felt it give a strange little pulse. Like following a trail, I traced the thread through my body.

"The Three-Faced God is great," she breathed. Her face was full of wonder, like I was some kind of miracle.

"Iona, what are you talking about?" I asked, but she didn't break the hold, and I felt the pulse again, stronger this time. Steadier. Even and low.

It wasn't my power, or hers. It was a heartbeat. And it was coming from my womb.

It shouldn't have been possible, but my daughter, my fierce daughter was still there, still clinging to life. She was a daughter of the desert, of me, of my murdered family that had sent their spirits like soldiers to keep her alive.

Even in the small, secret touch under the eyes of the guards, Iona's power rushed through me, healing me, healing *us*, and I sobbed, clinging to her, praying to every Sky and spirit I knew, thanking them.

My daughter was alive.

Sweeping the Stone

When we returned to the room, Calix stood there, smiling at me. I wiped my tears away, standing up straight, feeling a new kind of power rushing in my veins.

"Those two," Calix said. He pointed at me and Iona.

We looked at each other as they brought us forward. Calix locked me into the manacles from the ceiling and drew my arms up again. "You look thin, wife," he said. "Not enjoying your stay here?"

I drew a breath and shut my eyes.

"Don't worry," he said, his breath close to my ear. "You won't be here much longer."

I opened my eyes as I heard Iona's whimper. They tied her down to the table, and she looked at me, breathing rapidly, blinking back tears.

"Shalia, it's time for you to present your power. I hear you've become quite close with her, yes? I knew I could count on you to make friends, even in a place like this. So just know that every bit of pain she's about to feel will be your fault. Unless, of course, you want to show your power."

Iona looked up at the ceiling, and I glared at Calix. "I am not responsible for your choices, Calix," I told him. "You masquerade as a leader, but a leader would take responsibility for his choices. He would save people, not hurt them."

"Really?" Calix asked, smiling. "You're naive, Shalia. You have so many grand thoughts of leadership, but peace is always bought with death. Safety is inherently at odds with freedom. And you know nothing of what sacrifices leadership demands until you have fought for the lives of your people. You know nothing of what it takes to lead." He turned to his quaesitori. "Begin."

One of the men approached Iona with a small vial in his hand. Another came to the other side and blocked my view of her, holding a cloth and arranging it on her face.

She tried to buck and fight, but they held her tight.

"What are you doing?" I cried. "Calix, what are you doing to her?"

He didn't answer me.

She whimpered and cried, kicking her legs, but they opened the vial.

"Calix!" I yelled.

"Do it!" Calix snapped.

With only a glance at him, they dripped something onto her eye.

She screamed, a guttural, tortured noise, for barely a moment before her body went limp.

"Do the other eye too," Calix said. "Unless you want to show me something, Shalia?"

Desperate, I curled my fingers, trying to call up the threads, and I yelled out in frustration as the quaesitori switched places, opening her other eye.

The power is always there, she had told me.

Like my heart. Whether I liked it or not, even if it was shattered in my chest, my heart was still there. It wasn't as easy as saying I didn't know how to love anymore. The thought of my child, still growing inside me, was enough to make me believe that.

I shut my eyes and thought of her. My tiny girl, my little survivor.

My power had always been my ability to care for people. To love people, even in the bleakest of situations. Calix could say what he wanted, but that was truly what it meant to lead—to love people when they didn't deserve it, to love people when it wasn't in your best interest.

I would not let Iona die.

Like a thunderclap, the threads rushed back to my fingers. I tugged, and the chains tore out of the ceiling. The ground trembled and shook, and the quaesitori capped whatever dangerous liquid they held. My chains fell from me as cracks ran over the ceiling, and my husband turned to me, an evil light in his eyes.

"I *knew* it!" he crowed. "You see? I'm always right, *wife.* I will always be able to force you to show this filthy side of yourself."

"I'll be honest, Calix," I told him, holding my hands wide. "I don't know how well I can control this. You might want to run."

I pushed my hands at the doors, and some of them unlatched, but most shattered on their hinges. The other Elementae stumbled to the doorways. Someone ran for Iona, but most stayed where they were.

Calix started laughing. "Magnificent!" he crowed. "You are a fine specimen, aren't you? And you know, I considered what you said—what happens if I don't ever find the elixir? If I can't ever re-create it? Now I have my own answer to your little power. Danae!" he shouted.

A chunk of rock ripped free of the ceiling, and with a gasp I pushed it out of the way so it wouldn't hurt the others. As I put it safely down, Danae came out of the hallway. Her eyes were sunken and shadowed, and I saw bruises so dark her skin looked black spread wide around stitched cuts in her arms.

I stared at Calix, and suddenly the experiments, the cuts, the disappearing blood, and the dead girl made a stunning amount of sense. "You didn't. You couldn't."

He went to Danae, smiling at her for a moment. "Kill her. Meet us back at the City of Three," he said before disappearing into the tunnel behind her.

"Danae," I said.

She held up her hands, and fire wrapped around her fingers. "He made me one of you," she said, her voice choked. "He made me one of you so I have the power to stop you. To keep him safe." She swallowed. "He made me into the thing he hates most."

"Danae, please," I told her. "Your power is new; you won't be able to control it. You have to stay calm or you'll kill all of us."

"Don't tell me to stay calm!" she screamed, and fire shot from her palms, running over her arms as if flames were bleeding from her cuts. One of the others dove over Iona's body to cover her. "Galen—Galen turned from him *years* ago. But I have always loved him—he's my oldest brother!" she yelled. Her hands dropped, and the fire stopped flowing from them, but it raged out of control around us without anything to burn. She fell to her knees, covering her face. "My mother—my mother told me that he just needed someone to love him. That I had to love him after she was gone. And no matter what he did, I *loved* him. I did whatever he wanted. I protected him. *I killed for him*," she cried.

I called up dirt and dust and rubble, trying to tamp out the flames, but they just grew.

"Get out of here!" I screamed at the others. I couldn't see them. Fire was all around me, encircling Danae and me, forcing us closer together.

I could hear noises coming from beyond the fire, but I couldn't see through its glaring light enough to know what was happening. Someone screamed.

Coming forward, I knelt beside Danae. I pulled her into my arms, and fire burst from her hands. Crying out, I jumped back from her. The cave was thick with smoke, and I didn't think we could survive much longer.

Shaking, I touched Danae's face. "Come back to me," I told her. "Please, Danae—I love you. Galen loves you. No matter what, Calix did this because he trusts you more than anyone."

She didn't move, didn't look at me. The fire was burning closer to me, searing my back, and I cried out, shaking her. "Danae, please!"

Something cool rushed over me, so intense it hurt for the first stinging moment. Then I was drenched in water, and water was flying through the air, swirling around the fire and fighting it back, containing it.

The smoke began to clear from the cave, and I saw Iona sitting on the table, clutching another one of the girls, and both their hands were outstretched.

Beyond them, I saw men in black uniforms filling the tunnel. I gasped—I thought we were in the mountains, with few guards. I hadn't imagined contending with an army. I took a breath, turning, ready to fight back.

And then I saw Galen, and Kairos broke from the crowd, Kata and Rian behind him, and they ran for me.

As Kairos caught me in his arms, I saw that the men's uniforms also had a green dragon on them. Not the Trifectate. "The Resistance?" I asked, staring at Galen over Kai's shoulder.

"Put her down," Kata ordered Kairos sternly. He did, and Rian and he both began chattering as Kata put her hands on me.

"Quiet!" Kata barked, closing her eyes.

"Kata, the others need you. Iona, they did something to her eye—"

"Stop," she commanded. "I can heal you all."

Her power rushed through me, healing my burns, and her eyes opened.

"Oh, Shalia," she breathed.

The boys looked at each other. "What?" Rian demanded, his arm going tight on my waist. "She's going to be all right, isn't she? We just—Great Skies, tell me we got here in time."

"She's going to be a mother," Kata whispered. She looked at me. "Did you know? That the baby's alive?"

I nodded. "Just," I whispered.

Rian crushed me to him in a strong hug, and I felt Kairos wrap his arms around us both.

We were the last of our clan. The knowledge struck me hard, like a blow, and I squeezed them tighter to me.

After a long moment, I pulled away from them and turned to where Galen was kneeling, holding Danae limp in his arms. Wiping my face, I came over to them. "What happened?"

"She passed out," he said softly, looking at her. He touched her arms and the cuts there. "What did he do to my sister?" he whispered.

"I'll explain," I said. "But we should get her out of here. We should all get out of here."

He nodded, standing. He turned to the gathered force of the Resistance, calling them forward, and to my shock, they answered.

The Resistance—they were Galen's men.

Feeling dizzy and stunned, my eyes dropped to his chest. There, in careful stitching, was a green dragon.

"You . . . ," I managed, but I couldn't form the words.

The soldiers took Danae's small, slight body and started walking out of the cave. Other men were helping the Elementae as Kata healed them, and Galen glanced at me, swallowing.

He looked down. "Yes," he said, lifting his shoulders. "When my brother became king and named me commander, I realized that if I did what he asked, I would be committing terrible sins, and those acts would be on both our souls. And I knew that if I could play both sides of the coin, I'd be able to stop him before he went too far. So I started the Resistance. And when I needed someone else to be its face, I asked your brother."

I twisted around, and Rian was watching us, his arms crossed. He nodded once. I turned back to Galen, my mouth open but no words emerging.

Galen held up his hands. "I couldn't tell you, Shalia. It wasn't safe for you to know. I'm so sorry about that."

"You . . . I called you a coward," I realized.

His hands fell. "Fighting backdoor battles and lying to my brother's face doesn't quite make me a hero, Shalia. You weren't wrong. And I was a fool to think he could ever be redeemed." He stepped forward and raised his hand, then halted, looking at me. He swallowed again and touched my cheek. "Let's get you out of here," he whispered.

I nodded.

When we emerged from the cave, the fresh air was staggering. I shivered, and Galen looked at me. "I'll get you a blanket," he told me. "We don't have far to walk."

He was only gone a moment, but when he returned, Rian was already beside me and took the blanket from his hands, glaring at Galen.

Galen sighed as Rian draped it around me, putting his arm around my shoulders. "Rian," he said.

"No," Rian snapped. "You and I will have a very serious discussion later. Not now."

"About what?" I demanded.

Rian shook his head, rubbing my shoulder. "Come," he said. "You need food, and rest. Do you want me to carry you?"

I pulled away from him, crossing my arms over the blanket. "Of course not," I told him.

Kairos appeared on my other side with a smile. "Calix will never be able to take away the fact that she is desert born, Rian." Osmost called out above us, and Kairos tracked him with his eyes. "We need to move. There are soldiers on their way."

The Resistance had brought about twenty men, and they walked ahead of us and behind, some helping the Elementae to walk. Rian wouldn't stray more than a foot from me, and Galen stayed ahead, glancing back at me every few moments.

We walked for more than a mile through the forest and trees until an inn appeared in front of us. Rian touched my arm, pointing to the roof. "See?" he asked.

For a long moment I didn't see anything, but then I saw a small green dragon on the lowest shingle of the roof.

"Any place with that symbol is loyal," he said. "Only green. We've put other colors around as false signals. Just green—remember that."

I nodded, but caught his arm. "We're staying here? We're so close to the . . . Calix will know where to find us, Rian."

"He won't be looking. We've captured the guards and the quaesitori. Calix had already left for the Tri City; with no one to tell him otherwise, he won't have a reason to come back for at least two days, and we'll be gone by morning," Galen said. His eyes met mine more meaningfully. "You'll be safe here."

Rian grunted, shifting to block Galen from my gaze.

The innkeeper and his wife walked outside, giving Rian and Galen grave nods as they held open the door, looking around as we all went inside quickly.

Rian brought me to a room, and a few moments later Galen knocked on the door.

"No," Rian growled, standing between us as Galen opened the door, a pile of clothes in his hands. "You're not seeing her right now."

"Rian," I said.

"Rian, please," Galen said.

"Absolutely not!" he snapped, his hands curling to fists. "Are you going to tell me putting your hands all over her was some brotherly display?"

"No," Galen said calmly, shaking his head. "I love Shalia, Rian. I'm *in* love with her."

Heat filled my face, but Rian was slightly less happy to hear this. Before I even knew what he was doing, he launched his fist against Galen's jaw.

"Rian!" I shrieked as Galen reeled.

Kairos slid into the doorway, pausing for barely a second before grabbing Rian, twisting, and pushing him outside the room. "Move, Kairos!" Rian bellowed.

"Oh please," Kairos snapped, crossing his arms. "Let them talk."

"He *dishonored* our—"

"Shut it," Kairos said, pushing him back. "We need to talk about the plan for tomorrow anyway. She wants to talk to him, and you will respect that."

"You *knew* about this?" Rian demanded. "You *lied* to me?"

Kairos gave an exaggerated sigh, pushing Rian toward the stairs. "After all the misery of the past few days, Rian, you have a spectacular ability to focus on the inconsequential." Kairos turned back and winked at me before he shut the door.

Shaking my head, I went and sat on the bed with a sigh.

Slowly, Galen came and sat, his body almost a foot from mine. His hand was beside his knee, not near me, but after hearing those words, after all the horrors of the past few days, I wanted to touch him. I slowly reached across the space, edging my fingers over his.

He looked up at me and sucked in a breath as he turned his palm over, lacing our fingers together. "You're sure this is all right?" he whispered.

"Holding hands?" I asked.

He looked down, his throat working. "If you don't want to be touched, I'd understand. I'd respect that."

I curled my fingers tighter on his.

"How is Danae?" I asked.

A muscle in his jaw flared. "She's still asleep. I don't even understand how Calix could have done this to her."

"The blood," I said softly. "He probably tried it more than once—he tried draining a girl of all her blood, and that must not have worked. I don't know how he got it to work, but a girl—Dara, that girl from the communes, the one I thought—" I shook my head. "She died. And then Danae had her power."

His fingers squeezed mine. "I know what he's done in those experiments, Shalia," he whispered, his voice rough. "I've been imagining—" He stopped his words abruptly.

I slid closer to him. "No," I breathed, and even that called up tears. "He thought it would be more effective to hurt people and make me watch."

His arm let go of my fingers to curl around me, pulling me against him, holding me so tight that every time we breathed we inched apart, only to be brought close again when we exhaled. "Kata said your baby's alive?" he asked.

I nodded, and tears slipped down my cheeks. "My miracle girl."

His hand moved down my side, coming between us to touch my stomach. "You're the miracle, Shalia."

I covered his hand with my own. "What happens next?" I asked, trying to swallow all the things I felt with his big hand covering my tiny, hidden child.

"We have to get you out of the Trifectate's reach," he said.

I shook my head. "We need to go to the desert first. I need to make sure my people are safe."

"You broke the land bridge," he told me. "We can't cross into the desert."

"Calix will think that," I said. "But I'm sure I can find a way."

He nodded.

"What will we do about Calix?" I asked.

"It is time he was deposed," he said, looking to me. "And you are carrying his child."

I pulled back. "You want my daughter to be queen? An infant who hasn't even been born?"

He nodded. "With you as the regent. Yes. If we want there to be as little bloodshed as possible, we have to install a legitimate heir to replace Calix."

"We would still need an army," I said.

"Yes," he said, his hand stroking my back.

I looked at him. "You could be king, couldn't you?"

"No," he said. "It's either a legitimate heir or the crown reverts to the vestai."

"I will consider it," I told him. I took his hand from my cheek and clasped it in both of mine. "My family—the bodies—" I stopped, shaking my head.

"Burned," he whispered, holding me tight. "According to desert custom, yes?"

I nodded, pulling back. "Which you know, because you've known my brother. For years."

He sighed. "Yes."

I stood from the bed. "So even when we met in the desert—you *knew* him. You knew about me." My breath caught. "Did you know about the veil?" I asked.

He stood, frowning. "No," he said. "Of course not. And I knew you *existed*, but truly, does it seem like Rian gave me any opportunity to know you? Of course he didn't."

I rubbed my forehead. "Then what were you doing? The whole time—did you follow me in Jitra? Did you—all those times you defended me, you were doing it for him. I can only imagine he made you promise to protect me." My hand slipped to my chest, covering my heart, trying to keep something safe in there.

To my surprise, he chuckled, and I looked to him, his green eyes bright, his face unamused. "You think I could know you, touch you," he said, his voice slowing, "kiss you, and have any of those things be about your brother?"

Beneath my fingers, my heart sped up again. "Earlier, you said . . ." My words left me.

His head tilted, but then he smiled, a rare, precious smile. "That I love you," he said. "That I'm in love with you."

I nodded.

"I thought you knew that already," he said, his voice soft against my skin.

Slowly, I shook my head.

He came closer to me, pulling me into his arms. "That's despite your brother. And mine," he said. "Not because of them. I couldn't help loving you."

Releasing a deep breath, I felt my body melt against his. Tight, and close, and sheltered, just feeling each breath fill my chest and leave again. "I love you too," I whispered to him.

He went still against me. I looked into his face, and his throat was working wildly, but the rest of him was frozen and wide-eyed. "You do?" he asked.

I touched his cheek, the stubble rough against my fingers, then the soft patch of his cheek above it. His face showed the proof of his bravery, of his valor, his heart. I touched the scar on his eyebrow, and the one beneath his eye, where the stubble didn't grow. I trailed a finger over his craggy nose and touched his bottom lip. "I love you," I told him again. "Every bit of you."

He pulled me closer, pressing kisses to my cheek, my ear, my neck, murmuring so softly against my skin that I wasn't even sure what he said, but I knew what it meant. I knew that it made me feel safe and alive for the first time in months, and it made my heart feel swollen and even a little painful, to feel so loved when so many pieces of my heart were gone.

I felt the threads brush against my fingers, close and hesitant, desperate to believe that we could love each other.

"You've been through so much, Shalia," he said softly in my ear. "You need to rest."

Again, I nodded, and he started to pull away. "Please," I said. "Please don't go."

"Rian has been my closest friend for years. I treasure his friendship. I want to respect his wishes."

Tugging at his shirt, I shook my head. “That’s not the same thing as not wanting to stay,” I murmured.

“No,” he allowed. “But you do need to rest.”

“I think it would be easier if you’re here,” I told him. “I don’t . . . I don’t want to be alone.”

He stared at me for long moments, but then he eased us down, letting me lie in the bed before he fitted his body to curve around my back. I turned over, holding our clasped hands between us, feeling his breath warm on my cheek. He put his other arm around me, drawing me a little closer. I nodded, and his nose brushed my skin. “Sleep, my love,” he whispered. “I’ll always watch over you.”

I didn’t sleep long, but I had never felt as warm and safe as I did when I woke, Galen’s body and scent and breath surrounding me. Loving me.

As soon as I stirred, his beautiful green eyes opened, and his nose brushed mine. “You need more rest than that,” he whispered.

“I’m hungry,” I said back. “And I want to check on the others.”

He nodded, his eyes meeting mine in a way that made me feel warmer, shivering to life. He brushed my cheek, and looked at my mouth for a brief second before he moved slowly closer, touching my lips. I pressed forward to meet his mouth. It didn’t feel rushed or illicit like our other kiss.

When my cousin Cora married, her father gave her a home in Jitra. The night before her wedding I couldn’t find her, and I searched the whole house. When I still couldn’t find her, I went to her new home. It was empty, but she was there, sweeping the stone floors.

“What are you doing?” I had asked her.

She stopped, looking at me. She looked at the broom for a long moment. "I needed to make sure that there was room," she told me. "I just needed to clear room for him." She touched her heart, and then kept sweeping, and I always thought she meant something more than making room for his belongings.

As Galen kissed me, gentle and soft, I felt my heart opening, swelling, clearing some kind of room for him to come in and stay.

My Lovely Dragon

I dressed in the clothes that Galen had brought before we fell asleep—they were heavier fabrics than the silks of the Tri City; the styling was similar to the clothes the praeceptae wore, and I was grateful to have more fabric than the remaining shreds of the dress I'd been wearing, still dark with blood.

There were four other Elementae besides Iona and me—five if you considered Danae, though I wasn't sure she wanted to be called an Elementa. Everyone ate, and most went to their rooms to sleep. When I went to Iona, however, she was sitting up in bed, staring at the wall.

"May I come in?" I asked her.

She looked at me. The cavity around her eye was red still, and a little swollen, but Kata had healed it enough that she hadn't even bandaged it. There were uneven lumps of scar tissue, but otherwise it looked strangely smooth, like her eyelids had been fused together over a sunken space. The eye itself was gone.

She turned back to the wall, rocking a little on her bed, and I came and sat beside her. I touched her leg, and she jumped, but before I moved she covered my hand, holding it there.

"In the morning, we're going north," I told her softly. "To the desert, to make sure everyone's safe. You can come with us if you want, but I don't really know what to expect. There could be more fighting."

She shook her head.

"Galen's men can take you away from the Trifectate. Maybe across the sea."

"I'll be safe there?" she asked.

I squeezed her hand. "They'll send you somewhere safe."

"Will there be others like us?" she asked.

I hesitated. "I don't know. Why?"

She rocked a little faster. "I don't . . ." She trailed off so long I thought she had stopped talking before she continued, "I want to learn how to use it. How to heal, like you showed me." She nodded. "I can convince the others too. I think the rest of us should stay together."

"If that's what you want, I'll make sure of it."

"I want to *stop* him," she said. "And this power—he's *afraid* of us. I want to make sure he knows exactly what to fear."

Rubbing her hand, I promised her, "Then I'll make sure you know how to use your power."

I left Iona a little later, looking for Kairos to make arrangements. I found him out in the wood around the inn, reclining in the heart of a tree, looking at the sky. Osmost was making lazy circles, hunting, and we both watched as he swooped, silent and deadly, striking for a kill.

"So Galen says we're going to the desert," Kairos said without looking back.

"Yes," I said, coming beside the tree.

He nodded. "Good."

"What happened?" I asked, my voice low. "Since we parted."

His eyes swept down, but he still didn't look at me. His throat bobbed. "After you put up an epic fit?" he asked, but his joke didn't work. "I *had* you," he said, shaking his head. "I had you, and then your power just ripped me away from you. I couldn't hold on, Shy," he told me, and he finally looked to me. The pain in my brother's eyes tore at me. "I'm so sorry. I couldn't hold on."

I shook my head. "I'm sorry I couldn't save them, Kai."

He looked thoroughly confused. "What? How could you save them?"

I pushed a tear off my cheek before it fell completely. "What good is this damned power if I can't protect them? I should have learned to use it earlier. I was just so frightened of it—of *Calix*—"

Kairos waved his hand. "Unfortunately, my dear sister, you're not allowed to take credit for the actions of others." He rubbed his hands over his knees. "Even if it would make it easier to blame yourself. To feel like you had some kind of control in the situation."

I crossed my arms. "Then why do you get to be sorry for Calix capturing me?"

He looked at me with a sadder version of his sly smile. "I'm older; I get to make the rules."

I gave him the best smile I could muster.

But his smile faded. "And I should have known," he said softly, squinting into the forest rather than meeting my gaze. "The visions—I should have figured it out sooner. And I was so clouded trying to make sense of visions of our family buried in rock that I didn't look past it. I didn't know what was coming for you."

I wanted to tell him that like his vision of our family, there might have been nothing he could have done to change what happened to me, but it felt too much like rubbing salt in a wound. I put my hand on his arm, and tried to let that say everything I couldn't.

He cleared his throat. "So Galen?" he asked.

A piece of quartz in the dirt near the roots of the tree caught my attention, and I unearthed it with my shoe, delaying my answer. "I think Rian is going to murder him."

Kai smiled. "Not everyone is quite so enlightened as I am." I made a face, and Kairos's smile broke wider. "Rian wants you to be happy. Galen makes you happy—he'll see that eventually. But he's been lied to, and no one enjoys that."

I ran my finger over the tree bark. "I love him, Kai," I told him.

"I've known that for a while," he said. He sighed. "I think I knew that before you did."

"You did not!"

He looked at me and raised his eyebrows. "The day you selected the Saepia. Knew it then."

"I didn't love him then!"

"But I could see that you would." He shifted in the tree. "Go find Rian; Osmost is about to come back with something exceptionally bloody, and I'd rather spare you the violence of it all."

"Very well," I said, pushing off the tree. "I love you, Kai."

He didn't look at me. "Love you too."

I heard Osmost's cry as I turned away and didn't look back to see what he'd caught.

It wasn't difficult to find my oldest brother. He was in the common room of the inn, sharpening his sword and looking out the window to where Kairos was in the tree. When I came in, he looked down.

"Were you watching us?" I asked, sitting across from him.

"Yes," he said. "I'm not letting either one of you out of my sight. Ever."

"You punched Galen."

His jaw knotted with tense muscle, but he didn't respond.

"Rian."

"What do you want me to do, Shalia? I can only imagine what kind of advances he's made on you. You trusted him, and he abused that. He dishonored you—"

"No," I snapped. "Do *not* say that anymore. My *honor* has nothing to do with what man is married to me, or touching me, or loves me. I will not be broken or diminished or belittled by the choices of men around me. Do you understand me, Rian d'Dragyn?"

He stopped sharpening and looked up at me. His eyes darted over my face for a moment, and he said, "I understand."

"Good."

His hands moved on the blade again, slowly dragging the whetstone to sharpen the blade. "You sound like Mother, you know."

My eyes shut. That was everything I had ever wanted, but now—now—

"It's a good thing," he said, his voice rough. I looked at him, and he raised his head up, his eyes bright and ringed with moisture. He sniffed and fixed his eyes on his sword again.

"I'm worried, Shalia, and I have that right. You don't know him like I do. There's no one else I would want beside me in a fight, but he will hurt you."

"I've been hurt," I said softly. "And if he does hurt me, it won't be the same way Calix did. Galen's heart is strong and good."

Rian's throat worked. "What heart, Shalia? Galen may have emerged on the side of good in that family, but none of them are unscathed. Calix? Danae? They're damaged. They're broken. Galen has been lying to everyone he loves for years. He has killed for one cause while he believes in another. He is the most dangerous man I have ever met."

"And you don't have to see what I do," I told him. He opened his mouth, and I raised my hand. "I trust him, Rian. I trust him and his heart."

"Shalia," Rian said, frowning at me. "You've always been tenderhearted, but he is not a bird with a broken wing."

"Calix betrayed me in every way I can imagine," I told Rian, my voice soft. "He stole my will. My voice. He made me feel small, and quiet, and trapped. Galen has protected me, at great cost to himself. He's made me feel valued, and valuable, and precious, and loved. He doesn't see his own valor, his own worth, and I think it's shameful that you claim to be his friend and don't see it either." Rian scowled at me. "Galen may be broken, but I have been broken too. And if we can break and rebuild together, that's all I want."

Rian swallowed, shaking his head. "I want more for you. I will always want more for you."

"It's my choice, Rian," I told him. "After everything that's happened, don't take my choice away."

He sniffed. "I don't regret punching him."

I crossed my arms. "I suppose that's your choice."

Rian looked out at the darkening sky. "You should sleep. We're going to be moving fast tomorrow, and you've been through a lot. As has my niece," he said, looking to my stomach.

I smiled. "I'll try. Is there somewhere to send the other Elementae? They don't want to come to the desert, and they need to be safe. To heal in more ways than Kata can give."

He nodded. "I'll see to it."

"Are you going to stay here until Kairos comes in?"

"Yes."

"Very well. Good night, Rian," I told him, going around to kiss his cheek. He touched my arm for a quick moment and let me go.

I didn't go to my room. I drifted down the hallway, wondering how I could figure out which room Galen was in without bursting in, or knocking, or somehow making myself known. I walked the long hallway twice when a door opened.

Spinning around, I spotted one of the soldiers. He stopped when he saw me, and I froze. Blushing and feeling utterly foolish, I went back to my own room, shaking my head as I shut the door.

"Oh."

I knew his voice even from such a soft syllable, and I looked up to see Galen standing by the window.

"Galen," I said.

"I was just making sure no one can get up here," he said. "The windows seem sturdy, and I'm fairly certain that the pitch of the lower roof would take a while to climb. However, if we get ambushed, we might be able to make use of it for escape. But still, I'll have a guard outside, just to make sure." He was flushing, the red bright on his skin from his flimsy excuse, and he nodded once before starting to move toward the door.

"I was trying to find you," I said.

He halted, his eyes wide, watching me. "You were."

He was closer now, and I could see the redness near his eye where Rian had punched him. I touched it gingerly, and he smiled, a tiny, wry thing. "That doesn't hurt?" I asked.

His eyes swept over my face. "I can't really feel pain when you're touching me like that." The smile widened. "Or when you're touching me at all." Then he saw my wrist, and the white lines that remained from where Kata healed the wounds left by the manacles. He caught my hand in both of his, brushing his fingers over the scar.

His breathing was heavy and erratic as he touched me, not speaking. "Galen?" I whispered.

"He tortured you. He was supposed to love you, and he tortured you."

"No," I murmured. "Not in the way you think."

This drew his stark gaze to mine, and there was so much fear there. Fear for me. "Shalia, he knew how to torture you in a way that was far more effective. Just because he didn't strike you doesn't mean it wasn't torture."

I couldn't deny how true that felt. "Iona lost her eye. Because of me. Because I couldn't do it. I wanted to, but I just couldn't."

"Shalia," he said again.

"And another girl died. She couldn't have been more than thirteen. He was right," I told him, faster, trying to get it all out in a rush. "I was still able to use my power. I guess I just didn't—didn't care enough for them."

He stepped closer to me, and I nudged my forehead against his, closing my eyes and sinking into his touch. "No," he said, and his chest rumbled with the sound. "That's not your fault. Nothing he did was your fault."

"I should have *saved* them, Galen. If only I could have controlled my power." I shook my head hard, bringing my hands up to curl my fingers in his shirt.

He brushed kisses on my temple. "You said your power comes from your heart, didn't you?" he whispered.

I nodded.

"You can't control your heart. You can only trust it." He took one hand, and brought it to his lips, kissing my knuckles. "Like I trust you with mine."

He looked at me, slowly, for a long time. His eyes traced over every part of my face, and a slow smile came over his mouth. "I love you, Shalia d'Dragyn. Your heart is my heart." He took the hand he was holding and put it on his chest, like I could feel his heart there. He drew a long breath under my hand. "And I know right now, the only thing you can think of is surviving, and grieving, and being free of my brother. But when that happens, I will be there. I will keep you and your baby safe for the rest of your days."

My fingers eased on his chest, straightening and smoothing over his shirt, and I wondered if it were that easy, to take something and hold it. "I don't want that."

He looked like I had struck him, and my fingers wandered, finding the pulse at the base of his neck. This seemed more tangible, a brighter piece of his heart for me to hold.

"I went from being a sister and a daughter to a wife, a guarded queen. I have little idea what my life will be like if I'm free from Calix, but I don't want to be something you protect. I won't teach my daughter that her only choice is to be sheltered by the men around her. I want to stand beside you," I told him, running my fingers lightly over his chest. "I want to learn to fight with you. I won't accept you as a protector," I whispered. His eyes were wet, shining and bright green because of it. "But I will accept you as something else. Something far greater. Because with whatever scraps of my heart are left, I love you too, Galen."

My breath shuddered as it came out, but I leaned up, staring at his green eyes. I pressed forward, grazing his upper lip, opening my mouth to kiss his bottom lip.

Then he moved, and his mouth opened to meet mine. His tongue stroked into my mouth, and I raised my arms, twining them around his neck, our bodies sliding together. His hands ran down my sides, making my skin feel hot and alive everywhere he touched.

With relief so sharp it felt like pain, the threads strained against my fingertips, and I stepped back from his arms, holding up my hands.

"Your power?" he asked.

I gazed at him, his hair spiky and dark and slightly disheveled, his chest rising and falling hard. I nodded, and stepped back into his arms, pressing my mouth to the cords in his neck. His pulse hammered under my lips.

"Shalia," he said, catching my shoulders. "I shouldn't do this. I can't do this. You just lost your family, you almost lost your child—"

"You're not doing anything," I told him. "*We're* doing something. And after all the pain of the past few weeks, I want to know what this is really supposed to feel like. What it is to be touched by someone who moves the heaven and stars for you. Please give that to me, Galen."

His thumb touched my lip, and his eyes followed, like he couldn't look away. "It won't fix anything. It won't change anything he did."

"No," I told him. "It won't be about him at all." I kissed the pad of his thumb on my lip. "It will be different, with you, won't it?" I asked him, my voice quiet and small.

"I've never been so damn scared to touch a woman in my life," he whispered, his fingertips on my shoulder, barely grazing my skin. "So I'm fairly sure it's different for me."

My shoulders drew up. "I meant . . . with you, when you touch me, I feel things that I've never felt."

His fingers brushed my hair back, letting it slide over the skin of my shoulders, and following it with his fingertips. "I like the sound of that," he whispered.

His touch made me dizzy, but my thoughts sobered me. "Every time with him, it was awful," I breathed.

He swallowed, meeting my gaze, touching my face. "My sweet," he whispered. "It will be different. The only thing I want you to feel with me is pleasure. My love," he said, kissing my cheek. His lips moved to the corner of my mouth. "My lovely dragon." He pulled back a little.

Tentatively, I moved forward until our lips met again, and his hands fell, going to my waist and back, pulling me tight against him. His mouth left mine a moment later, kissing my chin, my jaw, my throat. His hands pulled up to slide under the coat and slip the garment off me. I shivered against him, and he kept kissing me.

I had never had a desire to touch Calix, but now my hands were restless and busy, trying to touch as much of Galen as I could. I pushed off his jacket and ran my hands over his shirt, feeling the firm knots of muscle as they moved and twisted and leaped up to meet my fingers. I loved how he couldn't seem to catch his breath, and I felt his heart beating hard under his skin, everywhere I touched.

He loosened the cords keeping my dress together beneath my breasts and around my waist, and as he pulled the knot, his fingers brushed my stomach and he stilled. He kissed his way down my covered body as he knelt in front of me, parting the cloth to show my stomach to him. His hands covered my child as he kissed me.

"You can feel her," he breathed, covering the spot where my skin had turned from soft to firm. He pressed a chaste, earnest kiss there, and stood up, looking at me. "You're a miracle, Shalia. And this child—it doesn't matter to me who her father is. I will love her like my own every day of my life. You know that, don't you?"

I ran my fingers through his hair and pulled his mouth to mine to keep from crying again, and I started tugging ineffectively at his clothes.

He broke our kiss to pull his shirt over his head and looked at me again. "You're sure?" he asked.

Nodding, I let the cloth of the dress slip off my shoulders.

He stared at me for many long moments, and then leaped into action, shucking his clothes in seconds and coming to me, wrapping his warm arms around me as he led me to the bed.

The threads crackled around me, but I let them slide away from my fingers. Galen was right; I had to put my faith in my heart, in my power, in him. I let it go, and I felt the power shimmering around us, soaking into everything that was of the earth as he touched me. I didn't have to try to control it; it was just there.

I couldn't help but think of Calix, and the way he touched me when I didn't want it, the way it was never my choice. Twice I stopped, touching Galen's face until I was sure it was him and not his brother, and both times Galen waited, halting until I asked him to continue.

The second time I felt embarrassed tears in my eyes, and I tried to laugh them away. "You have excellent self-control, you know," I told him.

He frowned at me, kissing me gently. "What control would I need? There's nothing exciting about the idea of hurting the woman you love, Shalia."

I stroked his back, pulling him closer to me. "You love me," I whispered.

He grinned, a sweet, bright smile. "I love you," he said.

I knew then what my mother meant when I was first married, when she told me that this was wondrous, the most intimate act that two people could share.

It had nothing to do with the closeness of our bodies. It felt like he saw everything I was, full of hope and scars and faults and love. He let me see him the same way, without his armor and masks. Open, and whole.

He continued when I asked him to, and as our lips met, everything seemed to shift inside that kiss, a new future spinning out in each other's arms.

Over the Edge

We woke in the night to shouting. My heart seized for a moment, the terror of the past few days overtaking me, but Galen caught me. "Hush," he said gently. "Something's happening. I have to go see what it is. Stay away from the windows and don't open the door."

He rushed out of the room, and I put my palm to my racing heart. Light caught my attention, and though I tried to stay away from the window, I saw the remains of a hot, fast flash of fire burning the leaves of a tree.

It wasn't long before Galen came back into my room, but I had guessed what he would tell me—Danae was gone, and by morning Calix would know where we had been.

We were all awake before the gray dawn, quiet and efficient in our preparations to leave. Ten horses had arrived in the night for us, but it meant that not everyone could come with us. Considering that Calix would never let me go willingly, it didn't put me at ease to have a smaller group.

The remaining men readied the Elementae to travel due east for the coastline and a ship to take them to the islands. Iona was trembling as she hugged me good-bye, but I told her I would see her as soon as I was able.

Galen hadn't spoken to me at all, but every time I caught his gaze—which was often—it felt like it was obvious in his eyes what had happened between us, and it made me feel hot and ever so slightly dizzy. He came and put his hands on my waist to help me onto my horse, and I couldn't breathe as he did.

"Let's go," Rian called gruffly.

I smiled at Galen, and he nodded at me and went to mount his own horse.

The ride was uneasy. It took us most of the day to make it to where the land bridge used to stand, and as we rode, I stretched my powers, clearing rocks from our path, piling up dirt when we were too exposed.

My power had shifted. It wasn't like reaching for threads anymore; it was like my body was made of threads itself, all part of the same fabric. Using my power was as simple as thinking, as wishing, as breathing—it was there with me, responding to me, part of me.

I didn't know if it was my growing relationship with Galen, or my child, or my freedom, but something within me had settled into my self, and my power grew exponentially for it.

When we saw the castle that Vestai Atalo lived in, we slowed, and I looked at its tall, strong walls with a shiver.

Kairos sent Osmost flying into the air to scout ahead of us, and I watched him, watching the bird, seeing how he turned and shrieked.

"You've gotten better at that," I told him.

He grinned and lifted an eyebrow. "Indeed I have."

He waited a few moments more and called out to Rian and Galen, leading the line. "No one's ahead, but if men are in the castle, Osmost won't be able to see, and we won't know until it's too late."

"Can we go north?" Galen asked. "If Shalia's building a bridge, can't we just do it anywhere?"

"It's not the bridge," I told them. "That shouldn't be too hard. It's the pass—this tunnel is blocked, but there's one about a hundred feet down in the cliff. If I can forge a bridge to that, we'll be in much better shape."

"An alternate exit in case of cave-ins," Rian told Galen. Then he seemed to remember they weren't on good terms and frowned.

"Shalia isn't the only Elementa here," Kata reminded, giving me an arch look. "And there's plenty of water in the river down below. If they come while she works, I can repel them."

"Very well," Galen said. "Move fast. Shalia, you go first; Rian and I will follow you. Kairos, stay to the middle and keep the hawk in play. Kata, toward the back so you can fight first. Men, you know what to do."

Everyone nodded, and I led my horse up between Rian and Galen. My heart was beating hard as I looked at the open stretch of road. "I just ride for the edge?" I asked, pointing. The road was still in shambles from where my power had wreaked havoc, and I couldn't ask if my family had been burned here or somewhere else.

Not in the sands of the desert, that was for sure.

"Yes. Wherever you need to be to use your power," Galen told me. He reached for my hand and kissed it, and Rian growled.

"You can do this," Galen said, ignoring my brother. "We'll keep you safe."

"That, at least, we can agree on," Rian grunted.

"We agree on much more than that, old friend," Galen told him. "If we die today, you need to remember that."

"We're not dying today, if only so we have more time to fight about this," Rian snapped at him. "Shalia, go!"

I went. I spurred my horse hard and covered the thousand or more feet between the castle and the pass. It seemed to take an eternity, long enough for my heartbeat to match the beat of the horse's hooves.

And then the edge of the cliff loomed before me, broken and jagged where the land bridge used to be.

I heard shouting, and I saw Trifectate soldiers swarming out from the castle, and then Kata holding her hands up and water cresting up from the crevasse and swirling in the air. With a rush, it arched down in front of her, hitting the road and knocking the soldiers off their feet.

With a deep breath, I reminded myself that the best way to help everyone was to get them across before the battle got much, much worse.

I turned back to the open air, the impossibly deep drop, even as I watched more water flying up to come to Kata's aid. I could see the dark smudge of the lower tunnel, and I shut my eyes, calling up stones and dirt, slamming the boulders into place to form a rough, uneven kind of stairway to bridge the gap.

The sound of rushing water behind me stopped abruptly, and I turned. Kata was on the ground, and Kairos was crouched beside her. The rest of the men were in a line, standing as soldiers ran at them. The two lines slammed together with a clash of violent steel.

"Shalia!" Kairos yelled, picking up Kata. "Focus!"

I looked back toward the crevasse. There were several stairs lifting up from the lower outlet. I lifted my arms, focusing again, watching the rocks rip out from the mountain and bash themselves into place.

"What happened?" I asked as Kairos came beside me with Kata limp in his arms.

"Arrow," he said, showing me her side. "And she hit her head."

"Leave her here. Keep fighting," I told him. He hesitated, but I shook my head. "Go!" I told him.

Kairos nodded, turning back to whatever was raging behind me.

Three more stairs slammed into place, the noise shuddering my feet.

"Shalia, hurry!" It was Galen's voice.

I turned for a moment. There were more soldiers rushing out of the castle, and the Resistance was about to be utterly overwhelmed.

"Almost done!" I yelled.

"Go!" I heard, and this was closer. Men peeled away from the line of battle, and the first one ran past me at full pace, leaping into the air to the uncompleted bridge. He caught the edge, slipping down, and with a gasp, I sent a rock up under him, pushing him higher. He popped up with it, running down the stairs as soon as he was able.

Men started running after him, but I could still hear fighting behind me. I turned again and saw Rian, Galen, and Kairos fighting men, and Osmost screaming and plucking at the eyes and face of another, who was flailing under the hawk's talons.

The next wave of soldiers was only seconds away. "Now!" I yelled. "We have to go! Kair—"

My words were cut off as something slammed into my side, pulling me to the ground and falling on top of me. The breath was knocked out of me as I saw my husband's face swim before my eyes.

He was faster than I was. He sprang up, wrapping his arm around my throat and hauling me up. I clawed at his arm as Galen, Rian, and Kairos halted in front of me.

"Brother," Calix growled at Galen.

Galen put up his hands, stepping forward slowly. "Let her go, Calix. You've done enough."

My eyes darted to Kairos. His eyes lifted up. *Osmost.* If I could knock him off me, Osmost would take him.

"You've betrayed me, brother. I always knew you would. So disloyal you would choose a woman—*my* woman—over your own brother."

Galen swallowed, and I called up a rock without any way to know how far behind Calix's head it was. "I didn't betray you," Galen said. "You have debased this family and this country for so long that this was all I could do."

The other soldiers had arrived, but they hung back, making a half circle around us and the edge of the cliff. Trapped. There was one extremely tall soldier, and I recognized him instantly. *Zeph.*

"Shy, now!" Kairos snapped, and I tried to hit Calix's head with a rock. It missed, but he dropped me to dodge it, and I ran forward as Osmost shrieked downward.

Calix hit Osmost's talons away, but Kairos was right behind him, tackling Calix around the waist and heaving him onto his back dangerously close to the edge. Kairos reared up, slamming punch after punch to Calix's face, and we all ran forward.

Calix bucked him off, rolling over to hit Kairos, but Kairos turned them once more and landed more blows.

Calix slammed his fist up through Kairos's jaw and pushed at the same moment, and Kairos's body flipped over the edge.

With a scream, I reached out with my power, and I felt rocks shearing off the cliff, but I couldn't see what I was doing. I couldn't tell if I had caught him or if I had hit him in the head with a boulder. I ran to the edge, kneeling to look over, but I couldn't see him.

"Shalia!" Galen yelled, snatching me back from the edge.

Galen dragged me toward the bridge and Rian ran to meet us as Calix yelled, "Kill them! Kill them all!"

There was still an unfinished gap on the bridge, but Galen jumped, and without a question, I jumped after him. He caught me, landing on the highest step and swinging me aside so Rian could jump after us.

The Trifectate men nearly caught Rian, but a big shape cut them off.

"You'll have to go through me," Zeph said, and I saw him turn to face the semicircle of men.

I saw Theron move forward, shaking his head. "This isn't how I wanted this to end, old friend," Theron said.

Zeph didn't respond, lunging forward with his khopesh. Rian jumped and stumbled down a stair as the men hesitated, then bellowed as they closed in on my brave guard.

"Go," Galen ordered Rian. He started running down the stairs, and Galen tugged my waist. "Shalia, go!"

"Not yet!" I yelled, raising my arms and calling up thousands of tiny stones as Zeph twisted and moved, fighting hard.

"Shalia, Calix!" Galen yelled, pointing to where Calix was approaching the stairs.

Taking one of the larger stones, I launched it at his head. It hit him square in the temple, and Calix fell to the ground.

Stretching my fingers, with a shout I sent the brute force of the rocks flying into the faces of the men around Zeph. It wasn't very precise or fatal, but it earned a moment of distraction.

"Run!" Galen shouted at him.

Zeph ran hard for us, barreling over the edge and hitting first Galen, then me, knocking us back.

Rather than falling onto the stairs, I fell off the side.

For long seconds, I fell through the air. Galen shrank in the air above me and I couldn't think. I couldn't breathe.

Was this what Kairos felt?

Suddenly, without my intention, a rock came up beneath me, cradling me and easing my fall before stopping it completely.

With a gasp of relief, I got to my feet, holding my hand to my belly as the rock began to rise. I looked down—I couldn't see Kairos, or where he might have fallen.

A shout from above drew my attention. Other soldiers had jumped across the rock, and Galen and Zeph were fighting them off, struggling to keep their foothold. Zeph drove his fist into a man's jaw, and the man careened off the rock.

"Down!" I shouted, pointing at the tunnel.

Galen pushed Zeph, and the two men started running down the stairs. I started collapsing it behind them as another soldier jumped and fell into air.

My heart seized, and I sent a rock out to catch him and send him back to the edge of the cliff.

Flying the rock back up to the tunnel, I saw Rian talking to Kata, pale and sitting, clutching her side as blood came through her fingers. "Go into the tunnel and get Kata to the water so she's stronger. I have to go look for Kairos!" I yelled.

I started to turn away when Galen leaped off the edge, landing on my rock and tilting it hard. I grabbed him, and he wrapped his arms around me. "Whoa," he said, steadying.

"What are you doing?" I asked.

"Coming with you," he said.

"Galen—"

His hands rubbed my arms a tiny bit. "No matter what you find, I don't want you doing it alone."

"Duck!" Rian shouted, pointing as an arrow flew, falling short and dropping into the crevasse.

"Go," I told him. "I'll be up as soon as I find him."

He nodded, fixing his stare on Galen. "Keep her safe."

Galen's throat bobbed, and his arm wrapped around my waist. "Always."

Galen brushed a kiss on my cheek, and I nodded at Rian, letting the rock drift downward. I curled my arms around him, leaning my head on his shoulder so I could look one way and he could look the other. I brought us all the way to the churning water in the bottom of the canyon, the wind blowing at my skirt and face and hair, cold where the rest of my body was warm against Galen.

I slowed the rock as it skimmed along the river.

"I didn't even know there was a river here," Galen whispered in my ear.

I nodded. "My father took me here once, when I was a child and we hadn't found food for a long while. We came to hunt." I pointed behind his back. "Far over that way, there's an old staircase. It took us hours to climb it." My fingers curled against him. "Maybe Kairos would go toward it."

"Shalia," he said softly. "Do you think he would have survived the fall?"

I shuddered against him. "I don't know. I tried to catch him," I said, my voice going so rough it barely escaped my throat. "But I couldn't see him. I could have—I could have hurt him."

"Or you could have caught him," he said.

"Keep looking," I said.

He nodded against my head.

We floated west first, going to where the mountains began to fold together, the river just emerging between the rocky crags. My eyes caught on rocks, and sticks, the movement of a fish, and every time, my heart leaped.

We turned east, going slower, looking at every inch of the riverbed. As we grew closer to the ocean, Galen pulled away from me to tug his jacket off his shoulders, putting it around me. I frowned up at him.

"You're shaking," he said, holding me tight again.

I looked up at his face and saw a sadness etched there. "I'm sorry," I told him. "That you had to fight your brother."

"I should have killed him," he said, but the words lacked fire and instead sounded defeated.

"He's your brother," I reminded him.

His throat worked. "Someday, I'll have to be the one to kill him, Shalia. I need to make peace with that."

I held his hand tight. "Maybe so. But it's all right if you haven't just yet."

He nodded, kissing my head, and I focused on the river again.

When we reached the ocean, the stone halted, faltering a little. "He's not here," I breathed.

"Not finding his body—that could be a good thing," he told me softly.

" 'Body,' " I repeated. "I can't—I can't lose him, Galen."

His arms tightened around me. "Let's check again."

"Rian will worry."

"He's safe. Worrying won't hurt him."

I nodded, moving the rock down the river again.

Legend

I didn't know how much time had passed when I finally gave up. The light was dimming in the sky and I couldn't feel anymore. I didn't feel cold, or tired. I couldn't look at anything anymore. Kairos was gone, and I had lost one more beloved thing, one more piece of me removed that I didn't know how to survive without.

Galen tucked me deep in his arms as I let the rock rise up.

I didn't trust myself to walk, so we stayed on the rock and floated into the tunnel. Within moments, the light behind us died and I shut my eyes. My power could feel the rock around me better than I could see it, and I just moved us along.

Rian wasn't in the tunnel. No one was.

"They're not here," I murmured.

Galen brushed my hair back. "They would have gone ahead. We've been gone a long while."

I nodded and kept the rock floating down the passage.

Soon we saw torchlight, and I slowed down. I saw Zeph first, his big body looming even larger in the flickering light.

"Something's wrong," Galen murmured, holding my hand as he jumped off the rock. I followed him.

"Zeph?" I called.

Zeph turned, and I saw blood cascading down his arm. "What happened?"

Kata came forward. She looked paler and weak. "He's wounded. It's bad. I couldn't heal it completely."

Zeph's uninjured shoulder lifted. "I can't really move my hand," he huffed.

"How are you standing?" Galen asked.

He pointed to himself. "Legend," he said with a heavy sigh, before instantly slumping against the wall. Kata sighed and caught him with her power, lowering him to the ground.

"He's fine," Kata told me. "Or he will be."

"Where's Kai?" Rian asked, walking around Zeph with a torch in his hand. He let it fall to the ground where it still burned, coming to me, looking around me. "Where is he?"

I covered my mouth. Words didn't come out—the horrible words, that I couldn't find him, that he wasn't *there*—but tears did, and Rian grabbed me, hugging me hard.

"We didn't find the body," Galen murmured. "But—"

"Of *course* he's alive," Rian growled. "You don't know anything about my brother."

I pulled back, nodding. "He has to be alive, right? Kairos—Kairos can't—"

Rian pinched my cheek. "Kairos is the most clever man I've ever known. Of course he's alive."

"There's a branch of the river close to here," Kata said softly. "If I can get to the water, I'll be able to try again to heal the guard."

I thought of Theron, and how only a few days ago I wouldn't have known which guard she meant by that. But now the two men were distinguished by their loyalty, a line I wished I'd never made them cross.

"Then we go," I told her. "We're not losing anyone else."

We walked for most of the night. We reached the river, and Kata waded into the water and out again a moment later as Zeph slumped down onto the ground.

"Zeph?" I called. "Zeph?" I touched his cheek—he was still breathing, but he had passed out. "Kata, please hurry."

We all waited, watching as she worked on him. Kata looked heartbroken as she said the arm was lost, and she couldn't heal it, so the men held Zeph down as Galen cut through the rest of it, severing his arm above the elbow. Zeph was so weak he barely fought against the pain, and as it was done, I went to his side, wiping his brow, speaking soft words of comfort to him, trying to protect him from pain as he had always done for me.

Kata's power took after the arm was gone, and she grew pale, sweating hard, pouring her power into him as his breathing eased and his heart grew stronger.

I stayed beside him as Kata went back to the water, pulling her strength from it. Galen sat beside me, tucking his body close to mine, and Rian sighed and sat down near Zeph. The other men of the Resistance came and sat with us.

Rian leaned his arms on his knees. "He'll be all right, Shy."

Galen grunted. "Please. He'll never be the same again. He will be lording this over me for years—lost his arm protecting his queen!—I'll never hear the end of it."

"Shalia," Kata said, and I met her eyes. She gestured toward the water.

With a deep sigh, I stood, going over to her. There was a frown on her face that made me think of Galen, and it was strange to think he was right behind me, right beside me in all things. "What is it?"

"Do you feel that?" she asked, running her hands in the water.

I dipped my hand in. "Cold?"

"No," she said. "Your power. Does anything feel strange with your power?"

I felt out along the rocks, along this place that hummed with threads. She was right—there was something there, like a break, like a place where threads had been cut.

"I think so," I told her. "What is that?"

Her eyes met mine heavily. "I've felt something like that once before," she told me. "In the islands. When I was . . . when they tried to get my powers to show."

"It feels stronger here," I told her, following the river upward. The stream disappeared into rock, and I pulled at it to make the space wider.

"What are you doing?" Rian asked from behind us.

But Kata was at my shoulder, and we pressed forward, going to the gap I created. More water was rushing out, and then something fell into the stream. I reached for it, but Kata snatched my hands away. "Rian," she called. "Grab that!"

I pulled away from her as he took it from the stream. He held up a glass cage, fused shut with gold, and inside an orb filled with red liquid shimmered, dark and dangerous.

"Blood?" Galen asked, coming closer. "What is that?"

I felt along it with my power. The gold was foreign to me, flat and unresponsive. All around the cage, I felt like the threads had been cut, and I couldn't use my power. Slowly, my fingers covered my mouth. "The elixir?" I breathed. "I think this is what Calix was looking for."

"This is the elixir?" Galen asked, taking it from Rian.

"This *was* a person," Kata said, her voice a snarl. "It's the blood of an Elementa. The blood of an islander." She shook her head, turning away from me. "It was a person."

"Kata," Rian said, going over to her. I stepped aside, wanting to move closer to Galen, but not wanting to get too close to that thing.

"Don't *touch* me," she snarled, turning to push Rian away. I saw tears in her eyes, and the sight made something crack inside me.

But Rian pushed forward, gripping her arms, pressing his forehead to hers. Her breaths were rough and shallow. "I'm here," he said. "You're safe. You've made yourself safe."

I felt totally lost, looking at them. Rian and Kata . . . *meant* something to each other that I had never noticed before.

Her breathing slowed, becoming even and steady. In his arms. I looked to Galen, wondering if he knew that's what he did for me too. "This whole time, he wasn't looking for some magic potion. It's not an object," Kata said softly, tugging my eyes from Galen. "It's a person. It's a fifth type of element."

"You said you felt it before?" I asked.

She nodded. "When he came to the islands. After he broke our numbers, they spent two days rounding people up and trying to get us to show our powers, and I tried, but I felt like this, almost as if it was severed. Like the power didn't even exist." She pulled away from Rian, wiping her face, shaking her head. "No.

It couldn't have been the same. I know he used something like this to *take* the islands, but they wouldn't have tried to make us use our powers with it nearby. They would have known I couldn't."

"Us?" I asked softly, looking to Rian. He shook his head. "Who were the others?" I asked.

She nodded. "At least two more. I didn't know them."

"Kata," I said softly. "One of them was probably this fifth element, some kind of void that can cancel out the other elements. And they didn't know it anymore than you did."

"How could it be?" she asked me. "I've never even heard of a fifth element. There are no more priestesses, my family is *dead*, and there is so much I don't know about my own heritage. About these powers."

"Your family is here," I told her fiercely, taking her hand.

"So we should destroy this," Galen suggested, holding it up over the river. "It doesn't look hard to break."

"Don't," I told him. "We don't know how that works, but it's like my power feels disrupted around it. Crumbled, a little. I think if that blood spills, it will be far worse."

Kata nodded.

"How did it get here?" Zeph asked, still sitting against the wall.

I pointed to the river. "That leads straight from the lake Calix was searching. It must have shifted."

"We're lucky it didn't break," Kata said. She took a deep breath, stepping closer to Rian and kissing him briefly. "We're going to have to hide it until we can figure out how to destroy it properly."

"Not here," Rian said.

"Definitely not. If Calix ever figures out a way across, this tunnel will lead him straight to it," Galen said.

"We'll bring it to Jitra for now. How are we going to carry him?" Kata asked, nodding to Zeph's limp body. "It's a long walk still."

"I can do it," I said, calling the flat rock we had used in the tunnel to me. The other men helped lift Zeph onto it, and I used my power to float him up.

"Do you—" Galen started, holding out the cage to Rian.

"You hold it," Rian said, a small smile on his face. "That way you'll keep your hands off my sister for a little while."

Galen's face soured. "You will have to accept this eventually, Rian."

"Yes," he said, moving ahead of Galen and me in the tunnel. "But not today."

With a sigh, I leaned forward and kissed Galen gently. "That's progress, at least," I whispered to him.

He nodded, chasing my lips for a moment before pulling back. "Go," he said. "I don't want this thing to do anything to you." His nose rubbed over mine, and in a soft, secret voice, he reminded me, "I love you."

I kissed him once more. "I love you too."

When the passage opened out onto the road, I saw that I had lost all sense of time. It was so dark it was nearly impossible to see. Rian and I didn't need light, sure of our steps back to Jitra, while the others stumbled along, and I found myself walking beside my brother, reaching for his hand as our weary steps grew faster, eager to go home.

The entrance to the carved city was cracked, the stone threatening to fall. Galen kept the blood out of range so I could use my power, lifting my arms to seal the rock back together, unbroken. Unharmed.

Inside the entrance more rock had tumbled down to block the narrow passages. Slowly, carefully, I pulled it all up, Kata close behind me. With the last stone moved, a path cleared into the center of Jitra, and I halted, unable to go farther.

"I can't," I breathed. "Not without him. Not without all of them."

Rian drew a ragged breath, tugging both of my hands. "Shy," he said softly. "What does your power feel like? When you use it?"

"What do you mean?" I asked.

"Kata's told me it's like strings, isn't it? Isn't that what it feels like?"

Sucking in a breath, I nodded. "Yes," I said, when I wasn't sure if he could see me in the dark.

"For wealth," he said. "For secrets. For ferocity. For a full stomach." His hands squeezed mine. "But most importantly, there is a thread because you're desert born, and you will never be alone."

I swore I could see them in the dark, my siblings and family coming forward to bless me just as they had the day I married.

Rian had been first, with his thread full of foreign coins that I now knew the cost of far too well. *For wealth, little sister. That you never want for anything.*

Then Cael. *You won't stand alone*, he told me. He gave me a white-and-black thread woven together. *You are desert born, and you will never be alone.*

Aiden was next, with a blue thread knotted around a mountain cat tooth. *For ferocity*, he said, and I could feel the ghost of his fingers pinching my nose. *Show them what the heart of the desert truly is.*

And then Kairos. Sly as ever, and as I remembered his words, they chilled me and gave me a thrill of hope. *Keep your secrets*, he had told me with a flash of his bright smile.

And then, last, the spirits of two small figures who would be together in death as they always were in life. Catryn and Gavan presented one thread, tied around a small purse. *I made the thread, and he made the purse*, Cat explained. She put it around my neck.

It's full of seeds, Gavan said. *In case they don't feed you.*

So you never go hungry, Catryn corrected.

Gavan shrugged. *Same thing.*

Their spirits stepped back and faded, but I still felt them all around me, felt the warmth of the clan, heard the women keening their low song to send me on from the desert with blessings and love.

I was not poor. I was not alone, or broken, or hungry. Their blessings had carried me through every challenge and horror I had faced; in truth, I had never left the desert at all, and my child would know the light, the warmth, and the love of her ancestors.

And yet. Passing through this doorway without Kairos and his secrets made my whole body ache, reminded me of the threat that was looming just beyond the desert, the hate of my husband gathering like a storm. I hugged Rian tight and hard, and I felt his chest shiver with grief against me.

"We must do this," he said. "Our feet will never fail to carry us home."

"But Kairos," I whispered.

"He's safe," Kata murmured, not far from us in the dark.

"You don't know that," I heard Galen tell her gruffly. "Don't give them false hope."

"I do know," Kata told him. "The world has been broken and hurt, lying shattered in pieces for years. And now the powers have all returned, and everyone here has a role to play. Kairos has a role to play. We'll find Kairos because not one of us can escape our fate."

I leaned away from my brother, remembering the last night I was here, when Kairos wished I would find someone who moved the heavens and stars for me. I looked up, knowing I had, knowing that those star spirits were the most eternal of all.

I prayed my family had found their places up there.

I prayed no more of my family would have to anytime soon.

"Maybe," I told Kata softly, "fate has only begun to play her hand."

Acknowledgments

This is my fight song.

So this book sold in March 2015; April 1 of the same year, I found out that because of a long and tumultuous history with diabetes, my retinas were bleeding into my vitreous fluid and blocking my vision. I spent almost a year with extremely compromised vision, getting laser treatments, injections, and surgeries in both eyes—I spent a year not knowing if I would be completely blind within a few years (I guess I still don't really know that, so keep your fingers crossed). I spent a month not lifting my head because to do so would disrupt a gas bubble that was keeping my retina attached.

Let me repeat—I looked at the floor for a *month.*

And all this while desperately trying to get my diabetes under control, and deal with an insidious sense of my own guilt and shame—*I had done this to myself.*

Through this all, I had this book. I worked on edits while I was facedown, making notes on Post-its since I couldn't even use a computer because of the angle of the screen. Thinking constantly about this book, primed for the day I could raise my head—ready for the chance to heal.

It's virtually impossible to, in a few public paragraphs, explain what a dark time that was for me, and the kinds of fear and depression I wrestled with. But in writing my acknowledgments, I somehow need to acknowledge what this book really became for me—it wasn't escapism. It was proof that I was still capable. It was my ability to function. It was my measure of worth for myself.

This is my fight song.

And yet, there's so much more to the story of this book, and this series. I wrote the first draft of Shalia's story when I was sixteen. It took me fourteen more years to learn how to tell her story the way it needed to be told—and I can't even express how many false starts and dead novels lie strewn in the wake of this final version. I mean, the first draft was handwritten across two composition notebooks. COMPOSITION NOTEBOOKS. I think one has my history notes from high school and plans to go to a party in my freshman year of college in the margins.

And now you're reading this in the back of a published novel. So for writers everywhere, never give up on a story that you want to tell. You may not know how to tell it just yet, but don't ever believe that you don't know how to tell it *period.* We learn craft and practice our skills to get better at *this.*

For myself, for many reasons and in many ways, I will always need reminding that my pen—and my heart—will never fail me. And this book is a testament to that.

But I didn't get here through force of will alone. So here is a paltry list:

To Mary Kate, thank you for never once making me feel like I was taking too long. Thank you for sending Word docs so that I could zoom in on the font and actually *see* things. Thank you for continuing to ask for excellence when it would have been so much easier to settle for less—not only did it, of course, serve the story, but it also reminded me what I was capable of producing. Thank you for believing in this book, but more than that, thank you for believing in *me.*

To Minju, thank you for being my incredible, dedicated agent—you are a tough-as-nails champion and a badass crusader, but you're also a loving and supportive friend. Your thoughtfulness and care have meant so much to me—thank you.

To the whole team at Bloomsbury that has had my back from day one, I can't believe the level of love and support you've shown for me and this book. Lizzy Mason, Courtney Griffin, Emily Ritter, Erica Barmash, Beth Eller, Melissa Kavonic, Oona Patrick, Pat McHugh, Christine Ma, Claire Stetzer, Charlotte Davis, Cristina Gilbert, Cindy Loh, and Donna Mark—you are the ultimate dream team. Thank you for making this beautiful baby a reality.

To the fans and bloggers who have been so excited for this book despite the long wait, your cheerleading helped me every step of the way. I'm looking at you, What Sarah Read, Melissa Lee, Andi's ABCs, Gail Yates, Mundie Moms, Gaby Salpeter, Jenuine Cupcakes, the Irish Banana Review . . . there are so many, many more. Thank you.

The funny thing about grappling with debilitating illness is that, while making me feel the most incredibly vulnerable I've ever felt—because I *really* do not like accepting help from others, and the need to do so was problematic at best and humiliating at worst—it also taught me how many people love and care for me. It's no coincidence that this book is all about the families you're born into and the families you make and choose.

To Annie Cardi, Tara Sullivan, and Katie Slivensky, you guys are just supposed to be my critique group. Where do you get off being some of the truest friends, confidantes, secret-keepers, and bitchfest arbiters I've ever met? Thank you for all the rides, all the love, and especially for my stuffed dragon to keep the other dragons out of my eyes. And of course, for getting this book shipshape. I literally don't know how I did this stuff before you guys came along.

To the Apocalypsies, the Class of 2k12, and the other authors, writers, and bookish people I have met along the way whom I now have the extreme privilege of calling dear friends, thank you for being excellent and inspiring more beautiful stories in your wake. Tiffany Schmidt; Diana Renn; Erin Cashman, Bowman, and Dionne (dude, there are a LOT of Erins I like); Gina Rosati; Sarah Aronson; Elly Swartz; Emery Lord; Trish Doller; and Cristin Bishara—thank you all for keeping my hope and my heart up.

To Nacie and Renee, my sisters from other misters (hi, Mr. C and Mr. D!), thank you for sitting with me and checking up on me and agreeing to eat no more ice cream with me when I gave up all sugar for eight months—it is so not easy to change up a friendship routine (especially involving sugar), but you never missed a beat. Seriously, that's love.

To Leah, Iggy, Ashley, Alex, Jenna, Emily, Nora, Robin, Andrea, and Beth, illness makes me a bad friend, and none of you cared. Thank you—that kindness and generosity is such a gift.

Holly, thank you for being my sounding board. Caitlin, Tyme, Leigh, Jo, Emily, thank you for the special brand of AIE love.

To Steve, Aysha, and Juliet, I was such a crappy employee for several months, and instead you made me feel like a fighter. Thank you for teaching me the meaning of a team—and thank you for reminding me that art is in fact the language of hope.

To the Girl Scouts, especially Liz, Lori, Emma, Jen, Christine, Sheila, Joan, Dianne, Danielle, Amy, all of Waltham—but really everyone because, seriously, what a team—thank you for taking me in and making me one of your own.

To Dr. Mark Dacey, Jen, Julie, and all of the incredible team at Eye Health Services, thank you for giving me my eyes back. Thank you for your expert care, your attentive concern, and your kindness. You are the closest I've ever come to miracle workers.

To Dr. Choong, thank you for answering my crazy e-mails and phone calls and helping me figure out diabetes when I had forgotten how to be diabetic. Your daily, excellent care is above and beyond, and I will be forever grateful.

To Mom and Dad—I am so sorry I scared the crap out of you. I know it's not easy to see your child struggle like that, but you each showed me in different ways that it's really okay for a thirty-year-old to need her mom and dad. Thank you, Mom, for literally caring for me for weeks, but also for reminding me how to do this whole diabetes thing and that I am perfectly capable of controlling this disease. Dad, thank you for making sure I never worried about anything other than being healthy—that was and is an incredible gift.

To Mikey, you know that whole poem "Footprints" about God and stuff? Mine to you would be similar, except it would be chairs. So thank you for sitting beside me in doctors' offices (even when I didn't tell you about the appointment), in cars when I couldn't drive myself, in movie theaters through good times and bad, on the couch even when there's not much to say, and in the very worst times, when I couldn't go anywhere without looking up, thank you for carrying a special chair for me to sit in.

And finally, to Kev and Alisa, thank you for the audiobooks and the regular books, for introducing me to the Royals and UnReal, and for always showing up and always being there despite being totally blissful newlyweds. Alisa, you totally went above and beyond the call of brand-new sisterhood (sorry about the hospital-gown incident) and I am so grateful and happy that you're family now. Kev, thank you for ordering stuff from Amazon when you feel worried about me, for rubbing my back when I'm fighting off tears, and for being there whenever I need you. I love you both.

Though, really, I love you all.

You are my fight song.